ANTHONY PRICE

The Hour of the Donkey

GRAFTON BOOKS

A Division of the Collins Publishing Group

LONDON GLASGOW
TORONTO SYDNEY AUCKLAND

Grafton Books
A Division of the Collins Publishing Group
8 Grafton Street, London W1X 3LA

Published by Grafton Books 1990

First published in Great Britain by
Victor Gollancz Ltd 1980

Copyright © 1980 Anthony Price

ISBN 0-586-20676-0

Printed and bound in Great Britain by
Collins, Glasgow

Set in Times

For Hugh Williamson

PROLOGUE

Saturday, 10 May 1940, to Tuesday, 20 May

'On the morning of Saturday, 10 May 1940, at 5.35, the German Army invaded the Low Countries, ending the "Phoney War" which had lasted in Western Europe since the outbreak of hostilities the previous September.

'Holland was overwhelmed before any help could reach her, but as in 1914, the Allies advanced hurriedly into Belgium, the French 1st Army and the British Expeditionary Force coming up alongside the Belgian Army on the line of the River Dyle in an attempt to protect Antwerp and Brussels.

'In fact, nothing could have suited the Germans better, for it was to the south, into France herself, that their decisive thrust was aimed. Having negotiated the supposedly impassable terrain of the Ardennes they burst like a thunderbolt on to the banks of the River Meuse in the region of Sedan on 13 May. Without waiting to concentrate their forces (as military prudence dictated), they at once launched a daring assault on the French defences across the river; and, having smashed through those defences, they then departed further from the rules with an act of even greater daring: instead of securing their breakthrough by attacking the broken flanks of the French line their armoured forces drove straight forward into France on a narrow front.

'Just as treason never profits because when it does so it ceases to be treason, so what seemed like military foolhardiness was transformed by success into military genius:

the eruption of Hannibal's elephants out of the snow-bound Alpine passes on to the plains of Northern Italy was scarcely a greater shock than the appearance of German tanks in the open country of Northern France. Preceded by the screaming dive-bombers which acted as their artillery – and also by equally unnerving rumours of their numbers and invincibility – these tanks now advanced with astonishing rapidity. While the cream of the Anglo-French armies were still closely engaged deep in Belgium, the German armoured divisions to the south did not so much drive back the French frontier defenders as simply leave them behind.

'Nor, to complete the surprise, did the Germans then seek either to threaten Paris or to swing eastwards to take the great defensive works of the Maginot Line in the rear. Herding thousands of panic-stricken refugees ahead of them to choke the roads and further demoralize Allied counsels, they swept irresistibly westwards, towards the English Channel.

'By the morning of Tuesday, 20 May, their exact whereabouts were unknown to the Allied commanders. In fact they had already – and incredibly – passed the line of the Canal du Nord, between Cambrai and Peronne. All that lay between them and the sea, some sixty miles distant, was a rolling peaceful countryside which, although strongly garrisoned by the dead of the 1914–18 War, was now only weakly held by the living soldiers of a handful of unprepared and unsuspecting British lines-of-communication units.'

– from *The Dunkirk Miracle*, by Sir Frederick Clinton
(Gollancz, 1959)

1

'Mad,' murmured Captain Willis at the Adjutant's departing back. 'Quite mad.'

Everyone at the breakfast table pretended to take no notice, except Captain Henry Bastable, who disliked Captain Willis almost as much as he did Hitler.

'Quite mad.' Now that the Adjutant was out of earshot Willis spoke louder. 'Probably certifiably mad, too.'

One day, when the war had been won and the washing hung on the Siegfried Line, and the Prince Regent's Own South Downs Fusiliers returned to its proper and more agreeable amateur status, there was going to be a new breakfast rule at the annual Territorial Army camp, Bastable vowed silently to himself: to the existing *Officers will not talk shop*, it would add *and at breakfast officers will not talk at all*.

'Mad as a bloody hatter', said Willis, more loudly still.

It was wrong to hope that Willis would be the first PRO battle casualty of the Second World War. And anyway, Willis would probably bear a charmed life, he was that sort of person. So that new rule would be needed to shut him up. But in the meanwhile, the best Bastable could do was to glower at him over his crumpled copy of *The Times*, and grunt disapprovingly in the hope that Major Tetley-Robinson would notice, and take the appropriate action.

'Drill!' exclaimed Willis, in a voice no one could pretend to fail to hear.

'Eh?' Major Tetley-Robinson looked up for a moment

from the piece of bread which he had been examining, but then looked down again at it. 'You know, we'll never get decent toast from this stuff, the composition's all wrong. We'll have to find a way of baking our own.'

'I said "drill",' said Willis clearly. '"Drill".'

'Eh?' Major Tetley-Robinson looked up again, but this time at Lieutenant Davidson. 'No more of this damn Froggie stuff, Dickie – I won't have it! It's all crust and air, and you can't make toast out of crust and air.' He switched the look to Willis at last. 'Talking shop, Wimpy? Or did I mishear you, eh?'

Bastable was disappointed to observe that Tetley-Robinson was trying to let Willis off. Normally the Major could be relied on to savage Willis at every opportunity, his dislike of the man dating from the discovery that Willis's fluent French stemmed from the possession of a French grandmother, and from Alsace moreover, which was dangerously close to the German frontier. 'Fellow doesn't look like an Alsatian – more like a cross between a greyhound and a rat,' the Major had observed *sotto voce* on receiving this intelligence. 'Probably runs like a greyhound too.'

But now the prospect of action appeared to have mellowed this enmity, for the Major was regarding Wimpy with an expression bordering on tolerance.

Willis returned the look obstinately. 'No, I said "drill". My company – '

'I heard.' The Major lifted his chin and looked down his nose at Willis. 'Shop – and you know the rule.' He leaned back in his chair and half-turned towards the mess waiter without taking his eyes off Willis. 'Higgins – fetch Captain Willis's steel helmet.'

Willis licked his lips. 'My company – '

'Not until you're wearing your steel helmet, *if* you please, Wimpy,' snapped the Major. 'Then you can talk as much as you like, if you can find anyone to listen to you . . .' He pointed down the table. 'Pass me the marmalade, will you, *Bar*stable?'

Bastable's blossoming joy turned instantly into dismay. The pot of Cooper's Oxford Marmalade in front of him was his own, his very own, his private pot and his only pot – and possibly the only pot in the whole British Expeditionary Force, if not the only pot in France. And also a bitter-sweet reminder of his mother, who had given it to him.

But Major Tetley-Robinson outranked Mother in this company, and Bastable watched helplessly as the Major spooned out a huge dollop of Cooper's Oxford Marmalade on to his plate, and proceeded to consume it in the proportion of three parts of marmalade to one of French bread.

Fusilier Higgins reappeared with the steel helmet, which he offered rather apologetically to Captain Willis. But to Bastable's surprise, rather than bow to the pressure of the mess rule, Willis put it on his head and returned to the fray.

'Drill – ' he began.

'Hah!' Tetley-Robinson assumed an enquiring expression. 'Very well then, Wimpy . . . since you choose to attire yourself so strangely at table . . . "drill"?'

Willis set his jaw. 'My company – what there is of it – is under orders to drill this morning, Charlie – ' the use of the christian name was permitted, but it always made the Major wince when Willis used it, ' – orders from the CO, relayed by the Adjutant just now, Charlie!'

'So I gathered.'

'It's bloody mad – *drill*, Charlie!'

'Nothing wrong with drill, my dear chap. When you can fight as well as the Guards, then you can stop drilling, I

13

always say – and your fellows have become a shower, an absolute shower. Worse than *Bar*stable's there, even.' Major Tetley-Robinson nodded at Bastable, noticed the marmalade pot again, and helped himself to another spoonful. 'Apart from which, drill used to be a PRO speciality – we've always drilled like regulars, not Territorials. And . . . if you ask me, that's why we've been sent out here, to France, when other chaps are still kicking their heels in Blighty. Because a smart soldier is a good soldier – '

Bastable raised his copy of *The Times* quickly to cut off the view. It wasn't that he disagreed with the Major, but he couldn't bear to see the Major finish his marmalade.

' – team-work, self-confidence . . . not having to think, because one already *knows* – '

Bastable tried to concentrate on his *Times*. It was nearly a week old, and he had already been through it twice, from cover to cover, so now he was rationing himself to one column per breakfast, nodding or shaking his head in exactly the same places and greeting remembered names like old friends.

' – and although most Territorial units are downright slovenly, we've always been different – '

Major Tetley-Robinson was moving inexorably into the History and Traditions of the Regiment of which he was the acknowledged custodian.

' – we do not bear the royal honour of "The Prince Regent's Own" for nothing – '

He was coming to the famous parade of 1811, when the Regent had reviewed the new regiment in the skin-tight uniforms of his own design – red coats with primrose-yellow facings and dove-grey pantaloons, snowy pipe-clay and glittering brass and leather; the only pity was that the Prince had subsequently taken his custom to Brighton,

14

which was a rather vulgar town, in preference to Captain Bastable's own native Eastbourne; but, to its credit, the regiment had done its best to correct that aberration in later years.

' – this lanyard, which every man wears as of right as a PRO – ' the primrose-yellow-and-dove-grey lanyard always formed the peroration of the Major's pep talk ' – is the symbol of his pride in his regiment and in himself for being privileged to belong to it. Which, as an officer of the regiment, you ought to know, Wimpy, by God!'

'But I do know that, Charlie,' protested Captain Willis wearily. 'Prinnie granted it to us on account of the exceptionally stylish cut of our uniforms – it wasn't a battle honour, it was a fashion honour, for heaven's sake.'

Tetley-Robinson raised an admonitory finger. 'But we wore that lanyard at the Somme, man – and at Gommecourt and Ginchy and the Transloy Ridges . . . aye, and on the Scarpe and Tadpole Copse and Picardy and the Sambre! By God, man! Where's your sense of history?'

'Yes, I do know – ' Captain Willis still seemed set on holding his indefensible salient, ' – but – '

'*And* they tried to take it away from us, too . . . Said it identified us – Huh! "So much the better!" says the Colonel. "Let the Hun know what he's in for!" Wrote to the Colonel-in-Chief, and *he* wrote to the King, who happened to be a relative of his in a manner of speaking. So *that* was the last we heard of *that* – after we returned their damn bit of paper marked "Kindly refer all future correspondence on this subject to His Majesty the King-Emperor" – *that* settled their little hash.'

'Yes, Charlie, I know – '

'So this lanyard means that we're different, Wimpy – and don't you ever forget it.'

'I won't, Charlie – I promise you faithfully that I won't.'

Captain Willis drew a deep breath and looked up and down the table presumably in the hope of finding a little moral support somewhere, and found none. 'But, you know, in a way that is precisely the point I am trying to make. I mean . . . drill . . . at a time like this. That's not just different, that's a clear case of *deus quos vult perdere, dementat prius*.'

'What's that?' At the furthest end of the table Major Audley roused himself from the copy of *The Field* in which he had hitherto been buried. Of all the officers in the regiment, Major Audley was usually the most elegantly silent. At the same time, nevertheless, he had established a reputation for possessing vast knowledge, both military and general, of the sort which could only be acquired by a perfect balance of practical experience, expensive education and natural-born intelligence.

'I said *deus quos* – ' began Captain Willis.

'Heard you. Euripides, Joshua Barnes's translation is the best one.'

It didn't surprise Captain Bastable that Major Audley could instantly identify Captain Willis's Latin quotation, which his own eight agonized years of Latin had left him incapable of translating. Indeed, it surprised him less than the quotation itself, though as a former schoolmaster Captain Willis was full of quotations, and as he had been a classics master, most of them were in Latin or Greek, and all of them might just as well have been in Swahili for any sense Captain Bastable could make of them. (It was an added coincidence, and the only virtue he had yet found in Willis, that the man had numbered Major Audley's only son amongst his pupils, and had spoken glowingly of the boy's intellectual capacity; but that had merely confirmed Captain Bastable's views on heredity – like father, like son, was the natural order of things; he himself, and the success and prosperity of Bastable's of Eastbourne, was proof of that.)

Major Audley squinted down the breakfast table. 'That pot . . . Cooper's?' he enquired.

'It is,' said Major Tetley-Robinson obsequiously. 'Help yourself, Nigel. Here, *Bar*stable – push it on down. There's still a good scraping in it, round the sides.'

Major Audley scrutinized the faces round the table. 'Whose pot?' he enquired.

Bastable examined the crumbs of bread on his plate. It was certainly true that the mess cook's attempts to turn French bread into toast had been disastrous. But the bread itself, although strange and foreign, was quite tasty when untoasted. It seemed to him (although he knew he would never dare advance such a suggestion in public) that it was a mistake to attempt to convert French food into English food: when in Rome – even though the thought smacked of Captain Willis – it would be more sensible to eat as the Romans did. Or in this case the French, deplorable people though they were in most other respects.

'Yours, Bastable?' asked Major Audley.

Bastable blushed to the roots of his hair: he could literally feel the blush suffuse his face. But he forced himself to look Major Audley in the eye because he did not wish the Major to think him a coward. 'Do please help yourself, Nigel,' he croaked, wondering only for a moment how Major Audley had identified him from the rest. But of course, Major Audley had identified him because Major Audley was Major Audley. The question contained its own answer, simply.

'Thank you, Bastable.' Major Audley applied the last of the marmalade to his bread. 'Since I assume the rest of you gentlemen have consumed Bastable's delicacy, then

17

his drinks in the mess tonight are on you.' He lifted the piece of bread in Bastable's direction. 'Meanwhile . . . your continued health, Bastable . . . the condemned man eats his hearty breakfast.'

'Hah!' said Captain Willis, with immense feeling, as though Major Audley had vindicated his protest. 'Precisely!'

Bastable experienced an indigestible mixture of conflicting emotions. Major Audley had acknowledged his existence, and in a most generous and gentlemanly fashion; yet he had done so in more words than were seemly, at least for him; and (what was worse) there had definitely been something in those words – a mere suggestion, perhaps, but an undoubted suggestion nevertheless – that his inclination was to support Captain Willis against Major Tetley-Robinson.

Bastable frowned at his plate again. Beyond the fact that Willis didn't want to drill his men he wasn't at all sure what it was which was so aggravating the ex-schoolmaster. The majority of the recent replacements were little better than civilians in uniform, notwithstanding their yellow-and-grey lanyards, and drill was something they could do straight away which at least might make them feel more like soldiers.

He clenched his fists under the table and nerved himself to speak.

'What is it that you want to do, Willis?' He couldn't bring himself to give the man the inexplicable nickname which had attached itself to him. Everybody in the mess had either a christian name or a nickname to distinguish him socially from the formal military world of 'sirs' and 'misters' outside – everybody, that was, except himself, who had somehow become frozen into 'Bastable' in the mess (and usually the more insulting variant rhyming with *bar*stard); which was a source of constant, nagging, irritating, bewildering and unfair pain to him. 'What's mad about drill, man?'

Captain Willis looked at him in surprise, as though he hadn't expected the faculty of speech in Captain *Bar*stable, but before he could reveal his heart's desire the burly figure of the battalion medical officer filled the doorway beside him.

'I don't know what you want to do, Wimpy – and frankly I couldn't care less,' said Captain Saunders. 'But I want my breakfast – Steward! Ham and eggs – three eggs – and don't toast the bread . . . And send across to the café over the road for a large pot of coffee on the double – and say it's for "M'sieur le médicin", don't forget that – a large pot!'

Captain Willis chuckled dryly. 'Trust the medical profession! I take it you have been feathering your nest with the locals, Doc? Touching up les jeunes demoiselles as part of the Anglo-French *entente cordiale*?'

Captain Saunders reached across the table and tore a six-inch hunk from one of the long French loaves. 'I have delivered a French baby – male. "Class of 1940" I suppose they'd call the poor little devil, when they finally call him up . . . in 1958 . . . which they probably will.' He ate a piece of bread from the hunk without benefit of butter. 'And the Germans are across the Somme, at Peronne.'

For a moment no one at the table spoke, or even moved. The medical officer's words seemed to hang in the air, like an unthinkable wisp of smoke over a dry cornfield on a still day.

'What?' said Major Tetley-Robinson.

'Where?' said Captain Willis.

'Who said?' said Major Audley simultaneously.

'Nonsense!' said Major Tetley-Robinson.

19

Captain Saunders munched his mouthful of bread. 'That's what the French say – the people I've just been talking to.'

'Refugees,' said Major Tetley-Robinson contemptuously. 'We've heard enough rumours from them to keep us going for a year. If we start believing what they say, they'll have the bloody Boche in Calais next week, queuing for the cross-Channel ferries.'

Captain Saunders continued munching. 'A week is right – ' he nodded ' – they say the Germans'll be on the Channel coast in a week. Hundreds of tanks, driving like hell – that's what they say . . . Actually, they said "thousands", but that seemed to be stretching it a bit, I thought.' He nodded, but then turned the nod into a negative shake. 'These weren't refugees though, Charlie. It was the station-master's wife's baby I delivered. He had it from an engine-driver – the information, I mean, not the baby. And all the lines are down now, he says – to Peronne.'

'Fifth Columnists!' snapped Tetley-Robinson. 'A lot of those refugees that came through on the main road, to the south, yesterday . . . they looked suspiciously ablebodied to me.'

'Peronne . . .' murmured Major Audley. He turned towards Lieutenant Davidson. 'You're alleged to be our IO, Dickie – so where the devil were the Germans supposed to be as of last night?'

Lieutenant Davidson squirmed uncomfortably. 'Well, sir . . . things have been a bit knotted-up at Brigade – or they were yesterday.'

'What d'you mean "knotted-up", boy?'

'Well . . . actually . . . things seem to be a bit confused, don't you know . . . rather.' Lieutenant Davidson manoeuvred the crumbs on his plate into a neat pile.

20

'No, Dickie,' said Major Audley.

'No, sir – Nigel?' Lieutenant Davidson blinked.

'No, Dickie. No – I don't know. And no, I'm not confused. To be confused one must know something. But as I know nothing I am not confused, I am merely unenlightened. So enlighten me, Dickie – enlighten us all.'

'Or at least – confuse us,' murmured Willis. 'What does Brigade say?'

'Well, actually . . .' Lieutenant Davidson began to rearrange the crumbs, '. . . actually, Brigade says we don't belong to them at all. So they haven't really said anything, actually.'

'What d'you mean, "don't belong to them"?' asked Major Audley.

'They say we should be at Colembert, sir – Nigel.'

'But we are at Colembert, dear boy.'

'No, sir . . . That is to say, yes – but actually no, you see.' Lieutenant Davidson tried to attract Major Tetley-Robinson's attention.

'Ah! Now we're getting somewhere,' Major Audley nodded encouragingly. 'Now I am beginning to become confused at least. We are at Colembert – but we're not. Please confuse me further, Dickie.'

Lieutenant Davidson abandoned the crumbs. 'This is Colembert-les-Deux-Ponts, sir. But apparently there's another Colembert, with no ponts, up towards St Omer. It seems the MCO at Boulogne attached us to the wrong convoy, or something – that's what Brigade says – '

'Good God!' exclaimed Major Audley. 'But St Omer's miles from here – it's near Boulogne.'

'Yes . . .' nodded Willis. 'And that would account for Jackie Johnson and the whole of "A" Company being absent without leave, of course . . . Only poor old Jackie

21

didn't lose *us* after all – he just went off to the right Colembert . . . and we lost *him*, eh?'

But Major Audley had his eye fixed on Major Tetley-Robinson now. 'So what the hell are we doing about it, Charlie?'

Major Tetley-Robinson almost looked uncomfortable. 'The matter is in hand, Nigel. That's all I can tell you.'

Willis smiled. ' "Theirs not to reason why – theirs but to do and die", Nigel. Same thing happened to the jolly old Light Brigade.'

'Same thing happens in hospital,' observed Captain Saunders wisely, nodding to the whole table.

'What same thing, Doc?' enquired Willis.

'Wrong patient gets sent to surgery to have his leg cut off. Always causes a devil of a row afterwards. Somebody gets the push, somebody else gets promoted. Hard luck on the patient. And hard luck on us if the Huns are in Peronne, I suppose.'

Major Audley considered Captain Saunders for a moment, and then turned back to Lieutenant Davidson. 'Are the Germans in Peronne, Dickie? What does Brigade say?'

Lieutenant Davidson looked directly at Major Tetley-Robinson. 'Sir . . .?' he appealed.

'Harrumph!' Major Tetley-Robinson brushed his moustache with the back of his hand. 'That would be telling!'

'It would indeed, Charlie,' said Major Audley cuttingly.

'They must be in touch with the French,' said Captain Willis. 'The French are supposed to be north-west of us here, and Peronne is . . .' he frowned, '. . . is bloody *south*-west, if my memory serves me correctly – bloody *south*-west!'

Willis's memory did serve him correctly, thought Bastable uneasily. In fact, Peronne was so far south as to be

22

impossible; there just had to be two Peronnes, in the same way as there had been two Colemberts.

'What *does* Brigade say, Dickie?' Willis pressed the Intelligence Officer.

'Well . . . actually, we've lost touch with – '

'That's enough!' Major Tetley-Robinson snapped. 'The disposition of the French Army – and the enemy – are none of our business at the moment.'

'I hope you're right, Charlie,' said Captain Willis.

Major Tetley-Robinson glared at him. 'We are a lines-of-communication battalion. Company commanders and other officers will be briefed as necessary – at the proper time.'

'Hmmm . . .' Major Audley exchanged glances with Willis, and even spared Bastable a fleeting half-glance. 'Well, I shall look forward to that, Charlie.' He extracted a cigarette from his slim gold case. 'I shall indeed.'

Major Tetley-Robinson brushed his moustache again. 'There's a lot of loose talk going around, Nigel. Damned loose talk.'

Captain Saunders stopped eating. 'Are you referring to me, by any chance? Or to my friends the station-master and his engine-driver colleague?'

'I didn't mean you, Doc,' said the Major hastily.

'No?' Captain Saunders pointed with his knife. 'Well, Major, my friend the station-master is a man of sound commonsense, and pro-British too, however contradictory those two conditions may appear to be at this moment, diagnostically speaking.'

Major Tetley-Robinson's expression changed from one of apology to that of bewilderment. 'I don't quite take your meaning, Doc.'

'But I do,' said Major Audley. 'Did the station-master see the Boche, Doc? At Peronne?'

'No. Not with his own eyes – that's true,' Captain Saunders shook his head. 'But he spoke to the driver who claims to have taken the last train out of Peronne. And *he* claimed to have been machine-gunned by tanks with large black crosses on them.'

'Tanks or aeroplanes?' Audley leaned forward intently. 'They've been bombing all round us the last couple of days, remember. We seem to be the only place they've missed out on, for some reason . . . But their dive-bombers will have been making a dead set on trains, for sure – could it have been planes, not tanks?'

For a moment Bastable was tempted to speak, to explain why Colembert – Colembert-les-Deux-Ponts – had been missed, if not overlooked, by the German Luftwaffe. Simply (which one glance at the map had confirmed) it was not worth attacking – a small town in the middle of a triangle of main roads, the destruction of which would block none of those roads. It had struck him as odd at the time that a Lines-of-Communication unit should have been despatched to a place on no line of communication. But he had assumed that the high command knew its business much better than he did, and that assumption was still strong enough in him to dry up his private opinion.

'Planes, for sure,' snapped Major Tetley-Robinson. 'It's just possible they could have pushed the French back over the Sambre–Oise line.' He nodded meaningfully at Lieutenant Davidson, as if to give his blessing to that admission. 'But that means they've already come the deuce of a way from the Dyle–Meuse line – their tanks'll be running out of fuel – the ones that haven't broken down . . . and their infantry'll be dead on its feet by now. And that's the moment when the French will counter-attack, by God! It'll be the Marne all over again!' He glanced

24

fiercely up and down the table. 'The Marne all over again – only this time we'll make a proper job of it!'

Nobody denied this aggressive interpretation of Allied strategy. Rather, there was an appreciative nodding of heads and a fierce murmur of agreement; and no one nodded more vigorously or murmured more approvingly than Bastable himself to cover the panicky butterflies which the mention of Peronne had set fluttering in his stomach.

'Only this time it'll be a Marne with another difference,' announced Major Tetley-Robinson expansively. 'Because this time the PROs will be "Up Front" with any luck, eh?'

He ran his eye round the table, until it reached Captain Willis. To his credit, Captain Willis met the eye bravely.

'Hah! Now . . . as to your drill, Wimpy . . . just what was it you wanted to substitute for your spot of drill? As I recall it you were dying to tell us all what you would rather be doing than drill – ?'

Major Audley took out his cigarette-case, clicked it open and offered it to Captain Willis. 'Smoke, Wimpy?' he enquired.

'No, thank you, Nigel.' Captain Willis smiled nervously at Major Audley, then erased the smile. 'Colembert-les-Deux-Ponts has two bridges, sir. D company, of which I am commander – '

'Acting-commander,' corrected Major Tetley-Robinson.

'Acting-commander . . . D Company has the southern bridge. I think the bridge should be wired for demolition, but we have no demolition charges.' Willis paused, swallowed. 'And even if we did have we don't have anyone who knows how to set them.'

Major Tetley-Robinson nodded gravely. 'I see. And

25

against whom are you proposing to blow your bridge, Wimpy?'

'Against any enemy forces who might approach from that direction, sir,' said Captain Willis tightly.

'From the south?' The Major's lip curled. And then he glanced at Bastable, and Bastable knew what he was thinking.

If any enemy – Fifth Columnists in strength, or possibly some roving armoured cars which might conceivably infiltrate the French Army by the web of minor roads which covered France – if any enemy approached Colembert, it would be from the west; and it was Captain Bastable's C Company which was supposed to be covering Colembert's western bridge. But it had never occurred to Captain Bastable to prepare his bridge for destruction. Lines of Communication (even to nowhere) had nothing to do with Plans for Demolition. And, in any case, demolition was for the Royal Engineers.

Yet he ought to say something –

Major Tetley-Robinson flicked another split-second glance at him.

Or, on second thoughts, nothing.

'Mr Davidson says there's an RE detachment at Belléme, where the 2nd Royal Mendips are, sir,' said Captain Willis. 'I was going to request permission to take the carrier, with PSM Blossom of the Pioneer Platoon, and obtain some demolition charges, with sufficient instruction in placing them . . .' He faltered under the Major's increasingly basilisk stare. 'And . . .'

'Yes, Captain Willis?' The Major's voice was glacial.

'I have two Boys anti-tank rifles. We were issued with them when we landed at Boulogne the day before yesterday. None of my men have ever fired a Boys rifle, sir. We have only eight magazines of ammunition – twenty

26

rounds, sir. But in any case it's only practice ammunition – full charge, but with aluminium bullets. It's bloody useless.'

Major Tetley-Robinson raised his eyes to heaven. 'Well, practise with them, Captain Willis. See the RSM – he's fired the Boys. And try not to kill any French civilians, or French livestock, for that matter. Is that all?'

Captain Bastable knew that it was not all. No one had trained on the Boys, but the horrors of its pile-driving, shoulder-dislocating recoil were widely known and feared. Other than the RSM, whose claim to have fired the weapon was generally discounted, no soldier had yet been traced who had operated it and lived to tell the tale. But even that was not the point.

'I'm in the same position, Charlie,' said Major Audley pleasantly. 'Except I haven't got a bridge – I've got a double line of nice thick trees, and they're all partially axed ready to block the road, I can tell you.'

'What!' exclaimed Tetley-Robinson.

'It's those infernal Boys rifles that are the trouble,' continued Audley. 'Same situation as Wimpy – exactly.' He glanced at Captain Bastable. 'And you too, Bastable, I suppose?'

Bastable nodded unhappily.

Tetley-Robinson shook himself free from the implications of Major Audley's unauthorized tree-felling preparations, to which the Anglophobe Mayor of Colembert would certainly take almost as great exception as to Captain Willis's ambitious bridge-demolition plans.

Captain Saunders pushed away his plate and wiped his hands on his napkin. 'And I've got good news for you too, Major,' he said. 'Twelve more cases of mumps this morning. Three in B Company, four in C and five in D. Making a grand total of eighty-one – all ORs, no officers

27

– excluding those in A, the whereabouts of which an informed guess would now place in Colembert, between Boulogne and St Omer, I agree . . . So I have commandeered a bus and despatched the new cases to the base hospital at Boulogne, in charge of Corporal Potts, who was one of yesterday's cases. Bringing our total fighting strength – if that is the appropriate term . . . which I doubt . . . to three hundred and thirty-five. Before long we'll probably have more officers than other ranks.'

Audley regarded the Medical Officer with interest. 'You're sending cases of mumps to the Base Hospital, Doc? But I thought mumps was a . . . childish disease? I mean – a few days in bed, and then up again and at 'em?'

'In young children – yes, Nigel. But in the case of adults . . . alas! Corporal Potts is – or was – a failed first-year medical student, and he has incontinently passed on his knowledge of Orchitis to the rest of the battalion, I'm afraid. So I've sent the sick to Boulogne to keep up the morale of the healthy.'

'Orchitis?'

'The Black Death would have been preferable to Orchitis.' Captain Saunders swung from Audley to Major Tetley-Robinson. 'Orchitis is an adult complication of mumps which inflames the testicles and can cause sterility. As a result of which the men are scared stiff for fear of having their balls swell up like melons, and then deflate for ever . . . And when Corporal Potts gets back from the Base Hospital I'll have his stripes off him if it's the last thing I do.'

One of the newest subalterns, a boy so new that Bastable couldn't even place his face, never mind think of his name, coughed politely.

'Sir . . . Sir, you said – or you implied, sir – that it's the

28

ORs who are getting it . . . the mumps . . . not the officers. Why is that, sir?'

Captain Saunders stared at the child for a moment or two. 'Where were you a year ago, Mr – Mr – '

'Chichester, sir.'

'You were at Chichester?'

'No, sir. I was at King's, Canterbury.'

'Ah-hah! And King's, Canterbury, is a public school, I take it, Mr Chichester?'

'Yes, sir.'

'Just so! Boarding cheek-by-jowl with other little boys – living in a perfect breeding ground for contagious and infectious diseases. So you have had mumps, Mr Chichester – '

'Yes, sir – '

'And measles, and German measles, and chicken-pox – you may well have braved scarlet fever and diphtheria and cholera and heaven only knows what other foul contagions.' As Captain Saunders leaned across the table towards the astonished Mr Chichester Captain Bastable picked up the strong aroma of brandy. He had not hitherto tagged the MO as a drinking man, but then (to be fair) the delivery of a French man-child, at least after the event, would not have been an abstemious event, he reasoned.

'You, Mr Chichester – ' the MO stabbed a finger at the subaltern, ' – are a product of natural selection. And the same almost certainly holds true for the rest of you – you are all inoculated by privilege and good fortune, unlike the other ranks of this exclusive unit.'

It was not the moment for the Adjutant to reappear, but the Adjutant had a knack of appearing when he was not wanted.

The MO swung round towards him as the door banged.

'I bet you've had mumps, Percy,' said the MO.

Captain Harbottle had no answer to that.

'They've got a problem with the Boys anti-tank rattle, too,' said the MO. He turned back to Major Audley. 'Just what is your problem, Nigel? You're the only one here who ever talks straight – except Willis there, and he talks too much. Whereas you don't talk enough.'

Major Audley grinned at the MO. 'I think you could say that our anti-tank weapons have contracted Orchitis, Doc,' he said.

The MO frowned at him. 'They've – *what*?'

'They've got no live ammunition,' said Audley. 'Twenty-four magazines of soft-nosed aluminium practice rounds between us – no armour piercing. If we meet any German tanks we might as well throw snowballs at them.'

Captain Harbottle decided to cut his losses. 'Company commanders to Headquarters at once,' he said. And then, to be merciful to everyone else, 'We've got two staff officers from GHQ. They say everything's going well.'

A not-so-distant rumble of exploding bombs at Belléme seemed to contradict this statement, but breakfast was plainly over, Bastable decided.

2

'Basically, it's a predictable situation, gentlemen,' said the CO in his best nasal military voice. 'The French have rushed in, and the Boche has given them their usual bloody nose – 1914 and all that.'

So Major Tetley-Robinson was vindicated. Bastable covertly examined the staff officers who had confirmed this predictable Scene One, Act One, of the Second World War. The younger of the two was a mere captain, fair-haired and ruddy-faced, but sharp-featured and sharper-eyed with it. He reminded Bastable of the up-and-coming area manager for Kayser-Bondor with whom he had had dealings just before the war – a clever grammar-school boy who had been to Oxford, or Cambridge, and was obviously destined for a seat on the board of directors by sheer force of intelligence; not quite a gentleman yet, to be asked home to dinner, but in four or five years' time he would have learned all the tricks and would pass muster; and in another four or five years after that he might well be running the whole show.

Bastable had no objection to such men so long as they knew their place at each stage in their career. Success in business was a healthy turnover, a fair profit margin for everyone and satisfied customers whose goodwill represented next year's turnover and next year's profits. His own particular innovation to that formula was the creation of a loyal, well-trained and adequately-remunerated staff, which in his opinion in turn created the conditions for

31

successful management. The recruitment of a trainee-manager like this young staff officer must be one of his post-war priorities if Bastable's of Eastbourne was to compete with Bobby's of Eastbourne successfully; and there would be plenty of men like this one looking for jobs then, no doubt.

He started guiltily. He hadn't been giving the CO his full attention.

'. . . but fortunately the French have plenty of men, and their tanks are generally superior to the Germans' – our information is that many of the German tanks are in fact light Czech machines, which proves that their numbers are not as great as rumour would have it.' The CO nodded to the senior staff officer, as though that had been a point he had been specially asked to make.

'*Which proves no such thing*,' murmured Major Audley. *It's a non-sequitur.*'

'What's that, Nigel?' barked the CO.

'I said, "I Hope we get some of them on our sector," sir,' said Major Audley. 'Czech tanks . . . just the thing for our Boys anti-tank rifles!'

The older of the two staff officers gave Major Audley a very sharp glance. Unlike his junior colleague, he had 'class' stamped distinctively all over him, from the cut of his uniform to the immense beak of a nose which dominated his face below the bush iron-grey eyebrows which overhung pale-blue fanatical eyes. It was, indeed, very much a fox-hunting, chairman-of-the-magistrates, lord-of-the-manor, High-Sheriff face, and Captain Bastable was damn glad it was now directed towards Major Audley and not himself, but concentrated on making himself as inconspicuous as possible just in case, behind the Adjutant's bulky shoulder.

Major Audley coughed politely. 'What is the present

position of the German advance units, sir?' he enquired of the beak-nosed Brigadier.

The Brigadier's expression became belligerent. 'That information is classified as secret, Major,' he said witheringly.

Major Audley refused to wither. 'Then they're not at Peronne, sir? Which, according to our non-secret information, they are alleged to be.'

The CO began to speak, but the Brigadier cut him off with a decisive gesture.

'Major – ?'

'Audley,' supplied Major Audley.

'Hmm . . . Major Audley – ' The Brigadier filed the name for future reference. ' – Major, enemy Fifth Columnist and some light motorized units . . . motor-cycle patrols and a few armoured cars . . . are deliberately ranging over wide areas, causing as much alarm and despondency as they can – choking the roads with civilian refugees, for example, and damaging communications . . . But I had not expected to find such alarm in any unit of the British Army, I must say!'

Bastable sensed a change of temperature in the room, and cowered lower. Even the unspeakable Willis, he observed, was maintaining an unusually low profile behind Dickie Davidson.

The Colonel said: 'Hah – now, well . . .'

Major Audley looked unblinkingly at the Brigadier, and when he spoke it was characteristically slowly and deliberately. 'With respect, sir . . . there is no alarm whatsoever in the Prince Regent's Own South Downs Fusiliers. And except for an outbreak of mumps in the ranks there is no despondency either. But if I may be allowed to speak for the fusiliers under my command, in my company, as senior company commander . . . I would

33

like to know . . . what exactly we are supposed to be doing in Colembert-les-Deux-Ponts . . . which I have just discovered – by accident – at breakfast – is not where we are supposed to be – Which is presumably why the local brigade refuses to accept us as one of its battalions . . . sir.'

The Brigadier stared back at Audley for a moment. 'I shall make allowances for the fact that you are a Territorial officer, Major.'

'I'd rather you didn't, sir,' said Major Audley. 'I'm sure the Germans won't.'

'But I shall, nevertheless. Your Commanding Officer has his orders: your battalion will hold Colembert until ordered to do otherwise.' The Brigadier turned to the CO. 'Thank you for your hospitality, Colonel. Keep your men . . . *and* your officers . . . hard at it. There'll be plenty for them to do before long, I shouldn't wonder . . . Come on, Freddie . . .'

'What the hell was that in aid of?' Willis whispered to the Adjutant in the wake of the Brigadier's departure.

'Raising morale, old boy,' murmured the Adjutant loftily.

'Well, he hasn't raised mine, I can tell you!'

'We also filled his Humber up with petrol,' continued the Adjutant. 'Seems he's been on the road since last night . . .looking for the Germans, *I* shouldn't wonder. No one quite knows where the blighters are, apparently.'

'I hope he finds them,' said Major Audley.

Captain Bastable eventually made his way back to his bridge and his company in a thoroughly depressed state.

It wasn't that he was frightened of The Enemy, because he found it quite impossible to imagine them – *they* merely

34

loomed impersonally in the background of his mind like an unpleasant but distant examination which everyone had to take sooner or later, like it or not.

No . . . fear (so far as he had observed it in the army) had nothing to do with the enemy and everything to do with one's own side. 'Will I be killed?' was in practice a ridiculous question compared with 'Will I make a balls-up of today's company drill in front of Major Tetley-Robinson?' Or . . . as the bridge drew nearer . . . 'Will I demonstrate my lamentable ignorance of the Boys anti-tank rifle in full view of Corporal Smithers and the anti-tank section?'

Possibly not, of course . . . since Smithers and his section had already, and loudly and unashamedly, expressed their fear and distaste of the bloody thing, which concealed their equal ignorance.

But that only made things worse, not better – the growing suspicion that his own lack of basic military expertise (as opposed to parade ground bullshit) was equalled by that of the rank and file of the battalion.

To be fair, he could think of plenty of excuses for this. Far too many promising NCOs and likely fusiliers had been posted away to officer-training and specialist courses, never to return; and far too many experienced officers also had departed . . . which almost certainly accounted for his own delayed and grudging promotion, for want of anyone better, to acting-company command.

(The bridge, and the reckoning, was getting ever closer: he could see them now, grouped round the slit-trench, pinching their dog-ends out while pretending not to notice his approach.)

And, to be fairer still (though there had been nothing fair about it), nothing could have prepared them for the demoralizing experiences of the last forty-eight hours, which had transported them from the comfort of the South Downs Depot to Folkestone, where they had been stripped of most of their equipment by grim-visaged Redcaps, and thence to Boulogne, via sea-sickness and mumps, where they had salvaged weapons and transport from the dumps on the quayside . . . strange and decrepit vehicles, and even stranger and quite unfamiliar weapons, like the two Hotchkiss machine-guns which had fallen to C Company . . .

And the two bloody Boys anti-tank rifles.

Thirty-six pounds' weight and five and a half feet long. And nobody ('owing to the absence of facilities') had ever fired a shot from them, armour-piercing or practice; and the men of the anti-tank section were obviously scared stiff of the thing, *and that had to be rectified*.

Captain Bastable lifted the weapon, not without effort.

'This is going to give the Boche one hell of a shock,' he said with false bonhomie, pointing past the bridge abutment to the gap on the skyline of the ridge ahead, where the road descended towards the little town.

'And us too, sir,' said Corporal Smithers, whose powerful shoulders had earned him the privilege of firing the monster.

'Nonsense, man,' snapped Captain Bastable, 'See here how the recoil reducer counters the effect of the recoil – and the buffer spring. *And* the padded shoulder-piece. Nine rounds a minute, the experts claim – and it's sighted up to five hundred yards.'

Nobody commented on these statistics, which Captain Bastable had quarried out of his copy of Ian Hay's *The Citizen Soldier* (which he hoped devoutly was the only copy of that work in the battalion) half an hour previously.

36

'It isn't the size of the hole it punches,' Captain Bastable elaborated. 'It's the effect of that bullet ricocheting round inside the tank, making mincemeat of the crew.'

Still no one spoke.

There was no alternative; he had known from the moment he had approached the anti-tank section that this moment of no alternative would arrive.

'Here – I'll show you,' he said.

The anti-tank section parted eagerly to allow Captain Bastable into their slit-trench.

It was a simple bolt-action weapon, little better than a monstrous rifle – with a truly enormous round of ammunition up the spout. Bastable hugged the shoulder-piece against his shoulder as though his life depended on the embrace.

Corporal Smithers cleared his throat. 'Are you going to designate a target, sir?' he enquired.

The bare hillside mocked Captain Bastable. On the crest, on either side of the gap made by the road, there was a thick belt of trees and undergrowth. That would enable the attackers to deploy under cover to fire down on the bridge and its defenders. Viewed from this slit-trench with the jaundiced eye of reality, the western defences of Colembert were a military nonsense as he had laid them out – an act of collective suicide.

'There's a goat on the hillside there, sir,' Smithers pointed a nicotine-stained finger. 'A white goat, by that bush . . . See that little shed, down by the stream – eleven o'clock from there, sir – white goat, tethered. Four hundred yards.'

Try not to kill any Frenchmen – *or French livestock!*

'Excuse me, sir – ' said a new voice, hesitantly.

Captain Bastable's finger twitched, then relaxed. It was an officer-type voice. He looked over his shoulder.

'Chichester, sir,' said Second-Lieutenant Chichester.

'Yes, Mr Chichester?'

'Second-Lieutenant Watson has the mumps, sir.'

Watson – the face was indistinct, but the name registered – Watson had been C Company's newest and least distinguished subaltern. But now he had distinguished himself by disproving Doc Saunders's theory, damn him!

'Major Tetley-Robinson has sent me to you as replacement, sir. He says he doesn't need me for Brigade Liaison, sir.'

Captain Bastable swallowed. 'Thank you, Mr Chichester.'

'What would you like me to do, sir?'

Major Tetley-Robinson had done this deliberately, Captain Bastable decided.

Well, then!

'I would like you to watch me fire the Boys anti-tank rifle, Mr Chichester. Observe how I engage the shoulder-piece firmly against my shoulder.'

'Oh – I have fired the Boys, sir. The full course, sir – at Aldershot.'

Captain Bastable knew then exactly how Hitler had felt – or claimed to feel – when his patience had become exhausted with Poland: only a violent act could purge his anger.

The loud crack of the Boys was eclipsed by the tremendous blast-and-flash from the muzzle and the smashing force of the padded shoulder-piece, which rammed Captain Bastable backwards in the slit-trench, lifting the slender barrel upwards into the pale blue French sky.

'Jesus-Fucking-Christ!' murmured Corporal Smithers blasphemously, reverently.

38

Tears of rage and pain momentarily fogged Captain Bastable's vision.

'Jolly well done, sir,' said Second-Lieutenant Chichester enthusiastically. 'Bull first time!'

'Goat, rather, old boy.' Captain Willis's familiar drawl, coming from just behind him, recalled Bastable to his senses and his duty. 'I say . . . I don't know what effect Mr Boys's instrument of torture will have on little Adolf's tanks . . . but if he sends goats against us we have nothing to fear, by God!'

Captain Bastable abandoned the instrument of torture and started to twist towards Willis. The pain in his shoulder made him wince involuntarily, but he managed to turn the wince into a grunt of simulated anger.

'What the hell are you doing beside my bridge, Willis?' he growled.

Captain Willis continued to examine the distant hillside through his field-glasses. 'Were you . . . pardon the question, if you will, Bastable, old boy . . . were you actually *aiming* for a headshot?' he enquired.

Captain Bastable frowned back at the hillside. The goat was no longer on the eleven o'clock line from the small shed which had been the centre of Corporal Smithers's fire order – it lay at about half-past two, apparently undamaged except for its head, which had disappeared.

Second-Lieutenant Chichester leaned forward. 'I've never seen a Boys fired like that before, sir – so accurately,' he said deferentially. 'Our instructors always claimed the prone position was most accurate. Obviously they were wrong!'

'Corporal – ' Captain Willis nodded to Corporal Smithers without taking his eyes from the field-glasses. He appeared to be scanning the hillside for other signs of life. 'Corporal, nip across smartly and pick up that animal, and we'll have it roasted for dinner tonight – I've never had roast goat, and it can't be worse than the alleged beef we had last night . . . Oh – and take a couple of buckets of water and swill the blood away, and find any bits of the head and dispose of them. With a bit of luck the owner'll think the creature's gone absent without leave. Or at least he won't be able to prove otherwise, and then we won't have to pay for it . . . Right?'

Corporal Smithers looked at Captain Bastable uncertainly, though whether this was because he was technically under Bastable's orders, not Willis's, or whether he considered that the disposal of the goat belonged more fairly to the marksman who had bagged it than to a mere onlooker, Bastable could not decide. What irritated him much more was that Willis had pre-empted the wisest (if not the most proper) decision with officer-like promptitude while he had remained silent. So now he had to retrieve his loss of face somehow.

'Hah . . . hmm . . .' He studied Smithers's face, but found no comfort in it. Smithers's expression bore that special blankness of the Other Rank who wishes his officer to believe that all Guilty Secrets are safe with him. Not that this culpable goat-slaying would remain secret for long, especially after Major Tetley-Robinson had sat down to his dinner.

And there, of course, was his solution!

'Hah – no, Willis!' he snapped decisively. 'This goat is a C Company animal. You can cut along and get it, Corporal, as Captain Willis says – and – ah – expunge the evidence to the best of your ability. But then take it to CQMS Gammidge with my compliments and ask him to have it prepared for the men's dinner tonight – with no questions asked, and no exchange of recipes with anyone from other companies. This is to be a strictly private matter between the Company and myself – understood?'

The effect on Corporal Smithers was gratifying. Like Captain Willis, he had obviously never tasted goat, but Captain Willis's planned annexation of the wretched beast for the officers' mess had turned it into a desirable delicacy – and one which now belonged to C Company's pot. So he grinned wickedly at Bastable – indeed, he came within a hair's-breadth of winking – and favoured him with a Brigade of Guards salute before gathering up the anti-tank section for its goat-recovery duties.

For once Captain Bastable felt he had done something right, and that unusual feeling emboldened him to face up to Captain Willis more confidently than he was accustomed to do.

'Now, Willis . . . what can I do for you?' he enquired.

Captain Willis regarded him curiously, as though they were meeting for the first time. 'Well, old boy, you can't actually do anything *for* me. But I'm afraid you've got to do something *with* me – in company with me, that is.'

'What?' The day darkened again. Of all the officers in the battalion, Willis got on his nerves most, with his endless chattering conversation on subjects about which he, Bastable, knew nothing, and cared less. He had heard it said, or he had read somewhere, that politics made for strange bedfellows, but war undoubtedly made for even stranger and less congenial ones, that was certain.

As he stared dispiritedly at Willis he was reminded once again of why he had applied to the Prince Regent's Own back in 1937: he had wanted to get away from Father, if only for short periods, because his ideas of running a successful business and those of the Guv'ner were diverging more and more. And he had also wanted to get away from Mother, on much the same basis,

41

because her ideas and his were also diverging, particularly on the subject of marriageable girls with fat legs.

'Bastable – ?'

It had all gone terribly wrong. The distant sound of bombing indicated that he was now very close to the sharp end of the war; and in a unit which was not so much under-trained and ill-equipped as untrained and unequipped. In fact, in fact . . . if the Prince Regent's Own had been a business, then the word BANKRUPTCY would have been uppermost in his mind now.

'Bastable!'

God! He was thinking thoughts of Alarm and Despondency such as the irascible Brigadier had explicitly stigmatized as cowardly defeatism. And he hadn't even seen a German yet – and there was the whole of the British Expeditionary Force, plus the French, with its thousands of tanks and millions of men, and its impregnable Maginot Line, between him and *them*.

'For Christ's sake, old man – do listen to what I'm telling you,' said Captain Willis. 'The CO has agreed that we should motor over to the Mendips and try and pick up some armour-piercing ammo for the Boys rifles. Nigel Audley had to have a blinding row with the old buffer, but – thank God! – he's a bit leery of Nigel ever since he discovered that Nigel's a friend of the CIG's brother, or sister, or someone. And when we're there I'm damn well going to pick up some gun-cotton and fuses to mine these bloody bridges of ours – the CO doesn't know that, but what he doesn't know won't worry him. And my CSM reckons he knows how best to do the job – we've only got to sling the charges under the keystone of the main arch and push it upwards, and then the whole caboodle'll fall down, he says – *are you listening*, old boy?'

42

'Yes,' said Captain Bastable shortly. 'I've looked at my bridge.'

'Good man.'

'It's pretty solid.' Captain Bastable came to himself with a jolt. 'Why is the CO sending two company commanders to get this ammunition? I don't know about you, Willis – but I've got a job of work to do here.' Bastable pointed to the indefensible bridge.

'Don't ask me, old boy.' Willis shrugged. 'He's sending me because I asked for the stuff, and I can speak French. But he doesn't trust me an inch, so maybe you've got to keep an eye on me. Or maybe Tetley-Robinson thinks we'll lose our way and he'll never see the pair of us again – maybe he thinks the Jerries will dive-bomb us both and blow us to kingdom come – God knows what goes on between Tetley-Robinson's protuberant ears! Probably very little, judging by the state of the Prince Regent's Own . . . But the sooner we're on our way, the better. Because I want to be snug in my billet again tonight, not fumbling around French roads in the dark.'

Bastable drew a deep breath. Ten months in the army had taught him that what could not be avoided was best done as quickly as possible – Willis was right there.

'I give you best over the goat, though,' said Willis with a sudden disarming smile. 'It *was* a damn good shot – and you were quite right to give it to your chaps. It'll buck them up no end, even though they'll hate eating it – it'll be tough as old boots.'

Bastable frowned. 'You've eaten goat?'

'Oh, yes. North African goat – Serbian goat – Greek goat. Greek was the best, that was merely awful . . . Kid is delicious, but that was an aged, stringy old nannie you decapitated. I only wanted to baffle Tetley-Robinson's dentures with it – *rather* naughty of me, I admit! But your

chaps'll think the world of you for giving it to 'em . . .
Even if they don't like it they'll give you the credit for
foisting it on them – they'll think you're a crafty blighter
if they don't credit you with generosity. You'll win either
way, I tell you.'

This was a world of complicated motives and machina-
tions which Bastable had never considered. He believed
the British soldier to be a simple soul, basically. The only
difference between running C Company and Bastable's of
Eastbourne was – equally basically – that it was frequently
necessary to turn a blind eye on the company's attempts
to 'annexe' material belonging to other companies, which
could be safely left to the senior NCOs to discourage
whereas the slightest evidence of dishonesty at Bastable's
resulted in instant dismissal without a reference.

Nevertheless, Captain Willis's approval was oddly –
almost inexplicably – heartening. And the prospect of a
trip in the only Bren carrier salvaged from the chaos of
Boulogne was not without its attractions, particularly as
there was a fair chance of finding out more about the
course of the battle from the Mendips than the beak-
nosed staff Brigadier had known, or been willing to
reveal.

There was some essential work to be done first, however; and young Chichester was still conveniently to hand
to do it, having been hovering in the background all this
time, pretending not to listen to the affairs of his elders
and seniors.

'Mr Chichester – ' the boy tautened up attentively, like
a gun-dog called by its master, ' – I've a job for you!'

'Sir!' Chichester almost saluted, and quite suddenly
Bastable felt himself to be enormously older and senior,
even if young Chichester did know a great deal more
about the Boys anti-tank rifle.

'What's your christian name, Chichester?'

'My – Christopher, sir. Christopher Chichester . . . Or Chris, sir, for short. Sir.'

'Chris . . . Well, our rule is formality in front of the other ranks and christian names among ourselves and in the mess, Chris. And my name is Henry – ' Just as suddenly Bastable knew that he had always disliked the name 'Henry', but had never been able to do anything about it – he had always been 'Henry' at home, and 'Bastable' at school. And – damn and blast it! – *Bar*stable in the Prince Regent's Own. But now, with this tall unfledged youth, he had a chance to start afresh. He had always wanted to be called 'Ronald', after Ronald Colman, who had always seemed to him the epitome of everything an English gentleman should be, and at least his carefully-trimmed moustache, neither too little nor too much, was authentic Ronald Colman. But he could not give himself a name which was not on his birth certificate.

'Henry, sir,' said Christopher – Chris – Chichester, with a look in his periwinkle-blue eyes which Captain Bastable had never seen before. It was – it was an adoring gun-dog look . . . except that Captain Bastable knew he had never looked into the eyes of an adoring gun-dog. In fact, that poor bloody white goat, minding its own business, munching its coarse French grass on its hillside four hundred yards away, was the first and only thing Captain Bastable had ever killed in anger.

Fraud, fraud, fraud! Incompetent fraud!

But not *Henry*. Not *Henry Barstable*. Never again *Henry Bastable*!

'Harry,' said Captain Bastable. 'My friends call me "Harry", Chris.'

'Harry.' Second-Lieutenant Christopher Chichester

pronounced the name as though it frightened him. 'Yes –
Harry.'

'I never knew that,' said Captain Willis. 'Harry?'

'Well, you know it now, Captain Willis,' said Captain
Bastable. 'Now, Chris . . . I want you to go to Mr
Waterworth – Lieutenant Waterworth – who is two i/c of
the company, and tell him that the bridge is untenable
. . . You'll find him upstream, by the old watermill, with
his platoon . . . Tell him to reconnoitre the trees on the
ridge – we'll have to defend the ridge first, whatever
happens. And until I get back with the Boys ammunition
the mortar section must cover the bridge, with PSM Gill's
platoon – do you understand that . . . Chris?'

'Yes – Harry.' Chichester nodded. 'Understood.'

'Off you go then.' Captain Bastable smiled fraudu-
lently. 'Now, Captain Willis – where's our carrier?'

'"Wimpy" to my friends,' said Captain Willis amiably.
'Back in the Classical Sixth it was "Willy" – not to my
face, of course . . . But now it's "Wimpy" – thanks to
Major Tetley-Robinson . . . Harry, old boy.'

Captain Bastable could think of no reply to that.

'And we haven't got the carrier,' added Captain Willis
apologetically. 'Major Tetley-Robinson would never give
me the carrier . . . We've got the Austin Seven – with
Fusilier Evans as driver – "Batty" Evans, as the most
unkindest cut of all!'

3

Of all the vehicles Captain Bastable had ever seen, the Prince Regent's Own Austin Seven was the least military-looking.

He could remember noting scornfully back in England that some less-favoured formations of the British Army had had to make do with transport which betrayed its recent and unsuitable civilian origin; and since arriving in France, on the one short expedition he had conducted beyond the immediate environs of Colembert to superintend the recovery of a broken-down ration truck, he had seen some French Army lorries which looked not so much as though they had survived the First Marne in 1914 as that they had been commandeered before that by Noah to victual the Ark.

Yet the least warlike of those vehicles seemed positively aggressive in comparison with the Austin Seven, which its hurried coating of khaki-drab paint somehow rendered even more pathetic and unmilitary.

Indeed, in the old halcyon days of less than a week ago, the Prince Regent's Own would have rejected such an addition to its MT as unbecoming to the battalion's dignity. But Folkestone had changed all that, and beggars who had arrived at Boulogne had ceased to be choosers: DPT 912 (its rear number plate was still readable under the khaki coating) had been scooped up with the rest of Old Mother Riley's relics, and was now judged quite good enough for two company commanders on a mission of gravity.

The trouble now, however, was not so much DPT 912 (which, to be honest, belied its appearance with a mechanical reliability not possessed by some of the other more imposing-looking relics), but its driver.

OFFICERS WILL NOT DRIVE was a strict Prince Regent's Own order, positively not to be disobeyed, ostensibly to free those officers for more important duties, but actually to prevent them killing themselves prematurely, rather than their men.

The defect of this order was personified in the person of Fusilier Evans, however.

It was not that Fusilier Evans was, like DPT 912, either pathetic or unwarlike; on the contrary, he was built like a steam traction-engine and aggressive with it. In repose he resembled nothing so much as King Kong with a yellow-and-grey lanyard; in simulated action his prowess with the bayonet on sandbags representing Germans was so destructive that he had been excused further bayonet practice (his standard of musketry was correspondingly appalling; he had never been known to hit a target, either his own or anyone else's; his natural weapon, according to his company commander – who was mercifully Captain Willis, and not Captain Bastable – was any smashing, crushing and skewering instrument from the Wars of the Roses); in drink – and there had been three memorable occasions when Fusilier Evans had been officially 'in drink', which were part of battalion legend – he was the terror of the Regimental Police, who on the last occasion had deliberately found pressing duties elsewhere, so the legend had it; he was in fact only amenable to Captain Willis, who played the part of Fay Wray to Evans's King Kong, controlling him by some strange personal magnetism possessed by no one else.

In spite of all this, and particularly in spite of his

manifest inability to drive any sort of vehicle, Fusilier Evans – 'Batty' Evans to those who knew him – had become a driver. And now, because of Tetley-Robinson's warped sense of humour, he was *their* driver.

Lord Austin and his Birmingham engineers had never designed the little car to accommodate the British Army. Even a normally-developed British soldier found it difficult to enter the Seven when in light marching order, and sitting down in it wearing a light pack, water-bottle and bayonet was quite impossible; such soldiers would have been forced to remove their equipment before entering, and it was no surprise to Bastable that he had to share the back seat with three sets of ammunition pouches, small packs, water-bottles, and a bayonet and rifle belonging to the driver; which, with his own and Captain Willis's Webley revolvers and the packed lunches provided by the mess corporal, did not leave a lot of room for him.

But fitting Fusilier 'Batty' Evans into the driver's seat, even after he had been stripped down to his unadorned battledress, was something different, and much more difficult; it could only be done be reducing the man to a constricted, almost crouching posture, with his knees jammed against the steering wheel and his face thrust down and forward towards the windscreen in a position which severely limited both his vision and his control of the vehicle.

Captain Willis circled the little car before climbing into the relative comfort of the front passenger's seat.

'If only you were a bit *bigger*, Batty,' he murmured, speaking more to himself than to anyone else, 'we could open the sun roof and you could see out of the top. But you aren't *quite* big enough . . . so you'll just have to do as I tell you, right?'

'Sir!' said Batty, in his inappropriate falsetto.

'So when I say, "Slow down", you come down to five miles an hour – that's about double-time . . . understood?'

'Sir!' squeaked Batty.

'And when I say, "Stop!" you jam the brakes on. And if you don't watch out bloody quick then you'll squash your face on the windscreen – understood?'

Batty grinned amiably at his company commander. His face, thought Bastable, already looked as if it had been continuously and brutally crushed against a succession of windscreens, if not something harder.

'Sir!' The squeak cracked into hoarseness, which seemed to indicate that Batty regarded both the order and the advice as something of a joke.

'Right. Maximum speed – thirty miles an hour when the road is clear. When any other vehicle approaches . . . and that includes horse-drawn vehicles and motor-cyclists and pedal cyclists – understood? – fifteen miles an hour. And also fifteen miles an hour at any corner where you don't have a clear view of oncoming traffic – *understood?*'

'Sir!' Batty grasped the wheel in his huge hands as though he planned to rip it from the steering column.

'I mean that, Batty,' said Captain Willis mildly. 'I shall be watching the speedometer – ' he reached across and tapped the dial, ' – and if you go faster than that . . . I shall be *very* annoyed.'

Batty looked down at the speedometer in surprise, like a man who had discovered a revolutionary innovation which placed a new and unfair responsibility on him. 'Sir?'

Captain Willis sighed. 'I shall say, "slower", or "faster", Batty. Just don't take your eyes off the road in front for a moment – not for a moment. Don't worry about your speed . . . just do as I say – right?'

'Sir!' Batty sounded much happier.

'Right-o, then! You know the way to the crossroads – you've been there twice with Sar-Major Brotherton. It's straight ahead, then turn right at the crossroads on the main road. And then five miles straight on, and we're there. Right?'

'Sir!' Batty peered ahead uncertainly.

Captain Willis swallowed nervously, and Captain Bastable remembered that Fay Wray had never really been comfortable with King Kong.

'Very well. Then off we go – start the engine and try to engage the gear quietly, there's a good fellow.' Willis's voice was beautifully steady. 'Slowly through the town, now.'

The gears crashed and the little car shuddered. And then began to move forward in a series of jerks.

Captain Bastable observed several grinning fusiliers carrying sandbags towards the Mairie, which because of its cellars had been appropriated partially by Captain Saunders as the Battalion Aid Post. So far the only casualties had been mumps . . . and road injuries, he recalled uneasily.

DPT 912 began to advance more smoothly – and also much faster. Another memorable phrase he had read somewhere popped inappropriately into his mind: faced with the prospect of sexual relations with her husband, Queen Victoria had allegedly lain back on her feather mattress and thought of England. At the time he had read it, it had occurred to him that she ought to have thought of the whole British Empire, rather than just England. But for now, England would have to be enough.

'Slower,' said Captain Willis.

'More smoothly' was relative. The streets of Colembert-les-Deux-Ponts were composed of pavé, a French road material inferior in smoothness to good British asphalt. So not all the juddering was due to Batty's incapacity.

'Good – well done, Batty,' said Willis encouragingly.

Captain Bastable decided to open his eyes again, and think of other things than England. After all, the northern exit from Colembert was as straight as a Roman road, and if Batty could avoid the line of trees which shaded it – Major Audley's trees, all ready for felling as an anti-tank obstacle – then they would soon be in open country.

There were the trees – slipping by at double-time.

And *there* were B Company's defences – there was even a momentary glimpse of the slender barrel of a Boys rifle, poking out of a camouflaged firing position that covered the road and the open fields which made the northern approach to the town so much more defensible than C Company's bridge-and-ridge.

'Faster,' ordered Captain Willis. 'That's enough – hold her at that, Batty!'

Captain Bastable settled himself among the weapons and equipment and packed lunches.

Willis half-turned towards him, while keeping one eye on the open road ahead. 'I know a bit more about those staff types at the Orders Group now, Harry – it was bloody brilliant, the way Nigel put down that hawk-nosed swine, don't you think?'

Captain Bastable – *Harry* Bastable – grunted to that. It wasn't a regimental officer's place to bait staff officers, but Nigel Audley had guts, undeniably.

'Reconnaissance from GHQ in Arras, Dickie Davidson told me. He thinks things are really beginning to move now,' nodded Willis. 'I should guess we're building up a major striking force there, for the big counter-attack. They'll let the Germans stick their necks out, somewhere between Valenciennes and St Quentin – and Cambrai too, where our tanks hit 'em in the last show – and then give them the bloody chop. Us and the French and the Belgians to the north, and the main French Army to the south. Gort and Gamelin have got a plan, he said – it seems Jerry is pushing on too far, beyond his supply lines . . . In fact, the younger chap practically spelt it out, Dickie said – we're letting them have their head to finish him at one go – he'll be in a huge salient, with his flanks open, trying to get to the sea. But the sea is *our* element, not Jerry's – that's the secret of it. With the Navy, we can come and go as we please. And when Jerry tries to swing his tanks northward, which he'll have to do – *then* the French will go in! Like the Marne – '

'That's what Tetley-Robinson said.' Captain Bastable didn't intend his interruption to sound like a criticism, but that was the way it came out.

Captain Willis shrugged. 'Well . . . the old bastard can't be wrong *all* the time. And he did see the last lot out – he's actually beaten them before, after all. He has to get something right, I mean!'

Bastable felt comforted. His morning-of-truth with C Company did apply only to C Company – or, at least, to the drill-obsessed Prince Regent's Own. There were dozens of other battalions – brigades, divisions even . . . and regular battalions too, at that . . . plus the whole French Army, to prove him a Doubting Thomas. And, after all, his total experience of the British Expeditionary Force in France had been limited to one demoralized evening in Boulogne, a single night's drive to the wrong Colembert, and then a couple of days in the middle of nowhere off the main roads, which more or less summed up Colembert's significance on the map of France.

Indeed, all his worries about C Company's bridge-and-ridge were demolished by that same reasoning: even if there were Fifth Columnists and odd Germans swanning about, they would hardly bother with Colembert-les-Deux-Ponts; as somewhere-in-the-middle-of-nowhere it simply wasn't worth bothering with, even supposing they could find it. Simply, the Prince Regent's Own was in no condition to go looking for the Germans – and the Germans had no reason to go looking for the Prince Regent's Own.

'Sir!' squeaked Fusilier Evans suddenly. 'Sir?'

'What is it, Batty?' asked Captain Willis testily.

'Crossroads comin' up, sir,' said Fusilier Evans, proving to Captain Bastable that he had more words in his vocabulary than 'sir', notwithstanding its variety of nuances.

'I can't see any crossroads, Batty,' said Captain Willis.

'They're comin' up, sir,' said Fusilier Evans firmly. 'I recognizes that oak tree, sir. That's the one, sir.'

'Which one?' Captain Willis peered ahead up a hillside bare of trees, hedges and even bushes.

'Just passed it, sir – big old oak,' said Fusilier Evans. 'Dead one, sir. Covered with ivy. Passed it before, I did – crossroads over the top ahead, sir.'

'Then slow down, Batty,' said Captain Willis.

'Sir!' Batty crashed the Austin's gears again, decelerating to a snail's march.

'Not as slow as that,' commanded Willis. 'For God's sake, Batty – *good God Almighty!*'

He stopped short as the little car laboured up the final yards of the rise – stopped short so unnaturally that Bastable instinctively craned his neck downwards to peer through the windscreen.

And then he understood why the command had been cut short.

On the morning when he had recovered the ditched,

broken-down rations truck on the road to the south of Colembert, Captain Bastable had seen refugees.

There had then been cars, and some trucks, and the occasional horse-drawn cart piled with goods and chattels, an intermittent but steady stream of them.

But this was different.

They had been gradually lifting up, undulation after undulation, from the river bottom of Colembert – what stream or river it was, he didn't know, from those two unimportant bridges.

But now they were at last on the top land of this French plain, where the main road ran east–west through the cornfields – the road they had planned to join –

Turn right, then five miles on, and we're there, Batty –

Five miles – craning left and right through the little Austin's windows – left and centre and right – he could almost see for five miles . . .

He could see miles of every imaginable variety of *vehicle* – lorries and trucks and cars and horse-drawn carts and hand-carts and bicycles and push-carts and prams, piled high with trunks and bags and cases and sacks and mattresses and bedsteads and – and *people* –

People walking and riding and leading and following, and being carried and led and pushed and pulled, old and young, men and women –

This was totally and terrifyingly different from what he had seen on the southern road twenty-four hours before, a deluge compared with a trickle, for which the trickle hadn't prepared him –

And soldiers!

French soldiers, from their helmets, with blue uniforms dusted to an indeterminate brownish camouflage, shambling along for all the world as though they were refugees too!

'My God!' whispered Wimpy. 'My God! Christ Almighty – what's happened?'

'They're runnin' away, that's what,' said Fusilier Evans.

Bastable pushed the equipment aside again and stared through the side window opposite him. There was a great dirty column of smoke away to the east, where his line of vision and the refugee column converged, and an incessant rumble of explosions.

'Jerry's bombing Belléme,' said Wimpy unnecessarily.

Bastable grunted. It didn't look like a garden bonfire.

'It'll take more than bombers to shift the Mendips,' said Wimpy. 'That's a regular battalion. They're shit-hot.'

'I hope they've got plenty of .55 armour-piercing,' said Bastable.

'Boys ammo?' Wimpy snorted. 'When I was there yesterday morning they were emplacing two-pounder anti-tank guns – they've got at least three of them, that I saw. They'll be reserving their Boys for the small stuff, after the main course, if Jerry ever gets so far. I tell you, they make our lot look like boy Scouts, Harry, old boy . . . So the sooner we get in there and find out what's cooking, the better.'

The damn butterflies were flapping again in Bastable's guts. 'You don't think we ought to get back to battalion?'

'Not bloody likely!' Wimpy emitted another snort. 'We still have to pick up that armour-plating, in case Jerry infiltrates round the side-roads . . . And besides, I want to see what's happening over there. Drive on, Batty!'

Batty Evans remained motionless.

'Drive on!' snapped Bastable.

'Can't, sir,' said Fusilier Evans. 'Bloody cart broken down in road.'

'So there is!' exclaimed Wimpy. 'Well – get it out of the way then, man!'

'Right, sir,' said Fusilier Evans, bursting open his door.

Without Batty's huge hunched figure in the way, half the windscreen became suddenly clear – and so was the accuracy of Batty's statement: a horse drawing a two-wheeled cart had chosen to founder precisely at the junction of the minor road with the major one. And the owners of the horse and cart were now grouped round the horse, attempting to cajole it to rise, while the rest of the traffic crawled round it regardless.

Batty Evans shouldered his way through the family group without attempting to discuss the matter and delivered a vicious kick to the horse.

The horse shuddered – and received an even more vicious kick. The aged owner of the cart remonstrated with Batty, and was sent spinning out of the way with an almost casual backhander. Batty went round to the front and took hold of the horse's harness alongside its mouth and jerked its head upwards. The horse did not wish to get up, but recognized *force majeure*: it rose first on to its hind legs, then on to its forelegs, as the only alternative to having its neck broken.

But having stood up, it positively refused to be pulled forward, and not even Batty's strength could move the combined weight of horse and cart (which, among the latter's contents included an enormous grandfather clock, Bastable observed).

Batty stood back and pushed his steel helmet back on his head, as though to let the air get to his brain. He stared at the horse for a moment or two, and then lifted his fist threateningly. The horse observed the fist and tried to back away from him.

This was exactly what Batty had wanted (so it seemed to Bastable), because he laid into the terrified creature like Jack Dempsey, first with one fist, then with the other,

57

backing it up until the cart tipped into the ditch at the corner of the road junction. The shafts rose brutally, practically lifting the unfortunate animal's feet off the ground, while the grandfather clock slithered off the pile of bundles on the cart, landing upright in the ditch with a musical crash.

Batty surveyed his handiwork for two satisfied seconds, and then doubled back to the car. The gears clashed again, and as DPT 912 moved forward Bastable caught a last, heart-rending glimpse of the owner of the cart holding his head in his hands.

'Well done, Batty,' said Wimpy. 'Now – right for Belléme.'

At first it looked as though that was a reasonable order, for the refugees passing at the moment were all on foot, weighed down by suitcases and bundles, and the car was able to nose through them, on to the main road, against the stream.

Then Batty stopped the car abruptly. 'Never get down through that lot, sir – ' he stared at the clot of heavier vehicles which was pushing its own way through the people on foot, ' – the bleeders are jammed solid, sir.'

Wimpy was still standing up in the front, chest and shoulders above the roof. He addressed a French soldier in the passing throng. 'Où sont les allemands, soldat?' he shouted.

The French soldier shrugged and continued to shuffle past. Batty sprang out of the car again, this time with astonishing speed: it was as though he had been coiled up into it like a spring waiting to be released – Bastable had never seen him move so fast. Before the astonished French soldier could react Batty had him pinioned against the radiator, facing Wimpy.

'Answer the officer when he speaks to you, you cheeky

fucker!' he howled in that unnatural voice of his, which anger raised to a hoarse treble.

Bastable had just about understood Wimpy's first French phrase – it was one of those in his private notebook of French phrases, in which 'où est' and 'où sont' were basic openers, with 'combien' and 'je ne comprends pas' close behind, and 'allemand' as essential as 'français'. But the French language in general had been almost as much of a crucifixion to him at school as Latin, and the Frenchman's replies to Wimpy's questions – punctuated as those replies were by gasps of pain every time Batty encouraged him to speak up – were quite beyond him, only serving to remind him that it was useless to learn questions if one couldn't make head nor tail of the answers.

'All right – let the blighter go, Batty,' said Wimpy finally.

'Sir!' howled Batty, propelling the Frenchman west-wards with a contemptuous kick.

There came a loud hooting from the vehicles they had delayed, while the smaller fry on two wheels and two feet had flowed round them. Batty turned towards the sound, feet apart, hands on hips, like a one-man roadblock.

'What did he say?' asked Bastable

'He said . . .' Wimpy tailed off as he surveyed the scene. 'Now if we go straight on, on to that other side-road ahead, we can take the first turning to the right, and maybe get to Belléme by one of the back roads . . .'

That obviously hadn't been what the French soldier had said; Wimpy was merely thinking aloud, trying to solve their problem.

'What did he say?' Bastable fumed impotently among the piled equipment.

'He said – ' This time Wimpy bit the answer off. '*Batty!* Back into the car double-quick – *drive straight on!*'

Batty moved back into his seat almost as fast as he had left it, driven by the urgency of the command.

'*Put your boot down, man!*' Wimpy shouted. '*Fast!*'

The car juddered forward, scattering the refugees ahead of it as it moved across the main road on to the other, minor arm of the crossroad which matched the narrow road from Colembert by which they had come. There was a crunch of metal as one wing caught the front of a hand-cart piled with possessions. The car checked for a fraction of a second, then the cart overturned, scattered its contents.

'*Faster!*' shouted Wimpy.

Loud cries of anger and sorrow mingled with the insistent hooting which filled Bastable's ears. Then, as though released from all restraint, the little engine roared into life under Batty's boot and the car shot away down the empty, dusty side-road, throwing Bastable against the rear seat and tipping his helmet over his eyes.

'What the devil – ?' Bastable swore, grabbing for the strap Lord Austin had thoughtfully supplied for nervous passengers and trying to pull himself upright.

'Messerschmitts!' snapped Wimpy.

'What?' Bastable twisted to peer out of the rear window, but the road was an impenetrable dust cloud behind them.

'Square wing-tips – remember 'em from the aircraft recognition posters. Quite unmistakable – saw 'em banking – make for those trees ahead, Batty.' He was back below roof level now. 'Hurricanes are rounded, Spitfires are pointed – Messerschmitts are square – the wing-tips. Saw 'em turning . . . Nearly there – *don't slow down, Batty!*'

Bastable had never seen a German aircraft for absolutely certain. During the last thirty-six hours plenty of aircraft had flown over Colembert, but always too far away or too high up to be identified beyond doubt, and even though the self-styled experts had all agreed that these had been enemy aircraft, he himself had remained unconvinced.

Besides, assuming every plane one heard to be an E/A was also in the realm of Alarm and Despondency. There were known to be a substantial number of RAF squadrons in the Advanced Air Striking Force, not to mention the two thousand planes of the French Air Force. So it was on the very tip of his tongue to say, 'nonsense', except that one officer didn't say things like that to another officer in the presence of another rank.

And, also, the Germans had undoubtedly been bombing Belléme – and judging by the continuance of that distant thunder were still doing so, too. So the aircraft Wimpy had spotted could very well be a German, whatever the shape of its wing-tips. . .

They were into the trees.

'Stop!' commanded Wimpy.

DPT 912 stopped abruptly with a squeal of brakes, in obedience to its driver's incompetence, and at once stalled.

The aircraft noise increased behind them, and was suddenly punctuated by a loud staccato rattling, at once quite different from and yet entirely reminiscent of the noise on the field firing range during the last Bren gun course.

Machine-gun fire. Machine-gun fire in bursts, growing louder – approaching – stopping . . . starting again and growing louder again – the sound pattern repeating itself behind him, along and above the road.

The road –

The road had been jammed with refugees – women and children, old women and young children, and old men – old men like the one with the smashed-up grandfather clock on the cart Batty had backed into the ditch – and the drab, dusty people who had wailed over the cart they had knocked over – Christ! even a single Bren fired down that line would tear them to pieces . . . and those Messerschmitts had three or four machine-guns each in them.

He had read about it all before. In Poland and Norway . . . and it had begun again in Holland and Belgium a week or so ago . . . But this was here and now, a quarter of a mile behind him, among human beings he had just passed – the old men in their shapeless suits, and the old women in their black shawls and the children in their dirty frocks – *Christ – oh Christ!* – but this was *real*.

'My God!' he said. 'My . . . God!'

'Harry – for God's sake don't be sick in the car, man,' said Wimpy anxiously. 'There isn't anything we can do – we've got to get round to the Mendips to stop the bastards, that's all – so don't throw up on me, there's a good chap! Start the engine, Batty – '

It wasn't theory any more. Bastable swallowed air. His breakfast was long since digested and there seemed to be nothing in his stomach but a painful contraction of its muscles.

'I'm okay. Start the engine, Fusilier,' snapped Bastable.

'Okay . . . we want the first turning to the right, that'll take us back to Belléme,' said Wimpy. 'So away you go, Batty, there's a good fellow. And take it slowly now – '

But there wasn't any turning to the right.

The road twisted and bent and forked occasionally, but

always more to the left than the right so that even by taking the right-hand fork they only maintained a northerly direction, when it was to the east – even increasingly to the south-east – that they wanted to go, by the tell-tale smoke from Belléme.

They stopped at a cottage, but it was locked and obviously empty; then at a farm, where a dog tried to bite Batty and received a boot in its face, and ran away whimpering; and there was no one there, either. The whole of France seemed to have emptied itself suddenly.

The land, which had risen up to the plateau that had carried the refugee road, now undulated downwards by a sunken road, into another and larger belt of trees.

'Stop the car,' ordered Wimpy.

This time there was no skid-and-shudder, for Batty hadn't needed to be told to drive slowly, he had driven like a man walking on thin ice across an immense frozen lake ever since the German planes had attacked the refugees. If Bastable had been able to credit Batty with anything like a sense of imagination he might have wondered whether the huge fusilier was a bit windy, but that didn't seem a tenable theory. More likely the further away he drove from home – home being Colembert – the less happy he felt, simply.

'There's another ridge up ahead,' murmured Wimpy. 'If only we had a map . . . I think I'll just scout it on foot – and if you hear me run into trouble, turn the car round and drive like hell. At least we know how to get back, even if we don't know how to go forward.'

Bastable was about to agree when he remembered that he was the senior officer present, at least technically, having received his acting-captaincy three weeks before Wimpy. Also (and rather more to the point) he had to recover his loss of face over that show of weakness during the Messerschmitt attack.

'It was a bit stupid of *me* not to bring a map,' he began, as a prelude to asserting himself.

Wimpy shrugged. 'We knew where we were going, that's all. Give me my revolver, will you, Harry?'

Bastable followed him out of the car. 'I'll go, Wimpy. I'm senior.'

'By two weeks,' said Wimpy. 'And it was my idea.'

'Three weeks,' amended Bastable. 'And if there is any trouble . . . you'll be able to get back through those refugees better than me – you can speak their lingo. So I'll go, and that's that.'

Wimpy considered this proposition for a moment or two. 'Okay – I tell you what, Harry . . . You scout up the ridge ahead – ' he unhooked the field-glasses from round his neck. ' – here, you can borrow these; you should get a pretty good view from the top. And I'll scout through these trees – this wood, more like – to the east. But you'd better take Batty with you, just in case.' He turned to Fusilier Evans. 'Now, Batty . . . I want you to go with Captain Bastable, and do what he says – right? And if there's any trouble, I want you to deal with it.'

Batty looked unhappy, but resigned. 'Sir!'

Wimpy nodded at him, as if to emphasize the orders, then smiled uneasily at Bastable. 'Any trouble – the first one back here takes the car and gets back to Colembert like a blue-arsed fly, without waiting . . . No trouble – and we'll have our lunch here – rather delayed, but still lunch, eh?' He paused. 'Okay, Harry?'

Bastable suddenly realized that he was quite hungry. The Messerschmitts were already a dream – a nightmare from a disturbed night in another time, another place. Almost, someone else's dream.

He smiled back. 'Right-o, Wimpy, old boy – agreed!'

He was Harry now. *Bar*stable had been left behind en route.

But as Batty unloaded the car, and then started to try and back it into a convenient space between the trees ready to move in either direction, Wimpy inclined his head towards him conversationally, rather as Nigel Audley had done after breakfast.

'If you don't mind me saying so, Harry – I hope you don't mind – I'd keep your eye peeled up there . . .' Wimpy scuffed the roadside dust with the toe of his boot. '. . . stay on the "qui vive", as they say, eh?' He didn't look up as he spoke.

'I beg your pardon?' Bastable stopped basking in his Harry-self and studied Wimpy. He found himself wondering how the chap had become 'Wimpy' – thanks to Major Tetley-Robinson, he had said it had been – after having been plain 'Willy' to his Latin pupils . . . yet whether he even liked being 'Wimpy' – he didn't seem to mind, but Tetley-Robinson was nobody's friend, and his least of all . . . Because if he didn't –

But that wasn't what Wimpy was worried about now, and he was surely worried about something.

'That French soldier said something?' Bastable remembered that he never had received any answer to that question.

'No, not really.' Wimpy looked at him at last. 'He said the Germans were everywhere. But he'd been running for a long time, that lad had. And he'd been bombed half out of his wits, I think, too . . . No, Harry – it's . . . it's more something I *feel* . . . It's . . . like, we're by ourselves, but we're not alone.'

Bastable shared the embarrassment. It didn't make sense, that; so he didn't know what to say to it.

'I read this story once, Harry – a sort of ghost story, by some foreign writer chap . . . never heard of him before – can't remember his name now . . . about this Austrian cavalry patrol in the fourteen-eighteen War, scouting in the Carpathian Mountains or somewhere . . .' Wimpy tailed off, suddenly even more embarrassed. 'Oh, damn! It doesn't matter, anyway.'

But it did matter, Bastable knew that as surely as he knew the wholesale and retail prices of soft furnishings, ladies' gloves and dining-room suites. The chap wanted to talk, and when a chap wanted to talk – especially a naturally talkative chap like Wimpy – it was better to let him get it off his chest. Batty was taking his time backing the car, anyway.

'No, do go on, old chap,' he said. 'Sounds a jolly interesting story – let's hear it.'

Wimpy remained silent for a moment. 'All right, then . . . They were scouting, and they ambushed a Russian force at a bridge – charged over the bridge and cut 'em to pieces . . . and then they pushed on. Only the country was empty, or almost empty – the people in it were strange . . . and so were the narrator's fellow officers – he was a cavalry lieutenant, the fellow telling the story – and they got stranger and stranger. And so did the countryside – kind of misty and shimmery as well as empty. Until they came to another bridge.'

He stopped again. He was no longer looking at Bastable, who now thought it sounded a damn funny story, and that Wimpy was behaving in a damn funny way, too. But then he hadn't exactly covered himself with glory back in the car. In fact, he had nearly covered himself with something else.

'Another bridge – yes?' If Wimpy was windy, it was best to know about it here and now.

Wimpy swallowed. 'A great golden bridge over a shining river of silver. And then he knew.'

'Knew where they were, you mean?'

Wimpy swung towards him. 'He knew they were all dead. *They'd* been ambushed at the first bridge, *not* the Russians – *They'd* been cut to pieces, *not* the Russians. All except him, and he was badly wounded, hovering between life and death. So that was where they were – he was still in the no-man's-land between life and death, where time stands almost stationary. Only they were fading as they crossed their final bridge, a second or two after they'd been killed, but he had a final choice – don't you see?'

Bastable didn't see at all. Except that it was a damn weird story, and this was not the time or place for it, and he was glad no one else was around to hear it.

'Don't you see?' repeated Wimpy.

'Yes.' Bastable humoured him. 'Jolly interesting . . . in a creepy sort of way – ghost story, of course, you said? So I take it he made the right choice, what? Obviously he did – otherwise there wouldn't have been any story!'

'No – I don't mean that – ' Wimpy gestured despairingly, and then swept his hand towards the ridge and the wood. 'It was like the country we're in, Harry . . . It's not *right*, somehow. And now we're making *our* decision.'

Bastable stared up the road which wound between its sunken banks and occasional bushes to another wood on the skyline. It was undeniably empty, but it was no stranger than any other bit of French countryside. It was rather dull really, not nearly as steep as his own beautiful downland above Eastbourne and between Polegate and Lewes . . . a bit like the Lewes road, maybe . . . But certainly neither misty nor shimmery. And with no golden bridges and silver rivers.

Perhaps Wimpy was sickening for the mumps, it occurred to him. It couldn't be drink, because the fellow had been in plain sight for the last hour or more, and there wasn't a whiff of it on his breath.

'Sir!' squeaked Fusilier Batty Evans at his elbow.

With a very great effort Bastable clapped Wimpy on the shoulder. Normally he hated touching people – anyone – beyond the obligatory handshake. But Harry Bastable wasn't Henry *Bar*stable. And there was that line from his favourite poem, by Sir Henry Newbolt, to remember –

> But his Captain's hand on his shoulder smote –
> 'Play up! play up! and play the game!'

– which really summed up the situation, literally. Because by those three weeks of seniority he, Harry Bastable, was Wimpy's Captain, by God!

'Don't worry, old boy – I'll keep my eyes open – "Qui vive" and "verb. sap." and all that. Don't worry!'

He had quoted those lines in the mess once, on a rather drunken evening a few months ago, and everyone had roared with laughter – Wimpy most of all.

But Wimpy wasn't laughing now, he was pleased to observe.

4

The road was definitely not misty and shimmery, any more than it was in the Carpathian Mountains. But it was deceptively steep in spite of its zig-zag and, because of that zig-zag, much longer than it had seemed from below, even to an officer used to Prince Regent's Own's route-marches. Or perhaps his legs had simply stiffened up in the constriction of DPT 912's rear seat.

Also, its high banks prevented ready observation of the land on either side except at the cost of regular side-scrambles, which further delayed the reconnaissance; and as Wimpy's scout through the wood must necessarily be more quickly completed, and the sooner they were on their way again the better, Bastable contented himself with cautious peerings round each blind bend after the first few hundred yards, with Batty crunching along stolidly five paces behind him.

At length, however, they began to get closer to the trees at the top, and through the thick spring vegetation Bastable made out the shape of what must be farm buildings.

The last turning revealed these as presenting a solid blank wall, topped by an orange-red tiled roof in a sorry state of repair, along some seventy-five yards of empty roadside – a barn, or stable, or collection of covered pens of some sort opening on to an inner courtyard, decided Bastable. He had seen run-down farms like this, more or less, on the outskirts of Colembert, unwelcoming from the front but with an entrance round the side. And in this case that entrance must be at the far end, judging by the lack of any side-track through the trees at this end. It would be at the far end, too, that he would most likely get a view of the plain – or the next empty undulation – beyond.

But now, quite clearly, was the moment of maximum danger, if there was any. Which there probably wasn't, because he could still hear no other sounds than the distant rumble of bombs and drone of aircraft engines which were as natural and unremarkable now as the birdsong in his own garden, and the raucous squawking of the gulls in Devonshire Park in the morning.

The memory was suddenly painful, as he longed for those other long-lost sounds, and smells, and all the sensations of England, Eastbourne, Home and Beauty – even girls with fat legs.

He turned back towards Fusilier Batty Evans and put his finger to his lips, and pointed to the scatter of weeds and coarse grass and young stinging nettles growing under the barn wall alongside the road, which would deaden their footfalls. Then he set out along the side of the wall.

Half-way along he thought he'd caught the sound of voices, but a renewed rumble from the east . . . or maybe it was from the north, he couldn't make out . . . overlaid the sound before he could confirm it in his mind. But at least it served to draw his attention to the emptiness of his hands. He unbuttoned the flap of his webbing holster and drew out the Webley.

This, it occurred to him, was the first time he had ever drawn the weapon in what might loosely be called 'anger', though now it was happening 'trepidation' seemed a more appropriate word.

Yet, oddly enough, it was not trepidation – damn it! that was only jargon for windiness – *fear* – fear of what might be round the next corner, but only of not doing things *right*, according to the book, and thereby making an ass of himself.

The book came vividly to mind: Lesson 2 of it, complete with diagram of British soldier in battledress ready for action:

– Fig 6 – Point-blank range –
Drill cartridges will NOT be used in this lesson.
The common faults in firing are . . .

He peered round the end of the building. There was a track here, between the end of the barn-like building and the next belt of trees, but it was quite empty.

And, as he stepped out on to the empty track, he could see that there was an opening in the farm wall – a gateway about ten yards down, opposite another gateway into a field, at the end of the trees.

So . . . so he would go down and peer into the gateway in the wall, and satisfy himself that the farmyard was empty. And then he would use Wimpy's field-glasses, which hung awkwardly on top of his respirator, to scan the countryside on the other side of the track, through the farm-gate of the field, which promised a fine view of the countryside below and beyond.

But, as it turned out, he didn't do things in that order at all.

As he came abreast of the farmyard gateway, edging cautiously along the wall, a flash of light from the sun on glass or metal drew his attention into the open gap of the field gateway.

The gap – the gate itself lay flat and crushed – did fulfil its promise of a fine view of the countryside below and beyond the farm buildings.

Bastable stared at the fine view with disbelief.

Rank upon rank of German tanks and vehicles were drawn up, motionless, in field after field for as far as he could see – as far as he could imagine – beyond his furthest imagining, because he had never seen so many vehicles at one time.

It wasn't possible that they could be there, his brain told him – without his having heard them – without everyone knowing it – or *someone* knowing it – *it wasn't possible –*

The sun flashed again on the same metallic surface, on a tank far down the valley, and suddenly it *was* possible, and Bastable graduated from disbelief to belief, and from belief to absolute panic.

He turned to run, and saw what was behind him.

In the centre of the farmyard was the Humber staff car he had seen that morning outside battalion headquarters. And he knew it was the same car because the same beak-nosed Brigadier who had barked at them that morning was standing beside it.

He had found the Germans right enough.

Or, since he was talking to two of them, they had found him –

As Bastable observed the tableau of the car and the Brigadier and the Germans talking to him in that split-second, one of the Germans raised his arm in the Hitler-salute he had seen in dozens of newsreels and photographs, and the Brigadier also raised his arm –

He had to rescue the Brigadier, it was his plain duty – the Webley came up automatically.

'Hands up!' shouted Harry Bastable. 'Brigadier – '

The three men turned towards him, thunderstruck. A German soldier in a steel helmet appeared from behind a farm cart, a rifle in his hands.

Bastable fired at the soldier in the helmet, and knew he'd missed even as he fired. And fired again, and missed again. The German soldier worked the bolt of his rifle feverishly, and the two German officers started fumbling with their holsters. The Brigadier pointed at Bastable and shouted in German to the soldier with the rifle.

Bastable fled back down the cart rack towards the road. Batty Evans appeared in front of him, rifle at the ready, bayonet fixed.

'Germans!' shouted Bastable. 'Run, Batty!'

Batty looked strangely at him, then threw his rifle up and fired it down the lane past him.

Bastable turned the corner. 'Run, Batty – follow me!' he shouted over his shoulder.

There was no time to run back down the road the way they had come. Bastable bounded up the side of the road-bank opposite him and threw himself over the top. The bank was considerably higher on the fieldside than the roadside because of the fall of the hillside, but fear made him as surefooted as a goat and he slid down it accurately on to both feet.

He heard another rifle-shot behind him, then more shots.

The field ahead of him was only a few yards wide at this point, owing to the zig-zag of the road, he supposed, and the next bank ahead of him was low enough to hurdle. Only after his feet left the ground did it occur to him that the drop on the other side into the road might be a painful one if the fall was as great as last time. But it wasn't the road into which he fell, but only another field, with another beautiful surefooted landing.

He was losing his sense of direction, but there was no time to worry about directions. Wimpy would have heard the shots, and Wimpy would know what they meant.

73

Not straight across the next field, then – that would only invite a bullet between the shoulder-blades – he would double to his right, under cover of this bank and in the opposite direction from which he had originally come, so far as he could make out any direction any more –

There was a low gap in the field-bank ahead of him, and then – like a crowning gift from God! – a thicket of small trees. He plunged over and into them, caught his foot on a tree-root, and fell sprawling. The fall half-winded him, and for a moment he lay gasping, waiting for sounds of pursuit – guttural German orders – or, worse still, the shrill squealing, clattering of the tanks.

There came the sound of another shot, but it was not very close to where he lay.

Hundreds of tanks – there were hundreds of tanks behind him!

He stuffed his revolver back into his holster – how he hadn't dropped it . . . stupid! it was on its lanyard! – and started off again.

The sound of the shot he had just heard suddenly registered in his brain. Batty was no longer with him, it reminded him.

He leaned against a tree, to get his breath back.

He had left Fusilier Evans behind.

He had abandoned Fusilier Evans.

He had run away in panic, abandoning Fusilier Evans to the enemy – *Captain* Bastable had deserted *Fusilier* Evans!

But no . . . that wasn't quite fair. He had ordered Batty Evans to follow him, and if Batty hadn't obeyed that order it was his look-out. They hadn't gone up the hill to fight the whole German Army –

The thought of the whole German Army started his

legs moving again and stopped him thinking about anything else except the lie of the land ahead of him and behind him. It was mostly flat now, and from the position of the sun, he was moving more or less westwards – the refugee direction. But also the direction in which the German Army was advancing.

He had to get back to the battalion!

Of course, Wimpy would be making for the battalion, and Wimpy had the car, God willing . . . And also Wimpy was no fool, schoolmaster notwithstanding – in fact Wimpy had smelt danger when he had felt nothing and had diagnosed a dose of incipient mumps, if not a bad case of windiness. And, by God, he knew what that last felt like now!

But not even Wimpy could take that Austin Seven past a German tank, and then it would be doubly his duty to get back to the battalion –

His head seemed to spin with the effort of thinking things out while steadily putting more distance between himself and the Germany Army.

There was something else that was his duty – there were probably lots of other things that were his duty. But getting back to the battalion was the first one, the most urgent one, and that meant bearing far more to the south than he was going at present. So bear southwards, Bastable, damn your eyes!

And southwards might even be safer from those tanks, too . . . The main road, with the refugees on it, would give him his bearings, anyway. But the important thing was to keep moving steadily at the trot, preferably with something solid between himself – dead ground would do best, but any cover was better than none – between himself and all those Germans –

All those Germans didn't bear thinking about when

75

one was running away from them. And, of course, that was why there had been no one along the route they had innocently and accidentally taken to get to Belléme. Because no one, positively no one, would wait about, milking cows or ploughing fields or preparing supper, right in the path of an army about to advance.

No civilians, that was –

No one, in fact, except the French Army whose job it was to stop the Germans.

But where was that army?

He settled down to another steady run, along the flank of a convenient fold in the ground, and could stop himself trying to think that one out as he ran.

There was still noise and smoke away ahead, to the left, in what must still be the direction of Belléme. But those Germans in the fields hadn't been heading – or pointed – in that direction, so they were obviously set to outflank or by-pass that hot-spot, with its regular Mendips and their anti-tank guns. So where were they heading for?

With a growing sense of military inadequacy, he began to realize that in so far as he had tried to imagine the Real War he had envisaged a war of trenches and barbed-wire, and great massed offensives – a war of lines and no-man's-land.

He was in a no-man's-land now, of a sort. But there was nothing to see, just empty farmland.

A sudden roar blotted out nothing, and two German fighter planes, their black crosses plain to see, snarled low across the empty landscape ahead of him – so low that they seemed to skim below the skyline of the ridge. Bastable flung himself flat and hugged the bare earth, cursing his respirator and webbing pouches which prevented him from flattening himself absolutely against the ground as more planes roared directly over him. And

76

more – and heavier ones, by the thunder of their engines, which concussed his eardrums. It seemed to him impossible that they wouldn't spot him, lying there on the open hillside.

But they wouldn't stop for one man, they would surely have other, much bigger and more important targets than Captain Bastable.

And they would probably think he was dead, anyway. He was lying as still as death.

Then they were gone, not as quickly as they had come, but droning away more slowly . . . But gone, nevertheless – he felt he had almost willed them on towards wherever they were going.

Only now there was another noise – a far more frightening and terrible noise which he recognized from way back: the clank and screech and roar of metal tracks. And it was coming towards him, the noise.

God! He could lie there, where he was, then they too just might take him for dead, as the pilots had done, and leave him. Or they might simply roll over him to make sure, saving bullets – no trouble at all, just one more squashed Tommy.

Or he could rise up on his knees and raise his hands in surrender. And because he'd at least given them a good run for their money, if they were sportsmen they might just take him prisoner –

The noise of the tracks was very close now, very loud, almost on top of him.

It stopped beside him.

'Is the poor bugger dead?' said a rich West Country voice.

'Naow! 'E's shammin' – I just seen 'im twitch. Get oop, mate!'

Bastable was already getting up before he received the order.

''E's an orficer!' exclaimed the second voice.

Bren carrier – of course, that was why the sound had been so recognizable! Bastable cursed himself, his stupidity, his cowardice; yet at the same time he wanted to embrace the machine and to kiss it, and its crew, out of sheer love and gratitude.

And with the Mendips' divisional sign on it, too!

'Bastable – captain, Prince Regent's Own,' said Bastable quickly with what shred of dignity he could find among the rags he had left. 'You're Mendips – from Belléme?'

'I didn't say 'oo we was.' The carrier sergeant whipped out a revolver and pointed at Bastable. 'And I didn't ask 'oo you was, neither.'

'Bastable, Sergeant.' The revolver bewildered Bastable. 'From the Prince Regent's Own South Downs Fusiliers – at Colembert.'

'That's them Terriers down south, sarge,' said the driver familiarly. 'That funny lot wot don't belong to no one, an' shouldn't be there – you remember!'

'I also remember there's a lot of dodgy boogers around 'oo ain't so funny, Darkie,' said the Sergeant. 'An' this one's a long way from home, if 'e's wot 'e sez 'e is.'

It was clear that they were going to take him for a Fifth Columnist until proved otherwise, Bastable realized.

'I have identification on me,' he said haughtily.

'An' you could 'ave got that from anywhere,' said the Sergeant suspiciously. 'You could be Adolf-bloody-Hitler for all I know!'

''Oo won the Cup in 1938?' challenged the driver.

Bastable stared at him in horror. 'Which cup?'

By the expressions on their faces he might just as well have phrased the question in German. Of course, it was a

78

football cup – and he was a crass idiot not to have realized it. All the other ranks were mad on football, of the soccer variety, so that it had been a source of dissension in the Prince Regent's Own that the regimental game was rugger. But he knew nothing about that either, although he had been forced to play it – at considerable cost to his person in bruises and contusions – and yet to admit knowing nothing about either sport now would be disastrous.

Fear honed up his wits. 'Who won Wimbledon?' he challenged the driver. 'The mixed doubles?'

'Wimbledon?' the driver looked to his sergeant. 'What's that?'

'Tennis,' said the Sergeant shortly. 'Who – ' He cut off the question unasked. 'No! Who's Len Hutton?'

So the Sergeant was smart enough not to ask a question which his Fifth Columnist could answer. Which was just as well, because he hadn't the faintest idea who had won the mixed doubles in '38. But he did know who Hutton was.

'Test cricketer.'

But he must retain the initiative. He plucked the only name he could think of out of his memory. 'Who's Sydney Wooderson?' he slammed the question in before the Sergeant could counter-attack him. Father had been a notable athlete in his youth, and Wooderson's record mile was one of his favourite Great British Triumphs.

The revolver drooped slightly. The Sergeant evidently didn't know who Sydney Wooderson was, but remembered the name.

'Look, Sergeant – ' Bastable pressed his advantage, ' – whoever I am – and I'm Captain Bastable of the PROs, I assure you – whoever I am, I suggest we all get the blazes out of here before the Germans arrive!'

The Sergeant's jaw tightened. 'Why were you tryin' to hide from us – shammin' dead?'

'From you?' Bastable looked round over the open field in surprise. 'I was . . . taking cover from those German planes!'

'But they'd gone – we took cover from them. An' you stayed flat . . . sir.' There was doubt in the Sergeant's voice.

Humiliation stared Bastable in the face – and he embraced it like a sinner in the Confessional. 'Because I was scared shitless, Sergeant – that's why! We haven't been bombed at Colembert – we haven't even seen enemy aircraft close up. I was heading for your chaps at Belléme, to get ammunition for our anit-tank rifles, when I ran into their tanks, just not far from here.'

Suddenly the Mendips sergeant's face cracked into friendliness. Not knowing who had won the Cup was one thing – but being frightened was a password he understood. 'Hop on, sir!' he commanded. 'Get moving, Darkie!'

Bastable threw himself into the carrier. 'Where's your Number Three?'

The carrier squealed and jerked forward. 'Lost 'im near Doullens,' shouted the Sergeant. 'Jerry armoured car – but we knocked the bastard out with the Bren then – God knows how . . . Where's Jerry, sir?'

'Over the ridge, back there somewhere,' shouted Bastable.

'In what strength, sir?'

Bastable had a sudden terrifying vision of cornfields filled with tanks. 'More than I've ever seen in my life,' he replied honestly at the top of his voice. 'Dozens of tanks – they looked like hundreds to me, but certainly dozens of them.'

The Sergeant nodded, not disbelievingly.

'What are you doing here?' shouted Bastable. The slap of the tracks on the underside of the carrier made conversation difficult.

'Tryin' to re-establish communications with Brigade, sir,' shouted the Sergeant. 'They got our wireless trucks – with the bombers, sir.'

Bastable nodded, as one unbombed veteran to another obviously much-bombed one.

'They tried their Stukas on us, sir,' shouted the Sergeant. 'All noise – but they didn't hit anything, and we got two of 'em with the Brens. But then they clobbered us with the big boogers – gave us a right goin' over.'

Bastable nodded again. The Stukas were the dive-bombers, whose hideous screech had reached Colembert briefly the previous afternoon. But he had heard nothing of them since then.

'We're going to RV with Mr Greystock and Corporal Titchener, sir,' shouted the Sergeant, lifting his map meaningfully. This was the difference between the Professionals and the Amateurs, thought Bastable, remembering Wimpy's regrets for their lack of a map: these men knew where they were going as well as what they were doing.

But he also had to remember what he was doing. That was also the beginning of professionalism.

'You can drop me off on the main road, Sergeant.' He wondered bleakly what had happened to Wimpy. 'I must report back to my battalion.'

The Sergeant merely acknowledged that decision with a nod. Professionalism was also the acceptance of another man's duty, without argument – that was another lesson learned: precautions, but no panic, no running away blindly in the most convenient direction without knowing where one was going.

And 'Darkie', the driver, was a very skilful operator too, he decided, as the carrier hugged the hillsides and slipped through each natural gap in the countryside, as though Darkie knew every hump and hollow in it like the geography of a NAAFI girl's body in the dark behind his billet.

'Not much further now, sir.' The Sergeant pointed to another copse ahead of them, alongside the stream they'd been following for the last quarter of a mile.

Bastable followed the line of the Sergeant's finger, and saw a Bren carrier like their own snugged under the overhanging foliage at the edge of the copse.

Darkie swung the carrier expertly round alongside the waiting machine.

A very young subaltern, who reminded Bastable of his own new Christopher Chichester, hailed them crisply. 'Good work, Sergeant Hobday – ' his eye registered Bastable quickly, and the absence of a third face he knew – 'you've had some trouble?'

'Armoured car, sir, Mr Greystock. They're pretty thick on the ground there, to the north – motor-cyclists too. No way through there, I'm afraid.' He looked his officer squarely in the eye. 'Corporal Titchener, sir – ?'

'Won't be coming with us any more, Sergeant . . . Who's your passenger?'

Bastable stood up. 'Harry Bastable, Prince Regent's Own, Mr Greystock. From Colembert-les-Deux-Ponts – Territorial battalion.'

'He was trying to get through to us, sir,' explained Sergeant Hobday. 'Met up with the Jerries, farm buildings 883768 and the fields north-east of there, so far as I can make out.'

'Oh, indeed?' The subaltern glanced down at his own map-case for a second or two, then up at Bastable enquiringly. 'In strength, I take it, Captain?'

It was a merciful question, thought Bastable. All those serried ranks of armoured vehicles could have been a regiment, or a brigade, or God only knew what – it had looked like a whole army to him.

He nodded. 'A lot more than I had time to count. They looked like the Grand National under starter's orders.' He had never seen the Grand National, except on the Pathé News, but that was the image which sprang to mind, horses transmuted into tanks waiting for the signal to spring forward to crash through every obstacle ahead.

The subaltern nodded back at him, wonderfully cool and composed in face of such bleak news. 'So they should be here pretty soon, I shouldn't wonder? Well – thank you, Captain . . . So we'd better tear ourselves away, back to Belléme . . . south first, for choice, back among those poor devils of refugees. With a bit of luck they'll steer clear of them now that they don't need them – is that anywhere near where you want to go?'

'That'll suit me fine.' Bastable tried hard to echo the composure and courage. 'I must get back to Colembert, and I can walk from there.'

'Jolly good!' The subaltern smiled. 'Right then, Sergeant – follow me!'

The Sergeant gave Bastable a half-nod, half-smile, half as though to reassure him that everything was all right now, half to register his own pride and confidence in his officer for the benefit of a stranger. When he could win that sort of look from a senior NCO, behind his back and in the imminent presence of the enemy, then he would have arrived in a military sense as an officer as well as a gentleman, Bastable thought enviously. That half-nod, half-smile, was what it was all about, without any requirements of words.

The carriers moved off again, wrapped in their own

noise at top cross-country speed, Darkie carefully holding their own at a fifty-yard interval behind Mr Greystock's.

Bastable had lost all sense of distance, and also geography; and, looking down at his wrist-watch, found that its glass was smashed in and its hands were frozen at ten to three – Rupert Brooke's honeytime at Grantchester, wasn't that? – which (it occurred to him insanely, as the carrier tipped and jolted) would be the recorded time of his death if he was now killed and anyone found him, and –

Christ! *That* was the other thing he had been trying to think about – which he had forgotten – which had been shocked out of his mind by subsequent events, but which was his other duty –

Christ! Which was even his *main* duty, beyond even that of getting back to the battalion – *Christ!* How could he have forgotten it –

The Brigadier –

Mr Greystock's carrier blew up with a shattering flash of orange-red fire, spattering pieces of metal and flaming debris in smoke-trails arcing out from the centre of impact.

'Hold tight!' shrieked Sergeant Hobday.

Darkie spun their carrier round almost in its own length as the sound of the German tank guns reached them. The road-bank just ahead mushroomed – Bastable lost sight of it as the carrier lurched sideways, the tracks on one side lifting off the ground with the force and momentum of the change of direction.

In the next fraction of time he was deafened by an even more shattering explosion – so loud that it had no sound at all, only force, as the carrier continued lifting, overturning sky and earth, to crash down in darkness on top of him.

5

Harry Bastable wasn't dead.

And yet, so it seemed to him afterwards, a part of him
did die some time during that long summer's afternoon,
as so many men of the British Expeditionary Force and
the French Army had already died, and were dying, and
were yet to die; and not on any golden bridge above any
shining silver river, but in pain and darkness and defeat
and despair.

And alone.

Certainly, he died so far as the Sixth Panzer Division was
concerned – the officers and men, armour, foot and guns,
who (so he afterwards decided) must have seen the legs
and boots of one more anonymous dead Tommy protrud-
ing out from under the overturned carrier.

Certainly, although they were in fact the living legs of
Captain Bastable, they must have seemed dead legs to the
swarming Germans. And not even any German Army
Medical Corps men, if any passed that way, could be
blamed for not bothering to investigate them: it must
have seemed to them that when a Bren carrier of several
tons' weight fell upside down on a man, then that man
could reasonably be left to some eventual burial detail,
with no great urgency involved in the matter.

First, he couldn't think at all, even when he was no longer
truly unconscious.

Then, though by no recognizable thought-process, he assumed himself to be dead – and was, to all intents and purposes, dead; and, having identified death as a final darkness, he lost consciousness again.

When he regained some consciousness for the second time, taste was the first thing he registered, and it was the taste of blood.

His blood! something told him.

It was in his mouth and on his upper lip – he could feel it, thick and congealing, with his tongue. But there was no sound to go with the taste, and when he opened his eyes there was at first no sight either, only darkness.

The soundlessness and darkness didn't frighten him; the fear only exploded in him when he realized that the darkness wasn't total – that there was a penumbra of not-darkness and not-light where he was – of not-death, but not-life.

The fear ignited his last sense in panic: he tried to move his arms – and found that he couldn't move, but touched something. And, as part of the same convulsive movement-attempt, raised his head – and hit his forehead on something hard and unyielding.

The panic and fear instantly became total and irrational. He struggled now, wildly but helplessly – and there came a sound now, and it was the sound of his own thick cries of panic and fear as he realized that he was trapped and bleeding.

How long that stage went on, he had no idea. But when it ended he knew more or less where he was, and despaired.

He remembered the carrier in front exploding. His own carrier had obviously been hit immediately afterwards, and he was trapped, half-blinded – almost totally blinded

– and dying under its wreckage, lying on his back – in pain –

Alone –

All the bitterness of dying and in pain and defeat rose up and engulfed him in a great wave of self-pity and misery and loneliness.

That was when Harry Bastable died.

And then, just as suddenly as he had realized that there was not total darkness round him, he realized that he wasn't in pain, and that he could move his feet freely – he could feel loose, gravelly ground under his heel – and he could almost bend his knees . . . he could bend them perhaps an inch or two, enough to give his heels purchase so as to push him – *ouch!* – the top of his head hit another unyielding surface.

Instantly he reversed the movement, scrabbling and contracting himself to move like a worm, backwards down the tunnel in which he was imprisoned.

The worm moved.

An inch. Another inch. Two inches. Each movement – contraction and scrabbling of the heels, then expansion – was a reflex instinct towards life.

Then the worm stopped moving: it had ceased to be a worm.

It was a worm which had turned.

And, in turning, had turned into a man again.

Harry Bastable was alive again!

The metamorphosis was completed in a fraction of a second. The worm had simply wanted to get out of its prison; the man immediately wanted much more than that – it wanted to get out, but also to escape and be free.

The man understood where he was.

The carrier had fallen on top of him, but because of its configuration, and the slight humps and bumps of the French roadside there had been just exactly enough room for one human body to lie under it at this point without being crushed by it. If that body had fallen an inch or two either way to the side, or forward, it would have been pulped; even if one of its arms or legs had been outflung – that also would have been the end of it.

But it hadn't. It had fallen as neatly and exactly as if it had been laid out in its grave.

So – it was alive and kicking – literally kicking!

And there was more light, too . . . Now that the fit of the body into its tunnel wasn't so tight, it could see daylight – Harry Bastable could see daylight down there, beyond his knees.

The light helped him to think. He turned his head sideways and put his ear as close to the ground as he could. And, as that was not close enough for the Red Indian trick to be really effective, he placed his palms flat on the ground and tried to *hear* them.

If there were any German vehicles still passing, they were far away, and he could hear no actual sounds, of jackboots stamping and scraping on the road, or voices, or even distant gun-fire. But it was better to be safe than sorry; they had passed him by so far, and he had been through so much pain and terror so far, that a little more time – a little more time for thought – made sense.

He deliberately stilled his feet in death again: one more dead, anonymous Tommy again!

* * *

Now he would think –

His head ached, but not very much. And the more he explored the different pieces of his body, the more he was certain that they all worked more or less normally. Even the blood on his lips didn't taste any more – his nose had bled every time he had played rugger for the battalion. At first he had been embarrassed by it, but a chance remark of the COs which he had overheard after one final whistle, when he had come off with his yellow-and-grey striped shirt disgraced with a stream of it, had changed all that:

'I'll say one thing for Bastable – he's got red blood in him, and he doesn't mind shedding it!'

That was two things, not one, he had thought at the time. But the voice had been approving (he had wanted to go off long before the whistle, but had been too scared of the CO to do so!), and thereafter he had spread the Red Badge deliberately over his face – and probably got his acting-captaincy and his company because of that too, by God! Because the CO and Major Tetley-Robinson preferred officers who could bleed to those who could think, that was for certain; Major Audley had his crown because he was too influential to be ignored, and Wimpy's third pip had been forced on them because there had been no one else remotely qualified: but Harry Bastable had got his because his nose bled easily.

But where was Wimpy now?

Dead in a ditch, most likely, poor chap! All those brains, all that knowledge of *hic, haec, hoc* and Caesar's Gallic Wars spilled into the French dust to mingle with the dust of Caesar's Romans and Gauls.

No! That was not what he must think about!

* * *

Vengeance is Mine, saith the Lord!

But not any more, Lord – Vengeance is Harry Bastable's now, Lord!

Promotion has been defined as the selection of an individual for a position of greater responsibility for which he has shown himself qualified by reason of experience and knowledge.

Until now, by reason of his birth and status rather than experience and knowledge, Harry Bastable had considered his promotion (at least in the Territorial Army) as a very reasonable and proper recognition of ability. Now, his considered opinion was that he was insufficiently experienced to conduct a party of Boy Scouts across Eastbourne Front on a quiet Sunday morning out of season.

But he possessed one piece of knowledge which now promoted him to a position of far greater importance than that conferred on him by birth or status (manager of bloody Bastable's of Eastbourne, and – purely by accident of birth – deputy managing director of same), or the three acting-pips on his shoulder.

Suddenly – and by accident – he was important for the first time in his life.

Check: the beak-nosed Brigadier had been having a friendly conversation with two German officers – and from their caps and their braid and their badges, and their whole bloody demeanour, high-ranking officers, too.

And – *double-check* – that hadn't been a British salute the Brigadier had been in the act of giving those high-ranking German officers. It had been the same goose-stepping *Hitler-heil* which they had just given him.

And – *treble-check* – although the German phrase the

Brigadier had barked at the German soldier with the rifle had been double-dutch to Harry Bastable, if there was one thing Harry Bastable could understand from its sound – and there were NCOs (the handful of reservist ex-Regulars) in the Prince Regent's Own whose shouts and screams were just as meaningless as double-dutch – it was a *direct order*.

An order – a command, then – and if Harry Bastable had been a betting man, he would have bet good money that the command in the King's English would have been *Shoot that man!*

And so *check* and *double-check* and *treble-check* added up to the blackest treason and treachery at the best, or the cleverest, most dangerous Fifth Column of all at the least: *an enemy in the uniform of a British brigadier, complete with a British vehicle and a junior staff officer, and the manner-born to go with them both which would take him anywhere and everywhere behind the lines to note units and their defences, and to give false orders at will.*

Such a man would be worth a division – an army corps – with the battle for France reaching its climax.

Such a man might make all the difference between defeat and victory!

And Harry Bastable was the only man in the whole British Army who knew about the bloody bastard – the fucking swine – the obscenity, the beloved multi-purpose adjective-adverb-noun-verb of the other ranks, surprised him in his own vocabulary, but only for a tenth of a second – *and also the only man who could identify him!*

He could wait no longer. Because, although not waiting was a risk, waiting was a bigger risk, with this load of responsibility on his shoulders.

The message had to be got through to someone in

authority – that mattered more than anything. He had already been culpably slow in not realizing it – he had seen it all with his own eyes, but had been too shit-scared for his own skin to put together what he had seen and heard. He should have passed it on directly to Sergeant Hobday and Second-Lieutenant Greystock –

Except that would have been no good, of course. Because Sergeant Hobday and Mr Greystock . . .

No.

It was risky, but he would just have to be that much more careful.

After he had assured himself, and then reassured himself, that there was no sound immediately around him, he wormed himself out from beneath the carrier.

He had lost his helmet. And he had long since lost Wimpy's field-glasses – he couldn't even remember where he had lost them, it was before Sergeant Hobday had picked him up, he realized now – possibly when he'd scrambled up that first bank, out of the road by the farm. He had felt something hard bump his knee – he'd gone over that bank like a rocket, as though it hadn't been there at all – most likely the strap had broken then; it was a rather thin strap, not army issue, like the field-glasses themselves, which had been Wimpy's own private property – Wimpy would be deuced cut up with his having lost them like that.

He swallowed miserably, ambushed by his own figure of speech: poor Wimpy was probably already cut up, much more literally than that, in the wreckage of DPT 912, somewhere around here . . .

Around here! He realized simultaneously that he didn't know where he was, but that Sergeant Hobday had had a map. And that meant . . . that meant he was going to have to do something which he hadn't intended to do, which he didn't want to do – but which he now *must* do . . .

He had lived thirty years – perhaps half his life . . . perhaps, in the next few hours, *all* of his life – he had lived thirty years, and he had never seen a dead man.

Suddenly he was in the buyers' meeting of the John Lewis branch where he had trained, staring at old Mr Plumb – 'Sugar' Plumb in his starched white collar, and black coat which always carried a tiny scatter of dandruff on its shoulders, against which old Sugar fought a constant and losing battle . . . not that he was really old, he could hardly have been more than forty, but he was prematurely grey, and anybody who was grey was old to young Mr Bastable.

Sugar Plumb was mild and inoffensive and pedantic, but he was a whizz in the hosiery and glove department – he had taught young Mr Bastable everything he knew about selling gloves . . . Morley and Dent's, Fownes of Worcester and Milore . . . and everything that went with the selling of them – the velvet cushion for the customer's elbow, the glove-stretchers, powder box – and the gentle patter which seemed to dull the customer's resistance . . . everything that he had used later on to make Bastable's glove department the success it had been, which had won him the Guv'ner's accolade and his spurs in the family business.

Old Sugar Plumb had taken him to lunch one day – brown Windsor soup, lamb cutlets and apple pie – and he couldn't face the brown Windsor –

'I thought you looked a trifle peaky this morning, Henry – a slight stomach upset, perhaps? I suffer from it myself at this time of year, my boy. Beecham's Powders is what

I take – take them for everything – ' Drone, drone, drone: outside the hosiery and glove department nobody in the world could be duller than old Sugar Plumb.

Young Mr Bastable looked down at his congealing brown Windsor soup and could take no more of the droning.

'I saw a dog run over in the High Street this morning, Mr Plumb, as I was coming to work – by a bus.'

'A dog? Tut-tut! Very nasty, I'm sure . . . But with the increasing number of motor vehicles there are on the roads these days, and the number of dogs allowed to run wild, snapping at cyclists and fouling the footpaths . . . we shall just have to get used to seeing them run over, my boy. You mustn't let a little thing like that put you off your lunch, otherwise you'll waste away.' Sugar Plumb spooned up the last of his soup with relish, quite unmoved.

Young Mr Bastable was surprised at such cold-bloodedness, even a little shocked by it. For, apart from being dull and having a weak stomach, Sugar Plumb was generally a gentle and considerate man.

'There was blood and – and bits of dog everywhere, Mr Plumb.'

Sugar Plumb wiped his mouth carefully with his serviette. 'So there would be,' he agreed. 'The entire contents of the wretched animal, no doubt. But we must still get used to such mishaps.'

'I don't think I'll ever get used to seeing *entrails*, Mr Plumb – outside a butcher's shop, anyway.'

Plumb looked at him over his spectacles. 'Nonsense, my boy! When I first went into the line opposite Spanbroekmolen . . .'

'Span – ?'

'Spanbroekmolen – on the right flank of the Ypres

Salient, under Messines Ridge . . . that was with the Londonderries, in the 36th Ulster Division – which was curious really, because I had never visited any part of Ireland – before the Third Ypres . . .' He paused as the waitress removed his soup plate. '. . . let me see now . . . that would have been early June in 1917 – 3 June, I believe it was . . . or perhaps it was the 4th . . . no, the 3rd, I'm almost certain, because my mother's birthday was on the 8th, and I recall feeling very badly about having forgotten to write to her early enough to be sure that she received my birthday congratulations – because the letters sometimes took some time to reach their destination in those days . . . and I was quite right to feel badly, because she received the telegram from the War Office about me – or not about me, as it happened – the day before she received my letter, which was after her birthday of course, and that letter gave her a very nasty turn, she told me afterwards – almost worse than the telegram, because she'd been half-expecting that . . . "Like receiving a message from beyond the grave, Edwin," she always used to say.' Mr Plumb smiled. 'And I always used to reply, "But it was *slightly* exaggerated, Mother" – the telegram, I mean, not the letter.'

'The telegram?'

'"Killed in action",' Mr Plumb nodded. 'It was an administrative error, of course – they had probably confused two E. B. Plumbs, I expect.' The surviving E. B. Plumb wagged his finger at the young Mr Bastable. 'And that's why I always emphasize the importance of administrative efficiency, Henry. The customer is always right, so however good we may be at selling, we must back that up with the same care and efficiency in administration – we must not shock the customer with bad administration.

That is a very important lesson which I cannot over-emphasize. Because, in this instance, we took the ridge – and with all those huge mines going up, that isn't surprising – but my mother was nevertheless a dissatisfied customer, you might say – eh?'

It must have been young Mr Bastable's look of frozen incredulity which recalled Mr Plumb to the original direction of his sermon.

'What I mean, Henry, is that God in His Wisdom has so constituted the human being that he can speedily become accustomed to *anything*.'

The waitress was hovering with Mr Plumb's lamb cutlets, but obviously didn't know what to do with young Mr Bastable's brown Windsor soup.

'Now – ' Mr Plumb ignored the waitress, ' – the things I saw around Spanbroekmolen that morning, and when we went on up the ridge too, would make a – would make a butcher's shop look like a – like a – like a florist's on a spring morning.' He paused in triumphant appreciation of his own simile. 'But I soon got used to it – and I had never seen a dead man before I went into the line. So eat up your soup before it gets cold, now.'

Harry Bastable turned Sergeant Hobday over. He wasn't so very terrible, really – he might almost have been sleeping, except that his eyes were open. He was just very dusty and somehow taller, though quite surprisingly heavy and difficult to turn.

But he had no map with him.

Bastable looked around for Darkie, but couldn't find any trace of him. So . . . while Sergeant Hobday had been thrown clear – though 'clear' wasn't the right word to go with 'dead' – Darkie must still be under the carrier.

With the map.

He went back to where Sergeant Hobday lay at the roadside, with the vague idea of closing those open eyes; and also because Sergeant Hobday hadn't frightened him as much as he had expected, and returning to what he knew, and what wasn't as awful as he had imagined, might somehow help the process of Mr Plumb's advice and God's infinite mercy and wisdom.

But when he got there he didn't see the point of touching the Sergeant's face (there would be other faces, plenty of them; and it wouldn't make any difference to them, closing their eyes, they couldn't see anything; or if they could – any golden bridges and silver rivers – they might just as well go on looking; and he had other things to do, anyway, than to go around closing eyes). He merely robbed Sergeant Hobday of his Webley revolver.

He did this in the first place because the Sergeant's revolver would have a full cylinder, and he had fired two rounds – or at least two – from his own weapon.

The firer must count his rounds as he fires them, to ensure that he will know when to reload. Never advance with less than two or three rounds in the cylinder.

And because he somehow felt also that a Mendips regular's revolver would be better than his own.

And also because his hands were shaking too much to reload.

And it was just as well, because when he examined his own revolver before abandoning it he found that its barrel was full of dirt, from when he had presumably jammed it into the ground at some time during his flight from the farm. As he poked instinctively with the nail of his index finger he thought of the earth in the garden of the house off the Meads – the earth which had got under his nails somehow as a boy, always just before meals, so that his father would send him from the table to scrub at them again. There was earth under his nails now – French dirt – and he would have given a million tons of it in exchange for one nail-ful of good Eastbourne soil.

He threw his old revolver over the bank, into a tangle of grass and weeds. Better to let it lie there, rusting, than that some German should come and pick it up and have it.

Second-Lieutenant Greystock had had a map.

He looked up and down the road. There was not a sign of movement still, but it had changed all along its length. It was scuffed and dirty now, with broken banks and clods of earth where the German tanks had smashed across it. And there, fifty yards further on, was the tangled ruin of the other carrier.

He gritted his teeth and commenced to walk towards it, willing himself to put one foot before another against his innermost wishes, because he could remember that vivid flash of bright fire which had engulfed it.

This would be worse. But he needed that map . . .

And it was worse – it was unthinkably worse.

There was a thing in the driver's seat . . . but it wasn't a thing he could recognize as ever having been a man, it was just a torn and blackened object where the driver had been.

He found Second-Lieutenant Greystock because there was a single cloth-pip on its red backing on something else which was half-impaled in a small thorn-bush near the carrier – something with no legs and trailing threads of what looked like pink wool –

He never looked for the map, his legs started to run without being told to do so.

They ran until they had carried him over the brow of

the rise, and down the dip on the other side. Then they simply stopped and sat him down at the roadside. He pulled up his knees under his chin and buried his face into them, and wept silently, rocking backwards and forwards, and wishing he could be sick because it must be like being ill – if you could be sick, once you had been sick you felt better. But he couldn't be sick.

The dying and living-again hadn't been completed under the carrier. There was a little more of both to be done, and he did it there, by himself at the roadside, alone.

Finally, he got up and continued up the road again, walking this time, and wiping his face, first with his hands and then with a handkerchief he remembered he had in his pocket.

He realized he was very thirsty, so he drank from his water-bottle.

He was aware of everything around him, and he had worked out approximately where he was without the aid of the map. There was a profound silence all along the road, not even any birdsong. But then there never did seem to be any birds in France, not as there were in England. All the same, he felt that he was carrying the silence with him, in a circle around him, as he went along. Beyond it, in the far distance, there was an almost permanent rumble-rumble going on somewhere, in one direction or another. There was even a very faint knock-knock-knocking which he fixed in the direction of Bel-léme. The Mendips were probably still fighting their last fight there, by-passed and surrounded, but game to the last, like the regulars they were.

But he wasn't going to Belléme, now. The homing pigeon had been winged, but only winged, and now it was going back to the loft for rest and refreshment before carrying its message abroad. That was the only thing it could think about, because that was how its mind was programmed. Besides, the pigeon didn't matter, only the message mattered, and there were others who could carry it once they knew its contents.

He was very tired now.

And this quiet around him – he had heard motor engines in the distance, but they had faded – this quiet all around him had a quality of its own which went with his fatigue. He had lost track of time under the carrier, and afterwards too, but the dusk was gathering and soon it would be dark; and once it was dark he would be hopelessly lost – even more lost than he was now.

Was this even the right direction?

If it was the right direction, then the main road *must* be just ahead, but he seemed to have been walking for hours in an empty world.

He stopped and listened intently. Far beyond the immediate silence surrounding him there was a distant thunder, to the west and to the north, on his right hand and behind him.

Ahead of him there was only the faint sound of a child, crying.

6

'Good God Almighty!' said a familiar voice.

Harry Bastable reached for his revolver, which lay on the blanket alongside the white rabbit. Then the words inside the sound and the familiarity of the voice itself registered simultaneously in his brain and his memory, and his hand stopped half-way to the weapon.

He peered uncertainly from one side of the road to the other, trying as best he could to establish the direction from which the voice had come. But the early dawn mist, still faintly blue-tinged with the dark of the night, lay thick in the fields: it was as though it had swallowed the sound before he had had time to hear it properly.

Just as quickly as brain and memory had taken up the information from his ears they now rejected it as being unlikely, if not downright false, and instinct took over again. He reached forward with his free hand and grasped the revolver, letting slip the multi-coloured shawl which he had draped over his shoulders to protect him from the morning's chill.

'Good God – it is!' came the voice again. 'Bastable!'

It came from half behind him, on his left. He swung himself and the revolver towards it, still only half-believing the repeated oral testimony.

'Willis?' His own voice sounded unnaturally loud – almost a shout.

A figure rose – loomed up – out of the roadside ditch fifteen yards behind him.

'Keep your voice down, man!'

'Willis?' this time he managed a whisper. 'Is it you?'

'The very same. And as bright-eyed and bushy-tailed as you could hope for this fine May morning!'

Yes, that was Wimpy right enough. If it had been pitch-black and blowing a gale, that was Wimpy Willis – with no need to ask him who had won the Cup in '38. There was only one Wimpy Willis in the whole wide world, and this was undoubtedly it, thought Harry Bastable with an engulfing feeling of relief and gratitude.

The figure detached itself from the mist into rose-tinted reality.

'Bloody marvellous – please don't point that thing at me, Harry, old boy – but bloody marvellous, all the same!' said Wimpy. 'Absolutely-bloody-brilliant!'

'Willis!' repeated Harry Bastable humbly.

Wimpy surveyed him, shaking his head admiringly. 'I wouldn't have thought it possible – I'm sorry, but I wouldn't, old boy. Not in a thousand years!'

He was obviously as grateful for finding Harry Bastable again as Harry Bastable was at meeting up with him, thought Bastable. And if he was also frankly surprised that a crass idiot like Harry Bastable could escape from the Germans, that was also fair enough. Because the crass – cowardly – idiot had escaped more by luck than good management and initiative: that was true, even though the idiot was not about to admit it.

'I'd never have thought of it myself, either,' said Wimpy. 'Not in another thousand years, by God!'

'Wh – ?' Bastable was suddenly aware that he had missed something in the exchange. At the same time he observed that if Wimpy was bright-eyed – and he was bright-eyed – he was something less than bushy-tailed. His face was filthy and his uniform a tattered, mud-stained ruin, with one arm of the blouse ripped open from wrist to shoulder.

102

Wimpy grinned at him. 'The shawl's damn good – I took you for for an old Froggie peasant until I could practically see the whites of your eyes, I tell you.' He pointed at the great multi-coloured thing where it lay at Bastable's feet.

Bastable stared at the shawl. Wimpy believed – Good God! – Wimpy believed that he had *disguised* himself in it!

'In fact, I wasn't absolutely sure it was you even then – because of *that* – ' continued Wimpy, pointing at the perambulator. 'That pram is your bloody masterpiece!'

As if she had heard this observation, and objected to the way it was phrased, the baby promptly awoke, letting out a single cry, quavering but piercing.

Harry Bastable immediately started rocking the pram, in as near as he could get to the way he had seen Eastbourne's proud mothers and nannies do on Sunday morning along the sea-front. As he did this with one hand, he replaced the revolver at the baby's feet with the other and moved the white rabbit up to a more comforting position alongside its owner.

The baby stopped crying.

'Good God Almighty, man!' exclaimed Wimpy in a hollow voice. 'You've got a real baby in there!'

Bastable leaned over the pram and scowled encouragingly at the baby. He couldn't stand babies – he disliked small children in general – but babies were worse. Where small children could occasionally be placated or threatened, babies were irrational. But this – rocking and smiling – was what women did with crying babies, and it sometimes worked, he had observed.

'It's a real baby!' repeated Wimpy.

'Of course it damn well is!' snarled Harry Bastable,

trying to contort the scowl into a smile. 'What did you think I'd got in here?'

For once Wimpy appeared to be short of something to say.

The baby smiled at Harry Bastable.

Wimpy peered over the side of the pram, and the baby stopped smiling. Her face began to pucker up.

'Keep off!' ordered Bastable, recognizing the sign from bitter experience. 'You're frightening her. Keep away!' He smiled and rocked frantically.

The smile returned.

'Let's move,' said Bastable. 'She likes being wheeled along.'

That, after all, was what had first stopped the poor little mite crying the evening before – and had also calmed her hunger down this morning. 'The sooner we can get her to Colembert, the better. I can turn her over to someone there.'

Without waiting, he started to wheel the pram forward once more. Wimpy caught up with them quickly, and promptly draped the shawl over Bastable's shoulders.

'There you are, Mum,' he murmured. 'How d'you know it's a her?'

'Because I know the difference,' hissed Bastable, his temper slipping and all his old antipathy for Wimpy flooding back.

'Oh . . .' Wimpy sounded chastened. 'Oh . . . I see – you haven't found it – her – just this morning, I mean?'

Bastable pushed in silence for a moment or two. There was no point in losing his temper, it was childish. And, more than that, it was ungrateful. And, most of all, it was *stupid* – because he needed Wimpy. And doubly stupid . . . to get angry with a chap for making a simple mistake

104

– the mistake of thinking that he was a damn sight cleverer than he was.

Hah! In fact, Wimpy's mistake had been for once crediting him with more wits than he had – that was almost funny, if it hadn't been another truth at his expense.

'Yesterday evening,' he said. 'Late yesterday evening, just as it was beginning to get dark.'

Wimpy digested the answer. 'On the main road?' he said at length.

Bastable nodded. 'At the crossroads.'

He didn't want to remember, but it wasn't something a man could easily look at, and once having seen forget at will – the pathetic bundles strewn over the road and along the ditches, some of which were not bundles at all, but the owners of the bundles; the smashed carts, with dead horses between the shafts; and the abandoned cars riddled with bullets, some of which had not been abandoned, because their owners were still in them . . .

And, in the midst of that desolation, the baby crying.

'It was bad, was it?' It wasn't just a question; Wimpy spoke gently, as though he understood what Bastable was seeing.

The baby had been crying in its pram on the edge of the road, miraculously untouched with all the bodies around it – he hadn't even been able to make out which body belonged to her – which was her father, or her mother, or her aunt, or her little brother, or a passing stranger. There hadn't been any way of knowing – or any *point* in knowing, they were all the same now.

He turned to Wimpy in the same agony he had felt then, with all his priorities in ruins around him. 'I couldn't just leave her, don't you see?'

'Of course not, old man. You did absolutely the right

thing – absolutely the right thing,' Wimpy nodded at him decisively, as if to reassure him that that was a man's proper duty, as laid down by the book, when the choice was between a French baby girl and the British Expeditionary Force in France. 'Quite right!'

Yet it hadn't really been quite like that at all, thought Harry Bastable.

Of course, she might have died there, on the road last night, without him. Of thirst, or hunger, or whatever it was abandoned babies died from.

Except – the fragment of conversation between his mother and her friends surfaced again in his memory, like all the other bits of overheard and observed child-lore and baby-care that he had overheard and forgotten, but not forgotten, which had surfaced these last few hours: *babies are very tough – otherwise they'd never survive all the frightful things young mothers do to them, my dear.*

The baby had been crying.

Any moment now there would be more Germans – armour, or those ubiquitous motor-cyclists, and motor-cycle-and-sidecar troops who scorned roadblocks and obstacles.

But he couldn't leave her to go on crying at the roadside while he passed by. And, after what he had seen there, he hadn't another hundred yards in his legs anyway.

He had to go back to her.

Of course, she was just *it* then – just an insistent noise in the dead quiet of the evening at the crossroads, which he couldn't leave behind him, and which drove the thought of all sounds out of his head.

He had been very busy after that: she had needed him and he had needed her.

* * *

106

'Well, you do seem to have a way with babies, I'll say that,' murmured Wimpy. 'Or is it with women in general?'

Bastable only grunted to that, neither denying nor admitting his expertise.

'Or this baby in particular?' said Wimpy.

Bastable looked down at the baby. Wimpy had got it right the third time, anyway.

'She's a good baby,' he admitted.

'And you know about babies?' Wimpy could never resist poking and prying, even if it meant occasionally listening instead of talking. And on this occasion, since he well knew that Bastable was a bachelor, he was certainly poking and prying.

'One learns about these things,' he murmured loftily.

'Younger brothers and sisters, eh?' Wimpy was more cautious about ascribing special qualities to Captain Bastable now. 'Has she eaten recently? Or do they only drink at that age?'

That was a problem which had specially exercised Harry Bastable's mind, and more this morning than the previous evening. Because the little mite had had a bottle of what he assumed was milk in her pram when he'd found her and it had been that which had eventually silenced her . . . Or very eventually, after he had discovered how uncomfortably damp she was.

(That was another memory from home, from an impossible other life: how Arthur Gorton's young wife attended to another shrieking bundle which had been disturbing one of those awful showing-off-the-new-arrival teas which his mother had insisted he attended.)

(*Why – my Precious is soaking wet, isn't he now!* – He had dredged that one up too, from his subconscious, never dreaming that he would do the same, so far as he could recall that Evelyn Gorton had done it, for another Precious in a French ditch two hundred yards from where Precious's parents lay machine-gunned to death with the flies already buzzing busily around them.)

Positively sodden, if not soaking wet, in fact. But the next morning – this morning – when there had been no more milk, and only the remains of what was in his water-bottle, and the rest of the stale loaf of bread he had rescued from the food left by the roadside, then he also had wondered, *Do they eat, or do they only drink, at this age?*

He had dried her up, and cleaned her up too as best he could, and had concluded that although she was a very little baby, with no teeth or anything like that, she was still substantially bigger than Evelyn and Arthur Gorton's Precious.

But she obviously couldn't eat hard bits of stale French bread (of the sort that didn't make satisfactory toast) with her soft little pink toothless gums – it would have to be crunched and crushed and *munched* to a watery pulp, and there was just as obviously only one way he could do that . . . with alternate mouthfuls of stale bread and army ration water, out of his own mouth.

But, then, she *was* a very good baby.

And, in a way – a rather wet, messy way – she was the first French girl that Harry Bastable had ever kissed, more or less, in the process.

But he couldn't tell Wimpy that, it was a private thing between him and the baby, a very personal matter and not the important matter at all, which he had been half-way to forgetting.

108

'Wimpy, I've got some extremely important information – vital information.'

'Join the club, old boy. The Sixth Panzer Division – at least, that was so far as I could make out. But there are others as well – I heard 'em mention the First and Second, I think.'

'Who mention?'

'Jerry, Harry – the Germans. And you know where the Second was heading for? Abbeville – *Abbeville!*'

Bastable could only stare at him. Yesterday *Peronne* had echoed like a thunderclap, because it was only sixty or seventy miles from the coast, as the crow flew. But *Abbeville* – Abbeville was on the estuary of its river . . . the Somme, was it? . . . *on the coast!* It wasn't possible that the Germans should be thinking of going there – it wasn't possible –

Wimpy read his expression. 'I know – that's what I thought. It's just too far . . . and I know my German's not perfect . . . But I tell you, Harry – these Germans were a bit windy too . . . Or the top brass one was – the younger chap was raring to go. He said the Second was going to be there by this evening – yesterday evening, that is – and his chaps were keen to be in on it, and they didn't want to be left behind by the lousy Second . . . And the brass-hat was all for a bit of caution and consolidation, but he gave in finally – that's as far as I could make out. So they went.'

Bastable blinked at him. 'What Germans were these?'

'The blighters who stopped on my bridge.'

'Your bridge?'

'Well, it wasn't exactly my bridge. It wasn't really a bridge, either – it was a sort of culvert. But there was water in it . . . and mud. And I was in it.'

Bastable could believe that: everything about Wimpy's appearance testified to the truth of that.

Abbeville – ?

'I saw these Jerries in the wood – they were coming towards the wood, that is – after you left me, old boy . . . Not the ones on my bridge, that was later on . . . they were in the fields, and there were tanks behind 'em. So I scampered back towards the car at the double, and I'd just about reached it when I heard firing from your way, up in the trees.' Wimpy looked at Bastable apologetically. 'Frankly, after what I'd seen I thought you'd bought it for certain . . .' He paused. 'So I ran for it.'

Wimpy still looked uncomfortable, almost guilty, and in doing so reminded Bastable of Batty Evans's fate.

'I couldn't have got back to you anyway.' He shrugged. 'Had to beat it smartly in another direction.'

Even that didn't assuage Wimpy's discomfort completely. 'To be honest, old boy . . . I was into that little car and away like a streak of greased lightning. I've never been so scared in my life!'

At least the disgrace was shared, then! So it was a proper moment for confession. 'I'm afraid I lost Fusilier Evans, Willis. That is to say . . . I told him to follow me, but he didn't.'

Wimpy accepted the loss of Fusilier Evans philosophically. 'Batty never was very quick on the uptake, you can't blame yourself for that – it would have happened sooner or later. We should never have taken him in the PROs – another of that old swine Tetley-Robinson's errors of judgement.' He nodded to himself. 'Like taking on damn useless schoolmasters . . . you know, you're absolutely right – she *is* a good baby. See how she's got her thumb in her mouth and her arm round that kangaroo!'

110

'Rabbit,' corrected Bastable automatically.

'Rabbit, is it? So it is, by golly! Alice's White Rabbit – we shall have to call her "Alice", Harry. Poor little Alice . . .' He trailed off. 'I just hope he got close enough to them to use his bayonet. That was all he ever wanted, poor old Batty – just to take one with him. I hope he got his chance.'

Under the cold-bloodedly philosophical Wimpy, so sharp and eloquent, there was another one he had never glimpsed before until now, thought Bastable. But there was nothing to be gained by mentioning that final burst of small-arms fire if that was the way of it.

Abbeville.

'You were under this bridge – ?'

'Culvert . . . yes.' Wimpy pulled himself together. 'I drove out of the wood like the clappers, over the next rise . . . And as I was going down the other side I saw a Jerry tank on the next skyline – a Mark Two – so I knew I wasn't going to make it. Thank God, he didn't see me . . . But when I pulled up at the bottom I could hear the blighters, they seemed to be all around me by the sound of them. So I whipped out of the car. But then I didn't know which way to go – the fields were so damn *open* . . . And there was this stream . . . Or it wasn't really a stream, it was just where the rainwater comes down under the road in winter, I suppose, and takes off down the lowest part of the land – that was open too, they'd have seen me for sure. I really didn't know where to go, as I said . . . but I naturally jumped straight into the ditch . . . And there was this culvert, under the road. So I thought, "The blighters haven't seen me yet, but they'll see the car any moment now, and if there's no one in it they'll think the driver has run away. So I'll just crawl into the culvert

111

and keep my fingers crossed." And I did. And *they* did, thank God!'

He drew a deep breath, almost a sigh.

'What actually saved me, you know, was these two Jerry officers, though . . . One of them was brass, and the other one sounded like a very young regimental commander – a real fire-eater. He was the one who wanted to go like hell, a proper cavalry-type. The older was more cautious, he said, "Just because you haven't had anyone to fight, you think war is all roses." Or something like that – they were pacing up and down right over my head. And the younger one said, "When I find someone to fight, then I'll fight him. I'm only trying to find someone."'

Another deep breath.

'During which I was lying in the mud with all my fingers crossed, hoping that it wasn't me the blighter was going to find – I was praying that he would win the argument – by that time they were arguing about how much fuel there was, and where the fuel-tankers were, I think . . . They lost me there rather . . . But I was hoping the young one would convince the old one quickly – and I was bloody lucky that he didn't. Or not right at that point, because . . .'

He took a deep breath, and little Alice sucked furiously at her thumb, her eyes closed tight, and hugged her white rabbit, oblivious of British and Germans.

'Because . . . then there was this sound of boots running on the road, and a new argument started with someone else – another officer. And the older fellow finally shouted, "No, no, no! We have been here all the time, you fool! Go away, and don't bother me!" And then they went back to the original argument, and finally the older one gave in and said, "All right, all right! Go and find someone to fight – and find this English officer for

112

that idiot – he'll be out there somewhere, running like a jack-rabbit" – '

Harry Bastable stared down at Alice's rabbit. That was just about how he had been running at the time, the description tallied exactly.

'Which was me, of course,' said Wimpy. 'Except I was burrowing into the mud by then – '

'Me, actually,' murmured Bastable.

' – right under their feet. And then the whole bloody Sixth Panzer Division and half the Luftwaffe came over. I was stuck there for hours, I tell you – '

By which time I was safe under a Bren carrier, thought Harry Bastable, *and dead to the world and the German Army both.*

'After which I had other adventures too boring and horrendous to relate. I could write a definitive monograph on the nature of French ditches and water-courses, Harry, I tell you. I even got quite close to Belléme before I gave up. But I'm afraid that's all finished now, though they must have put up one hell of a fight, the Mendips – there was a lot more dive-bombing at one stage. Real Stuka stuff . . . while I was face-down in another ditch, naturally, quietly shitting myself.'

Bastable had missed that. Or, he had been quietly dying under the carrier at the time, anyway. Time and Harry Bastable, and the German Army and Captain Willis, had all been inextricably mixed up yesterday afternoon and evening, more than somewhat at cross-purposes.

'Me, actually,' he said.

'What do you mean "me, actually"?' queried Wimpy.

'They were after me, I think,' he said. 'Not you.'

At that moment the front nearside wheel on Alice's pram came off, and Alice's rabbit jumped out of her grasp. Naturally she began to cry.

113

7

They knew there had been trouble a mile or more before they reached Colembert.

The first signs were clear enough to Harry Bastable, he could recognize them very well from his own limited military experience. Where soldiers passed through the countryside in any numbers there was always mess and minor destruction. Even back in England, the inevitable aftermath of any field exercise involving more than a dozen men was a rich crop of complaints from the farmers whose land they had crossed. It was only natural that where German troops were crossing the lands of their hereditary enemy their passage would be even more evident.

So all in all, it was just as well that he had been reduced to carrying little Alice in his arms, even though her dampness was beginning to penetrate the double-thickness wrapping of the shawl now, thought Bastable. The pram, even in its prime, had never been designed to cross the ruin of the road-bank which had been crushed into the road, which he had just negotiated; or the fallen branches of the young tree over which he was now stepping.

Wimpy came back down the road towards him. Bastable was glad to observe that he was returning from his scouting expedition confidently, not furtively. Indeed, allowing for the appalling state of his uniform, he really did appear quite bright-eyed and bushy-tailed, as he would hardly have done if the woods ahead were crawling with Germans.

Alice continued to sleep peacefully, thumb and rabbit in their regulation positions. One of the rabbit's ears tickled Bastable's chin slightly, rasping against his unshaven stubble. It embarrassed him to think what a sight he must look, not only filthy and dishevelled, but bare-headed and blue-chinned against the strictest PRO regulations. The obstinate growth of black stubble on his chin had always been a source of irritation to him, and whenever possible he had shaved twice a day for fear of Major Tetley-Robinson, so now he could only hope and pray that Wimpy's more outrageous appearance would take the first cutting-edge of the Tetley-Robinson tongue.

Wimpy grinned at him, and lifted something grey and black – a garment of some sort – which he had been carrying in his hand, trailing it in the dust behind him.

'Battle-trophy!' he lifted it for Bastable to see. 'One SS tunic, complete with Lightning and Skull and Crossbones – slightly shop-soiled.'

Bastable observed with a sick feeling that the tunic was soaked with dried blood.

'They came round from the west and attacked from the north, so far as I can make out,' said Wimpy. 'And – that was Nigel Audley's sector – and by God they must have taken one hell of a pasting . . . Attacked with infantry and armoured cars – no tank tracks that I can see. And then pulled out again double-quick, it looks like. One up to Nigel, if you ask me!'

Harry Bastable breathed a sigh of relief. Alice was safe, and so was C Company, and those were the only two things he cared about. And, while he had no doubts about Alice's abilities to face up to the harsh world, he had had the gravest doubts about C Company's capabilities, under that overlooking ridge and in the care of the diffident Lieutenant Waterworth. Even young Chris Chichester would have been a safer acting-company commander than little Waterworks, as Tetley-Robinson had dubbed him.

But that was an illusory worry now, thank God!

'I met an old Froggie peasant in the woods,' said Wimpy. 'He was picking over the remains of their forward Aid Post – blood and used bandages and field dressings everywhere! That's where I picked up this – ' he lifted the battle-trophy again, ' – I nearly brought along a very nice camouflaged cape . . . But then I thought – if I wear it I could get myself shot by Nigel's chaps . . . See the Lightning badge – that's the SS badge. Adolf's own special thugs – and the good old PROs scuppered them, by golly! Blood everywhere – great pools of it – '

His enthusiasm for blood was positively ghoulish. 'And the Germans have gone?' Bastable held Alice protectively.

'No Germans in Colembert – that's what the Froggie said. Only British . . . Typical Froggie – picking over the remains, like the Belgian peasants after Waterloo.'

'You think he was telling the truth?'

'Well . . . I put the fear of God up him – or tried to.' Wimpy nodded. 'I told him we were the advance-guard of the British Expeditionary Force, coming to drive the Germans out of France – with the help of the glorious French Army . . . And if he didn't speak the truth I would personally see that his own people would put him up against the nearest wall, and – *pouf-pouf*' Wimpy turned his hand into a pistol. 'I don't think he was very bright – but I'm damn sure he was very scared. So we'd best get moving again double-quick, for little Alice's sake, if not for our own.'

Bastable looked down at Alice. He could do nothing

116

more for her, except to give her away to someone who could give her all the things she needed.

Damn and damnation! The sooner Alice was where she ought to be, the better for her and the better for him – he had other things to do than to think about babies. Much more important things.

'Come on, Harry,' said Wimpy. 'It'll be better for her. And we've got to get that message off, about that Fifth Columnist swine of yours in the red tabs – we've really got to get that off double-quick, old man, before he does any more damage.'

Bastable was aware that he was being quite ridiculous, mooning over a small, damp, rather smelly baby, when the fate of thousands of British soldiers, and French soldiers, and even the war itself, was in the balance.

Little Alice and Harry Bastable counted for nothing in that reckoning.

'I'm coming, I'm coming!' He stepped out smartly down the road, the rabbit's ear scuffing at his chin.

As the trees thinned, at the last corner of the road, where it curved into the long straight stretch at the end of which Major Audley's trecs and his company had been waiting for the enemy, Wimpy cautioned him to halt.

Bastable crouched down carefully, so as not to disturb Alice, sinking on to one knee behind Wimpy.

'Place has taken a pounding,' said Wimpy over his shoulder. 'The church spire has gone – but I suppose that was only to be expected . . .' He reached back without taking his eyes off Colembert-les-Deux-Ponts. 'Give me my field-glasses, there's a good fellow.'

Even without Alice in his arms Bastable could not have granted that request.

'Wimpy . . . ah . . . I'm afraid I've lost them, old chap.'

117

Wimpy snapped his fingers. 'Field-glasses – quick!'

'I haven't got them.'

Wimpy turned quickly. 'I'm sorry – I forgot about Alice. Where are they, my field-glasses?'

Bastable closed his teeth. 'I've lost them. The strap broke when I was running away from the farm – I'm sorry.'

Wimpy frowned. 'Damn!' Then he shook his head. 'Damn – those were good glasses! My Uncle Tom gave me those glasses – '

'I'm sorry,' said Bastable. 'The strap broke.'

'Damn!' Wimpy swore again, sharply. Then the expected PRO nonchalance-in-adversity reasserted itself. 'Oh, well – misfortunes of war, I suppose. I don't expect I can ask the German Army if they've seen one pair of field-glasses marked "W. M. Willis" – and I'm damned certain the British Army isn't going to reimburse me.'

This was the Unacceptable Willis the Schoolmaster. 'As soon as we get home,' said Bastable stiffly, 'I will personally replace your field-glasses, Willis.'

'Nonesense, old boy!' replied Wimpy. 'It's just . . .' He swivelled back to scan Colembert again. 'It's just, I can't see anybody moving there at this distance, that's all.'

Bastable moved up alongside him.

Colembert, what he could see of it, certainly had taken a pounding, that was no understatement. But he could only see the northern and highest fringe of the little town – or large village would have been an equally accurate description of it, except that it had a mayor; it had developed on a loop in the stream between its deux ponts, and had only recently spread up the plain above its valley at this point, so there would never have been a lot of it to see from here. Yet . . . this had been the better part of the place, with the bigger houses of the more substantial

118

citizens – a sort of Colembert equivalent of his own Meads at Eastbourne . . . and now he couldn't see *any* of them, as they had been, only piles of rubble and shattered roofs. Also, the spire of the church – it had been built further down the slope, but the spire had still appeared above the skyline on the northern side – that had gone too, as Wimpy had observed.

'This was the side where they attacked, of course,' said Wimpy. 'It obviously took the brunt of things – you'd expect that.'

Bastable narrowed his eyes. 'There are people moving there.'

'Your eyes must be better than mine! What sort of people?'

'Civilians.' Bastable pointed. 'Over there – alongside the bit of red roof.'

'I've got them. Yes – those are civilians, you're right. No field-grey there, thank the Lord!'

'No khaki, either.'

'No. But our chaps'll be in their slit-trenches, ready for the next attack. If the Germans were there they'd be walking about in the open now.'

'Hmm . . .' Bastable had the uneasy feeling that there was something not right about the view. But it was Wimpy who had 'feelings' like this, and clearly he had none at the moment.

'On the other hand,' said Wimpy, 'if they did expect another attack, those civilians wouldn't be picking over the ruins either – they'd be down in their cellars.'

That was it! From what they had seen, and from the sad silence of defeat from the direction of Belléme, it was obvious that the Germans had been successful in this sector of the front. So, if they'd got a bloody nose at Colembert – then where were they now?

119

'I wonder why they haven't attacked again?' said Bastable half to himself.

Of course, Colembert wasn't important; and, it also had to be faced, the Prince Regent's Own presented no threat to the sort of German forces he'd seen. So perhaps they'd simply repelled a chance encounter with a smaller unarmoured unit which had lost its way and blundered off the main line of advance, and been thereafter left alone?

'My God!' murmured Wimpy suddenly. 'And we've got no patrols out, either – Nigel would have had patrols out in the woods, watching the road – '

No threat, Bastable was thinking grimly. The false Brigadier would have apprised the enemy of that, for sure. 'What – ?'

'They would have pulled out,' said Wimpy. 'I rather think they have, too.'

'Where to?'

'The South. Towards the Somme – where the French Army will be.'

'But if the Germans are at Peronne?' Bastable couldn't bring himself to mention Abbeville. Anyway, even if the Germans had set out for Abbeville, there was no proof that they'd reached it. The further they went, the more of the BEF they'd encounter. 'If they were at Peronne yesterday . . .'

'Christ! I don't know!' snapped Wimpy. 'But that old Froggie peasant said there were no Germans in Colembert – and I can't see any, either. So let's bloody well go in and find out for ourselves. Harry – come on!'

They advanced cautiously down the road, dodging in and out of the trees at its side.

Harry Bastable worried desperately for little Alice in his arms. He ought to have put her down, he felt. But

120

then, if he had put her down she would inevitably have woken up, and then she would have realized how wet and hungry and thirsty she was, and then she would have shrieked out as loudly as she had done when the pram had collapsed . . . until he had picked her up again.

This way, at least, they were approaching Colembert quietly.

There was a motor-cycle ahead, at the edge of the field just off the road – a big, grey-painted motor-cycle, smashed and surrounded by a scatter of earth.

But there was no sign of its rider . . .

And then a great tangled wall of fallen branches – the first of Major Audley's blocking-trees. In fact, the whole road from here on, into the ruins, was a mass of fallen trees.

'We got one of the blighters!' exclaimed Wimpy, pointing into the tangle.

There was a German armoured car in the tangle. It looked as though one of the trees had actually hit it, and from the shredded look of the tangle as though it had then been fiercely attacked with machine-gun and mortar fire. The hatch on the top was open.

'Good for B Company!' said Wimpy enthusiastically.

But still no German bodies, thought Bastable.

And . . . if the Prince Regent's Own had knocked out its first German armoured vehicle – and not a very big one, at that . . . it was a commentary on the state of the battalion that it had had to do the job with a tree. With a wooden club, in fact.

Bastable remembered that one awful vision he had glimpsed of the fields full of tanks, and thanked God that Colembert-les-Deux-Ponts hadn't been in their way.

* * *

121

They passed down the tangle of fallen trees. It was about here, Bastable recalled, that Audley had had one of his two Boys anti-tank rifles, in a camouflaged position. He searched among the chaos for the tell-tale signs of the more wilted leaves on the branches with which the firing position had been covered when he'd last seen it.

There it was . . . He pulled a branch aside with his free hand, but the position was empty now, except for the rifle itself and a scatter of used cartridge cases – Bastable knew exactly how many there were of them without any need to count. But, practice ammunition or not, they had used it.

'Empty?' asked Wimpy, and there was something in his voice which made Bastable look at him questioningly.

'Same with the slit-trenches. Seems they've scarpered – just cartridge cases, like here,' Wimpy nodded sorrowfully. 'The Prince Regent's Own appears to have found pressing business elsewhere.'

A dog started to bark in the town somewhere, beyond the great mound of rubble, and the barking noise emphasized the silence it had broken.

'In the circumstances, though, undoubtedly a prudent retreat . . . or, as they say, "a strategic withdrawal according to plan" . . . I suppose somebody higher up must have suddenly noticed that they'd left the poor old battalion behind in the wrong place and ordered 'em out – the Old Man would never had done it off his own bat with Tetley-Robinson to advise him,' continued Wimpy, more to himself than to Bastable and typically disparaging of his Commanding Officer's intellectual capacity.

Yet that must have been the way of it, decided Bastable – it must have been an order after what the false Brigadier had said – 'Your battalion will hold Colembert until it receives further orders' – that was the only way they would have moved out. And, when he thought about it, the false Brigadier's instruction to defend a position of no importance whatsoever in delaying the German advance substantiated its own treason: it was a perfect Fifth Column tactic.

'I wonder whether they got past the Germans,' he said aloud.

'Eh?' Wimpy misunderstood the simplicity of the remark. 'Yes . . . I see what you mean – they may well be in the bag by now, of course. They certainly wouldn't have stood a chance in the open . . .' He nodded thoughtfully. 'In fact they probably didn't get past the southern road, at that.' Then he brightened. 'Well – never mind!'

Bastable frowned incredulously. 'Never mind?'

Wimpy gave a slightly – very slightly – apologetic shrug. 'If they'd stayed here it would only have delayed the inevitable. Jerry would have come back again soon enough – ' he pointed past Bastable to the roadblock in which the armoured car lay, ' – after that. And if they held up the bastards for only ten minutes on the main road, that would have been better than waiting for them here.'

'What d'you mean?'

'Harry, Harry!' Wimpy spread his hands. 'To hold the Tiber bridge against Lars Porsena of Clusium – to hold the Pass at Thermopylae against Xerxes . . . *that* was worth fighting and dying for, old boy. But *Colembert* . . . not Colembert, Harry!'

The point didn't quite escape Bastable among the ex-schoolmaster's meaningless ancient Greeks and Romans – he had almost thought the same thing already, only a moment or two before, though in a different way. But now what had made harsh military sense was overlaid by the sobering thought of the Prince Regent's Own caught like a sitting duck in the open, with its one pathetic Bren carrier.

'Or they may just have slipped through – where there's life, there's hope, Harry,' Wimpy added quickly, as though he had read Bastable's thoughts. 'Apart from which, if they have been caught, then *we* are the Prince Regent's Own, old boy! They left us behind out of necessity, but maybe they saved us from Jerry in the process. *And* we've got a job of work to do, don't forget – how does that jolly poem of yours go, about the flaming torch?'

Bastable felt the blood rise in his cheeks under the coat of dirt and sweat. The blighter had no right to remember it, it didn't belong to him –

> This they all with a joyful mind
>   Bear through life like a torch in flame,
> And falling fling to the host behind –

'We're "the host behind" now, old boy. So we've got to play the game, eh?' Wimpy recalled the words with maddening accuracy.

Alice stirred in his arms, mewing weakly like a sleeping kitten, recalling him to reality once again as she had done before.

'Come on, then,' said Wimpy, taking the lead as he always did, damn it!

Bastable followed him round the mountain of rubble which half-blocked the road, picking his way carefully between the debris-covered pavé.

He almost bumped into the fellow –

'Good God Almighty!' whispered Wimpy.

Bastable was so intent on negotiating a shattered

window frame without risk to Alice that for a moment he didn't look up.

Then he looked up, past Wimpy's shoulder.

The whole of Colembert was in ruins.

8

Although there were no German soldiers visible in the ruins of Colembert-les-Deux-Ponts, there were still British soldiers there, but they would never be leaving.

Harry Bastable didn't see them in that first photographic flash of shock, when the scene imprinted itself on his memory: what one concentrated, uninterrupted aerial bombardment could do to one small unprotected town on one summer's afternoon –

His first unendurable thought, the stuff of nightmares ever after, was that *he was looking down Old Town into Eastbourne, past St Mary's* – St Mary's had no spire, but then neither did Colembert's church now; for bombs are great equalizers, and ruins have no distinguishing glories – *past St Mary's, down that narrow road to the sedate Goffs* – except that the Goffs were mounds of rubble now, and unrecognizable . . .

He didn't see the dead British soldiers in that first vision of ruined town, amongst the smashed and burned and fragmented litter of buildings and possessions and vehicles which choked the main street; khaki is designed to be dustily unobtrusive, and these dead soldiers were doubly well-camouflaged in their deaths.

He saw a dog – a thin, sharp-muzzled mongrel – sniff at something in the rubble and then look up alertly.

It didn't look at Bastable, but at an old Frenchman who sat in a shattered doorway five yards away from it.

As Bastable watched, the old Frenchman bent down and picked up a piece of broken brick at his side, feeling for it and finding it without taking his eyes off the dog. Then, with an incongruously quick movement for an old man, he flung the piece of brick at the dog.

The dog was ready for a missile, but not for the way the brick shattered on the jumbled stones above its head as it jumped to one side – nor for the second and more accurately placed lump which Wimpy threw, and which caught it squarely on the rump, sending it howling and whining down the street.

'Filthy beast!' growled Wimpy. 'M'sieur – '

In that instant Harry Bastable saw what the dog had been sniffing at: a blackened hand – a stained sleeve, and an arm – a dusty arm on which he could just make out the single chevron of a lance-corporal in the British Army.

It was as though that single discovery filtered out the wreckage from the dead, for he saw at once that there were other dead soldiers scattered haphazardly down the street. It struck him as very odd that he hadn't seen them straight away – they were so obvious now, with their helmets lying near them.

It struck him too that death didn't make men smaller, as he had been led to expect, so much as *flatter*, as though more than just life had been pressed out of them.

Wimpy started to talk to the Frenchman, gabbling undecipherable words with a fluency Bastable envied. He had been good at English Language and Mathematics, and that had been splendid for the drapery trade and good enough for the Prince Regent's Own. But now his total inability to string one French word to another once more made a half-wit of him in a world of foreigners.

But he wasn't missing anything this time, for the Frenchman looked up at Wimpy blankly, as though the words were as meaningless to him as they were to Bastable.

Wimpy waited for a moment or two, rocking nervously back and forwards. The lack of response seemed to annoy him.

'God Almighty! Où-sont-les-soldats-anglais? Dîtes-moi – ' he launched into another cascade of sounds punctuated with harsh k's and hissing sibilants, only different from his first attempt in their laboured clarity, which twisted his lips into unnatural shapes as he pronounced them.

The old man – but he wasn't really so old, he was just grey-white with dust – the man heard Wimpy out again without any further sign of understanding, his hands resting loosely in his lap. Then, just as Bastable was sure that Wimpy had failed once more, he answered.

'Les Boches – ' he began, but went no further. It was as though the thread of what he wanted to say had slipped out of his mouth the moment he opened it. Instead he looked away, staring down into the town vacantly. 'Les Boches . . .'

'He's lost his wits,' said Wimpy brutally.

Bastable stared at the Frenchman, and thought that if this had been at home – if this had been Eastbourne, and he had been caught in its destruction – he could see himself in much the same state. Yet Wimpy was wise to be callous, and the sooner he acquired the same hard shell, the better it would be for him.

'What did you ask him?'

Wimpy scanned the street ahead of them. 'I asked him where our chaps had gone, and when . . . I asked him how all this happened. There are some more people down there – let's try them, Harry.'

Bastable was aware of Alice in his arms. There were women down there, he could see them.

But there was something else to be done first. 'Wait!' He dredged in his memory for a moment, but came up without the words he must once have learned. 'What's the French for "For the dog"?'

Wimpy looked puzzled. 'What d'you mean – "For the dog"?'

'Just tell me. What is it?'

'Well . . . "pour le chien" – '

Bastable leaned down and touched the Frenchman's hand.

'Merci, monsieur – pour le chien. Merci.'

The man didn't look up. He didn't seem to have heard.

They picked their way down the street towards the small group of civilians. Half-way along Wimpy paused beside one of the bodies.

'Don't recognize him,' he said at length. 'But if they left a rear-guard, it would have been one of Audley's platoons, I'd guess.'

The guess took Bastable by surprise. The dead man was from the Prince Regent's Own, he could never have been anything else, even apart from the dusty once-yellow-and-grey lanyard. But somehow, until this moment, the dead had been anonymous British soldiers, no different from dead Mendips, and not fellow fusiliers.

Wimpy picked up the dead man's rifle, working the bolt to expose the chamber. 'Empty.' He snapped the bolt back with an air of finality, squeezing the trigger on the empty chamber.

They approached the silent group.

The buildings here had been very badly damaged – doors and window frames blown in, tiles smashed and disarranged on the roofs – but not quite totally destroyed. The group stood outside one of them, which looked as though it had been a shop of some kind; though what kind of shop even Bastable's professional eye could not

129

tell him, for the blast which had smashed its window had also blown away all its stock.

An old man – a genuinely old man – a youth, and three women of mature age . . . perhaps not grandmothers, but it was hard to tell under their enveloping shawls.

They all regarded Wimpy and Bastable with undisguised hatred.

'Pardonnez-moi, mais – ' Wimpy started again.

We are no different from 'les Boches' to them, thought Bastable. And to them we are just as much to blame for this as 'les Boches' – perhaps even more so. Because if we hadn't been here then this wouldn't have happened . . .

The looks didn't change as Wimpy spoke, if anything they intensified. And Wimpy faltered under them.

'Tell them about Alice,' said Bastable.

'Oh . . . right – yes . . .' Wimpy changed gear. 'Mon camarade – '

As the words spilled out of Wimpy, Bastable parted the edges of the shawl to reveal Alice's little face. It looked white and pinched at first, but even as the material parted it began to redden – and he knew what that meant: Alice was about to register her protest with the world again.

He rocked her desperately in his arms. 'There now, Alice – everything's all right now, Alice!'

Suddenly he wanted very badly to get rid of her. He had wanted to do that off and on, more or less continually, ever since he had acquired her – he recognized the desire. Harry Bastable carrying a baby, pushing a baby, *saddled* with a baby, was ridiculous . . . and she had already made him do things that sickened him when he thought about them, and she smelt, and she had wet his arm, and his shoulder ached, and she was just about to make that awful noise again.

One of the women moved in front of him. She made

130

noises – the sort of noises women made to babies, French noises not quite the same as Evelyn Gorton had made to her Precious, but the same noises more or less – as she reached up to relieve Bastable of his burden.

He smiled and nodded at the woman, who was rather ugly and had crooked teeth, but who also smiled and nodded back at him. The only French words he could remember were 'Pour le chien', and as they were hardly appropriate he went on smiling and nodding.

The baby started to whimper. She didn't cry – even to the very end of their relationship she was a very good baby, he had to admit that.

'Tell her – tell her I gave her a bottle of milk last evening, and some bread and water this morning,' said Bastable. 'I expect she's hungry.'

He wondered where the woman was going to find milk in this desolation. But that was her problem now, he was free of it; and at least she was better placed to deal with it than he was.

Wimpy translated, and the woman nodded. Then she said something softly to Bastable, touching his arm before she turned away.

Bastable thought that the old man and the youth didn't look a lot friendlier, but the other women clustered round the baby, and that seemed to take the edge off the situation.

'I told her you'd saved Alice under fire,' said Wimpy. 'There are times to gild the lily, and I rather think this is one of them.'

He turned back to the old man and gabbled more French at him.

The old man replied grudgingly.

'What does he say?' asked Bastable.

The old man spoke again, this time obviously putting a question of his own to Wimpy.

'He wants to know if we are the British coming back,' said Wimpy. 'He says the Germans have gone, whatever that means.'

'But where's the battalion?'

Wimpy addressed the old man again.

The old man shrugged, gestured eloquently up the road, and spoke briefly. Then he shrugged again, and said something else.

'What does he say?'

'They were in a cellar . . . hush!' Wimpy cut Bastable off.

More words, more gestures, all equally indecipherable. Wimpy listened and nodded, leaving Bastable in an agony of ignorance.

Finally the old man stopped, and then simply turned away, taking the youth's arm. Bastable realized that the women had disappeared into the ruined shop, with the baby, without his noticing their departure.

'Please – ?' It was a strange feeling to be unencumbered. 'What happened?'

Wimpy's shrug owed something to its French model. 'They don't really know. There was an attack, so they went down into the cellar – that was – must have been – when Audley got the armoured car – it was a shooting attack, he said. And then they came out, but after that the bombing started – dive-bombing it was, from the sound of it. That went on for a long time, and their house came down on them, and they had to dig themselves out – it took them a long time, he said . . . And then there was . . . this.' Wimpy's hand dismissed Colembert.

'So they don't know where the battalion went?'

'They know damn all about the battalion. As long as

there was noise on top of them they kept quiet. Even after that they sat still for some time, waiting to be rescued. Finally they set about rescuing themselves, and it was pitch-dark in the middle of the night when they broke out, so far as I could gather . . . The old boy was fairly incoherent, though.'

And small wonder, thought Bastable. One old man, a youth and three women entombed in a cellar, emerging at last into the middle of a devastated town – their town – in total darkness . . . What the first flaring match must have revealed to them would have been beyond their understanding – just as it had been beyond his.

'More to the point though, Harry, it seems the Mayor led most people out of town after the first attack. There's an old stone quarry about a mile to the west, with tunnels in it – that's where they went.'

Bastable thought quickly of the refugee road. The main road to the south of the town was probably much the same. The Mayor of Colembert-les-Deux-Ponts sounded like a sensible man.

'Good thinking on his part,' he observed. That was why there were so few people in the town, of course; and at least they were alive. Also, while they were alive, Colembert wasn't dead.

'You're missing the point, old boy. They'll be coming back soon – it's surprising they aren't back already. And the Mayor never did like us much.'

That was true, Bastable remembered. The Adjutant and the QM had both quarrelled with the Mayor, and had reported him as being cantankerously anti-British. So what he would be like now, after his town had been pulverized, Bastable had no wish to discover for himself at first hand.

133

'The bloody man's a Red, of course – a damn Communist,' said Wimpy simply.

Well, that fully explained what no longer needed explaining: the Communists were the allies of the Nazis, they had signed their pact just before the war – even though they had been at each other's throats in Spain only a few months before. But that was only to be expected of gangsters who were no more different from each other than the two sides of the same dud coin.

'The French should have jailed the bastard,' added Wimpy vengefully. 'But . . . as it is, the sooner we get out of this place, the better, I suspect.'

The prospect of having to argue politics with a damn Communist Frenchman – or, since it would be Wimpy who would be doing the arguing, listening to an argument he couldn't understand a word of, galvanized Bastable. 'Well, let's get to blazes out of here, then,' he snapped. And then thought; but where to?

He met Wimpy's eye, but to his dismay found only his own doubt mirrored therein. Faced with the same dilemma, and burdened with much the same harrowing experiences at the hands of the Germans, even the sharp-witted ex-schoolmaster didn't know what way to turn.

'Hmm . . .' Wimpy bit his lip. 'If Jerry was in Peronne yesterday . . . and if he was heading for Abbeville today . . . then it's not going to be very healthy to the south of here right now . . . I suppose we could head west, towards Doullens – that's probably our best bet, eh?'

Bastable shook his head, recalling Sergeant Hobday's report of his adventures. 'They were in Doullens yesterday.'

'How d'you know?'

'I met one of the Mendips coming back from there. He

said he couldn't get through.' Bastable clenched his teeth. 'He's dead now. He was their carrier platoon sergeant.'

'Oh . . . well that's that, then . . .' Wimpy took the point immediately: a senior NCO in a regular battalion could be relied on to report bad news accurately.

But that left only the prospect of retracing their steps to the north again, which after yesterday's horrors neither of them wished to do.

Wimpy looked around him, at the ruins and at the dead men in the street. 'We can't stay here, that's for sure, Harry.'

That was certainly for sure, thought Bastable bleakly. The inhabitants would be back soon, and even if they didn't prove hostile it was only a matter of time before the next wave of Germans arrived.

He tried to recall the geography of Northern France into his mind's eye. He could remember vaguely that the River Somme flowed from Peronne, past Amiens, to the sea at Abbeville. But south of that, it might just as well be darkest Africa – he had never thought to study the map south of the Somme, it had never entered his mind to do so. The territories of the British Army – of the British Expeditionary Force – lay far to the north in this war as in the Great War, beyond Arras into Belgium. It had been unthinkable that the Germans were all around them now.

Arras?

Arras!

The BEF was to the north – Arras was its great bastion, unconquered in the previous war and its GHQ in this one – where Uncle Arthur lay buried in an unmarked 1917 grave –

(Uncle Arthur, whom he couldn't remember, although he had always pretended that he did – Uncle Arthur who

135

had evidently been a trial and a tribulation to the family in peacetime, but who was always remembered now with proper reverence as One Who had made the Supreme Sacrifice . . .)

Arras – he should have thought of it in the first place!

'Arras,' he said decisively.

Wimpy looked at him. 'Arras?'

'That's where we'll head for.' The name carried its direction with it: it was vaguely to the north, or possibly slightly to the east of north. And not so very many miles either, the lie of some of which – and possibly the most dangerous miles, too – they already knew.

'Why Arras?' asked Wimpy. 'We'll have to cross the German line of advance again, Harry. You realize that?'

'That's where our chaps will be,' said Bastable.

Wimpy considered the proposition briefly. 'Rather than the French, you mean?'

The only French soldiers Bastable had seen had been running away with the refugees, without their rifles. That was obviously an inadequate basis for judging an army several millions strong, but he still had greater confidence in the smaller BEF. And, in any case, this wasn't a moment for indecisiveness, with which Wimpy would surely argue.

'Yes. If we go south it'll be no better.'

For a moment Wimpy stared at him, and then nodded. 'Fair enough, old boy. There are Jerries that way – but there are Jerries every which way, so it hardly matters . . . And I suppose there is a chance they'll steer clear of Arras for a bit – you're right there, Harry, possibly.'

That last hadn't figured in Bastable's calculations, but he hastily added it to them. 'A good chance,' he said.

'Right-o! Arras it is, then!' The force of his own logic

convinced Wimpy. 'Just give me ten minutes, or quarter of an hour, say . . . then we'll hit the road again – '

'What?' The delay, after they'd come to a decision – and against Wimpy's own advice, took Bastable by surprise. 'Why?'

'Oh . . .' Wimpy shook his head from side to side. '. . . I thought I might take one quick recce down to the bridge before we got out – or as far as battalion headquarters, anyway, in the square down there . . . I mean, we haven't seen much of the place yet, and there might be a clue down there – just a quick recce, old boy. You can stay here and hold the fort, and if anything happens here you can blow your whistle – and if I find anything, I'll blow mine . . . And I'll come back via the Mairie and see if I can pick up a map of some sort, eh?' He looked at Bastable sidelong, almost slyly. 'You can stay here,' he repeated. 'Just five or ten minutes – and then Arras.'

It was almost as though the fellow could read his mind, thought Bastable irritably, knowing that he didn't want to see any more of Colembert, and didn't want to stay in the place another minute longer than necessary. But these, nevertheless, were Wimpy's terms for agreeing to go north, he knew that also.

'Very well.' He surrendered ungracefully. 'But not more than fifteen minutes at the most.'

It was only after Wimpy had disappeared into the ruins that he remembered he had no way of telling the passage of time, since his watch was immovably fixed at ten to three. But then he knew that Wimpy would take whatever time he wanted, regardless of his promise, the fellow was like that – unreliable.

It also occurred to him then that one of the dead fusiliers might have a watch, which he might take for himself as a replacement. Yet, he decided, as not many of the men had wrist-watches that was hardly a possibility worth exploring. The corpse-robbing he had done already was enough to prove to him that he could do it when he had to, but he had no stomach for doing more of it.

He contented himself with the helmet of the nearest of them, which made him feel more soldierly, even though it had a dent in it. ·

He wished he had gone with Wimpy, even though that didn't make sense. If there was anything to find, Wimpy would find it. And if there was any danger –

'*M'sieur* – '

He swung round quickly towards the voice.

A woman's voice.

'M'sieur!' The woman stood in a gap in the ruins, which had once been a side-street, and was now three-quarters choked with fallen debris.

'Madame?'

He knew as he spoke that was only launching himself into fresh difficulties, since he would not be able to understand the answer to his question. He couldn't even tell her that if she'd just wait a few minutes Wimpy would be back.

She spoke, and it was as he feared. How in God's name had he studied French all those years and emerged so uselessly *ignorant*? All he could make out from the jumble of words was 'officier anglais' – which was himself.

'Je – ' he licked his dry lips, ' – je ne pas parlez français bon, Madame.'

Damn, damn, *damn*!

'Officier anglais,' she repeated.

He pointed at himself. 'Officier anglais?'

'Non!' She pointed down the side-street. 'Officier anglais – '

138

The other words were lost on him, but the pointing finger was enough: there was an English officer down there somewhere, probably a wounded one.

He nodded to her that he would follow where she led him.

The side-street was very bad. Here there had been fire as well as bomb damage, with a whole row of older houses blackened and still smouldering sullenly, though it looked as though the fires had simply burned themselves out with a quick fury of their own, unhampered by water from any firemen's hoses. Now he thought about it, it surprised him that there hadn't been more fire in the town, but then presumably the very completeness of the bombing had crushed the life out of the fires before they could take hold, strangling them with fallen stone and brick. But here, because the bomb damage had been less, the fire had been more destructive, to produce much the same final ruin.

This conclusion was confirmed by the change of scene at the end of the street, where a large bomb had cratered the road itself, bringing down the houses on each side so that their fallen rubble half-filled the crater. That was where the fires had ended, anyway, although beyond it everything seemed to be coated with a grey-black snowfall of ash from the conflagration up the street.

He followed the French lady across the crater and through a gap which the bomb had smashed in a stretch of fine ornamental iron railings, into a garden.

Like everything else in Colembert, the garden was a ruin now, fragments of stone and brick and wood scattered across its flower-beds, its surviving flowers covered with ashes, and its trees broken and shredded by the blast – it was strange how the bomb's effect hadn't snapped them cleanly, but had splintered them into frayed fibres of wood –

'M'sieur!'

Bastable realized he had been left behind – he had been stopped in his tracks, staring at the ruined garden which had been turned into a wilderness not by the slow action of neglect but in one hot, shattering blast.

'Madame!' He was in a world of new experiences, and every one of them was beastly, and this one in its way was no less horrible than those which had preceded it. Yet, although his imagination had failed to prepare him for the reality, he must grow accustomed to each shock at first sight, without ever being daunted by it again. This was what a bomb-blast did to a garden full of flowers and carefully-nurtured trees – he had already seen what the same forces could do to a steel Bren carrier and a carefully-nurtured human being. They would do the same to every garden, every human being –

To his own garden.

To himself –

'Coming, Madame,' he said.

The house was set back from the road – a good, solid, three-storeyed house, in its own garden.

His family house, it might have been, allowing for the difference in styles; instinctively, he knew that it was *her* house, for she seemed a good class of woman, with something of his mother's look about her.

A good, solid house: it had caught the blast, but had resisted it bravely. The stonework was chipped and pock-marked, every window was gone, the slates on the roof were disarranged and the front door was off its hinges. But it was still a house within the meaning of the word. He had seen worse.

The French lady led him up the steps to the buckled front door.

An absurd inclination to wipe his filthy boots checked Bastable for a moment. The absurdity of such an action was overtaken by the first glimpse of the chaos ahead, which triggered a hysterical fragment of a poem he had once been set to learn as a boy – a poem he had learned, but had not thought of again ever since –

> If seven maids with seven mops
>   Swept it for half a year,
> 'Do you suppose,' the Walrus said,
>   'That they could get it clear?'

The bomb had dislodged every fragment of plaster from the ceiling of the hall – and, indeed, from the walls too – to lay bare the laths to which the plaster had been attached.

His eyes became more accustomed to the gloom.

The bomb had also detached every ornament and every picture from the walls to smash among the plaster on the floor –

> 'I doubt it,' said the Carpenter,
>   And shed a bitter tear –

The French lady spoke to him again, and indicated a doorway, so that there was no time for bitter tears.

A big room – the lounge, if that was what the French called it.

A gloomy room – gloomy because the tattered curtains were drawn across the windows, admitting the light of what must still be early morning through innumerable rents.

Shattered china and glass. A fallen chandelier in the middle of the floor amongst the plaster –

Soft furnishings, furniture, china and glass – *if England is bombed like this*, thought Bastable, *then Bastable's of Eastbourne will make a fortune in replacements*.

There was someone lying on the huge high-backed settee, covered from chin to boots by a blanket.

The French lady whispered unintelligible words softly in his ear. All he could make out from them was the familiar 'officer anglais'.

He crunched across the floor towards the settee, skirting the chandelier. In the half-light all he could make out was a dirty white face – grey-white against the brown-white of the enveloping blanket – which he couldn't recognize. He realized that he had had the feeling, for no rational reason, that the wounded officer would be Tetley-Robinson, he couldn't think why. But this must be one of the new subalterns, like Chris Chichester, whose names and faces alike were still vague to him. This wasn't either Tetley-Robinson or Chris Chichester, certainly . . . yet – yet –

The eyes opened slowly, as though the crunching of his boots had awakened the wounded man from sleep.

The head moved and the eyes fastened on him.

'Who's that?' The voice was weak, but instantly recognizable. And yet the act of recognition only left Bastable more confused: how could he have failed to recognize Major Audley, whose face he knew so well, at that first glance?

He knelt down beside the settee.

'M – . . . Nigel?' he stared at the recognizable-unrecognizable mask. Audley's face had been stretched and had fallen in on itself, and then been covered with

142

sweat and grime and coated with fine dust which adhered to the twenty-four-hour bristles on his chin and cheek. The eyes, which had darker shadows under them, like bruises, had sunk into his head.

'Who's that?' Audley repeated.

'Harry Bastable,' said Bastable

'Harry . . .?' Audley could make nothing of the christian name.

'Bastable.' Harry Bastable swallowed. 'C Company – Bastable, Nigel.'

'Bastable!' The exclamation was little more than a whisper. The eyes closed, then opened again. 'Bastable . . .?'

'I'm here, Nigel. Captain Willis and I are here.'

The eyes disengaged from Bastable's. 'Willis?'

'We came back, Nigel. What happened?'

Audley moved his head, still peering past Bastable. 'Willis . . . Where's Willis?'

Bastable had the feeling that he had been rejected. 'He's not here at the moment. He'll be here eventually, Nigel.'

'Willis . . .' The voice trailed off and the eyes closed.

Bastable leaned forward and lifted the blanket, first a little, then more, and finally (when the eyes still didn't open to accuse him) enough to see what lay beneath it.

The French lady said something, and although Bastable didn't understand a word of what she said he knew what she was saying.

So this was another new experience, he thought as he lowered the blanket gently. He had seen dead men, so now he was seeing a dying one. It was just another new experience.

The French lady's presence behind him also had a steadying effect. He must not disgrace himself, or the

143

Prince Regent's Own. He was going to see a lot of this, and, at a guess, it would more often be worse than this, hard though that was to imagine.

Just another new experience. He had to hold on to that, and not be sick.

In the meantime . . .

'Nigel?' He paused. 'Can you hear me, Nigel?'

The eyelids fluttered, but remained closed. Bastable turned towards the French lady. 'Madame . . . s'il vous plaît . . .' he searched for the word, and as usual found nothing in his vocabulary except 'où est' and 'combien', and now 'pour le chien'. 'Damn!'

She looked at him questioningly. 'M'sieur?'

He turned his hand into a cup and lifted the cup to his lips. 'Water, Madame. Water?'

'Oui.' She nodded, and left the room without another word, crunching regardless over the wreckage of her treasures.

A brave lady, thought Bastable. Audley hadn't been hit here, or there would have been blood everywhere, so she must somehow have found him and brought him in – perhaps with someone's help, but into her house, to her settee, under her blanket . . . and a very good quality blanket too, as good as the best Witney blankets stocked by Bastable's of Eastbourne, by the feel of it. Would Mother have behaved so well, in the ruin of her house, with a dying French officer on her hands?

Well . . . well, perhaps she would at that, he thought suddenly with a stab of guilt at his disloyalty. Mother had sold her jewels, everything down to her wedding ring, in the bad times in the early thirties, when it had been touch and go in the firm, so maybe she would at that, by God!

He stared down at Major Audley's face. There was nothing he could do for Audley – and nor could Doc

Saunders have done anything either, for what lay under the blanket.

But there was still something Audley could do for Harry Bastable and for England, perhaps. And if there was, then he must do it.

He heard the familiar crunching sound of feet on broken plaster and china and glass behind him.

'M'sieur.'

Damn and damn and damn! He had wanted water, to moisten Audley's lips and wipe his brow – and she had brought him brandy in a mug, half a mug of it – he could smell it even before he could see it. Damn, damn, *damn*!

She smiled at him. It was for him, of course!

He took a gulp of the stuff, and coughed on it, and choked on it, as always, as it burned his empty stomach.

He couldn't give it to Audley, therefore. Audley had no stomach.

It was a bloody miracle Audley was still alive. With what was under the blanket Audley should have been dead long ago.

He took another, more controlled gulp, and felt it burn all the way down, and turned back to the dying *officier anglais*.

The eyes were open, and they were suddenly brighter, and they were looking at him.

'What happened?' asked Audley, pre-empting his own question with unbearable clarity. 'The battalion?'

Bastable stared at him in an agony of indecision. That was his question, and he no longer knew what to ask, if Audley didn't know the answer himself.

'Where's Willis?' asked Audley. 'I want to talk to him.'

'What happened?' The question sounded empty now, but it was still the only one he could think of.

'Where's Willis?' The dirt-encrusted lips compressed themselves obstinately.

'Nigel – what happened?' Bastable bent over the dying man, pushing aside the question with his own. 'Tell-me-what-happened?'

'Willis – ?'

'Captain-Willis-is-coming. The-Germans-attacked . . . ?' Under desperation Bastable could feel anger rising.

The lips trembled. 'Amateurs . . . Came across the fields . . . and down the road . . . open order – like, they didn't care – like, we weren't there . . . But we were . . .' The lips quivered again.

'Yes?' Bastable willed the lips to open again. 'Yes?'

'After that . . . bombers . . . Stukas – smashed up everything . . .'

'Yes?'

'Tanks . . . infantry . . . *professionals* . . .' The eyes lost Bastable's face, and the voice trailed off again.

He had to get both back again. '*Sir* – Nigel?'

He couldn't shake a dying man. 'Sir?'

'Bloody shambles, naturally.' The eyes transfixed him. 'Where's Willis?' The voice seemed stronger.

A horrible certainty loomed out of the mist in Harry Bastable's mind – and advanced into the clear light of inevitability as he stared at it.

He recognized it, because it had been there all the time, waiting to show itself to him – he had known about it and had expected it, but had refused to look at it. Instead, he had made pictures in his imagination and shared them with Wimpy, and they had both believed in those pictures because they had both been unwilling to accept the reality, even when it stared them in the face.

That was why Wimpy had insisted on 'scouting around', with that sly, withdrawn look on his face – Wimpy was

146

much brighter than he was, much quicker on the uptake, so he had needed to have those pictures (which he didn't believe in) proved or disproved by the evidence of his own eyes, which he knew he would find.

The battalion had never left Colembert-les-Deux-Ponts.

That was really why he had wanted to go north, to Arras – because there wasn't anything to the south to follow.

And that was why Wimpy had said, 'To the French?', and not, 'To catch up with the battalion?', of course.

'Where's Willis?' repeated Major Audley, almost petulantly.

And . . . *a bloody shambles, naturally* . . . naturally.

That was how it would have been, with tanks up against soft aluminium anti-tank ammunition, over the ridge against C Company – *a bloody shambles, naturally* –

But there was no time for tears for C Company, and poor incompetent acting-acting-company commander Waterworks, and young Christopher Chichester, whose knowledge of the Boys anti-tank rifles would have availed him nothing with that bloody-fucking-useless practice ammunition up the spout – *Oh God!*

'I'll go and get him,' said Harry Bastable.

'*No* –'

There was a slight, impossible movement under the blanket, as though Major Audley had found the use of one blackened claw.

'*No*. No time . . .' The feverish eyes truly transfixed him now. 'My boy, David . . .'

Bastable was pinned down by those eyes.

'Tell Willis . . . My boy, David – he knows my boy, David – ' Audley stopped abruptly.

Suddenly, Bastable knew what Audley was talking about: he had a son named David, and Willis was an acquaintance, if not a friend, and more than that a schoolmaster, if not an acquaintance, who had admitted teaching Audley's 'my boy, David' – that was who he was talking about.

'Yes, Nigel – ' he leaned forward again. ' – your son, David – ?'

'Not my son – not my son – but my boy, damn it – ' Major Audley took one great rattling breath, and then a second shallower one.

Bastable couldn't make head nor tail of that, for the man was obviously rambling now, but he forced himself to lean over to place his ear closer to catch the words.

'Your son, David?' He found himself staring at the heavy brocaded cushion on the back-rest of the settee. It was old-fashioned, but very high-class material, he noted. And very expensive too – not unlike the curtains he had sold to Mrs Anstruther last spring – was it only last spring?

Major Audley seemed to have had second thoughts about the message he wished to pass on to Wimpy about his son, David, or the propriety of giving it to someone else, perhaps. ·

'Your son, David?' Bastable felt himself belittled by such lack of confidence. 'Tell Wimpy what?'

In the far distance, faint but clear enough in the silence surrounding them, there was the sound of someone kick-starting a motor-cycle. The engine roared for a moment, and then stalled.

That would be Wimpy, thought Bastable. Wimpy's passion for riding motor-cycles was unbridled, and he had even been known to break battalion rules to satisfy it. But if there was no battalion any more, then the rules no

148

longer applied – and if the battalion had left a motor-cycle behind then Wimpy was the man to nose it out, like a dog sensing the presence of a bone.

The French lady had touched his shoulder, he realized. And she was speaking to him again.

He turned towards her. 'Ne comprenez pas,' he said.

She stared at him for a moment. Then she reached past him and drew the·blanket up over Audley's face.

Bastable looked down at the blanket, then back to the French lady, then down at the blanket again.

'He can't be dead. He was just speaking to me – ' He pulled the blanket down.

The motor-cycle started up again in the distance.

9

But it wasn't Wimpy on the motor-cycle.

It was one of the khaki machines the battalion had
acquired at Boulogne – British Army property, and
certainly not the property of the spotty-faced French
youth who was sitting proudly astride it outside the shop
where the old man and the women had been standing.

Bastable felt a sudden vicious danger well up inside
him. There were dead British soldiers lying in the street –
he had only this moment left another one of them, newly-
dead – killed in France and not yet buried. And the dirty
bastards were already picking up the spoils – the dirty
thieving swine!

He launched himself down the street in a red haze of
rage, kicking obstructions out of the way, and fetched up
within striking distance of the youth before another
coherent thought could cross his mind.

'Get off that machine!' he barked. 'Get off – d'you hear
me – *this instant!*'

And that might not be an order delivered in French,
but – by God! its meaning ought to be plain enough, he
told himself hotly.

The youth tossed his head insolently and rotated his
hands on the handlebars.

'Get off!' shouted Bastable. 'At once!'

The youth smirked at him – he was hardly older than
the errand boys Bastable's retained for their parcel deliv-
eries – and pronounced a single word. And although it

was a French word its vulgar meaning was also immediately clear to Bastable.

His anger passed the point of incandescence, consumed itself and suddenly became deadly cold. He knew now, as he fumbled with his webbing holster – he knew now with a horrible icy certainty that he would shoot this youth dead in five seconds if he refused to get off the motorcycle.

Then something hard poked him in the back, just below the right shoulder-blade.

'Non,' said someone behind him.

Bastable swung round and found himself staring into the twin mouths of a double-barrelled shotgun.

The shotgun was held by a villainous-looking bandit whose expression indicated not only that he was quite capable of squeezing both triggers but also that it would give him great personal satisfaction to do so.

Bastable's own murderous anger dissolved into fear as he identified the emotion behind the expression: it was the same one that he himself had experienced seconds before – the mad glare of impotent rage which had at last found something to expend itself on. It was his own finger on the trigger of the gun that was pointed at him.

The understanding of his own imminent death froze him into immobility, hand on holster.

'Levez . . . Poot up . . . the 'ands.'

There were other men behind the man with the shotgun, and it was one of them who spoke. It seemed impossible to Bastable that he should not have seen or heard them behind him, but he hadn't.

He put up his hands so quickly that for a heart-stopping moment – as he did so, but before he could stop himself – he thought the shotgun man would blow him to pieces.

Someone detached himself from the blur of individuals:

a short, fat little man in a dusty black suit but no collar and tie, only a gold collar stud.

Not the face, but the whole man and the air of authority he still carried, sparked Bastable's memory. He had seen this one before, only once and from afar, but the image was there – of a short, fat little man arguing with the Adjutant outside the Town Hall of Colembert.

It was the Mayor.

This deduction fanned a quick flame of hope in him. The Mayor might be anti-British – he might even be a damn Red, if Wimpy was to be believed. But he was still an official of local government, and presumably a man of substance as well. Even in Colembert – even if Colembert wasn't Eastbourne – that must count for something.

God! He could remember the last time he had talked to the Mayor, when he had offered the services of Bastable's lady assistants to help assemble the town's sixty thousand gas masks just after Mr Chamberlain had come back from Munich, not long after the first air-raid siren trials –

Somewhere below, in the lower town, there came a rumble and crash of falling masonry.

Colembert wasn't Eastbourne.

And the Mayor of Colembert wasn't the Mayor of Eastbourne.

The Mayor of Colembert was speaking to him now – hissing those meaningless words at him, which he couldn't understand. If only Wimpy was here!

Assassin. That was a word he could understand.

Assassin?

That wasn't fair.

'I am a British officer!' he snapped back. 'Britain and France – '

He felt a movement at his side, where his holster was: the youth was relieving him of his revolver! But before he

152

could think of lowering his arm to prevent the theft the shotgun jerked menacingly at him, countermanding the movement.

God! It wasn't possible – it wasn't happening to him!

One of the other men came forward from behind the Mayor to take the revolver from the youth. And then, before Bastable had time to think, let alone to duck, the man slapped him hard across the face.

'Assassin!'

The shock of the blow brought tears to Bastable's eyes, even more than the stinging pain of it. He wanted to cringe, but his body wouldn't cringe, it only swayed upright again, tensing itself against the next blow.

The man swung his arm back. Bastable closed his eyes.

But the blow never landed – he heard a sound at his side, a scrunching footfall and then the sound of another slap, loud as a pistol shot, yet not on his own cheek.

He opened his eyes quickly, and caught a black blur. For an instant the tears obscured the blur as it passed him, then his vision cleared.

The black-shawled woman hit the man with the revolver again.

Well, it was more of a vigorous push than a hit, but it was just as good: in backing, the man tripped on the pavé and fell over in a wild confusion of arms and legs into the rubble behind him.

The woman swung round and knocked the shotgun barrel up. The shotgun exploded with an ear-splitting concussion as the owner staggered back.

The Mayor stepped forward and shouted at the woman.

The woman shouted – screamed – back at the Mayor.

The Mayor took another step forward, and it proved to be an unwise step. As he lifted his finger at her and opened his mouth to speak she back-handed his arm out

153

of the way, putting him off-balance, and then caught him on the side of the head with her return swing. Something pink-and-white shot out of his mouth and fell at Bastable's feet.

Bastable looked down at a set of false teeth.

As he looked down the woman stepped sideways and trod – either deliberately or accidentally, he never knew which – on the Mayor's teeth.

Then she started to revile them. As usual, as always, the words were lost on him, and he couldn't even guess at their exact content. But their effect was as concussive as the shotgun blast, he could see that.

Finally she swept an arm out to the side, pointing past and behind him. And as she did so there came a shrill answering wail which Bastable recognized instantly.

Alice!

There was another woman alongside him now, on his left side, with the unforgettable shawl-swathed bundle in her arms which she held up for him to inspect, as though for his approval, quite unmoved by the increasing noise which came from it.

He lowered his arms, and lifted one grimy finger to touch the little, scarlet, unrecognizable face. He felt that that was what the woman wanted him to do.

'Alice – little Alice,' he said, nodding at the woman.

Alice. Little nameless, parentless, lost, unknown, bereaved and abandoned Alice –

'Al-ees?' The woman looked at him questioningly. 'Al-ees?'

'Alice,' said Bastable. 'Alice.'

At which Alice, being Alice, quietened down in her arms, her crying trailing off into hiccoughs punctuating a tearful chuntering sound, which expressed only mild dissatisfaction where before there had been angry protest.

'Al-ees.' The woman nodded at him and lifted the baby high on her shoulder, out of his view once more, rocking her vigorously.

The first woman started to speak again, addressing the men contemptuously now, as though the matter was settled, and there was really no more to be said. Indeed, when one of them started to say something she cut him off before he had reached the third word, in the same contemptuous tone, completing her own sentence with a two-handed gesture of dismissal which seemed to cow them utterly.

The Mayor, who looked as if his head was still ringing from the buffet he had received, mumbled something, and pointed towards her feet. Bastable realized that if he had been able to catch the words he might have been able to add 'false teeth' to his French vocabulary.

The woman was implacable. She ignored the Mayor, pointing at the man who had received Bastable's revolver and then opening her hand to receive the weapon. Only when she had it in her hand did she shift her ground, turning without a second look at the men to return it to Bastable.

She was the ugly woman with the crooked teeth, who had taken Alice from him in the first place, and he could have kissed her. But as it was, he didn't know what to say, and knew that even if he had known what to say he wouldn't have been able to say it to her in a language which she could understand.

'Merci, Madame,' he said. And because he could think of nothing else to do, he saluted her, touching the brim of his steel helmet in salute with the tips of his stiffened fingers.

'Merci, Madame,' he said again, aware as he spoke that the would-be lynching party behind him was dispersing.

She scrutinized him for a moment, this time neither speaking nor smiling. Indeed, he could see no friendliness in her face at all: it was as though they were back where they had been when he first saw her, before he had revealed Alice to her. So perhaps that was where they were, with all debts settled – his life for Alice's – and nothing left for him but to leave her alone in the ruins of her town, to go away and never return.

'M'sieur,' she said finally, and then nodded, and turned away into the dark interior of her wrecked shop. He heard her picking her way carefully over its littered floor, but eventually the crunch of her footsteps on fallen plaster faded into silence.

Now he was alone again, with the motor-cycle, and he felt oddly light-headed. It must be the French lady's brandy, he decided. He had drunk rather a lot of that, and on a stomach containing only the bread he had shared with Alice in the half-light of early dawn . . . though by the position of the sun it was still only early morning, even though so much had happened to him since then. Indeed, the French lady's brandy must also be to blame for that sudden blinding, murderous rage he had surrendered to, which had nearly been the death of him.

He started to wonder what else would happen to him, but resolutely stopped wondering when the first instant possibility to occur to him was that this could be the day of his death – the odds on that lay all around him.

Wimpy must have wandered out of earshot, or out of range of the sound of the motor-cycle's engine-noise anyway, for *that* would surely have summoned him back at the double.

But . . . supposing Wimpy didn't come back?

Then he would truly be alone. The last, the very last,

of the Prince Regent's Own South Downs Fusiliers, outside death and captivity.

That thought was unbearable, so he turned his mind away from that too, and busied himself with examining the motor-cycle. He had never ridden a motor-cycle – Father had refused point-blank to permit it. But if . . . but it shouldn't be too difficult to work the thing out, one way or another. If . . .

'Hullo there,' said Wimpy, conversationally, from behind him. 'You've found one of the bikes, then.'

'Yes.' Bastable was surprised at Wimpy's lack of enthusiasm.

'Where did you get it?'

'Oh . . .' Past time flowed for an instant before Bastable's eyes, as for a drowning man, and then was gone. It didn't really matter: it was over. '. . . The Frogs supplied it, old boy.'

'They did?' Wimpy looked at him incuriously. His face had an unnatural look; it had lost its healthy tan, and was like the piece of upper arm which showed through the tear in his battledress blouse – pasty white under dirt. 'That was deuced civil of them.' He bent down to examine the motor-cycle.

'Yes, it was.' Wimpy's lack of interest decided Bastable finally to keep the details of his own experiences to himself.

'The 500 cc Norton . . . I would have preferred the Ariel,' murmured Wimpy ungratefully.

'The Ariel?'

'Only 350 cc, but more nippy . . . And damn good front suspension . . .' Wimpy tweaked the machine. 'Petrol's okay, that's one good thing. Right!' He stood up. 'Hold this, will you?'

157

He threw a battledress blouse to Bastable, and then started to unbuckle his equipment. Bastable stared at the blouse, which belonged to a captain in the RAMC.

'Is this Doc Saunders's?' It was a stupid question, really.

Wimpy stripped off his own blouse and held out his hand for the exchange.

'He won't be needing it.' Wimpy handed his own blouse to Bastable in exchange for the RAMC one.

'What?'

'My need is greater than his.' Wimpy buttoned up the blouse and picked up his equipment. 'Wrap it up and put it on the baggage thing at the back and sit on it. I'll take my stuff out of it later – ' he pointed to the metal carrier on the back of the Norton ' – it'll protect your arse in the meantime. Let's get the hell out of this bloody place.'

Bastable blinked unhappily at him. This was a strangely-altered Wimpy, and he preferred the old one.

'For Christ's sake, come on, Harry!' snapped Wimpy, throwing his leg astride the Norton. '*Let's get out of here!*'

Even before Bastable could reply he stood fiercely on the kick-starter. The engine turned over, but didn't fire.

'Fuck!' spat Wimpy. 'Start, damn you!'

He kicked again, and the engine roared explosively. Bastable wrapped the battledress blouse into an untidy bundle and placed it on top of the metal carrier, and himself on top of it, astride it.

'Hold on,' commanded Wimpy.

Bastable clasped him desperately. The road ahead was scattered with rubble and pock-marked with holes in the pavé, but before he could protest at Wimpy's assumption of command the motor-cycle was moving, and all consecutive thought was jolted out of his mind.

Except – *the last time I rode up this road was in DPT 912, with Batty Evans at the wheel* –

Wimpy was a skilful rider: the Norton bumped and twisted and swerved, but it never faltered over its obstacle course.

Sergeant Hobday's driver in the carrier had been a skilful man, but that hadn't saved them –

Think of England –

Or, not of England, but his duty, which transcended survival, but survival was essential to it: *he had to tell someone in authority about the false Brigadier – that was his sole reason for existence.*

The Norton negotiated the last scatter of debris; the fallen trees – Audley's trees – were ahead; Wimpy twisted the machine between two empty slit-trenches, out into the open field alongside the road, and opened up the throttle. 'Hold on!'

The wind whipped Bastable's face, sweeping away the smell of Wimpy's sweat and the faint medical smell – so faint that it might only be in his imagination – of Doc Saunders's battledress blouse, which mingled with it.

He held on for dear life. He couldn't look back, and he didn't want to look back, at that hated skyline – that ruined skyline, without its spire, without anything that he wanted to remember –

Alice?

The ugly woman with the bad teeth?

The Norton jumped and jolted his own teeth, so that he rolled his tongue back for fear of biting it, as they swept up on to the road again – he must hold on for dear life, because life *was* dear – *surviving* was dear – he had felt that already, because there had so far been his duty to survive – to pass on his message – and he hadn't yet had to make the choice between the one and the other, and he hoped he would never have to make that choice, because –

God! All he had to do now, at this moment, was to hold on tight, and hope Wimpy knew what he was doing!

They were in the wood now, bumping over and round the fallen branches he remembered from their original approach to Colembert – and Colembert-les-Deux-Ponts was gone at last – out of sight, out of mind, all the guilt of it!

Never again – never again – *he that outlives this day and comes safe home* (he had learned that line somewhere, or heard it somewhere, and it had stuck in his memory in readiness for this moment) – *never again!*

And if he looked back now it wouldn't be there, thank God!

Wimpy was slowing down, and he didn't want him to slow down. At this speed they were only two hours from the Channel ports – straight down the road for Boulogne, or Calais, or even Dunkirk, and then England – with only the German Army in the way –

Wimpy was slowing down.

He shouted meaningless words in Wimpy's ear, urging him on, but they coasted to a stop, nevertheless.

'What's the matter?' asked Bastable

'Oak tree,' said Wimpy.

'Oak tree?'

'Batty's oak tree – poor old Batty's oak tree,' said Wimpy. 'Don't you remember?'

Bastable couldn't remember. The last memory of Batty was that final burst of firing at his back, when he had run away and left Batty in the lurch, to hold off the whole German Army.

Wimpy pointed to the bare hillside above them. 'The

crossroads are ahead – we've just passed Batty's oak tree. So we'd best have a look and see what there is on the main road at the top there, old boy – eh?'

Bastable had no choice but to dismount from the Norton, since that was plainly what Wimpy intended. He stared round him, but saw only the open, empty country-side, so bare of real hedges and trees, unlike his own Sussex landscape. For the first time – but with surprise that it was the first time – he saw it as an alien land, in which he was as much an invader as the Germans. It was not their country, but it was also not his either, and he didn't want to die in it. Because if, in the next second of time, that same mushroom of smoke and flame enveloped him that had enveloped the young Mendips' subaltern in the carrier, then he would die and rot in foreign dirt, and be lost and forgotten for ever.

Wimpy was staring at him, yet seemed curiously reluc-tant to meet his eyes. There was something wrong with Wimpy.

'I'll go this time,' said Wimpy. 'My turn, eh?'

He didn't wait for Bastable to agree, he simply went, and Bastable watched him go without protest. At least he didn't have any premonitions about silver rivers and golden bridges this time; and they certainly weren't in that no-man's-land of his, between life and death, either.

Nevertheless, there was something wrong with Wimpy. It had been apparent ever since he had returned from his reconnaissance of the lower part of Colembert: he hadn't been Wimpy at all, only a pale, forced copy with the stuffing knocked out of it. Even, he hadn't enthused over the Norton as he ought to have done – Wimpy of all people, whose obsession with motor-cycles was almost childish.

Bastable stared miserably at the big motor-cycle, and

thought of Nigel Audley, and Sergeant Hobday of the Mendips, and that young officer, whose name he could no longer remember; and also of the men of his own company – young Chichester, and poor frightened, incompetent little Mr Waterworks, and old sweats like Sergeant-Major Franklin and CQMS Gammidge, and Corporal Smithers, the ex-boxer whose prowess in the ring had won him his stripes.

It was painful to imagine them now, mostly as prisoners, shambling to the rear of the enemy, dishevelled and exhausted, but some of them inevitably dead, like Nigel Audley – young Chichester would be dead for sure in that damned badly-sited slit-trench by the bridge, firing that damned useless ammunition from that damned anti-tank rifle in full view of the ridge.

Damn, damn, *damn*! He should never have sited the slit-trench there, by the bridge, like a grave ready to receive its occupants. Whoever had died there, he had killed them with his stupidity and inexperience as surely as if he had pulled the trigger on them himself –

Not that it would have made any difference. They had all been lambs for the slaughter, doomed from the start, from the moment they joined the wrong convoy, for the wrong place.

No! He mustn't think like that!

Thinking like that betrayed his own military inexperience, even more than the badly-sited slit-trench by the bridge. Just because he and his battalion had happened by accident to be in the direct line of the German spearhead – just because the Allies had been forced to retreat at that point – he was demoralizing himself with defeatist thinking.

It had happened like this before.

It always happened like this –

It had happened like this in 1914, when the Germans had smashed through Belgium in just the same way. And now, the very speed of their advance in open country – Wimpy's Panzer commander had said he hadn't fought anyone yet – meant that the Allied armies must still be intact and undefeated.

'*Their tanks will be running out of fuel, and their infantry will be dead on its feet now. And that's the moment that the French will counter-attack. It'll be the battle of the Marne all over again!*'

The Prince Regent's Own didn't matter.

The only thing that mattered, so far as he was concerned was that he must get through to someone in authority with his information about the false Brigadier before the false Brigadier could betray any more Allied plans. It was as simple as that.

Wimpy was coming back, at the double.

'It's okay!' he shouted. 'The road's clear at the moment.'

Relief flooded over Bastable, washing away the sludge of defeatism which had settled over his sense of duty while he had been in Colembert. He was not alone, and they were not so many miles from Arras. With the right mixture of caution and luck – if the Germans were still pushing to the west – they might still get past them to the north.

'Jerry's been on the road,' said Wimpy breathlessly. 'He's cleared all the refugee stuff off the road into the ditches, to give him a clear run, I suppose. But there's nothing moving on it at the moment.'

He seemed a bit brighter too, thought Bastable gratefully, watching him reclaim the Norton. And if that was just the fellow's natural ebullience coming to the surface again, for once it could pass as a virtue. A little ebullience was what they both needed now.

'Where's my bloody battledress blouse?' Wimpy looked at him accusingly, pointing to the metal carrier which had served Bastable as a pillion-seat.

'Oh . . .' The carrier was bare. It had been uncomfortable when he had first sat on it, on top of Wimpy's old blouse. It had become more uncomfortable as they had bumped over the scattered debris of Colembert, and the field, and round the obstacles on the road, but he had expected that and had been much too busy holding on for dear life to notice any change in the degree of discomfort.

Wimpy stared back the way they had come. 'I suppose the damn thing's back there somewhere . . . Oh well – I had two hundred francs in my wallet – but I'm damned if I'm going back to look for it . . . and I don't suppose money's much use in France at the moment, anyway, come to that – oh well . . .' He shrugged at Bastable. 'That means you owe me two hundred francs and a pair of field-glasses, old boy.'

Yes – Wimpy was definitely almost back to normal. And so now was the time to transmit his own bad news.

'Audley's dead.' For a fraction of a second he had searched for some way to wrap up the bad news, but instinct told him that it would be a fruitless exercise.

Wimpy looked at him.

'He died . . . in my arms.' That wasn't quite the way it had been, but it was close enough.

The corner of Wimpy's mouth twitched. 'Did he say anything?'

The ruined room filled Bastable's memory: the fallen chandelier and the smashed china, the tattered curtains and the rich brocade of the settee, the litter of plaster everywhere in the half-light.

'He said . . . they drove off the first attack. Then they were dive-bombed . . . Then the tanks attacked.' Bastable moistened his lips. 'I think . . . I think he was buried in the rubble, and this woman found him and dragged him into her house, somehow . . . afterwards.' He still hadn't got round to telling Wimpy what he believed had happened to the battalion, the words kept escaping from him.

'Yes . . .' Wimpy nodded, as though he already knew what that 'afterwards' concealed: that Audley had been left behind by the victors only because they hadn't found him. Though, with those wounds, it wouldn't have made any difference, either way.

'Then he died . . .' That also wasn't quite how it had been. But this wasn't the moment to pass on the dying man's rambling, incoherent message to Wimpy about his son, David.

Wimpy was staring at him with that same look, white under dirt. He had been a friend, possibly even a family friend, of Major Audley's. Only, there was no room for friendship now.

'He's dead, anyway,' said Bastable brutally. 'And the battalion – the battalion – '

'They're dead too,' snapped Wimpy suddenly.

'What d'you mean?'

'What do I mean?' Wimpy's voice rose uncharacteristically, 'What do I mean? I mean what I say – what else should I mean? I mean they're *dead* – the battalion's *dead* – the Prince Regent's Own South Down Fusiliers is *dead* – they're all *dead* . . . All except you and me, Harry – and A Company back in that other Colembert of theirs – and Lance-Corporal Jowett, back there in *our* Colembert . . . and he'll be dead before long, if I'm any judge of wounds – they're all bloody well *dead*, Harry – that's what I mean.'

Bastable opened and shut his mouth without managing to get any words out of it.

'They're dead, Harry,' said Wimpy. 'They're all dead.'

'But – ' the words when they finally came were as shrill as Wimpy's ' – but they can't all be dead. There must have been prisoners – and the wounded?'

'Oh, there were – yes, there were – prisoners *and* wounded.' Wimpy had recovered his voice, or something like it. 'Not a lot of them, Jowett said. The bombing and the machine-gunning had already knocked out a good many – the Aid Post was full before the tanks attacked . . . But they did their best, all the same – they fought the bastards, Harry, they fought them . . . They couldn't stop them, but they fought them – there's even one of their light tanks knocked out on the approaches to your bridge – God only knows how your chaps knocked it out, even though it's only a little one, but they did, somehow . . . But they couldn't stop them.'

Professionals –

A bloody shambles, naturally!

'The ones who were left – the ones who could – fell back into the town, towards battalion headquarters, Jowett said. He was one of them. And Nigel's chaps came from the top of the town to reinforce them. But with the tanks, they didn't stand a chance – they were just too damn good, the Germans, he said – "They went through us like a dose of salts," he said – '

Professionals.

Professionals versus Amateurs.

'So they surrendered. There wasn't anything else they could do, because there was a tank in the street outside, and another at the back . . . There were about fifty of them, plus the walking wounded who hadn't reached the Aid Post. And more of them turned up afterwards – he

reckoned there were about seventy or eighty there in the
end – '

In the end?

'The Germans weren't bad to them – then. There was a
bit of pushing and prodding, but nothing to speak of. One
of them even gave Jowett a cigarette . . . And then they
herded them down to the river, first – Jowett thought that
was while they searched the town, because they brought
in some more prisoners while they were sitting there,
beside the bank.

'And then some more Germans came up, in a car –
different ones from the fellows who had done the fighting
. . . Or different uniforms, anyway. Officers, of some
sort, Jowett thought. And they talked to the officers who
were already there. He couldn't understand what they
were saying, of course, but at first it seemed friendly, and
then suddenly they were arguing – and the new lot,
particularly one of them, started to shout at the ones –
the officers – who had been in the fighting.

'Then some lorries came down the hill, full of more
soldiers – '

THE SURVIVORS' STATEMENTS TO THE JUDGE ADVOCATE
GENERAL'S OFFICE
William Mowbray Willis

*I, William Mowbray Willis, formerly of the Prince Regent's Own
(South Downs) Fusiliers and latterly of the 2nd/8th Royal West
Sussex Regiment (Army Number 1047342) and now discharged
from the Army and resident in South Ampney, Sussex, make
oath and say as follows:*

   . . . the aforementioned Lance-Corporal Jowett then said to
me: 'Shortly after this German soldiers from the lorries took
over from those who had been guarding us. The new guards
wore black uniforms with camouflaged caps, and had "Skull and
Crossbones" on their collars. Their officer had two bands of
silver braid, between the elbow and the wrist, on his tunic, with

167

some lettering between the bands, to the best of my recollection. The new guards treated the prisoners very roughly, driving them into a barn close to the bridge.'

Paragraph 4. Lance-Corporal Jowett then continued: 'After some minutes two of the guards took Major Tetley-Robinson from the barn. Major Tetley-Robinson, who had been wounded in the shoulder, was the senior officer present and had been commanding the battalion since the death of the Commanding Officer. Shortly after this I heard a shot outside the barn. The Adjutant, Captain Harbottle, was then taken from the barn by the same two guards. Then, after a while, there was another shot.'

Paragraph 5. Lance-Corporal Jowett continued: 'The guards came back a third time. This time they took away an NCO, I think it was Sergeant Heppenstall of B Company, but I'm not sure as he had a bandage round his head. Corporal Pollock came to me and told me that there was a hole in the wall of the barn behind some sacks nearby, and that he intended to try to get through it and make a run for it. He said, "I think they're going to do for us one by one, Bill, and I'm not about to wait and find out." I said I would go with him. The hole was not very big and Corporal Pollock couldn't get through it, but when I tried I did get through.'

Paragraph 6. Lance-Corporal Jowett continued: 'There were no Germans directly outside the barn by the hole, but there were some standing around a lorry about fifty yards to my right. There wasn't any cover, so I started running towards the river bank, trying to make for a big clump of reeds to my left. I'd got about half-way when I heard shouts behind me, and looking over my shoulder I saw that two other men had got out, but I don't know who they were. Then there were shots and screams. I went on running, but just as I reached the reeds I was hit in the upper leg and I fell into the river. The water came up to my chest and it was all red, and I couldn't stand properly, but I held on to the reeds growing next to the bank.'

Paragraph 7. Lance-Corporal Jowett continued: 'I don't know how long I stood there, it seemed a long time. I heard the sound of grenades going off, and then a lot of firing, in bursts, like from an LMG. Then a German soldier finally appeared on the bank above me. He was very young and he had a zig-zag badge on his collar, on a green patch. He looked at me like he was sorry for me, and while he was looking at me there were more shots, single ones, which sounded as if it was further away, but I think they were inside the barn. Somebody shouted something at the soldier and he pointed his gun at me. It was a little machine-gun, with the magazine underneath it which he had to hold on to. He said something to me, and then he fired into the water just alongside me. I don't know why he did this, but I'm sure it was deliberate, because he couldn't have missed at that range. So he saved my life – '

'One good German – even in the SS,' said Wimpy. 'But he didn't, I'm afraid.'

Bastable swallowed. 'Didn't what?'

'Didn't save Jowett's life,' said Wimpy. 'He stayed there in the reeds until they cleared out, and then he pulled himself on to the bank – God only knows how, he must have been as weak as a kitten, with all the blood he'd lost, with that smashed leg of his . . .'

Bastable tried to swallow again, but found he had nothing to swallow. 'You found him – but you found him – '

'And he talked, yes.' Wimpy stared at him, almost belligerently. 'Some woman found him, actually. And she did what she could for him . . . I don't know what hit him, but it wasn't just one bullet, poor devil. And it wasn't just in the leg, either.'

Bastable stared back at him, speechlessly.

'But he talked,' said Wimpy. 'He talked – and I shan't forget what he said.'

'You . . . left him?'

'Of course I bloody well left him!' snapped Wimpy. 'What d'you think I am – a bloody surgeon, complete with an operating theatre? Do you think I carry a needle and thread to sew his leg back on – or a hacksaw to cut it

169

off? Or you think I should have given him a fireman's lift and put him on the back of the Norton instead of you? Don't be bloody stupid, Harry – of course I left him. The man was dying – loss of blood, shock, exposure – take your pick, for Christ's sake! He was dying – *and the rest of them are all dead* – can't you get that through your head, man?'

It wasn't possible, was all Harry Bastable could get through his head – *it wasn't possible* –

'The barn's a shambles – a slaughterhouse . . . Grenades – and they must have fired machine-guns into it too . . . And the Aid Post under the Mairie, in the cellar there – '

'The Aid Post?'

Wimpy's expression was frozen. 'I picked up Doc Saunders's battledress blouse off the peg at the top of the stairs . . . It was dark down there, but it smelt – it smelt – Christ! I can still smell it, Harry – they did the same thing there . . .' He trailed off helplessly. 'Let's go – let's get moving. I can't be sick again, I haven't got anything to throw up – *let's go, Harry* – '

They went.

If Wimpy had ridden fast before, now he rode furiously, as though all the devils in hell – or all the ghosts in Colembert – were after him, as well as the whole German Army.

Up, over the brow of the hill, and across the main road.

The crossroads, which they had passed once before . . . and he had passed again the previous evening – where he had found Alice bawling weakly in her pram – the crossroads were gone like a dream before he could recognize them properly.

Never again –

The motor-cycle bucked and jumped and jarred under them, the noise and the wind deafening and blinding him.

But why?

Why?

Dear God – it had been hard to think before, to do anything but hold on, as though the speed and the incessant bumping jumbled all his thoughts into one indistinguishable porridge of thought where nothing made sense. But now there were too many thoughts, and all of them were out of nightmares.

The wind stung tears from his eyes, he closed them tight and smelt that same antiseptic smell on the coarse material of Doc Saunders's battledress blouse.

Doc Saunders, too – Tetley-Robinson and Captain Harbottle and Chris Chichester and Corporal Smithers and CQMS Gammidge and Nigel Audley – and – and – and –

Why?

He had to think however hard it was to think, because there was something in the back of his mind, like a lump in the porridge, and if he could only isolate it he would know what it was. But every time he came close to it some bone-jarring bump and the terrifying wheel-wobble which followed the bump drove coherent thought out of his head, and he could only hear Wimpy cursing and praying as he fought to control the Norton.

But *why* – ?

'Oh, God!' said Wimpy suddenly, in a voice quite different from the one in which he had been cursing and praying.

171

The motor-cycle decelerated sharply, began to wobble again – then accelerated again.

'Oh, God!' repeated Wimpy.

Again he decelerated, and this time the wobble came close to becoming uncontrollable. As Bastable opened his eyes he caught a glimpse of something huge and grey flashing past them – or they were flashing past it – a vehicle – and white faces –

'We've had it,' said Wimpy, almost conversationally.

The wobble was uncontrollable now –

'Let's go!' shouted Wimpy.

There was a grating metallic screech, and then a loud *bang* as they heeled over and the machine seemed to slide out from under them. Bastable bounced on to the road in a great starburst of shock which turned suddenly green.

Then oblivion –

10

There were shapes, moving –

And he looked up, and said, I see men as trees, walking. And after that He put His hands upon his eyes, and made him look up: and he was restored, and saw every man clearly –

But the men he saw clearly were Germans.

Bastable closed his eyes again.

This was the reality. It was what had always been going to happen: what had happened since he had left the battalion had only delayed the inevitable. He had escaped the enemy once by the purest fluke, but his plans – his plans and Wimpy's plans – for escaping them again . . . for crossing the line of march of a whole army as though it didn't exist . . . had been innocent and childish to the point of idiocy. They had had as much real hope of success as two lambs from a scattered flock in the midst of a pack of wolves.

His head ached abominably. And his soul ached abominably too, with the humiliation and helplessness of failure and defeat and captivity. A tide of misery washed over him and pulled him down into darkness.

'Are you all right, Captain?' said Wimpy.

As Bastable opened his eyes again something cold and wet touched his forehead. Wimpy was kneeling beside him, wiping his face with a damp rag.

'Don't move, there's a good chap,' continued Wimpy.

'Just lie still while I check you for broken bones . . . Captain.'

Instinctively, Bastable twitched his arms and legs to find out if they were still under his orders.

'I said . . . don't move.' This time Wimpy's tone had a hint of command in it as he ran his hands over Bastable's legs. 'I'm the doctor, remember – and you're the patient, *Captain*.'

'I'm all right,' said Bastable hoarsely. 'I'm – *ouch!*'

'So you are, so you are,' murmured Wimpy gently, in strange contrast with the fierce ungentle squeeze which he had just applied to Bastable's knee-cap. 'No bones broken . . . but just remember that I'm the doctor, and you're the patient, *Captain* . . . So – lie back again – '

Before Bastable could protest Wimpy pushed him down flat, placed one thumb on his eye, lifted his eyelid, and bent over him at close quarters.

'Look up . . . look down . . .' Wimpy's face was two inches from his own. '*And don't say anything* – up again . . . *not a word more than you have to* – and down again – ' Wimpy's instructions fluctuated between a barely audible whisper and the unnecessarily loud up-and-down command, ' – that's fine! Now . . . just you lie still there for a moment or two, Captain. Doctor's orders – do you understand?'

Bastable didn't understand at all, but he nodded weakly. With German soldiers all around him it hardly mattered what he did, in any case.

'Good!' Wimpy nodded back at him and straightened up, wiping his hands on the damp rag.

Bastable rolled his eyes to the left and right of him. He seemed to be lying on the grass verge in a gap between two lorries. There were German soldiers sitting in the lorries, and others standing beside the tailboard and

174

around the cabs of the vehicles, but they didn't seem to be taking a lot of notice of their prisoners. As he watched one group they burst out laughing, as though one of them had cracked a joke. Then, just as suddenly, they stiffened into attention – he could even see, from his worm's-eye-view, how one of them, who had been smoking, palmed his dog-end between thumb and forefinger into his hand.

Wimpy cast one quick glance down at him. 'Steady the PROs,' he hissed out of the corner of his mouth. 'Top brass in sight.'

The blood rose to Bastable's cheeks as he glimpsed the newcomers in the gaps between the rigid soldiers. As they reached the open space in front of him one of them spoke conversationally, and Bastable knew what he had said even before the casual words had been translated into a command by an NCO –

'*Stand the men easy, Sar-Major!*'

'*Sir!*' Pause. '*STAND – EASY!*'

The German soldiers relaxed. The speaker addressed them again, in the same easy voice. For a moment there was silence, then there was a burst of laughter as the soldier with the dog-end realized he was the centre of attention and sheepishly produced what he had hidden.

So that must have been . . . 'And Fusilier Arkwright may smoke,' or something very like . . . which wouldn't have happened in Captain Bastable's company, because he had never been able to make such a joke of Fusilier Arkwright's weakness; but which just might have happened in Wimpy's company, or Nigel Audley's, because they had the gift which he lacked – which, when he had tried to exercise it, had always fallen flat on an unappreciative audience.

The soldiers laughed again, and Bastable thought: *So*

they're no different from British soldiers, to be led or driven – no different.

Then he remembered Colembert-les-Deux-Ponts.

Misery and despair weren't the worst things any more: now it was *I picked Doc Saunders's blouse off the peg at the top of the stairs, but it smelt down there – Christ!*

Fear choked Harry Bastable's throat. He was going to die now – this man with the nice casual voice was about to kill him, as they had killed Major Tetley-Robinson and Captain Harbottle and Sergeant Heppenstall and Corporal Pollock, and all the rest of them – Dear God! Dear God! – *God – Mother! everything that was Harry Bastable was about to be wiped out and extinguished as it lay there in the gutter now, like a dog in the street –*

The fear was paralysing. He felt his muscles relaxing, and knew that if there was anything in his bowels he would be shitting himself now – but instead there was only choking fear.

'Well, Doctor?'

'Sir . . .'Wimpy drew a deep breath. 'This officer is in shock. And he is also mildly concussed – perhaps more seriously in shock as the result of a blow on the head . . . And under the Geneva Convention he cannot be subjected to interrogation, sir.'

'Cannot, Doctor?'

'Under the Geneva Convention, sir . . . All that is required of him is his name, his rank and his number. And as a wounded combatant, not even that is required of him, I believe . . . sir.'

The German officer looked down at Bastable, and Bastable blinked back up at him in fear and confusion.

'He looks . . . un-wounded to me, Doctor – if I may say so.' The German officer paused. 'Captain – ?'

'Bass-tabell,' said someone else, out of the group.

'Bass-tabell?'

The someone – from his peaked cap, another officer – offered the German officer some evidence to support this contention.

Bastable was aware that he had lost his equipment. His webbing belt and his pouches, and of course his revolver, had all been removed, and his battledress blouse gaped open on the chest.

The German officer studied the documents –

My dear Henry,

I hope you are well. Your Father and I are in the best of health and although business is slow we are in good spirits. Since the 'Barnhill' was bombed off Beachy Head (it finally drifted ashore at Langney Point) we have had the cellar strengthened with timbers very kindly supplied by Mr Stone, and when the practice warnings sound Mrs Stone comes to keep me company while your Father does his duty as an ARP Warden, so that I have someone to talk to now that Yvonne has joined the WRNS. Your Father said that Mr Smith, who is the ARP Controller, and Brigadier-General Costello, who is the Chief Warden, think that Eastbourne will not be bombed, because we do not have any War Industries, so you must not worry about us. That is exactly what Mr Taylor said at the Junior Imperial League meeting in the Hartington Hall before the war, and as a Member of Parliament, he should know! But if it happens we are ready!

Please let me know if you have received the string vests I sent to you, but you must not put them on until the Autumn –

'Captain . . . Bast-abell?'

Bass-tabel or *Bast-abell*, there wasn't any denying that – not with Mother's letter, and with what they had taken out of his pockets, in their hands.

He nodded. The war had ended here for Captain Bastable.

'Of . . . the Prinz Regent's Own Fuziliers?'

That wasn't in the book of words. Name, rank and number was all he had to give – Wimpy had said as much.

Bastable held his head steady on *name* and *rank*.

The German pointed to his shoulder. 'Die Abuzsleine – die . . . Abuzsleine . . . the string, Hauptmann – Captain!'

Bastable glanced sideways. His shoulder strap was undone, where his equipment had been stripped off him, and his lanyard was half-way down his arm. The disarray of his appearance added to his humiliation, contrasting as it did with the smartness of the German officer's uniform under its coating of dust. With clumsy fingers he buttoned the blouse together, as well as he could – half the buttons had gone – and pulled up the lanyard on to his shoulder again.

'That is right – die Abuzsleine, Captain,' said the German.

Bastable looked down at the lanyard in his hand, the proud primrose-yellow and dove-grey which had once taken the Prince Regent's fancy all those years ago.

Which every man wears as of right, as a South Downs Fusilier – the symbol of pride in his regiment and in himself for being privileged to wear it – Major Tetley-Robinson's words echoed out of the grave.

The lanyard marked him for what he was: he could no more deny being an officer of the PROs than he could fly to heaven with RAF roundels on his wings and claim they were swastikas.

He frowned up at his captor. So the enemy had identified his unit; but since his unit no longer existed that was hardly of any consequence to the German Army now.

'I must protest, sir!' said Wimpy. 'This officer is injured!'

'Your protest is noted, Doctor,' the German cut him off.

Doctor? Bastable looked at Wimpy in baffled surprise.

'Under the Geneva Convention, sir – ' Wimpy refused to be overawed ' – under the Geneva Convention this officer cannot be interrogated.'

The German officer continued to look at Bastable. 'Under the Geneva Convention, Doctor, atrocities are punishable by death . . . Captain Bast-abell – you are an officer of the Prinz Regent's Fuziliers?'

Bastable blinked at the German. The pain in his head hammered on his brain.

'You are an officer of the Prinz Regent's Fuziliers,' said the German, dropping the question mark.

'Sir – !' exclaimed Wimpy.

'Be silent, Doctor. Do you know an officer named Willis, Captain Bast-abell? Captain W. M. Willis?'

Bastable rolled his eyes helplessly from the German to Wimpy, and then back again to the German.

'Captain-W. M.-Willis?' The German officer repeated the name carefully.

'I told you – Captain Willis is dead,' said Wimpy quickly. 'Captain Bastable and I were trapped in this cellar during the bombing and the attack on Colembert – we went to treat a wounded fusilier – it took us half the night to dig our way out – Captain Willis was killed in the bombing – '

'*Doctor!*' The German officer's voice cracked with exasperation. 'One more word from you and I shall have you placed under arrest in spite of your status, Captain Saunders!'

God! *The battledress blouse* – Captain Saunders's

blouse – *Wimpy had been wearing it!* thought Bastable feverishly.

Atrocities?

What had Wimpy done?

Captain W. M. Willis?

But –

Wimpy had told him, in that breathless pack of lies a moment ago, what he must say. But he could never stand up to any prolonged interrogation in support of it – what cellar, where? What fusilier?

What had Wimpy done?

But –

'Captain Bast-abell – do you hear me?' The German officer leaned over him. 'Do-you-hear-me?'

Bastable groaned realistically, and heard himself groan, and reflected that the sound was convincing because most of it was made up of genuine pain and fear and bewilderment.

'Bastable . . . Captain . . . 210498,' he whispered feebly. 'Bastable . . . Captain . . . 210498 . . .' and closed his eyes.

One of the other Germans spoke, snapping out harsh words which sounded uncomfortably like disbelief in his performance.

'He can't tell you anything about atrocities,' said Wimpy sharply. '*But I can.*'

For a moment no one spoke. Bastable didn't dare open his eyes, but he could feel the pressure on him lifting.

'What?'

'I can tell you about the atrocities,' said Wimpy. 'But you won't like what I have to tell.'

'What do you mean, Doctor?' The German officer seemed to have forgotten his earlier threat. But then Wimpy had side-stepped that neatly, and not only with

180

that promise to tell all, thought Bastable admiringly. For by also telling the blighter that what he had to say contained an unpleasant surprise he had challenged him to listen to it.

'I thought you would already know – when you asked me about Captain Willis I thought you knew,' said Wimpy. 'But when you mentioned . . . atrocities . . . I realized at once that you didn't know.'

There was a pause. Bastable wondered fearfully whether Wimpy wasn't overdoing the mystery.

'Know what, Doctor?' The suggestion of irritation was there, but the German had it well under control.

'Who is it that wants to interview the late Captain Willis so badly . . . sir?' Wimpy remembered his military manners belatedly. Bastable opened one eye wide enough to examine the German officer more carefully. The man looked hard as nails, no longer young but still in the prime of life, and carried an air of authority which established his seniority as surely as the badges on his collar. There was also something else about him which eluded Bastable for a moment – it was almost a touch of Nigel Audley . . . an indefinable touch of *class*, if the Germans had such a thing.

Or perhaps it was simply that his present silence was reminiscent of Audley's self-control when he was beginning to get angry. With Audley it was often the quieter, the angrier.

'Not the fellows with the skull-and-crossbones and the zig-zag lightning flashes, by any chance . . . sir?' enquired Wimpy almost casually.

'Doctor . . .' now the self-control was like a danger-signal.

'They would.' Suddenly Wimpy was grim. 'And I can guess why they want to lay their murdering hands on

181

every man who wears that lanyard – ' he pointed at Bastable's shoulder, ' – every man who wears that lanyard and who's still in the land of the living – because they don't want one of them to live to tell the tale, that's why!'

One of the other German officers, a fresh-faced young man, said something then, and there was a brief instant of silence. But when the young man opened his mouth again the senior German officer cut him off with a raised, leather-gloved hand.

'You want to know about an atrocity, sir – ' Wimpy plunged straight into the gap. ' – well, I can show you one! It's just down the road, in Colembert-les-Deux-Ponts – by God! if you want to know about an atrocity, I can show you one! My battalion – the battalion in which I was medical officer . . .' he stumbled over his mistake, suddenly incoherent, lifting a hand which Bastable saw was skinned and bloody from contact with the road '. . . *my* battalion – *my* battalion, sir – ' his voice lifted ' – we are the battalion now. There's no need to send us back to the skull-and-crossbones brigade. You can shoot us both here, by the roadside, and have done with it. At least we'll have been shot by soldiers, not bloody butchers!'

Bastable sensed that everyone was listening to Wimpy, the soldiers beside the lorries as well as the knot of officers in front of them. And that, he supposed, was what Wimpy intended, if Wimpy was still play-acting: to make what he was saying as public as possible, for all to hear and remember.

If Wimpy was still play-acting –

'Control yourself, Captain Saunders!' said the German officer sharply. 'There is no question of your being shot. You are a prisoner-of-war – and a medical officer – '

Wimpy gestured eloquently, almost insultingly, with his bloody hand. 'So were my orderlies in Colembert –

182

medical orderlies in the Battalion Aid Post. And they're dead. And there's a barn full of prisoners-of-war in Colembert – and they're dead too. They're *all* dead – shot down in cold blood!'

He wasn't play-acting, Bastable decided. He might have been to begin with, but he wasn't now. He was mixing lies with truth, but he wasn't play-acting any more: he was speaking for the real Captain Saunders, RAMC, as Captain Saunders might have spoken, to the life – to the death. The clever lies were blotted out by the fouler truth. Wimpy was Doc Saunders now.

The German officer stared at him, stone-faced. 'You . . . you saw this, Doctor?' He paused. 'You saw it happen?'

Wimpy stared back at him uncompromisingly. 'If I had seen it happen I wouldn't be here to tell you about it. But it's there for you to see . . . sir. In Colembert-les-Deux-Ponts. Just down the road from here.'

The challenge hung between them, unarguable.

'We were in the cellar,' said Wimpy, recalling himself to his original story. 'We had to dig ourselves out.'

The young German officer stirred uneasily. 'Prisoners . . . haf . . . haf been known to . . . to try to escape, Hauptmann Saunders,' he said with slow concentration on his English.

'Prisoners?' Wimpy echoed the word contemptuously. 'And my wounded in the Battalion Aid Post? Most of them couldn't walk a yard.' He let the words sink in. 'They threw grenades into the Aid Post – it was in a cellar . . . They threw grenades down the stairs.'

Silence.

'It's there for you to see,' Wimpy spoke only to the young officer, as though they were alone together. 'The cellar is there – and my wounded are there. They are not going to escape, I assure you.'

My wounded was a brilliant touch, thought Bastable. It was so brilliant that, if it hadn't been true for Doc Saunders, it would have been an obscene lie for Captain Willis –

Captain W. M. Willis?

The senior German officer drew himself up, taking back the control of the situation which he had momentarily lost. The other Germans stiffened instinctively.

The senior German officer addressed the young officer. The young officer clicked his heels.

'Captain Saunders . . . you have made a very serious allegation. There will be an immediate investigation of that allegation. A report will be made.'

Wimpy drew a deep breath. 'Thank you, sir.'

The German nodded. 'Also . . . you are a prisoner of the Wehrmacht – the German Army. If you have nothing to hide, then you have nothing to fear. You have my word on that. And that applies also to this officer.' He pointed at Bastable.

'Th-thank you, sir.' Wimpy swallowed almost audibly.

In the circumstances, Wimpy took that well, thought Bastable. But they were both still in the deepest trouble, that word-of-a-German-officer meant.

'You will remain here, for the time being, while we remain here.' The German nodded, saluted, and turned away.

Bastable closed his eyes and relaxed himself on to the grass verge. There was nothing he could do any more to shape his destiny, he was as helpless and as useless as little Alice in her pram, a prisoner not only of the Wehrmacht, but also of circumstances and events he could no longer control. Truthful lies and lying truth held him like a web in the midst of his enemies.

* * *

The cold touch of the damp rag on his forehead aroused him again.

'That's the ticket,' murmured Wimpy. 'Look as though you're dying, old boy!'

If you could have died according to orders, and mingled with the roadside dirt, that at least would have solved all his dilemmas and swallowed up all his fears, thought Bastable miserably.

'You're not really crocked, are you, old boy?' murmured Wimpy gently in his ear. 'No broken bones, or anything?'

Bastable opened his eyes to gaze at his tormentor. 'You're the bloody doctor – you tell me,' he hissed.

Wimpy was sitting down beside him. 'Can you feel your toes and your fingers? No pain anywhere?'

'Only in the neck,' said Bastable.

'In the neck?' For a second Wimpy sounded solicitous, then he got the point. 'Jolly good . . . because . . . I thought I did that rather well, actually.'

There was no denying that, temporary though their survival might be: the ex-schoolmaster had run away just as quickly as the ex-businessman, but he had talked them both out of a very tight corner brilliantly for the time being.

He nodded, and Wimpy nodded back.

'Yes . . . the trick is to twitch the rear wheel to the left and put the front wheel over – and send the bike on ahead of you, instead of getting hit by it from behind . . . that's how most silly blighters get themselves crocked, you know,' confided Wimpy in a self-satisfied whisper. 'It's quite violent, but it doesn't really require a lot of skill. You just skate off on your own, with abrasions – and I've certainly got them, on my hand and my arse . . . but my elbows are okay, and I haven't quite dislocated my thumbs, though damn nearly . . . though it does feel as though I've sprained my ankle, which is a bit of a bind . . . But I've never done it with a pillion passenger . . . Are you sure you're okay, Harry?'

Bastable could only stare at him. In the midst of their troubles . . . in the midst of everything, here was Wimpy congratulating himself on his skill in surviving motor-cycle accidents, for God's sake!

'You probably have got a touch of shock,' said Wimpy. 'You came off harder than I did.'

'I'm all right,' said Bastable. 'I've just got a headache, that's all . . .'

Wimpy looked at him apologetically. 'I couldn't do anything else. They had this staff car alongside a lorry, right in the middle of the road – I couldn't get between them.'

Bastable's head throbbed. He wasn't at all interested in the circumstances of their crash; but what he needed most desperately was some explanation of the incomprehensible events which had followed it, yet somehow he couldn't find the right question to start with.

Wimpy flexed his thumbs for a moment or two, and then set about massaging his right ankle. 'My thumbs are just about workable – last time I came off I dislocated both of them . . . but I think this ankle is going to be a problem,' he murmured to himself.

Bastable gave up trying to find the right question. 'What did you . . . why did you say . . . what you said?' he whispered inadequately.

Wimpy stared at him. 'Well . . . it seemed the right thing – for him, I mean, don't you know . . .'

'Who?'

'The German officer, old boy – the Colonel chappie

186

. . . he's one of your old-fashioned regular-soldier types –
an officer and a gentleman, you might say.'

'What?'

Wimpy stopped massaging his ankle. 'A regular, Harry
– a regular. And they're all the same, aren't they!'

'What d'you mean?'

'A regular – a professional . . .' Wimpy looked round
furtively to make sure no one was listening. 'Don't you
remember that time we did that exercise with that battalion of the Rifles – they were regulars . . . And I was with
their CO – a real fire-eater, absolutely covered with
medals and that sort of thing. But when he heard the
Divisional Commander was in the next field he went quite
white with terror – it was pathetic really, because I wasn't
at all scared, but he was *white* with fear, in case he'd
blotted his copybook – I didn't know any better, so I
didn't care. But he did.'

He continued massaging his ankle. And, very strangely,
his hands were shaking.

'I mean . . . if I complained to you about the Geneva
Convention, Harry, you wouldn't know what I was talking
about – I might just as well quote the Thirty-nine Articles
of the Church of England at you. But *he* knew about it –
it's his business to know about it.'

'You know about the Geneva Convention?'

'Good God, no! But I assume it draws the line at
shooting prisoners, and bombing hospitals and killing
doctors, and all that . . . And the point is, proper soldiers
have to follow the rules, it's a matter of professional ethics
for them when they're winning, and pure self-preservation
when they're losing, don't you see?'

'But – ' It seemed to Bastable that Wimpy was forgetting their own hideous experience. 'But – '

'Colembert?' Wimpy nodded. 'But the swine who murdered our chaps there weren't the ones who captured them, Harry. Those murdering bastards weren't real soldiers, they were SS thugs in uniform. Like . . . suppose we had a unit made up of the worst of the Reds or Mosley's Blackshirts . . . But these fellows here, they're *soldiers* – and the Oberst is a soldier too – if you put him into khaki battledress he'd pass for one of ours any day, old boy. He knows the rules, and he has to obey them – *that* was what I was betting on. What would his Divisional Commander say if he caught him shooting prisoners? And, what's more, I've read somewhere that the proper German Army doesn't much like the Nazis and the SS – did you see the way the Oberst went rigid when I mentioned them? And how he went out of his way to tell us that we're the prisoners of the German Army – the Wehrmacht?'

That hadn't been quite how Bastable had interpreted the German Colonel's reaction at the time. But the anger he had sensed in the German could – just *could*, by an additional stretch of the imagination – have been directed at someone other than Wimpy himself.

Except that if the German Colonel discovered that Wimpy was no more a medical officer than Harry Bastable was a Chaplain to the Forces, then that anger would be very quickly re-directed in their direction.

'Why are you trying to pass yourself off as Doc Saunders?'

Wimpy grimaced at him. 'I didn't start it, old boy: when they picked me up and dusted me down – while you were out cold – I didn't know whether it was Christmas or Hogmanay . . . But they had poor old Doc's book of words off me before I knew what was happening. It didn't occur to me that they'd add two and two together and

188

make five, I assure you. But it was bloody lucky for both of us that they did. Because . . .' He paused, and for a moment his eyes left Bastable's, to stare at something else.

'Because what?'

'Because it was you they were interested in, Harry.' Again Wimpy paused, and his eyes came back to Bastable's. 'Or rather, it was your lanyard that excited them – the good old PRO yellow-and-grey badge of distinction, that's what!'

Die Abuzsleine.

'When they came back to me, they called me "Doctor", and they asked me about Captain Willis straight off. And as they seemed rather disappointed that you weren't Captain Willis, old boy, I decided that I wouldn't volunteer for the job. Because if they want Captain Willis so badly I reckoned it'd be safer to find out why before owning up.'

At last they had come round to the question which Bastable had wanted to ask all the time, but which had eluded him.

'I know it's a hell of a risk, claiming to be poor old Doc,' admitted Wimpy. 'And it's an even bigger risk to throw Colembert at them – if they're wrong 'uns, then we've had it – they'll shut us up, and that'll be that . . . And if they duck the job themselves, and hand us over to those bastards who did for our chaps, we've had it too . . . But if I'm any judge of character, *he* won't, not after saying we're prisoners of the German Army – and in front of his officers, that's a good sign, I think . . . Besides all of which, once I'd answered to being Doc, I couldn't let you talk too much. I had to say something, just to take the heat off you, old boy!'

'But if they find out you're not Doc . . .' Bastable

trailed off as he remembered that wasn't what he had intended to say a moment before. But everything was so confusing that he was unable to hold anything in his mind, it seemed.

'No reason why they should.' Wimpy shrugged. 'And what we've got to concentrate on is giving them the slip before that can happen, anyway.'

Bastable's wits returned to him with a jolt. To his shame, he realized that the idea of escaping hadn't even occurred to him. But Wimpy was right, and doubly right too: it was not only their duty to try to escape at the first opportunity, as British soldiers – it was also an absolute necessity that they did so in order to stop the false Brigadier in his tracks before he could do irreparable damage.

'And . . . the sooner we do that, the better.' Wimpy took a surreptitious glance around him. 'No chance at the moment, I'm afraid. But we can't afford to wait too long . . .' His eyes came back to Bastable. 'Old chap I knew at school – taught physics and chemistry badly – he was taken prisoner twice in the last war, once near Ypres in 'fifteen and again near Bapaume during the retreat in 'eighteen. Got away both times . . . and he said the longer you put it off, the harder it is. His formula was to make 'em think he was glad to be out of it, that put them off their guard . . . We can't very well do that . . . but so long as they think you're injured and I'm in the RAMC they may not watch us too closely. That'll be our best chance, so don't recover for the time being, Harry, old boy, while I mop your fevered brow.'

He leaned over Bastable and applied the damp rag again, and winked encouragingly as he did so. Bastable felt hope rekindle inside him like a tiny candle flame which had almost been extinguished by a fierce draught, but which was now burning more steadily behind the shield of Wimpy's irrepressible confidence. He recognized, with a twinge of guilt, that his dislike of the fellow in the past had been grounded on pure envy – impure envy: Wimpy was cleverer than he was, but he had always half-suspected that and had even tried to devalue it into mere schoolmasterish general knowledge which he could dismiss as being inferior to the practical commonsense of businessmen like himself. Now he could acknowledge that cleverness for the resourceful intelligence it really was, and the natural leadership that went with it.

'And when we do start running, remember that it's every man for himself,' murmured Wimpy casually. 'I shan't worry about you, and you mustn't look for me – that'll double our chances of getting away. Agreed?'

Bastable frowned up at him.

'Agreed, old man?' Wimpy pressed him, massaging his thumbs again one after another. Once more Bastable observed that his hands were trembling.

Suddenly, with unbearable clarity, he remembered that Wimpy had complained of a sprained ankle, and he knew exactly what lay behind that casual, selfish-sounding insistence. When it came to running, Wimpy didn't think that he could make it. But he was doing his utmost to see that his sprained ankle didn't ruin Harry Bastable's chances, even though he was scared half out of his wits. The casual voice and the endless chatter concealed the reality and the desperation which the hands betrayed.

An emotion which was more than mere admiration flooded over Bastable. He himself was too stupid and too unimaginative to know what real fear was like – his pale version of fear was simple self-regarding cowardice. But Wimpy was too intelligent not to recognize his own fear for what it was, and to fight against it for all his worth.

191

Up until yesterday, Bastable realized, he had never had any doubts about his own courage – he had taken it for granted, because there wasn't any choice in the matter. In the battalion, courage was a group activity; the only thing that had frightened any officer was that he might not do his job properly in full view of the CO, or Major Tetley-Robinson, or his own company sergeant-major.

But courage wasn't like that at all, and now he knew that he was a coward, and that Wimpy was a brave man.

'Agreed, Harry?' said Wimpy for the third time.

Bastable knew that he couldn't agree, but that he couldn't not agree – and that he couldn't let Wimpy know that he *knew* –

But he had to say something.

'Why does everyone call you "Wimpy"?' He plucked the question out of his subconscious in desperation. It still wasn't the question he wanted answered, but it was the first one to answer his call for volunteers.

'What?' Wimpy was clearly taken by surprise. 'Oh . . . That . . . that was that old b – . . .' he caught the *bastard* before it could escape his lips '. . . no! *De mortuis nil nisi bonum* applies to the late Major Tetley-Robinson, I suppose . . . I never thought it would, but it does . . .' He cocked his head on one side and gazed thoughtfully at nothing. 'They must have asked him the ultimate *viva voce* question!'

'What?'

Wimpy looked at him. 'They pulled him out of the barn, Harry. And then I think they asked him where Captain W. M. Willis might be found – at least, that's what I suspect they asked him, just as they asked you about Captain W. M. Willis, Harry – don't you remember?'

'W – ?' This time the idiotic *what?* stifled itself.

'Poor old bastard!' Wimpy shook his head sadly. '*De mortuis* and all that, but he was an old bastard . . . And it must have been the last straw if they did – with the battalion in ruins around him . . . to be reminded of Captain Willis, of all people! The ultimate *viva voce* question: even if he'd answered it, they'd probably have shot him. But I'll bet he didn't answer it – not him!'

Wimpy continued to stare at him, and through him into the past of yesterday evening, outside the barn beside the stream, beside the bridge, on the edge of Colembert-les-Deux-Ponts, in the middle of nowhere that mattered in the whole of France –

'I'll bet he told them to get stuffed. So they shot him *pour encourager les autres*,' said Wimpy. 'And of course that's exactly what it did, by God! But not in the way they expected. Because once they'd shot Tetley-Robinson, they got the same answer from the next man – *get stuffed* – and the next man –'

Abruptly he was no longer looking through Harry Bastable, but at him. 'He coined "Wimpy", old boy, did Major Tetley-Robinson, because he was a man of limited reading. *The Times* was much too difficult for him – too many words, and not enough pictures, don't you know. He pretended to read it but he always preferred the popular papers – the yellow press. Don't you remember how he used to grab the *News of the World* in the Mess at breakfast on Sunday, Harry? "Vicar's daughter tells of Night of Terror" and "Scoutmaster jailed after campfire Orgies", that was his favourite reading. And first look at *Lilliput* and *London Opinion* for the girl with the bare tits? Don't you remember?'

Bastable remembered. Everybody in the Mess knew which papers and magazines not to touch until the Second-in-Command of the Prince Regent's Own South

Downs Fusiliers had abstracted them from the array on the huge mahogany table and tossed them down, crumpled and dog-eared on the floor beside his chair. Green subalterns had been mercilessly savaged (since, by custom, nobody warned them) for contravening that unwritten law.

But what did that have to do with 'Wimpy'? And 'that ultimate *viva voce* question', whatever that meant? And outside the barn at Colembert-les-Deux-Ponts, where it had all ended in senseless bloody murder?

'My dear chap – "Wimpy" is a character in a comic strip in one of those awful rags,' said Wimpy simply. '"J. Wellington Wimpy" is one of Popeye's friends – he has a weakness for eating some sort of American toasted meat bun – a sort of hot sandwich, I suppose . . . *And* for speaking in complete sentences – that was what Tetley-Robinson found so absolutely outrageous in me . . . Let's say . . . let's just say he thought that I talked too much, old boy, eh?'

He regarded Bastable with the merest twitch of a smile. 'Which I do, of course. But then, it comes from being exposed to whole generations of small sullen boys – and larger boys too, I'm sorry to say – who don't know the subjunctive of *amo* and haven't mastered their reflexive pronouns in any recognizable form of the Latin language . . . I'm afraid that a captive audience of recalcitrant middle-class boys is bound to bring out the worst in a man, he has to fill the silence with his own voice . . . It isn't often that one encounters a really clever boy like Nigel Audley's young David – Latin irregular verbs were a Goliath well within reach of that young David's slingshot. He had no trouble with them, but then he was an exception – ' he caught the expression on Bastable's face ' – but have I said something wrong now, old boy?'

'No . . . no . . .' Bastable tried not to look at him. That mention of 'young David', 'Nigel Audley's young David' – *my boy, David – not my son, not my son – but my boy –* took him back hideously to the room in the French lady's house, and that final bubbling death rattle which had cut off Audley's last message to Wimpy. But he couldn't pass that on now, this was not the time and the place for it, if there was ever a time and place.

Yet now he was in another situation where he had to say something to head Wimpy off from any further question about Nigel Audley, or Nigel Audley's young David, who had known all the answers to Wimpy's questions, and was therefore exceptional among his fellow schoolboys – like father, like son, for God's sake: Nigel Audley had never been at a loss to know what to say – unlike Herbert Bastable's young Henry, who could never make head nor tail of *hic, haec, hoc* and Caesar's Gallic Wars, any more than he could conjugate *être* and *avoir* in all their variation, or handle the Boys anti-tank rifle properly –

'What did you do?'

It was exactly like *Why are you called 'Wimpy'?* except that it was the real question at last, inadequately phrased but still the one he had been searching for all along in the midst of the other questions.

'What d'you mean – what did I do?' Wimpy frowned.

Bastable seized the chance of elaborating what he had said, necessity cancelling out the delicacy of the enquiry. 'Why do they want . . . Captain Willis? What have you done?'

'Oh – I see!' Wimpy's face cleared. 'You haven't got the point, old boy – I thought you had! I haven't done anything – '

'What?'

'Not a damn thing! Except run away, that is – and hide in a drain, and a lot of other uncomfortable places, like in hedges and behind dungheaps, don't you know.'

'But – but . . .?'

'You haven't got the point at all. But then neither did I at first . . . But . . . it's *you* they want, Harry – don't you see? It isn't me at all – ' Wimpy cut off the explanation quickly ' – now, just lie back and take it easy, Captain – and that's an order . . . doctor's orders, in fact. Right?'

Bastable was aware that there were Germans in his immediate vision, to Wimpy's left. He rolled his eyes uneasily to take them in more accurately as Wimpy rose to his feet to face them.

They were new Germans – or at least not the senior officer and the young fresh-faced one, certainly. With a sudden spasm of fear he searched their collars for the deadly lightning zig-zag which he had first seen on the tunic Wimpy had exhibited as a trophy on the edge of the wood outside Colembert. But these soldiers, he saw with relief, had no such distinguishing marks of death: they were heavily armed, and dusty and dirty like the men lounging among the vehicles a few yards away, but they appeared to be ordinary, run-of-the-mill soldiers.

Also, they bore themselves deferentially, almost apologetically, not like captors with prisoners but more as other ranks in the presence of officers.

The foremost one, who was built like a tank and had badges of rank on his arm, came to attention in front of Wimpy, clicking his heels and raising his arm in a military salute.

'Yes?' said Wimpy sharply, half-lifting his arm to return the salute, and then remembering at the last moment that he was wearing nothing on his head. 'But nicht . . . nicht speaken . . . Deutsch, old boy. Understand – comprenez?'

Evidently Wimpy was not going to reveal that he had a good working knowledge of German, as well as French and Latin and Greek, so long as that secret might be of service to them.

The German started to say something, the tone of his voice matching his bearing, but then thought better of it and stood to one side, gesturing to the men behind him. The ranks parted to reveal two men carrying a stretcher.

'Oh, Christ!' murmured Wimpy.

The stretcher-bearers advanced towards the ex-schoolmaster and deposited the stretcher at his feet. Bastable lifted himself on to his elbows to get a better view of its occupant.

The wounded man was a German soldier.

Bastable craned his neck. The German was dark-haired and white-faced, and very young, and his tunic and trousers were undone, but there was no sign of any wound on him. As Bastable stared at him the boy moved his head and for an instant their eyes met. Then he twisted his head away, as though embarrassed, and at the same time arched his body and gripped the side of the stretcher as if the sudden movement had hurt him.

'Oh, Christ!' murmured Wimpy again, even more under his breath.

The German who had saluted and spoken to him launched himself into a pantomime of slowly-pronounced words and exaggerated gestures, such as a white explorer might have used to communicate with an African tribesman, the burden of which seemed to be that his comrade had eaten something that didn't agree with him and had a bad stomach-ache as a result.

Wimpy listened and nodded gravely at intervals until the German had completed his description of events.

'Has he been sick?' He pointed to his mouth. 'Sick?'

The German frowned at him. 'Bitte?'

'Sick – ' Wimpy pantomimed the act of vomiting.

'Ja, ja!' said one of the other Germans, nodding vigorously.

'Uh-huh . . .' Wimpy nodded again. A curious change had come over him: where the usual Wimpy expression was one of casual, almost cynical detachment from the world, as though he found its events somewhat ridiculous and was taking part in them against his better judgement, now he displayed an almost magisterial gravity, with his chin tucked down and his lower lip thrust out.

'Uh-*huh* . . .' He nodded to himself again. 'Uh-*huh*!'

This, decided Bastable, was how Wimpy imagined doctors ought to act, even if it was nothing like how Doc Saunders had ever behaved. And, in spite of the awfulness of their situation, it would have been laughable if the hands clenched behind Wimpy's back hadn't been trembling as uncontrollably as ever.

But the effect on the Germans did seem satisfactory: they waited respectfully for Wimpy to pronounce on their comrade.

Suddenly Wimpy straightened up. He brought his hands out from behind him, held them up in front of him for an instant – one was blood-stained and both were filthy – and then went through the motions of washing them.

The German sergeant-major – by his stripes that was what he must be – barked out an order to one of his men.

A tin basin was produced, and a lump of greyish-looking soap. The German NCO uncorked his water-bottle and offered it to Wimpy.

Wimpy drank from the bottle greedily, and Bastable was aware that he too was horribly thirsty.

'Can I have a drink?' he said. 'Can I have some water?'

Before Wimpy could offer him the bottle, one of the German soldiers came over to him and squatted beside him, uncorking his own water-bottle.

'Wasser, Hauptmann?' The German soldier held the bottle to Bastable's lips. The water had a strange chemical taste, but it was marvellous, nevertheless.

Wimpy had finished washing his hands and was drying them on what looked like a strip of grey blanket.

He knelt down beside the stretcher. 'Now, young fella, let's have a look at you,' he said confidently, parting the patient's clothing.

Bastable watched, fascinated, as Wimpy probed the fishy-white stomach, pressing and tapping as though he knew exactly what he was doing. Several times he saw, by the expansion of the boy's chest and the in-drawing of his breath, that a tender spot had been touched; and when Wimpy pushed down the boy's knee, which had been raised, he was rewarded with a grunt of agony.

'Uh-*huh*!' Wimpy welcomed the grunt as though he had been expecting it. Then he leaned forward over the boy's face. Without speaking he stuck out his tongue to indicate what he wanted.

'Nasty . . .' murmured Wimpy, sniffing at the boy's mouth. 'Pooh! Very nasty!' he sat back on his heels, wrinkling his nose.

Bastable was aware of a sudden stir in the audience, who had been similarly engrossed in Wimpy's performance. The ranks stiffened and parted as they had done once before.

'Was ist denn hier los?' The German Colonel appeared in the gap. 'What is this?'

Wimpy looked over his shoulder. 'Ah, Colonel! Just the very man I wanted! Would you be so good as to ask this young chap when the pain started? And you might also ask him when he last went to the lavatory, too.'

The Colonel took in the scene, and his eye settled on the NCO, who managed to stiffen himself even more rigidly.

'And there's one more test I'd like to make,' continued Wimpy. 'Only it does need some explaining –'

The Colonel addressed a sentence to the NCO, who replied at some length while staring at a fixed point slightly above his commanding officer's head.

The Colonel nodded finally, and looked down at Wimpy. 'What is it that you wish, Doctor?'

'When the pain started – how long ago? And when . . . is he constipated?'

'Constipated?'

'Has he been to the lavatory at all recently?'

'Ach – so!' The Colonel addressed the NCO, who evidently found the question extremely embarrassing.

'So . . . He was in pain last evening, but only now and then . . . I suspect that he did not report it because he did not desire to be left behind, Doctor. But now the pain is bad . . . And he has been – how do you say? – constipated . . . constipated for several days.'

'Good.' Wimpy nodded. 'Now . . . I want to turn him over on his face, Colonel, if you please.'

The Colonel translated the order, and the sick man's comrades accomplished the task, though not without pain to the patient as they straightened his right leg again in the process.

Wimpy moistened his right index finger in the tin basin, pulled down the German's trousers with his free hand,

200

and then, to Bastable's consternation, proceeded to stick the finger up the lad's back passage.

He was rewarded with another groan of pain.

'Excellent!' exclaimed Wimpy, washing his hands again. He nodded to the NCO. 'You can turn him back right side.' He fitted a gesture to the words.

'Well, Doctor?' enquired the Colonel politely.

'Field hospital, as quick as you can, Colonel. He needs surgery, but any of your field hospitals can do it.' He held up his hands apologetically. 'I can't do it here – my hands aren't up to it after coming off the motor-cycle, anyway. But the pain's still generalized over the abdomen, and so he should be all right until it localizes over the – ah – the area of the trouble.'

'And . . . just what is the trouble, Doctor?'

Wimpy assumed his Aesculapian expression. 'Simple appendicitis, Colonel. He has all the classic symptoms – the generalized pain is quite normal, and the vomiting . . . and the furred tongue and the stinking breath – *foetor*, Colonel, *foetor* – from the Latin, naturally . . . and finally I was able to tweak the offending object from the back, of course. You can't always do that, sometimes it's tucked out of the way, but in his case it was just ready and waiting to be tweaked.' He nodded wisely at the Colonel. 'I trust you have a field hospital to hand – or a French hospital will do, you should be in a position to insist on immediate surgery. Because if you don't the lad will die of peritonitis in due course, inevitably. Your medical officer will confirm all this, I'm sure – ' He frowned suddenly. 'Where is your medical officer?'

'The British killed him, Doctor,' said the Colonel. He swung on his heel and snapped an order at the NCO. The stretcher-bearers lifted their burden obediently and trotted down the road, away in the direction from which they had originally come.

The NCO started to move, then stopped in front of Wimpy and gave him a smart salute. Wimpy acknowledged the salute gravely.

'Accidentally, of course,' said the German Colonel. 'One of your bombs – outside Maubeuge.'

'I'm sorry,' said Wimpy.

'There is no need to be. It was an accident, as I have said . . . And we shot down the bomber.' He flicked a glance at Bastable, then came back to Wimpy. 'I thank you for your service, Doctor.'

Bastable watched him continue on his way until he passed out of sight between the lorries, followed by his entourage, rippling his men to attention as he passed them. Wimpy could be right about the fellow, at that; what was certain was that it was a good motorized battalion, this one, smart and soldierly and keen – and, what was more, with men in it who weren't in a hurry to report sick when they had stomach-ache, who would rather stay and fight . . . If there were too many battalions like this one, then the Allies were really in trouble.

'Phew!' whispered Wimpy, breathing out deeply and then drawing in his breath again. '*Phew!*'

Bastable looked at him for a long moment. 'Did he really have appendicitis?'

Wimpy raised his eyebrows. 'How the hell do I know?'

Bastable stared at him wordlessly.

'At least he had all the symptoms, old boy,' said Wimpy.

'Those . . . were the symptoms?'

'Of course they bloody were! Did you think I made them up?'

Again, no words presented themselves to Bastable.

'I had appendicitis when I was young . . . I can't remember much about it . . .' Wimpy drew another deep breath. 'But . . . when I was acting-schoolmaster at school the year before last, we had a boy go down with it in the middle of the night – I was terrified he was going to die on me . . . but I remember how the doctor came out to us, and stuck his finger up the poor little blighter's arse. And he gave me a running documentary on what he was doing, too – I'd clean forgotten all about it . . . except about *foetor*: he insisted that I should have a smell of it, because I was the boy's Latin master – they have the smell of shit on their breath . . . And *he* had the same smell too, that's what brought it all back to me.'

He looked at Bastable in silence for a second or two. Then he half-grinned. 'If you want my opinion, old boy . . . I think we were lucky, and that young fellow wasn't – or maybe he was, at that: I mean, I think my diagnosis was spot on . . . And if it wasn't – well, Harry, you could say I've inflicted my first casualty on the enemy. Besides which, it isn't everyone who gets the chance of sticking his finger up a German and lives to tell the tale – eh?'

It was about ten minutes later, no more than that, when the German Colonel came back to them. Only this time he was alone.

Wimpy rose from where he had stretched himself out by the roadside near Bastable.

'Doctor . . .' The Colonel glanced at Bastable. 'Are you able to walk, Captain?'

Bastable swallowed. 'Yes, sir – I think so.'

'Very well. We shall be moving on in . . . not a long time. So it is . . . not convenient that you remain with us – either of you.'

'Sir!' protested Wimpy. 'You said, sir, that we were prisoners of the German Army.'

The Colonel lifted a gloved hand. 'So you are, Doctor.

203

And so you will remain. I am sending you to the north, towards Arras.'

'Arras – ' The name came to Bastable's lips involuntarily, almost like a groan. 'But . . . but . . .'

'Towards Arras.' The German regarded him with a flicker of sympathy, which only made the news more unbearable. 'Oh, yes, Captain . . . your comrades are still in Arras. And they defend the town as you would wish them to do – with great courage.'

The very fact that he was sugaring the pill finally confirmed Bastable's fears about its fatal contents.

'But I do not think they will be there very long. General Rommel's column is already to the south-west of the town, he has only to swing northwards, on to Vimy Ridge . . .' The gloved hand completed the encirclement of what had been the General Headquarters of the British Expeditionary Force only a few days earlier, and Bastable's heart sank finally into the bottomless hole in the centre of that circle. For four unconquerable years in the last war Arras had been Britain's other Gibraltar, second only to Ypres. Now it was about to fall, with all that blood-soaked ground, in a matter of hours – that ground in which his own flesh-and-blood already lay in Uncle Arthur's unmarked grave – not in a matter of days and weeks and months and years, but in a matter of hours, perhaps even minutes.

Bastable stared at the German with a despair which made what he had experienced under the wrecked Bren carrier seem like a happy time. Every disaster, every humiliation, had been a false crest, concealing a worse one behind it; but this was too much, the last straw, the final reality of defeat. And now even the slim chance that he could do anything to avert that awful reality was gone – even worse, it was revealed to him for what it really was and had always been: a silly, hopeless, useless gesture that would have made no difference either way, even if he had succeeded.

'Defeat is something every soldier must learn to accept, Captain,' said the German Colonel, his voice hardening suddenly as though he could read Bastable's face, and despised the weakness he saw on it. 'Now, Doctor – there will be other prisoners . . . wounded prisoners, too, who will require your skill . . . and you will be able to join them. And . . . I will naturally send the Captain with you, of course.' He paused. 'I think that will be . . . better for you both – do you not agree?'

Wimpy glanced quickly at Bastable, then back to the Colonel. 'If you say so, sir.'

The Colonel nodded. 'I do say so. Also . . . there has not yet been time to investigate . . . that which you spoke of earlier, I must tell you, Doctor.'

Wimpy opened his mouth, but then closed it again without saying anything, which struck Bastable as being quite out of the ordinary, and very odd indeed.

The German gave him a long look. 'In war . . . in war, Doctor, there are things which happen, which should not happen – which are to be regretted. And also there are things which ought to happen – which ought to be done – which cannot in the circumstances be done . . . For which there can be regrets also.' He paused again. 'And there are also times to remain silent, Doctor – in the best interests of one's patient, shall we say?'

Before Wimpy could reply to any of that incomprehensible advice (and, just as incomprehensibly to Bastable, Wimpy showed no sign of wanting to reply to it), the German Colonel turned to look down the road. 'Ah!' His manner changed. 'I think your transport is ready – it is even being backed up the road to save you unnecessary

205

exertion, Doctor!' He smiled frostily. 'I suspect that is a way of showing gratitude for your service, perhaps . . . The soldier you treated is . . . what is your word – "mascot", I think . . . he is only seventeen years of age. They think I do not know, naturally.' He looked down at Bastable. 'I was nineteen years of age, Captain, when I was captured at Bourlon Wood in 1917 – I remember that I wept at the time, it was my first fight . . .' He looked away, and then back to Wimpy. 'My men are still senti-mental, Doctor – they haven't been properly blooded yet – which is just as well for both of us, I think . . . *You do understand, Doctor?*'

'I understand, sir,' said Wimpy. 'Thank you, sir.'

'Good.' The Colonel turned away without another word. His men made way for him as he passed between the parked lorries and the smaller truck which had backed up the road towards them. Bastable caught a last glimpse of him as he stopped for a moment to speak to one of them. There was a sudden burst of laughter, the slightly forced laughter of men who required half a second to work out whether it was proper to laugh and had decided that it was, and then he was gone.

'Get up, Harry,' murmured Wimpy, 'But try and look groggy.'

Bastable levered himself off the grass verge. It didn't take much acting ability to simulate grogginess, his knees were like water and Wimpy's supporting arm was for a moment a necessity.

'Ouch!' said Wimpy sharply in his ear. 'My bloody ankle!'

Instantly shamed by a genuine injury, Bastable swung his own arm to support Wimpy and they hobbled together to the dropped tailboard of the truck. With clumsy gentleness, almost with embarrassment, a large German soldier helped him up on to the vehicle's floor.

The German grinned at him and breathed a mixture of alcohol and garlic into his face. 'War over, Tommy!' said encouragingly. 'Goot – yes?'

Whatever it was, it wasn't *goot*, thought Bastable desperately. But he could feel the thought weakening him, that he was still alive when so many others were dead, and that being alive was immeasurably better than being dead – yet when he thought that he would be a total prisoner, and as good as dead, and that would add treason to cowardice.

'Thank you,' he said stiffly.

Wimpy scrambled in after him, and two German soldiers followed Wimpy. The tailboard clanged back into position. Someone threw a blanket into the truck, into Wimpy's hands, and someone else shouted and banged the side with the time-honoured 'ready-to-go' signal.

The truck juddered forward and Bastable hit his head on the floor, and remembered Batty Evans in an agonizing flash of memory. 'Phew!' exclaimed Wimpy, hugging the blanket to his chest. 'A good German, that one, old boy!'

Bastable thought confusedly of the man who had helped him into the truck, then hit his head again as it lurched forward. 'A gentleman, in fact,' said Wimpy. 'I was right about him – eh?'

Just in time, before the next bump, Bastable cushioned his head with his hand.

Wimpy nodded at him. 'Saved our lives anyway, old boy, I shouldn't wonder – or did his best to, anyway,' he said.

11

Saved our lives –
Saved our lives!
The truck bumped up and down on the road, and the
floor bumped Harry Bastable's knuckles, and the shock
of the bump transmitted itself to his aching head.
Saved our lives – saved our lives – saved our lives –
'I wonder what this General Rommel he's sending us to
is like,' said Wimpy. 'I hope he's a gentleman too – have
you ever heard of a Jerry general named Rommel,
Harry?'
Batable had never heard of a German general named
Rommel, but then he couldn't recall the names of any
German generals at all. Even those of whom he had
heard, but couldn't now remember for the life of him,
had all had 'von' in front of their names, anyway.
'No,' he said, carefully not shaking his head.
One of the German soldiers, who was cradling a lethal-
looking little sub-machine-gun rather as Wimpy held his
blanket, pricked up his ears.
'General Rommel?' The harsh *G* came out explosively.
Bastable stared fascinated at the sub-machine-gun. It was
a little weapon with a pistol-grip and a straight magazine
sticking downwards from the firing chamber, quite unlike
the big round drum on the Tommy-gun he had seen a few
months before, which Major Tetley-Robinson had dismissed as a gangster's tool.
'General Rommel – ja!' said Wimpy. 'I mean . . . that
is to say, General Rommel – yes?'

Bastable continued to study the sub-machine-gun. He remembered having agreed with Major Tetley-Robinson about the Tommy-gun, but in this German's hands – one on the pistol-grip and one grasping the slender magazine – it looked like a devastatingly effective close-quarter weapon, and he found himself coveting it and wondering why the British Army didn't have anything like it. Of course, the Bren and the Lee-Enfield and the Webley were the best weapons of their kind in the world, but . . .

He wondered whether the Germans had anything like the Boys anti-tank rifle, and hoped fervently that they did.

'General Rommel – ' The German plunged into his own language enthusiastically.

Wimpy spread his hands, after having listened carefully.

'Nicht – nicht comprenez, old boy,' he lied apologetically.

The German soldier shrugged. 'General Rommel – goot,' he said, and made what looked like the sign of the cross at his throat with the hand which had grasped the magazine. 'Pour le Mérite – ja?'

Wimpy nodded. 'Pour le Mérite – jolly good!' He leaned sideways towards Bastable. 'He says that General Rommel has got the Pour le Mérite – that's the Jerry equivalent of the Victoria Cross, Harry, old boy. So he can't be a bad type, what!'

Now it was the German's turn to nod again. 'Victoria Cross – goot!' he agreed.

Bastable felt that something was required of him, and for once what was required was perfectly obvious.

He lifted himself on to his elbows. 'General Gort – goot!' he told the German.

'General – Gort?' The German obviously knew no more about the Commander-in-Chief of the British

209

Expeditionary Force than Bastable did about *General* Rommel. And Bastable could have wept at his inability to tell the blighter how 'Tiger' Gort had led his Grenadiers through the Hindenburg Line in 1918, winning the medal they had given him three times over if half of what the history books said about him was true – that would put the Jerry in his place, by God, with his references to this *General* Rommel of his!

'General Gort – Victoria Cross,' he said as clearly as he knew how. 'General Gort – VC!'

'Ah – ah!' The German bobbed his head in sudden agreement. 'General Gort – *gut, gut!*' He turned towards his comrade and spouted a stream of German at him.

Wimpy bent over Bastable, spreading out the blanket as he did so.

'Do be a good fellow and stop talking about the Fat Boy, and try to look as though you're dying, Harry,' he murmured conversationally.

'What d'you mean "the Fat Boy"?' said Bastable, outraged.

'That's what they call him – our esteemed and revered C-in-C – "Fat Boy",' said Wimpy. 'Didn't you know?'

'But – but he isn't fat – ' Bastable moved from certainty to doubt in one bound as he tried and failed to recall General Gort's measurements from the newsreel and newspaper pictures which were the closest he had come to his commander ' – is he?'

'Don't ask me, I don't know. But that's what they call him, according to Nigel Audley anyway.' Wimpy started to push him back ungently.

'But – '

'Forget about him. Lie back – ' Wimpy increased the pressure on his chest and lowered his voice to a whisper ' – lie back and be a casualty, for God's sake!'

Bastable surrendered to the urgency in the whisper rather than to the awful possibility that his tiger might be . . . portly. It was probably only a nickname, anyway: lots of people had nicknames, and the names were not always accurate, as Wimpy's was – they were often deliberate reversals of the truth, like that which had been fastened on one of his own fusiliers, a six-foot-six beanpole of a man who answered more readily to 'Shorty' than to his own name. Indeed, nicknames could also be signs of affection and good fellowship among equals (unlike Wimpy's). In his own heart of hearts he had always hankered after one like that as a sign that his brother officers accepted him as one of them, and because he could then reassure himself that he was not a dull nonentity.

'That's better,' continued Wimpy softly, pretending to busy himself with making his patient comfortable. 'I don't think either of these two fellows can understand English, but I'm not prepared to bet my life on it.'

Bastable looked up at him questioningly.

'We've got to get out of this *quam celerrime* – ' Wimpy seized Bastable's wrist and went through the motions of taking his pulse ' – because I do rather suspect we're in a damn tricky situation, Harry, old boy. In fact, I'm bloody sure of it!'

'What?' Bastable floundered. 'But why – '

'Ssh! No need to shout.' Wimpy's lips hardly moved. 'Why d'you think our good Colonel shunted us off double-quick to this tame general of his? Who is by way of being an old friend-of-the-family, if I've understood our talkative guard's obscure German dialect aright . . . Can't you guess, old boy?'

'They were moving out, weren't they? He said – '

'Poppycock, Harry. They didn't show any signs of that – apart from what he spelt out himself very loud and clear

211

. . . No, old boy – we were just too hot to handle. Or *you* were, at any rate, Harry – too hot for a mere colonel, but maybe not too hot for a brass-hat like this Rommel-chappie – don't you realize?'

Bastable rolled his eyes helplessly.

'They knew my name, man – for God's sake – they knew my name *and my initials*!' hissed Wimpy. 'Don't you understand what that means? *Don't you understand why they bloody well wiped out the battalion?*'

The truck lurched and bumped bone-jarringly over a pot-hole in the road.

'We've had it all back-to-front – ' Wimpy dropped the wrist and applied a sweaty palm to Bastable's forehead ' – We've been trying to get your information about that fucking bastard of a Brigadier back to our people . . . But – can't you get it through your head, Harry – *can't you understand that the Germans are trying just as hard to stop us doing just that?*'

He nodded and grinned reassuringly – incongruously – as he delivered this information, and Bastable was aware of one of the guards looming up behind him. Prisoners who talked too much – and they couldn't know that Wimpy always talked too much – even doctors who talked too much to their wounded – were obviously cause for concern.

Wimpy grimaced at the guard and rubbed his chest and stomach meaningfully. 'Hauptmann . . . internal injuries . . . der – der *ribs* – ' he pointed to his ribs ' – der ribs *kaput*, bitte?'

With his free hand he pinched Bastable painfully, and Bastable winced in support of the diagnosis, his eyes clamped on the muzzle of the sub-machine-gun which pointed unwaveringly in Wimpy's direction.

'Groan, old boy, groan,' murmured Wimpy.

The German snapped out a harsh word.

Bastable groaned, and arched his body as he remembered Wimpy's previous patient had done, and closed his eyes.

Wimpy's words fed the groan –

My initials?

The battalion –

The battalion was a genuine agony: he had thought of Fusilier Dodsworth – 'Shorty' Dodsworth – in the present tense, but that was just another pathetic attempt to refuse a truth too crushing for acceptance: that the whole of the Prince Regent's Own was gone – Tetley-Robinson and the CO, Captain Harbottle and Corporal Smithers and CQMS Gammidge, and Nigel Audley and young Chichester, and Dodsworth –

All of them – it still wasn't possible – *all of them –*

Suddenly he understood what Wimpy had been droning on interminably in his ear about.

It was because of him – it was all because of him!

He had seen the false Brigadier, in that split-second in the farmyard on the hill.

And, of course, the false Brigadier had seen him, too.

Had seen him – had remembered him –

But hadn't known who he was, of course; he had been just another face among the officers of the Prince Regent's Own South Downs Fusiliers – a nonentity until seen again for that split-second in the farmyard on the hill –

But he had dropped Wimpy's field-glasses at the first fence, complete with Wimpy's initials –

And then the face had had a name as well as a battalion, and a place in which to die.

* * *

213

He opened his eyes and found himself staring into those of the German soldier who was in the act of bending over him.

The German's gun wasn't pointing at him, but for a mad fraction of a second the gun didn't matter anyway, all that mattered was that his enemy was there within his reach. But as he started to move he discovered too late that he was imprisoned in the blanket which Wimpy had tacked around him, so that the movement degenerated into a wild convulsion before he could control it.

The German sprang back in panic, and Bastable's momentary insanity froze into fear as the gun swung towards him.

'Steady there – for Christ's sake!' exclaimed Wimpy in alarm. 'Nein! Nein!'

The German waved the gun menacingly at them, swinging it from one to the other, and barked an order which raised Wimpy's arms into the air like rockets.

'Nein! Nein!' he protested. 'Hauptmann sick – crazy . . . damn it – verrückt – verrückt, bitte?'

'Eh?' The German regarded Bastable with a mixture of suspicion and apprehension.

'Verrückt.' Wimpy lowered one hand sufficiently to tap the side of his head with one finger. 'Mad as a hatter – verrückt!'

The other guard, the more friendly of the two, murmured something in his comrade's ear, and received a growl and an unwilling nod in return.

'And crazy is right,' snapped Wimpy, lowering his hands cautiously. 'Lie back, Harry. They don't want to shoot us, but they will if they have to, so don't push them.'

Bastable lay back in his cocoon and stared miserably at the canvas hood above him. That was another black mark on his record: he could never have reached the German quickly enough, and even if he could have there was still the second one. He had acted without thinking, and all he had achieved was to put their guards on guard.

Wimpy was right again, as usual. Indeed, if he'd been on guard and a German prisoner had thrashed about like that right under his nose, he'd most likely have shot first in a blind panic and that would have been that. In fact, probably the only reason why that hadn't happened just now was because these men had been specifically ordered to deliver their prisoners to General Rommel's head-quarters, and German soldiers were proverbially exact in carrying out their officers' commands to the letter. So once again he had been lucky as well as stupid.

But he couldn't continue to rely on his luck – he had to learn to *think* more, and ahead, instead of simply reacting (and too slowly) to each catastrophe as it occurred.

Think, then – calmly and logically –

Wimpy had put most of the pieces together for him.

From the moment he had seen the false Brigadier, the battalion had been doomed.

They had chased him – or maybe they hadn't chased him at all, but had chased Wimpy by mistake and Wimpy had got away.

Only they had found Wimpy's field-glasses, with his name on them – that was the only way they could have learned his initials.

And the false Brigadier had reasoned quite correctly that the only place Captain W. M. Willis could go was back to his battalion, the precise whereabouts of which – and the distinguishing mark of which – he already knew.

So one quick radio message had directed the nearest German unit to Colembert-les-Deux-Ponts.

And that had been the SS unit, which had been given a bloody nose for its over-confidence.

After which, however, there had come the devastating Stuka attack, and then the Panzers, who had made no mistake about the job.

And then the SS unit – probably the same one, and in a vengeful mood – had set about finding Captain W. M. Willis . . . in their own way.

But they hadn't found him.

But –

Think –

They hadn't found him, but they hadn't given up looking for him. In fact, the bastards had even invented some false atrocity story to encourage other nearby units to join the hunt – he could just imagine how that would have redoubled his own vigilance, if the roles had been reversed, and he had been fed a similar story.

But once more they'd been lucky – and damned lucky, too! – to fall into the hands of a German officer who clearly didn't like the SS and didn't particularly *dis*like the British . . . at least sufficiently to give them the benefit of the doubt, and pack them off out of harm's way to the custody of this brass-hat friend of his –

No! He was being simple again, and not thinking logically at all. German colonels didn't disobey orders on the grounds of their personal likes and dislikes. This Colonel hadn't shot them out of hand – or sent them back to the SS, which amounted to the same thing – not because he was an officer and a gentleman, who didn't do such things, but because he had believed Wimpy and had disbelieved the thugs on his own side.

But why?

Bastable stared up at the stained canvas, and discovered to his surprise that the answer was staring back at him, and it was simple.

He had always been suspicious of people who were clever, because they often turned out to be too clever for everyone's good, including their own. Only this time he was grateful for the too-cleverness of the SS (whatever 'SS' stood for, but it did have the right hissing snake-in-the-grass sound about it, anyway), which had had precisely the opposite effect from the one they had intended.

Simply – once Wimpy had challenged the German Colonel with a genuine atrocity which he could go and see for himself, and an atrocity committed by the SS too, then the Colonel had quite reasonably deduced that *that* was the real reason why the SS was so hell-bent on eliminating Captain W. M. Willis.

Obviously – *simply* – Captain W. M. Willis knew too much – had seen too much – and had escaped to bear witness to it.

Which was the exact truth.

Except, it wasn't an atrocity that Captain Willis had seen.

And it hadn't been Captain Willis who had seen it.

The truck was slowing down, and there were other sounds outside it, of other engines labouring in low gear.

Bastable resolutely blocked the noises out of his mind. There wasn't anything he could do about his predicament at the moment now, if there ever had been. But at least he could still think for himself, and he was aware that he was not yet satisfied with his thoughts. Somehow, he hadn't got it right yet; or, he had got it right as far as it went, but somewhere along the line of thought he'd missed the point; because sorting out what had happened wasn't really important – it was the *why* before the *what*, that was the point he had missed, somehow –

The truck stopped with a jolt.

He back-tracked feverishly. He had worked out why the German Colonel had disobeyed his orders, which was because duty was one thing but conniving with a bunch of gangsters to cover up murder was another – and that had to be right, because if the Colonel had known what was really at stake, what Captain W. M. Willis had really seen, and why the SS wanted him so badly, his duty would have been inescapable.

So he had not known – the SS hadn't told him.

'Are you okay, old boy?'

Bastable screwed his eyes tighter.

'Harry?'

Why hadn't they told him?

'Harry!'

All the other whys didn't matter compared with this one.

Bastable opened his eyes. Wimpy was leaning over him, wearing his worried-doctor face, as well he might: and he was staring into Harry Bastable's face as plainly as the truth was staring into it.

The SS hadn't told the Colonel the truth because the truth was too important.

'I'm fine,' said Bastable.

And too secret. Too secret and too important.

So important that they had destroyed the Prince Regent's Own South Down Fuseliers and were still pursuing its survivors with murderous lies to preserve that secret.

He had come to it at last, what he ought to have realized straight away, but had been too full of revenge and fear – and also too stupid – to understand: if it was vitally important for him to report the treachery of that damned false-fucking-bastard Brigadier to his own people, it was just as vitally important for the Germans to stop him reporting.

This was all only the confirmation of what he had feared, and yet at the same time much more than the confirmation. For now he knew that whatever the Brigadier was up to, it wasn't run-of-the-mill Fifth Column stuff. It was something so big that the Germans weren't even prepared to trust their senior field officers with its true nature, by God!

He lifted himself on to his elbows to get a better view of the rear of the truck. The guards were fumbling with the tailboard pins, and beyond them he could see brick buildings. The intermittent sound of those other engines resolved itself into the familiar noise of a heavily-loaded MT column not far away. But beyond that, further off yet not so distant that it was not instantly recognizable against the lorries' roar, was another sound: the *pop-pop-pop* of a machine-gun. Even as Bastable listened to it, and was surprised that he hadn't distinguished it more quickly against the racket of the vehicle in which he had been travelling, it was punctuated by the heavier sound of gun-fire – not the vague thunder he remembered from the previous day, but the distinctly different cracks and concussions of shells being fired in one place and arriving in another.

Wimpy leaned towards him. 'Arras,' he whispered.

'Arras?' Bastable peered wildly at the redbrick building.

'Not here, man – *there*.' Wimpy jerked his head towards the sound of the guns. 'We're still four or five miles away, on the outskirts. I saw a road sign just back there – "Arras, ten kilometres" . . . Don't you remember what

219

the Jerry Colonel said – how this friend of his . . . what's his name? Damn it! – '

'Rommel,' said Bastable, pleased that he could remember something Wimpy had forgotten.

'Rommel, that's right. Well, he's supposed to be swinging round behind Arras, to outflank our chaps.' He nodded again in the direction of the firing. 'That'll be him, probably attacking Vimy Ridge – I swear those are anti-tank guns. It's just the same sound I heard yesterday when I was near Belléme, and the Mendips had some two-pounders there . . . and if they are, I hope we're giving the blighter beans, by God!'

Bastable suddenly felt ashamed. His brief flash of pleasure at remembering the German general's name had been extinguished in the next second by the realization that they were so very near their objective, yet so immeasurably far from it at the same time. If Arras was about to fall to the Germans, then in reaching it they would only be swapping one captivity for another and greater one.

And yet here was Wimpy as bright-eyed and bushy-tailed as ever – Wimpy, who had always looked on the black side of things and had nothing but cynical comment for the generals and the conduct of the war, almost to the disgraceful point of defeatism – yet here was a quite different Wimpy, fierce and defiant in adversity, almost to the point of idiocy, undefeated.

'We've got to watch for our chance now, Harry – ' Wimpy cut off his final hiss of advice so quickly that the last words ran into each other as his lips closed tightly on them.

Their guards were shouting at them.

''Raus! 'Raus!' The tailboard of the lorry clanged in unison with the peremptory shout. They were no longer officers and gentlemen, the shout told Bastable: they were

220

prisoners on the edge of a battle, and when any German soldier howled an order at them – any German Batty Evans, no matter how moronic – they had to jump to it, or else they could be shot out of hand and nobody would think twice about it.

'Come on, Harry, old boy – and play the wounded hero for all it's worth, for God's sake!' Wimpy murmured urgently in his ear, pretending to help him on to his feet. 'Get the blanket round your shoulders, that's right . . .'

In the bright sunshine of the harsh world outside the truck it wasn't difficult to simulate false injury, Bastable discovered; there were awful internal wounds, to his pride and his self-respect and his very soul, which made him lurch and stagger like a drunken man.

This was the true face of defeat –

They were on the edge of a courtyard, flanked by the brick buildings he had glimpsed from the truck, tall on two sides and wrecked by bombing or shell-fire on the third, and there were German soldiers all around them, standing in groups – officers and men – waiting, talking, but all animated by the same sense of excitement and purpose, dusty and dirty and rumpled, yet for all the world like men on an outing . . . or – the image pierced Bastable's heart – like a rugger team at half-time in a game they were winning.

Oh God! It was the face of defeat because it was the face of victory!

Wimpy grunted with pain as Bastable leaned against him. For a moment neither was supporting the other, and they teetered unsteadily as Bastable's boots skidded on the pavé. Bastable found himself staring into the face of a passing German soldier as he fought to get his arm under Wimpy's armpit: the expression on the man's face was neither hostile nor sympathetic, it was simply incurious, as though they were debris of war to be avoided or stepped over, but not human beings.

'Damn!' groaned Wimpy, throwing his weight back at Bastable. 'Bloody ankle – '

The blanket slipped from Bastable's shoulders and he felt his knee buckling in the opposite direction. But then, just when he was within an ace of collapsing altogether, a strong arm came out of nowhere to support him.

'Coom on, sar – had oop noo! Aah've got yew!' a strange voice close to his ear encouraged him deferentially. 'Aaah've got yew noo!'

The voice was almost unintelligible, but it was British – and the arm was khaki-clad and indubitably British too – and each in its different way recalled Bastable to his duty, reminding him that he mustn't let the side down in the midst of the enemy.

'Aye, that's reet, sar – tek it aisy noo, aah've got yew.'

One of the guards appeared in front of them suddenly, snapping angry words and making threatening gestures with his rifle.

The British soldier at Bastable's side made a rude gesture at the rifle. 'Why man – wee the fukken hell d'ye think ye are? Haddaway and shite!' he snapped back, and then transferred his attention to Bastable again. 'Divunt tek ainy notice uv him, sar – had oop noo – that's champion!'

Another figure loomed up: it was the young German officer who had attended the Colonel at the roadside where they had been captured.

'Hauptmann – Doctor . . .' He exhibited exactly the same degree of irritated concern Bastable himself would have felt if charged by his commanding officer with such a mission, which had to be done properly but which was a great waste of valuable time.

'Right-o!' said Wimpy through clenched teeth. 'Let's go then, Harry.'

They lurched forward towards the main door of the building ahead, their five good legs producing an erratic crablike motion which made precise steering difficult. For the greater part of the journey the Germans they encountered took not the least notice of them, even when stepping aside to let them through; it was only when they had almost reached the doorway that they came upon a group of officers who evinced any interest in them.

First, it was borne in on Bastable that this group was not going to give way, and that the crab would have to navigate round it. Then a quick glance terrified him: one of the officers carried the lightning zig-zag of the dreaded SS on his collar, and he was accompanied by a civilian in an oddly-cut leather driving jacket who frowned at them with sudden curiosity which made his heart miss a beat.

For a second he was undecided as to which way to manoeuvre the crab. Then his mind was made up for him by Wimpy, who had hitherto allowed himself to be pulled or pushed without demur, but who now changed direction with a sudden and wholly unexpected burst of energy to propel the crab past the obstacle.

'Halt!' shouted a voice from just behind them.

'Keep going!' hissed Wimpy into Bastable's ear.

'Halt!' repeated the voice.

'*Keep going!*' repeated Wimpy urgently. 'Pretend you haven't heard – *keep going!*'

The main door was only two more steps ahead of them. Almost against his will, in deadly fear of being shot from behind, Bastable was swept through it by the combined efforts of a suddenly desperate Wimpy and their rescuer, who apparently needed no encouragement to disobey German commands. The swing doors banged open and then swung shut behind them, cutting off the sunlight. Wimpy swivelled on his good leg to look back through the shattered glass panes.

'Thank Christ – the Jerry subaltern's talking back to them!' Wimpy turned to the British soldier. 'Who are you?'

'Adwin, sir. First Tyneside Scottish – '

'Is there a way out of here, Adwin?'

'*H*adwin, sir.'

'*Had*win – *Had*win, is there a way out of here? Quickly now!'

'Sar?' The soldier goggled at him. 'A way oot?'

'In ten seconds from now those SS blighters are coming through that doorway, and they're going to shoot us, Hadwin. Now – *is there a way out?*'

The Tynesider continued to goggle at him, and so did Bastable.

Wimpy pointed. 'Your bloody lanyard, Harry – you're still wearing it. And they saw it, by God, too – if we don't get out of here right now, Hadwin, the two of us, we've had it. Is there a way out, man?'

Bastable looked down in horror at the treacherous yellow-and-grey snake on his shoulder. How could he have been so stupid as to forget it? *Die Abuzsleine* – how could he have been so criminally stupid! Feverishly, he tore at his epaulet to get the thing off.

'There's mebbe a rood oot, if yah ganna tek a chance, sar,' said the Tynesider. 'Mind, it's oonly 'aff a chance, aah'm tellin' yew, sar – '

'We'll take it,' snapped Wimpy.

'Reet, sar. Coom oon, then!' The Tynesider led the way down the debris-littered passage ahead.

They followed him down the narrow passage, Wimpy hopping painfully, supporting himself with one hand on the wall, until they reached a door.

The room beyond was a slaughter-house at first glance. At second glance . . . it must have been a wash-room or a laundry-room of some sort once, with large stone sinks beneath antique brass taps . . . but at second glance it was still a slaughter-house, with its huge table stained with blood – there was blood everywhere – and the floor was thick with blood-stained bandages and dressings.

'Aye,' said the Tynesider, nodding at Wimpy, 'yew'll nah this place reet enough, Doctor. They patched oop some ov thor aan, but it were mostly wor lot, more's the pity. The buggers cut us to bits, theer fukken tanks did, cut us to fukken ribbons . . . Mind, they did thor best for wor lads, aa'll say that for thum – trayted us the same as theer aan.' He pointed to the outside door. 'But the garden's full uv them they could dee nowt wi', them that was ower far gone, sar.'

'Where are the German medical people?' asked Wimpy.

'Buggered off and left iz this mornin', sar, wi' the fukken tanks. Left iz in charge, wi' one uv theers an' me, an' one uv wor aan from the Durhams – tha' wi' the poor wounded in the front rooms noo, waitin' ter be moved oot.'

The front door banged in the distance.

'Quick man!' exclaimed Wimpy. 'They're coming!'

'Get oonder the tebble, sar!' Hadwin pointed under the huge operating table. 'Twa stretchers – yew lay yorsels doon on them, an' aah'll cover yew wi' blankets, an' the tebble wi' a shayet. Then if they see yew they'll think yor joost twa more deed 'uns, like them poor buggers oot there, mebbe.'

'Harry – ' Wimpy began. But by then Bastable was already half-way on to his stretcher under the table.

'That's reet, sar – that's reet!' The Tynesider arranged a blanket over him. 'Noo – leave yer byuts sticken' oot the end thar, an' cover yer face – there, that's champion! Noo, divunt mek a noise, an' aah'll coom back for yew when aah can. Mayntime, aah'll gan oot th' back way – '

For a moment, there was silence, but then Bastable heard the beating of his heart, his tell-tale heart, which he must still somehow.

This was the second time that he had been dead, and with his boots showing too – passing for dead among the dead once again, except that this time he knew what he was doing and was not at all sure he could act the part with the conviction it required if the Germans looked under the table.

The blanket against his face wasn't soft, it was strangely stiff, almost like cardboard.

At first he had hardly understood a word the Tynesider had said, it had almost been a foreign language. But then, quite suddenly, he had understood every word, *every fukken* word.

In the silence he could still hear the distant *pop-pop-pop* of machine-guns, and the heavier *poop* – it was not a rumble, but merely a gradation up from the *pop-pop-pop* – the *poop* of heavier guns.

And now the crunch of footsteps in the passage, much closer.

It seemed that all he had left was his sense of hearing –

The blanket against his face was stiff with blood, of course. But he could no longer feel that, it was the knowledge inside his head, mixed with equally sickening fear.

The door cracked open.

German voices. Once again Bastable experienced the humiliation of hearing only guttural sounds, without the least understanding of what they meant. Wimpy would be lying there beside him, making sense of those sounds, while all he could do was to lie like a block of wood, like a dead man, like a donkey – like a dead donkey – and understand nothing.

He forced himself to listen to the harsh voices. It was incredible that this was the same language as in the German *lieder* – those meaningless, but heart-wrenchingly beautiful songs Mother loved to play – the language of Goethe and Bach and Beethoven, about whom he knew next to nothing except that they were great men like Shakespeare and Milton and Newton, and that it would be in their language that the orders for his death might come in the next moment.

He knew that he was trying to keep sane, and to stop screaming with terror in protest that he hadn't been born and brought up with love and gentle kindness, and trained and educated, to lie under a blood-stiffened blanket in a French laundry on a summer's afternoon with the fear of death sweating out of him through every pore – this wasn't Harry Bastable at all – it was a stranger, because this couldn't happen to Harry Bastable –

Bastable!

One of the Germans had said his name –

Bast-abell - schwisser - glutzig - aben - geruber - begegen - schlikt - wollen - nachtvice - *Bastabell* - gabble - gabble - gabble-*abuzsleine*-gabble-gabble-gabble-gabble-*Willis*–

Willis!

There was more than one voice, in fact there were three voices: there was the subaltern's voice, which was now deferential, almost scared, with only the shreds of obstinacy left in it – the voice of a junior officer who knew his

227

orders, but also knew that he was overmatched; then there was a bullying voice, before which the subaltern's voice retreated; and finally there was a third voice, softer than the bullying one, yet somehow more frightening, because it seemed to require no loud threats to make its points – it was this voice which finally reduced the subaltern to heel-clicking obedience.

After that the door opened and shut again. But just as Bastable was about to breathe out a full shuddering lungful of relief the second voice started up again, only more conversationally, as deferential as the young officer's had been.

The third voice replied, and as Bastable caught his own name and Wimpy's he became conscious again of the fear that had been pulsing through him all the time. He could also feel the lanyard, which was screwed up into a sweaty ball in his right hand, which he had had no time to get rid of – *the symbol of his pride in his regiment and in himself for being privileged to wear it*, which had become the mark of Cain for every man who wore it, the insignia of death in primrose-yellow and dove-grey.

The voices droned on and on, back and forth, until finally the door banged open again and heels clicked.

The bullying voice challenged the heel-clicker.

The heel-clicker spoke, and it was the young officer again, only now he wasn't scared, he was terrified.

For a second neither of the SS officers replied. In the stifling darkness under the blanket Bastable heard the *pop-popping* of the machine-gun once more, and because of the sudden silence in the room – and also presumably because the door was still open – it sounded much louder. And then, in the last fraction of that same second, he knew why the young officer was frightened, and also why the SS officers had been struck momentarily speechless, and even what was going to happen next, all these thoughts travelling through his brain with the speed of light to fill the slow-moving instant of silence with time to spare in which his own terror was transformed into panic.

The bullying voice roared out in exactly the tone of incredulous rage that he had expected – that he even recognized from his own experience of bullying senior officers, so that although every word was still unintelligible to him he knew their sum total down to the last syllable.

'What the bloody hell d'you mean – "they've gone"?'

He lost the rest in the tide of hopelessness which engulfed him. They had vanished – they had passed through the main door into the field hospital, and their guards simply hadn't thought to follow them, and now they couldn't be found so the Germans would search for them more thoroughly, and in no time at all they would be found again without difficulty. All they had to do was to look under the table –

The door banged and boots stamped and scraped metallically on the stone floor within inches of his ear.

Now they were going to be discovered. It was impossible that they could escape, it had always been impossible – he might just as well throw back the blanket himself, rather than wait to have it ripped off him, and surrender to the inevitable with dignity and courage . . . except that it wouldn't be dignity and courage, it would be in the fear and horror of death, shaking like the coward he was – he could feel his hands shaking at the very thought of it and his body turning to water in physical rejection of what was about to happen to it.

Oh God – he'd wet himself! He could feel the uncontrollable spasm of the muscles in his penis as they relaxed, and the warm damp spread in his trousers as his bladder emptied itself, the warmth turning colder even as he tried unavailingly to stem the flood.

Oh, God – oh, God – oh, God –

Now he couldn't stand up even if he wanted to. If he stood up now they would see a great dark patch in his trousers, and they would know he had wet himself – the great dark hateful badge of shame –

'*Listen to me carefully* – '

An English voice – ? Bastable's senses reeled with the shock of it.

'I will ask you a question. You will answer it.'

Not an English voice: it was too perfect – each word was too distinct and complete in itself, not like the related parts of a whole sentence, but like carefully chosen samples picked deliberately from a rack in order to make a sale to a customer who didn't really know his own mind.

And he knew the voice, too –

'If you do not answer . . . correctly . . . *truthfully* . . . I will have you taken out and shot – do you understand? Shot – do you understand that?

No answer.

'You do understand.'

Not a question, but a promise. And with such pure and careful English, without either accent or passion, it was impossible not to understand.

'Two of your soldiers entered this building – officers. You assisted them. One of them was wounded, the other was an officer of your medical . . . corps.'

Not questions, but facts, the words stated.

'Now . . . and think correctly before you answer – remember that which I have told you . . . that if you do not answer . . . truthfully . . . you will be shot. Yes?'

Not a sound. But then, the question had not been asked yet.

'Where-are-those-officers?'

The cold feeling round Bastable's crutch spread upwards.

'I ask one more time. Where – '

'Ootside.'

'What?'

'Ootside.'

There was a pause, while both Bastable and the SS officer worked out the meaning of *ootside*.

'What is that?' *Ootside* was evidently not in the SS man's dictionary.

'Ootside in the garden, man – ootside!' The Tynesider addressed the SS man with a mixture of incredulity and contempt, as any intelligent man might do to a hopeless idiot. 'Ootside – divunt yew understan' plain English? Do yew not naa what aah'm sayin'?'

There was a pause.

'In . . . the garden?'

'Aye. Ootside in the fukken garden – oot there, man. Aah left 'em oot there, aah'm tellin' yew. Thar!' Now pity joined contempt.

'Where? Show me!'

Footsteps passed on each side of Bastable.

'*Thar,* man!'

It was a nice distinction, thought Bastable hysterically, that the Tynesider was refusing point-blank to call the enemy 'sir'.

'But they are not there now.'

'Well, that's where aah left them – settin' thar.'

'Why did you leave them there?'

'Haddaway, man! They wor fukken officers, an' aah'm oonly a fukken orderly, aah niver had aany say in it. Aah told them aarl the beds is full oop. So the one says, "Alreet, we'll set doon ootside until yew find me marra'

231

somewhere to lay." An' they set doon thar, aah tell yew – an' aa doon't care. It's no ma job to lewk after fukken officers, aah've got men *deein'* back inside . . . an' this one, he canna walk, but he's no deein', aa can see that. So aah doon't care where they set.'

Pause. As well as there might be, thought Bastable, as he struggled to disentangle the sense of it, from which 'It's not my job to look after fucking officers' rang clearest and loudest and truest to life.

'So you have no idea where those officers are now?' The SS man sounded more desperate than angry.

'Aah doon't noo – haddaway, man – aah'm tellin' yew – aah've got better things t'doo than lewk after the likes of them. "Fukken find me marra' a bed," he says to me. But aah'm not after findin' a bed for a man that's no bad hurt – fukken officers!' The Tynesider loaded a world of bitterness into his words, the weight of their deeper truth adding conviction to the lie. 'So aah left them settin' thar ootside, an' that's the last aah see uv them like aah said. An' if they've buggered off it's none uv ma dooin' – aah'm noo their keeper, aah've got better bliddy things t'doo.'

The SS man digested that in silence again for a moment, as he had done the Tynesider's previous outbursts, and Bastable could almost conjure up a tiny spark of sympathy for him out of his own bitter experiences with other ranks whose ability to lie their way out of any situation had always defeated him.

Except that this man was lying to save his own life – and theirs!

Then fear took over again, and he lay bathed in it as the voices and sounds snarled and shouted and cracked and stamped all around him in the darkness, beyond fear and

despair and understanding – it couldn't be Harry Bastable, Captain Bastable, Mr Henry Bastable of Gloves and
Hosiery, *wash-your-hands-and-comb-your-hair* Henry – it
couldn't be any of those – oh, God! it couldn't be any of
those lying now in sweat and urine under a blood-stiffened
blanket.

'Harry!' The whisper reached him in the darkness.

They had gone. It seemed impossible, when they only
had to look under the table – it seemed so impossible that
perhaps that was why they hadn't looked under the table.

'Harry!'

Why couldn't Wimpy leave him alone? Anger stirred in
Bastable at the prospect of being forced into activity, with
the Germans all around them, when they didn't stand a
chance. And anyway, one thing he had learned was that
however bad things were, whatever happened next was
bound to be worse. So, better to lie here and hope – that
was preferable to any madcap scheme Wimpy might have
in mind.

He felt the anger spreading, engorging him.

'Harry – ' Wimpy cut off abruptly.

The door banged again. He knew the sound of that
bloody door by heart, and the loud, insistent firing beyond
it, and hated both sounds, and hated Wimpy and hated
himself –

The blanket was ripped from him before he had time to
draw breath, and he found himself staring at a German
face which had been thrust under the table.

The German's eyes widened in astonishment and his
mouth opened even wider. All Bastable's rage transferred
itself in that instant from the rest of the world to this one
man, the final disturber of his misery.

The German dropped the edge of the blanket, and

started to draw back and to shout at the same time as –
Bastable caught his wrist. The grip was too weak – it was
too slow off the mark to tighten in time – but it held the
man just long enough to destroy his co-ordination: instead
of ducking back and straightening up and shouting, he
failed to clear the table in time and caught the back of his
head with a loud crack on the underside of it, which
reduced the shout to an exclamation of pain. At the same
time his soft forage cap tipped over his eyes and he let go
his rifle, which fell with a clatter on the stone floor.

Bastable grabbed wildly with his other hand, and felt
his fingers close round the leather ankle of a jackboot. He
pulled back with all his might, felt the German begin to
overbalance, and rolled himself violently off the stretcher
against the man's legs in an attempt to sweep him off his
feet.

The space between the table and the wall on this side
of the room was so constricted that for a desperate
moment he thought the man wasn't going to fall. Then
the hobnails on the jackboots lost their purchase with the
stone, and the man fell with a scrape and a crash in the
narrow aisle, with Bastable's face between his legs. A
field-grey knee raked the side of his head in passing, and
then a thigh pressed against his face: he bit into the thigh
savagely, like an animal, through the thick material. One
of his arms was now imprisoned under the German's leg,
but with his other he could reach upwards, towards a face
– a snapping mouth, like his own – a rough chin – and a
throat –

He clamped his fingers on the throat, but as he did so a
hand fastened on his own throat, the thumb digging
agonizingly into the soft angle of his jaw. He lashed out
furiously with his leg, which was half across the German's
chest. For a moment the fingers on his throat lost their

grip, but then the German managed to wrap his other arm round the leg and the fingers tightened again, pushing his head back. He abandoned the attempt to free his leg and concentrated on his enemy's throat, but the pain of the grip on his own windpipe was too great.

Suddenly, he realized that he was no longer trying to subdue the German, he was fighting for his life. The realization caused him to heave wildly in an attempt to break free, but the convulsion failed to loosen the pressure – it was his own grip that was weakening as his neck was forced back towards breaking point, which he could only relieve by pressing downwards into the very neck-grip that was squeezing the life out of him. He could feel his strength ebbing.

His enemy was the stronger man – his consciousness was slipping into darkness – he had taken his enemy at a disadvantage, but his enemy was the stronger man – and defeat was red agony as the carrier burst into flame and came crushing down on top of him –

A great fiery gulp of air, more painful than anything he had ever experienced, burned his chest, straining it to breaking point.

And now another gulp of air – and light and shapes swimming out of focus in the pain, under a crushing weight –

'*Harry!*'

The air was cold now, and he was swimming in sweat, and the weight was gone, and Wimpy was bending over him – Wimpy's face expanding like a balloon, then receding, then expanding again, and finally stabilizing.

He tried to speak, but the words clogged around a great lump in his throat.

'Come on, Harry – we've got to get out of here, old

boy – come on!' Wimpy pulled ineffectually at his hand from far away.

His throat hurt abominably, and his ears were ringing. Wimpy's voice, and other voices, came from beyond the ringing, muted by it. He felt sick, and utterly confused by his surroundings.

Wimpy was supporting himself on a rifle, steadying himself with it. He reached out again.

Bastable came to himself with a jolt. He was still lying between the table and the wall, alongside the German – his right arm was still imprisoned under the German's legs.

There was a loud bang, and the house shook under him, around him. Pieces of plaster fell from the ceiling, exploding on the table.

'We're being shelled – come on!' Wimpy's voice rose. 'For Christ's sake, Harry – come on, man! Now's the time!'

Bastable struggled to his feet from under the dead weight of the German, steadying himself on the edge of the table. Wimpy turned, and began to hobble towards the outside door. Bastable could see the bright sunshine through the glass panels of the door. It surprised him that the glass wasn't broken. It surprised him that he was still alive. The glass ought to be broken, and he ought to be dead.

He looked down. The German's face was grey-white, except where there was a great bloody contusion on his temple, just above his left eye – the blood was bright red, and as he stared at it a globule of it rolled sideways into the hairline above the man's ear, into a congealing clot.

Dead men didn't bleed – the thought came into Bastable's brain as a matter-of-fact observation, divorced from reality. Then, suddenly, he remembered everything, and was very frightened.

Wimpy was fumbling with the door handle. As he opened the door Bastable's fear had resolved itself into its component parts; he didn't want to go out into that fearful outside world of sunlight and Germans, but he couldn't stay here, where there were those great strangling hands coming for him again – or where there would be other Germans any moment now – *Oh, God!*

He lurched forward, steadying himself between the wall and the table. The German groaned under him, and the groan added panic to the lurch, making his final decision for him.

The sunlight was blinding.

Wimpy was hopping ahead of him, half-way across, using the German's rifle to steady himself –

Bastable checked in mid-stride: *the garden was full of dead bodies!*

Wimpy was negotiating the first of two lines of bodies, two neat lines of corpses – British soldiers lying shoulder to shoulder with their boots towards him, wedged so close together that Wimpy was having difficulty getting between them, standing with his good leg while he stretched his bad leg across to place it alongside the butt of the rifle –

God! now he was losing his balance – he was sitting down in the middle of the dead men!

Bastable heard himself cackling hysterically as he raced across the open space towards the living and the dead . . . And he could hear Wimpy swearing incoherently as he dragged him off the dead man he was sitting on –

Something had fallen out of his hand. On the trampled grass between the two lines lay the yellow-and-grey lanyard he had clasped in his hand. He frowned stupidly at it: it seemed impossible to him that he hadn't dropped it

237

when he had fought with the German – it must have been clenched in the hand which had been trapped under the man's body – but there it was, the symbol of fucking pride and death, still with him!

He reached down automatically to pick it up and stuff it back into his pocket – he mustn't leave it there, whatever he did, he must keep it secret and hidden, no one must ever find it.

'Harry!'

Why wasn't anyone shooting at them? The house reared up behind him, with its blank windows staring at him – the open door out of which he had run still swinging on its hinges – why wasn't anyone shooting at him?

'*Harry!*'

Wimpy had reached a door in the brick wall at the bottom of the garden. The second line of bodies had been easier to traverse, they weren't packed so tight, there were gaps in it. Through the open door Bastable glimpsed a dusty track running parallel to the wall and then open country – desperately open country, with no hint of cover.

As quickly as Wimpy opened the door, he closed it again.

'Get back – Germans!' he cried.

Bastable heard the sound of men running beyond the wall. He looked round hopelessly. If there was no cover on the far side of the wall, there was even less on his side; there was only the house itself, and that was too far away, and he didn't want to go back inside it anyway.

Wimpy came hopping towards him, blank-faced and empty-handed. Bastable saw that he had wedged the rifle against one of the struts of the door in an attempt to hold it shut.

'Get down, man!' snapped Wimpy, and threw himself

on to the ground in one of the gaps in the line of dead men.

The latch on the door clicked like a gunshot. Almost simultaneously there was another crash of an exploding shell not far away, just outside the garden. The door rocked as someone put his shoulder to it.

Once again, choice vanished into necessity: before the door could shudder again, Bastable sprang towards the nearest gap and dropped down alongside a dead lance-corporal whose face was swathed in blood-stained bandages, black-spotted with flies. He turned his head away in horror and disgust. The sun blazed above him in a huge pale-blue sky. He closed his eyes against the glare, but it still burned red and hot into his brain.

The door burst open with a splintering bang. He held his breath in the red darkness while a whole new range of sounds swirled around him – the thud of heavy boots on the ground, the jingling clank and scrape of equipment, and the gasping and grunting of men who had been running hard in that equipment, in those boots. He had been dead and blind so often recently that he seemed to be able to understand what was happening in the living world of light outside him much better now: these were sounds he knew and had heard before many times, with only minor variations, though he had never registered them in his memory at the time – the harsh, untuneful noise of fully-equipped soldiers at full speed, with the fear of God or the sergeant-major at their backs, desperate to escape from one or the other –

His chest was bursting again, not under the vice of those terrible fingers at his neck, but under the pressure of fear which sustained his will beyond its ordinary strength, to the point where his senses reeled as they had done without choice before, but now – sound-blotted-out-by-the-train-in-the-tunnel-rumbling-in-his-ears – but now – now-now-now-*now* –

He breathed out with inexpressible relief, beyond fear, grateful to himself for surrendering to life, however brief that surrender might be.

For a second or two he could hear only the sound of air flooding into him. Then there was the endless intermittent *pop-pop-pop*, pause, *pop-pop-pop*, far and near, which was so much part of his existence now that he couldn't tell whether it was inside his head, an echo louder than the reality, or on Vimy Ridge –

Vimy Ridge! *On Vimy Ridge* –

Arras –

Bastable sat up, jerked into life by *Arras*.

The garden was empty again, except for the rows of British dead.

Life and determination flared up in him – *he was alive and free again, against all the impossible odds* – he didn't know why, but he didn't care – *Harry Bastable was alive*, and that was all that mattered!

He leaped to his feet and swung towards the door –

Wimpy?

But Wimpy could only hobble. Wimpy would hold him back, damn it! Without Wimpy he could run like the wind – to Arras –

'Harry – wait for me!'

Damn! The door was open, inviting him through it. And the field beyond, at second glance, was much more promising than his original glimpse of it had suggested: there was a farm cart parked in the middle of it, and the thick grass – or maybe it was young corn of some sort – hid the wheels up to their axles. A dozen yards into that, and a man could drop down and be invisible, and crawl to his heart's content!

All the man had to do was get there.

'Harry!' Wimpy appealed again from behind him. 'Wait for me, Harry!'

Damn the bloody man! thought Bastable savagely. He'd said *when we get the chance, it's every man for himself*, but now, when the chance was here, it was *Harry, wait for me*, damn it!

He cast a last despairing look at the field, and then turned back to Wimpy.

'Come on, then,' he said brusquely, offering his hand.

Wimpy caught the outstretched hand in a fierce grip, his face screwed up with pain. 'Thanks, old boy – but listen – did you hear them back there? Did you understand what they said?'

'Who said – where?' Bastable slid his hand round Wimpy's back, under his arm, to support him. 'Come on –'

'Back there – in the house,' Wimpy cut him off urgently. 'About the Brigadier – did you understand?'

Bastable understood only that Wimpy was talking when he should have been hopping, and nothing else mattered.

'Come on!' he snapped, propelling Wimpy forward through the doorway.

'No, listen – *aargh!*' Whatever Wimpy wanted to say about the Brigadier was lost in the pain of his damaged ankle, which collapsed under him as Bastable dragged him out into the dusty road.

But now Bastable was merciless: pity for Wimpy's aches and pains was blotted out by the sound which shrieked at him from the far end of the track, to his left – the powerful engine-roar and the unmistakable squeal-and-clatter of a tank.

He wanted to drop Wimpy and run, but Wimpy's arm was wound round him too tightly, and at the same time his own panic infected Wimpy, so that they rolled drunkenly against each other in the middle of the track, cursing incoherently at each other, like the losers in a three-legged race.

And they had lost the race – oh, God! they had lost the race –

It wasn't a tank – Bastable was transfixed by the sight of it – it was a weird half-tank, the like of which he had never seen before, with wheels at the front, and tracks at the back, and Germans on the top –

He urged Wimpy forward, knowing that it was hopeless, and they were finished.

And doubly, finally finished: there were tanks – real tanks – issuing out of the trees on the far side of the field directly ahead of them, dust and debris rising from their tracks as they jerked and swivelled on to a diagonal course across the field to cut off their escape. The shallow ditch by the roadside, on the edge of the field, was at his feet, but it might as well have been a thousand miles away, on the other side of the Channel, in another world lost for ever now. Wimpy had been right –

He let go of Wimpy, no longer conscious of his weight, as the leading tank halted abruptly a few yards from the abandoned farm cart. Its gun began to traverse towards him.

Wimpy had known from the start, instinctively: they had been dead from the start, back in the little wood beside DPT 912, but they had been a long time dying, that was all. *How* didn't matter, only *when*. And *when* was *now*, and that was the end of it at last.

Nevertheless, he flinched as the bright spout of fire

242

issued from the tank's gun, and closed his eyes against his death, in the hair's-breadth of time between the sight and the sound he knew he would never hear –

Now!

The crack of the gun, like a magnified rifle-shot, was part of the much louder scrap-metal *bang* of the solid armour-piercing shot hitting the German half-track.

12

Bastable managed one half-second glimpse of the half-track's destruction – one indelible impression of fragments rising up from it and bodies tumbling out of it – before Wimpy saved his life by clasping him around the knees and toppling him into the ditch.

For an instant, as he fell, Bastable was furious with Wimpy for cutting off his vision; then the crack of bullets overhead, only inches away, restored him to sanity.

The tank fired again, punctuating the shouting and screaming with a second clanging metallic *bang*. Bastable pressed himself into the ditch, digging his fingers through the vegetation and the damp mud into the soft earth and fibrous roots beneath in an attempt to hold himself down as close to it as possible, away from the bullets.

Wimpy pushed at him from behind.

'Go on – go on! Move, Harry – for Christ's sake – *move!*'

Move where?

'*Go on!*'

There was only one way he could go, and that was down the ditch, the push indicated. Above them, the tall grass was no longer inviting: the fact that those were now British bullets which were cracking through it didn't make it safer, if anything that only made Bastable more determined not to be hit by them. To be shot by the Germans when the Germans were winning was bad enough, but to be shot by the victorious British, accidentally, was infinitely worse, and wholly unacceptable.

The victorious British!

Bastable started to crawl down the ditch, hugging the mud joyfully. The thought of victory reanimated him, giving him strength and purpose again. All he had to do now was to keep his head and think straight. He didn't have to get away any more – or at least not very far, only to a less-exposed position – he only had to survive until the main force arrived, following the tanks, to rescue him.

The victorious British!

The earth trembled under him, and the rumble of a heavy explosion passed above him. Something big, like an ammunition carrier, had blown up not far away – something big and something German, by God!

The Marne all over again – that had been Tetley-Robinson's phrase. And here, outside Arras, was where the tide of battle was turning at last!

Now, at last, he understood all the noises he had been hearing in the distance, which he had taken for granted had been the sound of a German offensive. But those German soldiers who had burst into the garden had not been searching for him, they had been running away, of course! That heavy breathing and desperate speed had been panic – he ought to have distinguished that, just as he should have realized that the machine-gun fire had been getting closer all the time. And, once again, his slowness in understanding what was happening had nearly been the death of him on the track a minute or two back, when it had been Wimpy's quick thinking that had saved him, as usual.

But now Wimpy was tugging at his boots, trying to hold him back – ?

'W – ?' He held his tongue as he saw Wimpy put a finger to his lips, and then point upwards with the same finger.

The ditch was fully three-foot deep now, and the coarse vegetation growing along its banks almost met above their heads, reducing the sky to a narrow strip of blue and the sunlight to a lattice of brightness dappling green shadow.

The noise of battle outside was still loud, and almost continuous, so that for a moment he was unable to distinguish which sound in it had aroused Wimpy's unerring sixth sense. Then, just as he was about to turn back to Wimpy for explanation, he heard a sharp German word of command snapped out not far away.

Cautiously, against his better judgement but driven by a curiosity that was too strong to resist, Bastable raised himself to his knees in the slimy mud and peered through the fringe of weeds on the lip of the ditch.

At first he could see nothing but the rough surface of the road at ground level, magnified at close quarters, with the red blur of a brick wall on its further side. His eye focused on the bricks and travelled along them until they ended in a pile of rubble. Beyond the rubble, amidst a scatter of single bricks and brick fragments, half a dozen German soldiers strained to manoeuvre an anti-tank gun into position. As he watched them, they finally got the gun where they wanted it, and sank down all around it – all except one, who remained half-crouching with one arm raised.

The crouching man shouted again.

Bastable swivelled in the mud, to search through the screen of weeds on the other side of the ditch for the German's target.

There in the field, not two hundred yards away, was a British tank, alone and stationary, pumping bright fire-flies of tracer ammunition into its own chosen target further down the road, oblivious of its peril.

Bastable wanted to shout out a warning, but his tongue

and his mouth were dry, and he knew that nothing he could do would make any difference. It was as though he was watching an event which had already happened, a preordained tragedy which nothing could alter.

The anti-tank gun went off behind him with an ear-splitting crack, and he stared in horror, waiting for the tank to explode. But to his unbelieving surprise it remained unaffected, and something small and black ricocheted up, spinning end over end with an extraordinary screaming whine, high above it.

Wimpy was pulling at him, but he beat off the clutching hands.

The tank's turret was beginning to traverse –

The anti-tank gun fired again, pushing Bastable's chin into the weeds. He felt the sharp sting of nettles on his nose and cheek, but the pain was lost in the wonder of seeing a second shot bounce off the tank's armour, with the same hideous screech.

Wimpy succeeded in dragging him down in the very instant that the tank fired back. In the midst of a wild moment of concussive noise beyond the ditch they were locked together in a wrestling match in the mud, oblivious of everything.

Bastable stopped struggling abruptly, letting Wimpy hold him down. He was surprised to find how strong the fellow was.

Someone was screaming hoarsely – scream after scream, each one starting before the previous scream had properly died away, as though the agony could only be released in a continuous cry which the injured man was unable to achieve.

'D'you want to get us both killed?' snarled Wimpy into his ear. 'Have you gone mad?'

Bastable looked up at Wimpy's face, three inches from

his own, and found it barely recognizable, at least not as the face belonging to someone who had been a brother-officer for so many months: it was the face of an angry stranger – filthy and scratched and unshaven and frightened as well as angry, with strands of sparse hair plastered down sweatily across its forehead, and black rings under its eyes – the unshaven face of a tramp, with the foul breath and sour smell of a tramp, not the face of Captain Willis, of the Prince Regent's Own, which he knew.

'Old boy – are you all right?' The anger clouded into concern, and the face was Wimpy's again – not Captain Willis's, but that of the Wimpy he remembered coming out of the mist this morning, on the road to Colembert.

Only a few hours ago . . . could it be only a few hours ago?

The screaming had turned to groaning – the groaning was being drowned by the squeal of tank tracks so close to them that the ground shook beneath his shoulders.

The tank was coming in close to examine its handiwork – he pushed up against Wimpy unavailingly.

'Don't be a fool, man – they'll shoot us down as soon as look at us,' hissed Wimpy. 'They'll shoot everything that moves, don't you understand?'

Bastable relaxed. Wimpy was right, of course – as always. Inside that tank, after having survived those two shots at point-blank range, the crewmen would be bound to fire at every movement without a second thought. All he had to do was to wait for the infantry following behind – all he had to do was to keep his head, and be safe at last . . .

He nodded at Wimpy, and tried to grin at him. Tramp or not, smelly or fragrant, Wimpy had saved him once and twice and ten times over – and once was all a man needed to turn a comrade into a blood-brother – and he

248

loved every filthy line and seam on that stranger's face
above him more than he had loved anything in his life
before, and it was incomprehensible to him that he could
ever have disapproved of Wimpy, never mind actually
disliked him. But that had been in the lifetime of Henry
*Bar*stable, who was also a stranger, not in Harry Bastable's shorter, truer span of existence.

Wimpy reflected the grin back at him, and relaxed the
pressure. 'Your trouble, old boy, is that you're too bloody
brave by half – that's your trouble. I suppose it comes of
having no imagination.'

Brave?

'No good frowning – I've seen you in action, and I
know,' Wimpy nodded at him, smiling half-ruefully. '"Up
and at 'em" is your motto, and that's all very well when
it's a battalion attack, but it won't do now, Harry – it
won't do at all. Because that's not what's required now.'

Brave? But that wasn't true – it was the exact opposite
of the truth.

'No good rolling your eyes and denying it.' The half-
grin was sad now. 'It takes a coward like me to know a
brave man – "cowards die many times", and I've been
dying with quite monotonous regularity recently, I can
tell you . . . Only we can't afford for you to die just yet,
Harry, old boy – you wanted to go up the hill, and you
wanted to have a go in the lorry . . . and you wouldn't
leave me back there – *I know* – and thanks for that, old
boy – even though you were wrong there . . . except that
you were also right, as it happens . . .'

Once Wimpy started to talk nothing would stop him,
that was something Bastable – Harry Bastable – *did* know.
But, for the rest, it was hard to understand how a bright
chap like Wimpy could get everything so bloody well
back-to-front, even to the point of believing that he had

deliberately lingered back in the garden and at the garden gate, when the very opposite had been the true case – when he, the heroic Harry Bastable, had wanted to leave Wimpy in the lurch, only Wimpy had been too quick for him, hanging on to him like the Old Man from the Sea.

'Except that you were right, Harry,' repeated Wimpy. 'Because you've got to run for it now. Or at least crawl for it, anyway!'

God! And now he couldn't even understand what Wimpy was driving at, with his being *wrong* and yet *right* at the same time.

The tank was moving away. He could hear it clattering and its machine-gun firing intermittently, but the sounds were no longer so close, and as he listened to them they faded until they were almost part of the continuous background firing further off.

'Now . . . listen to me, Harry – ' Wimpy relaxed the pressure on him, but still pinned him down into the ditch's muddy bottom ' – with my ankle I'm not going to run anywhere. So you'll have to go on without me – do you understand?'

That was what they had agreed on in the first place, and it had been Wimpy himself who had thought better of it, thought Bastable. But now the emergency was over, and all they had to do was wait for the troops advancing behind the ranks to reach them, such heroics hardly seemed necessary. And if Wimpy would just shut up, then he could concentrate on listening for the first sounds of their rescuers' approach.

'So listen to me now. We were damn lucky under that table back there . . .'

Bastable only half-listened to the droning voice. He didn't need Wimpy to tell him how lucky they'd been . . .

'Incredibly lucky . . .'

250

Incredibly lucky. What would advancing British troops sound like? Like Germans, except that they would be speaking English . . .?

'. . .so if things do go wrong, it's essential that you know what he said too – just in case – do you understand?'

Bastable focused on Wimpy suddenly. He who? He who said – ? 'What?'

'For God's sake, man! Don't you understand what I'm saying? Haven't you been listening?' snapped Wimpy angrily. 'Those two Germans – those SS men – when we were under the table?'

'What about them?'

'Christ! I've just been telling you – about the Brigadier!'

The mention of the Brigadier – Wimpy had never mentioned the Brigadier! – cleared the mists from Bastable's mind instantly.

'What about the Brigadier?'

Wimpy closed his eyes for a moment. 'I'm trying to tell you, old boy – for God's sake!' Bad breath wafted over Bastable. 'When we were under the table one of them asked the other why this Captain Willis had to be scuppered so smartly. And the other one said it was because he had overheard information about the rendezvous the British brigade commander had with the Führer's representative tomorrow. Now – for God's sake – have you got *that*?'

Bastable had that. He just didn't understand it.

'He meant you, Harry, obviously,' said Wimpy. 'At the farm.'

'But . . . but I didn't overhear a damn thing!' protested Bastable. 'I saw him – that's all. I didn't hear anything!'

'They think you did.'

'But I didn't – '

'It doesn't matter. What matters is that the Brigadier is

251

apparently going to give them something so bloody important that they're hell-bent on tomorrow's meeting, whatever the risks – and in the meantime anyone with the PRO lanyard gets the chop just in case.' Wimpy nodded meaningfully.

'But . . . what?'

'What d'you mean "what"?'

'What's so important?'

'I don't know – he didn't say. But he did say where the meeting was. It's at noon tomorrow.'

'What?'

'For Christ's sake don't keep saying "what". I said *where*!'

'I meant "where" – '

'At the bridge between Carpy and Les Moulins, that's where.'

Bastable blinked unhappily. 'Where's that?'

'I haven't the faintest idea, old boy. But it must be somewhere they reckon to have reached by noon tomorrow.'

'How do they know where they'll be then?'

Wimpy frowned back at him. 'Christ! I don't know. They seem to be going where they please – maybe they're leaving that bridge alone for the time being – I don't know . . . It sounded to be quite a step from here, the way he spoke about it . . . But it doesn't matter, anyway. What matters is that you must get to our people and tell them about it – the bridge between Carpy and Les Moulins – got it?'

But all they had to do was to wait for 'our people' to get them, thought Bastable. Yet he owed Wimpy – and more than he could ever manage to repay. So the very least he could do at this moment was to humour him . . .

And anyway, even if that swine of a Fifth Columnist-Brigadier was no longer so important now that the Allies were successfully on the offensive at last in spite of him, there was still vengeance for the Prince Regent's Own – for their murdered comrades – to be extracted.

So Wimpy was still right: whether the swine was a German masquerading in British uniform or a damned traitor to King and Country, the sooner they got him up against a wall in front of a firing squad, the better. That was still their plain duty.

'Yes – ' The word came out as a croak: his throat was raw, and it was painful to swallow, so he completed his acceptance with a vigorous nod. And that hurt almost as much, reminding him how close the German soldier had got to killing him in the house before Wimpy had applied the rifle-butt.

'Good man!' Wimpy rolled off him and pulled back up the ditch, arranging himself more comfortably. The whole of the front of his uniform, what remained of it, was covered with thick pale-yellow mud. Looking down at himself, Bastable discovered that he presented a similar spectacle: when he brushed ineffectually at it he found that it was slimy and glutinous, a mixture of clay and chalk which caked between his fingers.

He looked up again, and met Wimpy's eyes. Wimpy looked down at himself, and then back at Bastable.

'Good thing the Adjutant can't see us now, eh?' The eyes bored into him. 'But never mind, old boy – *at ingenium ingens inculto latet hoc sub corpore*, as Horace has it . . . Except that this is more of a Virgil occasion, I venture to think – more *nunc animis opus, Aenea – nunc pectore firma*, and all that. Time to move the dauntless spirit and the stout heart, right up your street.'

Bastable didn't understand a word of it, but he didn't

253

need to. All they had to do was to survive until the infantry caught up with the armour, but that could be tricky if the infantry was trigger-happy – as they well might be on the edge of the village here. Yet, at the same time, he was loath to move from the relative safety of the ditch, disgusting though it was.

But Wimpy intended them to move on, and what Wimpy wanted was usually best.

He raised himself up gingerly, to peer through the weeds again.

It took him a moment or two to find the German anti-tank gun, which was not where he had last seen it, but overturned in ruin among a scatter of bodies several yards away from its firing position. He reflected fleetingly that the gun-crew had been either very brave or very foolish: they had seen their shot bounce off the tank, and the tank's gun traverse inexorably on to them – and he knew how terrifying that was – but they had stood by their gun like heroes, and had been destroyed with it.

Or perhaps they had been simply rooted to the spot, too frightened to move – as he had been?

He preferred that explanation. Yet it didn't change the insight which went with it: if it had been that gentlemanly German Colonel and his men here, they would have stood by that gun too, and fought it to the last out of duty and courage, he had no doubt about that.

So . . . being brave and skilful – and, what was worse, being decent and ordinary – wasn't a monopoly of the right side. And he should know that better than most other people, because he had abandoned Batty Evans and had wanted to abandon Wimpy, and was fucking useless as a soldier –

A high-pitched whine in the sky above, different from the battle-sounds which banged and thumped and popped ceaselessly not far away – which were even increasing, judging by the crash of exploding shells – wrenched him back to the immediacy of the scene along the road. He pushed his face further through the coarse leaves until he could see up and down it.

The half-tracked vehicle lay silent at one end, with a scatter of bodies like that beside the gun, but with one man hanging two-thirds out of it, as though his feet were trapped; at the other end, in the direction they had been crawling, fifty yards beyond the wrecked gun, a lorry was burning brightly, shreds of flaming canvas dropping off it on to the road. But along the whole length, from one end to another, nothing moved but the flames and the smoke, there wasn't a sign of life anywhere.

He shifted his attention to the other side of the ditch, to the field.

It was empty, except for the farm cart. There was no sign of British infantry, and the tanks had disappeared, leaving no sign that they had ever been there.

The high-pitched whine turned into a shriek which he recognized instantly as one he had heard before. It had been in the distance then, over Belléme, where the Mendips had been – that was only yesterday, but it seemed a much older memory. Now it was closer, uncomfortably closer, but still not directly overhead, and he was heartily glad that it wasn't, and that whoever was at the receiving end of that shriek, it wasn't him.

The ground shook as the bombs exploded, and columns of smoke rose in the distance, one after another.

'They're dive-bombing our chaps.' Wimpy had pulled himself up beside him. 'Naturally.'

Naturally. It was only to be expected. They were bombing our chaps, of course – the RAF wasn't bombing *their* chaps – naturally.

Bastable craned his neck towards the blue sky to try and get his bearings. Without a watch he had lost all track of time, and it seemed to be crawling with impossible sluggishness, so much had happened to him in so few hours. But the sun was lower now than it had been when he had last stared at it, and the sky was paler. Yet . . . yet if the sun was to be relied on those columns of smoke were still between them and where Arras ought to be . . .

'Come on, Harry. You've got to be moving,' said Wimpy softly.

Bastable was already resigned to the inevitable. What he didn't know was which way the inevitable ought to be. But that, at least, he could leave to Wimpy.

'Okay.' He looked expectantly at Wimpy. 'Let's go, then.'

Wimpy shook his head. 'Not me, Harry, old man. You.'

The thunder of the bombs was getting louder: he had lip-read the words, but had misunderstood them.

'What?'

Wimpy held out his hand. 'Good luck, old man – ' his voice rose against the thunder ' – *Audentis Fortuna iuvat* . . . or *Fortis Fortuna adiuvat*, if you prefer Terentius to Vergilius – it comes to the same thing, anyway. You'll get through somehow.'

It wasn't the bomb-sound that was ringing in his ears, it was consternation verging on panic.

'No!' he shouted, as the bombs got closer.

'Yes!' Wimpy shouted back at him. 'You're a good chap, Harry – I TAKE BACK ALL THE THINGS I'VE EVER THOUGHT ABOUT YOU – DO YOU HEAR? ONE OF THE BEST – I KNOW YOU DON'T WANT TO LEAVE ME, BUT YOU'VE BLOODY WELL GOT TO – DO YOU HEAR?'

'NO!' He shook his head vehemently. Leaving Wimpy

didn't come into it: without Wimpy he would be as helpless as a baby – he would do the wrong thing at the first opportunity. 'NO!'

The earth shook so violently around them that fragments of soil fell from the lip of the ditch into the bottom, displaced by the shock wave.

Wimpy shouted at him, but this time the words were lost in noise, Bastable was aware suddenly that he was kneeling almost upright, and crouched down quickly to Wimpy's level. Clods of earth showered down, descending through the half-canopy of vegetation like bombs all around them.

Bastable cowered down beside Wimpy on the bottom of the ditch until the thunder died away. For a moment or two he was unable to think clearly of anything, but then his brain cleared and he was conscious that he was miserable, not frightened.

Wimpy looked at him, white-faced under the grime. 'Phew! That last one was close!'

Obstinacy was what was called for, decided Bastable.

'No,' he snapped.

Wimpy regarded him curiously. 'God! Doesn't anything frighten you?'

Everything frightens me. The words stayed unsaid because Bastable was too miserable to say them. *And not having you to tell me what to do frightens me more than anything else.*

Therefore – obstinacy.

'No,' he said.

'That's what I thought. I just find it hard to believe,' said Wimpy, banging his ear with his palm and then trying to extract dirt from it with his finger.

'We'll go together, or not at all,' said Bastable, abandoning the idea of trying to explain what that 'no' had referred to; if Wimpy had the wrong notion, maybe it would be better not to disabuse him of it, just so long as he stopped arguing as a result of it. 'Come on.'

Wimpy shrugged. 'All right. If you think you can carry me, I can't stop you trying, I suppose . . . even if it doesn't make sense – I shall only hold you back – '

Once Wimpy got started, there was no way of stopping him, he could argue the hind leg off a donkey. All Bastable could think of was to ignore him by standing up and looking around again.

Except for the farm cart, which stood untouched, the field was still empty, but it was different now: there were several large bomb craters in it, the nearest of which was so near that it surprised Bastable that he was still alive to see it.

Down the road, the German lorry was still burning; and now columns of black smoke were also rising up from the village itself in several different places, beyond the trees on the other side of the road. Either accidentally or deliberately there was another Colembert in the making.

He wondered what had happened to the Tyneside soldier who had baffled the Germans, and to the wounded men in the house down the track. So far as he could make out, the house wasn't on fire yet, but he looked away deliberately from it before he was sure, putting the wounded out of his mind. He couldn't do anything for them, so there was no point in thinking about them.

What was worth thinking about was that if they were going to move, then now was the time to do it, while the coast was quite miraculously clear.

He reached down and dragged Wimpy to his feet.

' – and together we'll stand out like sore thumbs, too – ' Wimpy had been rabbiting on all the time down below, but the effect of being raised up into the open closed his mouth at last.

He looked around him jerkily, pivoting on his good leg while leaning against Bastable for support.

'Oh, Christ!' he murmured, and sat down again in the mud.

Bastable ducked down to join him. 'What's the matter? It's all clear, damn it – '

'All clear?' Wimpy grimaced. 'So – we're in the middle of bloody no-man's-land then, old boy, that's what. So we'll probably get the chop from whoever arrives here first – "if it moves, shoot it", that'll be the order of the day.' Wimpy's voice trembled as he spoke.

Bastable felt disappointed that Wimpy had nothing better to offer than a conclusion he had already reached himself, more or less. 'So what do we do?'

Wimpy grimaced again. 'We get out of here – this bloody ditch is too handy, whoever comes this way'll be certain to take cover in it. If we can hide somewhere less obvious we can wait and see how things turn out, maybe.'

This time it was Bastable's turn to grimace. 'Hiding somewhere' sounded like going back into the village, and that was the last thing he wanted to do. Also, waiting to see how things turned out struck an uneasy note of doubt in his mind from which he shied away instinctively.

'There's a house all by itself on this side, just down the road – ' Wimpy indicated the direction with a nod ' – maybe we can find something to eat there, I'm famished – and something to wear, too – ' He pushed at Bastable ' – so get moving, Harry – go on, go on! Crawl, and I'll follow – go on!'

Bastable started crawling. Food was something he hadn't thought about for hours, and even now, although his stomach hurt, he wasn't noticeably hungry. But he was, he realized, quite desperately thirsty and his tongue filled his mouth like a sausage.

To wear?

Wimpy pushed him from behind. 'Go on, damn you – go on!'

To wear? What did Wimpy mean – to wear?

Fifty yards down the ditch, level with the smouldering lorry, a dead German soldier lay waiting for them.

Sweat had rolled down Bastable's forehead into his eyes, until the way ahead had become a green-and-brown blur which he had wanted to clear, but which, with his hands slimy with mud and Wimpy pushing and grumbling at him from behind, he was unable to attend to so long as no obstacle barred his way.

But then there was an obstacle, and the obstacle was the dead German.

Bastable knew the German was dead even before he had wiped all the sweat from his face, not so much because the German didn't move as because nothing could lie there in the mud so uncomfortably – so ridiculously – contorted, regardless of where legs and arms ought to be, and still be alive, so he wasn't frightened, only momentarily shocked, and the shock was momentary because it was overtaken first by revulsion at the thought of having to navigate across the body and then by irritation with the dead man for being where he was, quite unnecessarily occupying the ditch when he hadn't any use for it.

Wimpy had half overtaken him by the time all this had gone through his head.

'Go on – get past him!' The blighter sounded positively eager. 'He won't bite you, poor bastard!'

Passing the German was much more horrible than he had imagined: the body was unbearably soft and for one sickening instant it seemed to be actually trying to embrace him as he squeezed past it, pushing it sideways against the ditch so that an arm flopped over on to his back.

Wimpy had no such qualms; no sooner had he clambered over the body than he turned back to it and started fiddling with its equipment.

'Hold on a tick, Harry . . . we'll have his water-bottle, he doesn't need it now . . . Damn! It's got a bullet through it!' He dropped the water-bottle in disgust and began to pat the dead soldier's pockets. 'Well, then . . . we'll see what else he's got that's worth having . . .'

Bastable closed his eyes on the scene. He knew that it made sense – he himself had robbed the first dead man he had ever encountered, he remembered. But there was something too unpleasantly businesslike about the way Wimpy was setting about the job, as though it was the most natural action in the world.

'Ah!' Wimpy let out an exclamation of pleasure. 'Just the ticket and *two* of them *and* my favourite sort as well! Here, Harry – one for me and one for you, old boy!'

Bastable opened his eyes, and found he was being offered a large bar of Nestlé's milk chocolate.

Wimpy was already eating his, positively wolfing it. 'Here – go on, take it, man – bags of energy and whatnot in it – take it!'

Bastable took the chocolate bar. It was limp and broken, and distorted by heat – the body-warmth of the man who had carried it – and the very thought of eating it sickened him. Even the sight of Wimpy munching made his throat contract painfully.

'I'll eat it later,' he mumbled thickly, stuffing the bar

into the breast-pocket of his mud-encrusted battledress as he plunged down the shaded tunnel of the ditch again, unable to decide which of them daunted him more, the live Wimpy cramming chocolate fragments into his mouth with muddy fingers, or the dead German with his bloody hands and face.

But now, at least, he was able to leave Wimpy behind, first because Wimpy was too busy finishing his revolting meal and then because the ditch became so deep that he didn't have to crawl, but could squelch along upright, screened by the nettles, while Wimpy still laboured on hands and knees behind him. Indeed, he was just beginning to wonder, as the distance widened, if he hadn't been perhaps a teeny bit too quick to discount the liability of that damaged ankle against the advantage of the undamaged wits that went with it . . . when the end of the ditch came in view.

Or not the end, but here it vanished into a drain-pipe, and the drain-pipe carried the bridge which connected the road with the driveway of the house Wimpy had selected as their destination.

On the bridge, canted up at a steep angle with its handles sticking in the air and its pathetic bundles mostly tipped out, was a crude hand-cart which looked as though it had been knocked together out of orange boxes and a pair of old bicycle wheels.

Bastable raised himself cautiously, and saw that one of the bundles wasn't a bundle at all: inside the hand-cart, stretched out in the dust, lay a little old Frenchwoman in a black coat with an imitation fur collar, black woollen stockings and brown carpet slippers.

Bastable frowned at the carpet slippers, and the frown released a rivulet of sweat which ran down between his eyebrows into his right eye, the salt stinging it sharply. Carpet slippers really weren't the sensible thing to wear. He had seen women in the poorer part of Eastbourne wearing carpet slippers just like these, down along Seaside.

Now the sweat had got into his other eye. He blinked at it in an attempt to dislodge it.

He wasn't sure whether the old women down along Seaside wore slippers in the street because slippers were more comfortable, or simply because slippers were cheap: he'd just never thought about it before.

Blinking didn't shift the sweat. He raised his arm and wiped his face carefully with the inner part of his sleeve.

Someone ought to have told the old Frenchwoman not to set out in carpet slippers. It was one thing just walking round the corner to the shops in them, but when it came to walking any distance they'd be worse than useless. She wouldn't have got far in a silly damn pair of carpet slippers –

'What's that you said?' Wimpy's voice came from behind and below. 'Carpet slippers, did you say?'

'I didn't say anything,' said Bastable.

'Yes, you did. You said . . .' Wimpy trailed off doubtfully as he began to pull himself up beside Bastable '. . . something about *carpet slippers*, it sounded – ' He stopped abruptly.

Bastable shook his head angrily and transferred his attention to the house. It was a typical French house, ugly and foreign and quite out of proportion. In his observation, detached houses in France, other than the more substantial better-class ones, were either squat cabins, more like dilapidated stables with their shutters and half-doors, or fussy boxes with one storey too many and no taste in design. This was one of the boxes, only it was no longer fussy, but half-ruined by bomb-blast, every tile shaken loose and every window blown in. Even as he stared at it, a small avalanche of displaced tiles slithered and scraped down the roof, to fall with a crash into the garden below.

'It must have been the bombs just now,' said Wimpy softly. 'The shock, most likely – she doesn't look as though she's got a mark on her, poor thing.'

'Yes,' agreed Bastable automatically.

Eat up your brown Windsor soup before it gets cold, now.

'All right, then – let's get inside, and see what we can find – help me out, old man, there's a good chap – '

The inside of the house was like every other half-bombed house, full of broken things and fallen plaster which crunched underfoot.

Brown Windsor soup.

He leaned Wimpy against the nearest bit of open wall, between a barometer and a tall mahogany hat-stand which had a mirror in the centre of it. The mirror was blemished and pock-marked with age, where its silvering had peeled away, and he resisted the temptation to look at himself in it: whatever Wimpy looked like, he, with his blue jowl, must inevitably look worse, and there was no point in confirming that image.

'Find the kitchen,' commanded Wimpy, pointing down the hallway, 'Don't wait for me, man.'

There were two doors opposite each other at the end of the hall, both ajar, and Bastable took the right-hand one, putting his shoulder to it when it grated and stuck on debris beneath it.

It wasn't the kitchen, it was a parlour of some kind, and it was almost filled with an immense table covered

264

with a beige moquette cloth on which a bowl of artificial fruit was the centre-piece. Both were covered with fallen plaster.

In the corner of the room, by the window, an old man with white hair and a bushy white moustache sat staring at him from the depths of an armchair. A gold watch on a chain hung down from the centre button of his waist-coat. Like the moquette table-cloth and the bowl of artificial fruit, he was covered with dust and fallen plaster.

Bastable pushed back out of the room so hurriedly that he ran into Wimpy in the passage.

'W – !' Wimpy staggered on one leg, reaching for the support of the wall. 'I say – steady on, old boy!' he protested.

Bastable shouldered the second door open without bothering to try the door handle.

This was the kitchen.

Pots and pans, a sink with a hand-pump for water, a great black range – there was still a fire smouldering in it.

They had left it too long, they had left it too long and too late, the old couple had! They had been too old to take the road – too old and too foolish and too afraid – and too late . . .

Or . . . this had been all they had, everything they had in the world, and they hadn't wanted to leave it, couldn't bring themselves to leave it – the barometer and the hat-stand and the artificial fruit and the pots and pans –

And the British had gone, anyway.

And the Germans had come – God! Maybe they could remember another time, the old couple – maybe they had been here that other time, when the British hadn't gone, and the Germans hadn't come – but this time the British had gone, and the Germans had come, and they had been safe after all, because not even the Germans would bother about an old couple in their ugly little house on the edge of the village.

And then the British had come back and it had been too late.

God damn and blast it all to hell!

'The old boy's dead too, poor old bugger,' said Wimpy from the doorway behind him.

Bastable turned towards him.

'Is that a parcel of food on the table there?' Wimpy pointed with one hand. In the other hand, with the gold chain dripping down between his fingers, was the old man's watch. 'And what's in that jug?'

'What are you doing with that watch?'

'It's still going – is that milk, by any chance?'

'What-are-you-doing-with-that-watch?'

'Don't shout, Harry – the Germans took my wrist-watch – we need a watch . . . Is that milk?' Wimpy frowned at him. 'Don't be a fool. Harry – *he* doesn't need it. And we do.'

The blood stopped drumming in Bastable's head. He had been about to make a fool of himself by losing control, like the coward he was, while Wimpy was behaving like a soldier.

There was an untidy parcel on the green-and-white chequered oil-cloth which covered the kitchen table, and a tall white jug beside it – all in the inevitable litter of plaster.

He reached forward and picked up the jug. There was plaster also on the thick yellow cream, and a large black fly moving feebly in it, drowning slowly in the midst of plenty.

He stuck a dirty finger into the cream and flicked the fly out of the jug, and lifted the jug to his lips.

The milk under the cream and plaster was thin and

266

sour, and marvellously, gloriously cool and refreshing as it ran down his sandpaper throat, and out of the corner of his mouth down his chin. He had never drunk anything so beautiful in his life, it was all the drinks he had ever drunk, on all the occasions when he had been thirsty, rolled into one blissful quenching.

'Hold on, old boy – leave some for me then,' said Wimpy reproachfully, reaching across the corner of the table.

Bastable looked down into the jug, and found that he had drained two-thirds of it already.

'Thanks – ' Wimpy hopped round and grabbed the jug from him – ' – thanks *a lot* – ' he tipped the jug against his face, the watch-chain swinging from one hand in a spatter of overflowing milk.

Well, fuck you too, old boy, thought Bastable unrepentantly, aware that he was still thirsty – and there was the pump at the sink, just waiting for him!

For the first dozen strokes the thing only squeaked and wheezed as he banged the handle up and down with increasing fury. Then he felt the pressure draw and pull against the plunger, and in the next instant a powerful stream of water splashed into the sink beside him.

He lowered his face into it, still pumping with one hand; this was better than the sour milk even – it went into his mouth and on to his cheeks and into his eyes and down his neck, slaking his thirst and washing away mud and sweat at the same time, making him alive and almost human again.

He was aware that Wimpy was waiting his turn, but Wimpy could bloody well wait his turn, and that was that – he managed to get his neck under the jet, and felt the delicious coldness spread across his scalp, soaking in and saturating, and driving everything out of his head with the relief of it, even the awareness – just for a moment, the awareness – that the whole bloody world was full of dead people – dead Fusiliers – dead officers and dead men – and dead Mendips and dead Tynesiders, and dead Germans, and old women dead in the dusty road and old men dead in the chairs – *dead fucking everyone, except him and Wimpy, who ought to have been dead ten times over, but weren't, but were alive – alive –*

In the end, he let Wimpy have his turn under the pump, starting him off and then fastening his hand on the pump-handle as he also spluttered and porpoised with relief under the deluge.

He was hungry now – dripping wet, and with his uniform still caked with mud – but too hungry to care about that.

He tore open the parcel on the table. There were the usual long French loaves – yesterday's bread, or maybe last week's by the crumbly hardness of it – and a smelly round cheese, and an even smellier sausage, full of garlic, which he hated, but which he bit into nevertheless.

'*Harry!*'

Wimpy grabbed him by the arm and swung him round just as the panic in the cry got through to him.

'What?'

'*Christ* – ' Water was dripping down Wimpy's face, but words for once had failed him, he could only point through the broken window, down the length of the kitchen garden at the back of the house, towards the field beyond.

Tanks –

German tanks –

Oh, God! Oh, God! Oh, God!

Panic again!

* * *

268

'Wait for me – help me!' cried Wimpy.

Bastable was already at the door, and he had no intention of coming back, but Wimpy had no intention of being left behind either and he had somehow reached Bastable before Bastable was able to get through the door into the hallway, and he hung on like grim death once he'd made contact.

They lurched down the passageway, bumping from one side to the other.

'Up the stairs – up the stairs,' cried Wimpy, pushing him sideways towards the newel-post.

Bastable looked up the staircase. It was steep and it was narrow, and he was never going to be able to haul Wimpy up there, one step at a time . . . But he was also never going to get Wimpy out through the front door and down to the safety of the ditch in time, either: this was the moment to drop him and run – it had come at last –

Clear through the open front door came the hideously familiar squeal-and-roar, terrifyingly loud.

They were trapped. They had waited too long, just as the old couple – the old man and the old woman – had done before them. They had left it too long and too late, and now they were trapped – just as the old couple had been.

'Up the stairs – ' Wimpy pawed at him ' – *carry me!*'

Batsable bent down automatically at the word of command, and Wimpy followed it himself by flopping down across his shoulder in obvious preparation for a fireman's lift.

'Okay – *oof!*' The next part of the command was cut off as Bastable stood up and Wimpy's head crashed against the barometer.

Bastable found himself staggering round in a circle. It wasn't that Wimpy was too heavy – he was actually much lighter than he looked . . . but there was a mouthful of sausage stuck in Bastable's throat which he had forgotten about, but which now refused either to go down or come up while all his muscles were concentrating on holding his burden in position: he gagged and choked, and Wimpy's head hit something else – either the newel-post or the hat-stand – or maybe it was Wimpy's feet . . .

The sausage went down with a painful gulp; the stairs reared in front of him and he took them at the double, in a rush, driven upwards by the sound of the tanks outside. It occurred to him as he went up that the cellar – if the house had a cellar – would be a safer place in which to take refuge. But then, of course, that would probably be the first place the Germans would look.

The rush took him to the top of the stairs – and also to the bleak thought that if the cellar wasn't safe, the bedrooms were hardly likely to be safer; he had come up here simply because Wimpy had told him to, and he was now accustomed to doing whatever Wimpy ordered for lack of any initiative on his own part. But unless Wimpy had another bright idea to go with his last order they were even more hopelessly trapped up here than at ground level.

There were only three doors to choose from on the tiny landing, and he was just about to ask if Wimpy had a preference when he caught sight of another stair through a gap in a curtain which at first glance he had dismissed as concealing a cupboard. Of course – the house had another floor above this one!

Driven by the same instinctive obedience which had taken him up the first stair, he plunged through the curtain up the second. It was much narrower and steeper – so narrow and steep that with Wimpy on his shoulder he could only keep his balance by accelerating up it with his face only inches from bare wooden treads in front of him, until he issued out through the square hole of a trap-door and fell sprawling on to the floorboards of the attic above.

The sole contents of the attic were two large tin trunks, wide open, with clothes strewn around them.

In between them, crouched under the eaves, was a little girl.

13

Harry Bastable and the little French girl stared at each other in dumb horror.

Little girls, of all the different species of children, were the worst, the very worst –

LOST CHILDREN . . . *in the case of female children, male staff will at once summon a lady assistant to deal with the child. On no account –*

The very worst. Where he hated the mindlessness of babies he actively feared little girls – had feared them ever since that hideous occasion during his time as a trainee manager in London when one irate mother had reclaimed her lost child not with gratitude but with foul suspicions and wild threats –

'Stop pawing at 'er, you dirty rotter – I saw you! I'll report you, I will – I know your sort – I'll report you, I will!'

He had only been trying to comfort her. She had put her arms round his neck, and she had seemed to like him, and he had only been trying to comfort her – he hadn't known what else to do to stop her crying.

In Bastable's of Eastbourne it had been different, it had been easy:

'Miss Brown! Miss Hartland! Mrs Summers – see to this child, please – at once!'

* * *

The little French girl's chest inflated with one long shuddering breath, and Harry Bastable didn't know what to do – was incapable of either words or action – to stop her from crying it out, to quench the sound before it burst forth from her.

Miss Brown, Miss Hartland, Mrs Summers –

'Sssh! Sssh, ma petite – nous-somme-de-amis – *ssh!*'

Wimpy had rolled off him like a sack of potatoes, as though half-stunned, as he collapsed on to the attic floor a moment before. But now, incredibly, Wimpy was on his hands and knees – or on one hand and two knees, the other hand lifted into a finger at his lips cautioning the frightened child into silence.

'Sssh!'

The child lifted her hands to her face – two small, grubby hands tipped with black finger-nails – and subsided noiselessly through them. Bastable looked quickly from her back to Wimpy, and back to her again, and back to Wimpy, torn apart by relief, and by contempt for himself – *Sssh!* was a universal sound: why hadn't *Sssh!* come to his lips? – and admiration for Wimpy's astonishing resilience in adversity, which made time stand still when there was no time left.

'Clothes!' said Wimpy.

'What?'

'Clothes, man – clothes!' Wimpy rummaged in one of the tin trunks. 'Clothes, by God!'

He was ignoring the child now: he was kneeling beside the trunk, holding up one garment after another, throwing this one aside, measuring that one against himself, feverishly, as though his life depended on outfitting himself.

'What?'

'Look in the other one – don't just lie there, old boy – find yourself some togs . . . Ah! Now *that's* more like it . . . and *that* – go on, man, for Christ's sake – look in the other one!'

Wimpy spread his arms, crucifying himself against a blue-striped shirt as he spoke, then throwing the shirt down in a growing pile beside him. 'Yes – ? No . . . *Ah* – '

It was unreal – it was a nightmare.

Bastable rose to his knees and swivelled to the second trunk. He knew what Wimpy was about, but he didn't want to do what Wimpy intended, yet there was nothing he could do to stop the blighter, he knew that too: the nightmare wasn't unreal, it was truly and irrevocably what was happening to him.

An overpowering smell of camphor assailed him.

Layers of tissue paper, crumpled and uncrumpled –

A feather boa – long cylinders, which he knew contained ostrich feathers: his mother had ostrich feathers in cylinders just like that – *ostrich feathers* – from Grandmother's day.

Dresses . . . he tore the tissue paper from them. White silk – white, but with a touch of yellowing age: white silk and lace fluffed up . . . It was a wedding dress – a wedding dress –

The old woman lay in the road in her black coat with the fur collar, her thin legs in their black stockings – and the carpet slippers, the carpet slippers –

The camphor-smell sickened him, and he felt his throat contracting and rising, summoning up the undigested garlic sausage from his stomach.

The wedding dress between the tissue paper – the carpet slippers in the dusty road, beside the ridiculous

274

hand-cart piled with bundles – and the sweat cold on his forehead, and the vile garlic in his mouth – *nightmare!*

'You've got the woman's trunk – there'll be nothing in there . . . Here, try this . . . try these, Harry – go on, take them, man – ' Wimpy thrust garments into his hands.

Bastable looked down at what he had been given: a jacket of some sort . . . or more like a tunic . . . of coarse blue denim cloth, old and patched and faded to a pale indeterminate blue-grey, with trousers to match. He had seen French labourers wearing clothes like these in Colembert; if they belonged to the old man downstairs – the old man lying dead in his parlour, in the ruin of his home, with his wife lying dead in the road outside – they must date from another age, another time, many years ago, before the old man had come up in the world to the dignity of this ugly little house; and yet, for some reason, the old woman hadn't thrown them away, but had washed them and ironed them, and stowed them away in the old tin trunk in the attic – for some reason, for some reason, for some unfathomable reason –

He didn't want to put them on, but more than that he didn't want to take off the wreckage of his battledress: that would be to burn his boats finally, to cross the last frontier between Captain Bastable and a nameless fugitive.

'I say, Willis – look here . . .'

Wimpy had already stripped himself down to a filthy string vest, and was unbuttoning his trousers.

'What is it?' Wimpy frowned at him.

'I mean . . . is this . . . wise?'

What did he mean? He searched in his confused thoughts for what he meant, that would make sense to Wimpy.

'If we're not in uniform they can shoot us, I mean.'

275

The frown became pitying. 'I rather thought that was their general idea anyway, old boy.' Wimpy transferred his attention to removing his collar studs from his shirt and attaching them to the civilian shirt. When he had completed that task he rummaged again in the trunk and finally produced a collar-box.

Batsable watched him with a growing sense of desperation. In another moment it would be too late, he felt.

'Out of hand, I mean – Willis!'

'Eh?' Wimpy upended the box and selected a stiffly-starched wing-collar. 'Out of hand? Yes . . . I haven't worn one of these since Repton . . . And one size too big, I'd guess – but better too big than too small . . . Yes, well, that's what I meant too, Harry – out of hand or in hand, it amounts to the same thing now that we've done a bunk, I shouldn't wonder.' He looked up at Bastable. 'Frankly, old boy, I don't believe we've got a prayer together – in uniform. But out of uniform . . . as civilians – as refugees – the Jerries don't give a damn for refugees, they're too busy winning the war . . . out of uniform, maybe we *do* have a chance still – that's what I mean.'

'But – I can't speak a word of French – '

'Then don't speak at all. Let me do the talking – I'll say you're dumb.' Wimpy gave him a calculating look. 'I'll say you're a half-wit too, if you like, old boy.'

That was too close to the bone, and Bastable had a shrewd idea that it was intended to be so. 'You think you can pass as a Frenchman, then?' He tried to infuse sarcasm into the question.

'Not among Frenchmen – no. But to a German, Harry – could you tell a French-speaking German from a French-speaking Frenchman? Because I'm damned if I could.' So saying, Wimpy pulled the civilian shirt over his head and plunged his arms into its sleeves, as though to

276

leave unsaid but clearly stated that the matter was over, the conversation ended and the decision made.

Bastable eyed the faded work-clothes on his lap. Wimpy had set aside a smart black coat and pin-striped trousers for himself, which, with the wing-collar, was the universal uniform of the bank manager and the senior civil servant – which, taken all together, must have been the old man's very best suit for formal occasions, presumably – while leaving him, Harry Bastable, with the role of the dumb servant, the stupid peasant, the half-wit!

It was a damnable, downright offensive thing to do without consultation. But the bitter truth which he had to face, although it was nonetheless insulting for being true, was that if this was what they were going to do, then this was the way it had to be done: without one word of French he was no better than an idiot – he had learned that already. And, what hurt even more was that beneath that humiliation there was a dark suspicion about his own lack of sense and courage, which the last twenty-four hours had raised within him.

He closed his eyes and stripped off his battledress blouse and shirt – ripped them off, rather, spilling buttons and feeling the filthy sweaty material tear, hating what he was doing and what he was about to do with equal misery.

Harry Bastable was dying again: just another death to add to all those previous deaths he had submitted to, on the way to that one real, inevitable one, waiting for him somewhere ahead –

'That's better . . . a bit big, maybe, but I can hitch them up as high as possible – not bad, though . . . not bad at all – '

Wimpy was mumbling to himself in the background, against another background of the noises of war which were still all around them, but which the pounding of his own head blotted out as he fumbled with the buckles of his gaiters and tore his mud-caked trousers down over his equally muddy boots.

Damn, damn and damn! Where Wimpy's borrowed clothes were too big, his were almost too small: one heavily-patched knee, the stout material thinned down by a thousand wash-days, stretched and split under the pressure, to reveal the dirty white leg beneath – damn! And the final buttons of the trousers were impossible, and even though the gap was covered by the tunic, which was mercifully designed for a looser fitting, there were three full inches of hairy wrist sticking out of the sleeves.

'Ooof!' Wimpy exclaimed. 'My bloody-ankle!'

Bastable stopped looking at the travesty of a French working-man which was himself and looked at Wimpy.

He knew, as he looked, that there had been one part of his mind which had been chattering in the background all the time while he had been stripping off his own uniform and cramming himself into the denim tunic and trousers . . . which had been chattering all the time, *What will Willis look like? What will Willis look like?* because this mad scheme depended on what Wimpy looked like, and because he knew in his heart that there was no chance, no possibility, that Wimpy in an ill-fitting black coat and pin-striped trousers and wing-collar could look anything other than . . . ridiculous and laughable and utterly impossible.

And yet, it wasn't so – even standing there without his boots on, balancing himself on one leg in his stockinged feet, it wasn't so –

The clothes *were* too big, not much too big, but no floor-walker in the men's department of Bastable's of Eastbourne would have dared to send a customer out in those clothes and still hope to keep his job when the customer's wife stormed back into the store: they had the

278

same effect that such over-sized clothes always had on their wearer, shrinking him smaller than his own size – just as the clothes he himself was wearing would make him bigger and more awkward than he really was.

'Well?' said Wimpy, brushing dust from one black sleeve. 'Well?'

He was smaller, and he wasn't Wimpy – Wimpy, whom he had only ever seen in well-fitting tweeds, other than in the different uniforms of the regiment, from sharply-pressed battledress to the immaculate mess-kit of the Prince Regent's Own, with its primrose-yellow-and-dove-grey facings – it wasn't that Wimpy, those Wimpys, whom he already knew.

But it was another Wimpy.

'Well?' repeated Wimpy.

Another Wimpy – adam's apple prominent as it never had been before above the too-roomy collar, with its tightly knotted black tie: a Wimpy from behind some desk stacked with invoices and printed forms and bank statements, whom he didn't know.

'For God's sake, Harry – '

'You look all right. Except for the feet, Willis.'

'You look . . . bloody marvellous, old boy – feet and all.' Wimpy looked down at his own feet. 'But my ankle's going to be a problem again, I'm afraid.' He shook his head. 'I don't think I can even get my boot back on again, either.'

'Marvellous?'

Wimpy raised his eyes. 'Ferocious, let's say – if you could just manage to look a bit more frightened and stupid, that would be more proletarian . . . But you damn well don't look like a British officer on the run, old boy. In fact, all you need is a cloth cap, and I've got one here . . . It's a bit too clean, but if you rub some mud from

279

your uniform on it – and then some dust from the floor
. . . then, you'll do, Harry, you'll do, by God!'

Bastable accepted the cap, half-reassured, half-choked
with distaste. He had never worn a cloth cap in his life,
clean or dirty –

'Pull it down a bit more – and push the peak up . . .
that's it – marvellous! Bloody marvellous – you look
absolutely bang-on now, if you can only get the right
expression . . . The only trouble is . . . my . . . bloody
. . . ankle – ' Wimpy set his stockinged foot down flat on
the floor and gingerly put his weight on it ' – *aargh!* It's
no good, Harry – you'll have to go without me. Even with
a stick – even if we could find a crutch – I shall only hold
you back.'

The ankle wasn't the only trouble, thought Bastable
savagely: it was only the beginning of their troubles. But
now, dressed as he was, he was finally committed to
Wimpy beyond any alternative plan of escape. Without
Wimpy to speak for him he was helpless. Even if he had
to carry the fellow – even if he had to drag him . . . Or
even –

Or even?

'Sit down, man.'

'It's no good, Harry – '

'*Sit down!*' Bastable turned back to his own trunk,
throwing out the feather boa and pushing the wedding
dress aside. The old woman had thrown nothing away –
there were garments here which hadn't been stocked on
Bastable's shelves for twenty years – but he had caught
the feel of something he recognized down there at the
bottom – damask table-cloths at worst, but . . . sheets at
best – ?

Sheets. Fine linen sheets, not common-or-garden
cotton!

He commenced ripping the fine linen sheets into strips.

'Harry . . . it's still no good. If you wrap it up like a football I still won't be able to walk more than a dozen yards on it – it's no good – '

'Shut up!' Bastable piled all his bruised self-esteem into the order, and felt the better for it. For this moment at least, if only for this moment, he was in command. For he had seen what Wimpy had missed, or had remembered what Wimpy had forgotten.

He was further rewarded with an indrawn hiss of pain as he drew the sock off the foot: the injured ankle was discoloured and hugely swollen, to the point of being misshapen. If it was only a very bad sprain, then Wimpy was lucky. So much for being such a clever motor-cyclist, then!

'This is going to hurt.'

'Tell . . . ahh! . . . Tell me something I don't know . . . old boy!' Wimpy drew a deep breath.

Bastable frowned over his work, trying to remember what he had learned in his first-aid lessons about bandaging. Under there, and over there, and round there – that was it.

'It . . . still won't . . . keep – keep . . . me going more than . . . a few yards – ' Wimpy was gritting his teeth now; there had to be a broken bone there somewhere, for an uninformed guess.

'I only want a few yards. Just as far as the road.'

'What?'

'There's a hand-cart in the road there. You can sit in that.' Bastable split the end of the bandage, knotted the split, and then knotted the ends. The foot did look a bit like a football now, or the swollen extremity of a gouty admiral; and as a bandaging job it lacked the layered neatness by which the first-aid instructor had set such store. But it would do – it would have to do, anyway. 'There!'

'Oh . . .' Wimpy's face was beaded with sweat, and chalky white under the sweat, so that Bastable was suddenly ashamed at his professional disregard of the pain he had caused. 'That's good thinking – I'd quite forgotten about that, Harry. That's *very* good thinking!'

Bastable looked at him quickly, and the shame was cancelled by the surprise in the voice: one thing Wimpy didn't expect of him, apart from bull-at-a-gate courage, was thinking of any sort, clearly.

'There's a pair of old shoes here – I'll put one on my other foot, it doesn't matter if it's too large . . . And you get rid of the uniforms – stuff them down somewhere out of sight, just in case.' Wimpy's voice had regained its sharp note of command before the sweat had dried: the three weeks' seniority had only been momentarily re-imposed and the reality was back again.

'And take a look out of the window, too . . .' Wimpy rose carefully to his feet. 'Remember to stand well back, or they'll see your face – *aaah!* Not so bad . . . bad enough, but not so bad . . . until Boadicea can reach her chariot – go on, man, go on!'

Bastable fished around among the ruined finery and the heirlooms from the old woman's bottom drawer for the fragments of his uniform. As his hand closed on the battle-dress blouse he felt something hard in one of the pockets, which surprised him for a second; of course, the Germans had taken everything from him – his identification, Mother's letters, his money and his pocket-knife, and even his broken watch from his wrist – but this . . . what was this?

This was the bar of chocolate from the dead German

soldier, which Wimpy had plundered – it reminded him that he was still hungry.

It reminded him also that there was one other thing in his pockets; there was still the lanyard of the Prince Regent's Own in his trousers. It was something he could neither safely take with him nor safely leave behind, damn the thing!

He was ravenously hungry: he tore at the wrapper on the chocolate, his fingers suddenly clumsy with desire.

He stuffed a piece into his mouth, and then remem-berred guiltily that he ought to be disposing of the uniforms and peering out of the window, and looked towards Wimpy – up towards Wimpy, who was still gently trying his ankle above him.

'Do you want some?' He offered up a wedge as an expiation for not doing what he ought to be doing.

'Give it to her,' Wimpy nodded to his right.

To her?

Christ! He had clean forgotten about the child! She was still crouched there in her little ball of fear under the eaves, to one side of the broken windows – hands lowered now, clenched in front of her cheap print dress, dirty little dried-tear-stained face turned towards him now – and he had forgotten about her so completely that he had stripped off down to his filthy underwear, right in front of her as though she hadn't been there at all. It didn't seem possible that he could ever have done such a thing. But he had.

'Go on, man – ma petite – ' Wimpy switched into a string of French words, soft and soothing, amongst which Bastable was only able to distinguish 'shoc-o-la', and then chiefly because Wimpy pointed to the chocolate in his hand.

'Say something,' murmured Wimpy.

Bastable opened his mouth, but no words came to him:

he could think of nothing to say in English, let alone French. The child was plainly terrified anyway, and therefore beyond reasoning with, even if he had known what to say, if indeed there were any words for such a situation, she was in no condition to understand them. The soothing sounds Wimpy had made hadn't registered in the slightest. All he could communicate was his own helplessness and fear, which could only make matters worse.

'Give her the chocolate.' Exasperation edged Wimpy's voice. 'I'll look out of the window – you calm her down, Harry. You know how to handle kids.'

It was useless to protest that this was the very reverse of the truth, before he had even finished speaking Wimpy had pivoted on his good leg and had commenced moving down the attic towards the other window.

Meanwhile, the chocolate was melting into a sticky mess between Bastable's fingers. He looked at the little girl hesitantly, extending his arm towards her, offering her the mess.

'Chocolate . . . chocolate . . . er . . . pour . . . vous?' he managed.

No recognition. If anything, the poor little thing seemed to contract into an even tighter ball.

'Bon . . . chocolat – bon?' Their eyes were almost on the same level. Hers were huge and round and dark, looking at him and yet not looking at him – not properly focused on him. Her hair was black, under a coating of dust and small fragments of plaster – blacker even than his own. It was unusual to see a child with such black hair . . . not that he had ever been in the habit of staring at children, or even noticing them. But that was the sort of hair which would shine like a raven's wing with proper brushing.

He was being stupid, offering her his chocolate at this

distance, a yard beyond her reach. Even if she wanted it, she wasn't going to move.

But it would be a mistake to stand up, above her.

Why was he doing this?

It would be a mistake, therefore he must crawl that yard, through the wreckage of her grandmother's linen sheets, through the tangle of her grandmother's wedding dress – her mother's wedding dress? – which she would never wear in her turn.

Mustn't take his eyes off her, either.

He moved on knees and one hand, the other still extended towards her.

'Chocolat?'

She was focusing on him, and the little clenched hands moved as the flat chest behind them inflated with a long fearful breath.

Poor little mite, thought Harry Bastable – *poor little mite and poor Harry Bastable, both equally stretched beyond endurance!*

The chocolate was disgusting – revolting – a dead man's possession; he flung it to one side with a twitch of his wrist and stretched out both arms to her, opening his hands to offer her the only thing he had that was his, the comfort of his own loneliness, his own confusion and fear.

She was in his arms.

'Good man!' said Wimpy. 'I knew you could do it, old boy.'

'What?' Bastable moved his head just enough to take Wimpy in, without disturbing the child more than was necessary.

'I said, "I knew you could do it" – you've got a way with them, Harry – that's all. But now we must go.'

'What?'

'We must go – downstairs – on the double, too – '

'Why?'

'The fields are crawling with Jerries, old boy – tanks and infantry – crawling with the blighters . . . what we want is . . . something white to wave – ' Wimpy bent down and picked up the remains of the torn linen sheet ' – this'll do fine.'

'Why?' With the child hanging on to him so desperately, Bastable was unwilling to move from the safety of the attic.

Wimpy tore savagely at the sheet. 'I told you – the Jerries are all around . . . and if they start searching the houses for our chaps before we can get outside, then I want to be ready for them, old boy. That's why!'

'But . . . won't we be safer here?'

'I wouldn't like to bet on it – here, take this strip – ' Wimpy thrust a large square of sheet into one of Bastable's hands ' – wave that as you go out – '

'*Out?*' The word squeaked.

'That's right – out. Now's the time to go through them, if there's ever going to be a time – before they've got themselves organized, don't you see?' Wimpy examined the piece of sheet he had torn for himself. 'If I could attach this to a stick or something . . . Now's the time: we'll just be civilians running away – with a bit of luck they won't bother about us, they must have seen thousands of civilians trying to beat it out of the line of fire. The sooner we get out of their way, the better – for them as well as us – don't you see?'

Bastable saw. But now, he also saw, things were different. The little limpet which was attached to him made them different.

'But what about the child?'

'We take her with us – of course.' Wimpy frowned at

286

him. 'It was your idea in the first place, Harry – and a bloody good idea, too, by God!'

'My – idea?' Bastable stroked the little girl's back with his empty hand, feeling the back-bone through her dress, quietening the sobs to an irregular trembling.

'With the baby – our little Alice that was.' Wimpy peered down the trap-door opening. 'The child will take Alice's place, that's all.'

'What?'

'She's part of our disguise, don't you see?' Wimpy looked up at him. 'Come on.'

Bastable tightened his own hold on the limpet protectively. 'No, Willis. I won't have it! We can't risk her.'

'We won't be risking her. The Germans won't shoot a child. They're not savages.'

'No, damn it!'

'She'll double our chances . . . They'll not look twice at two civilians *with a child*.' Wimpy shook his head in surprise. 'You took the baby, Harry – what's the difference taking the child?'

Bastable blinked at him. 'I . . . I couldn't leave the baby – on the road . . .' He trailed off, baulking at the truth.

'Then you can't leave *her* – here.' Wimpy gestured round the attic. 'What'll happen to her if our chaps counter-attack again? For God's sake, Harry – what'll happen if they don't counter-attack, come to that? Do you want to leave her behind?'

Whatever they did would be wrong. To stay here was out of the question. But to take her with them . . . or to leave her behind . . . each of those alternatives was equally monstrous, the way Wimpy had put them to him. If there had been no Germans outside he would surely have reversed his argument, but so long as there were

Germans to be bamboozled the child wasn't an encumbrance – she was the best part of their disguise.

And Wimpy was right, of course – as always.

But that didn't make it *right* –

'Harry . . .' Their eyes met, and Bastable understood that Wimpy already knew exactly what he was doing, and why he was doing it, and the price of the doing. 'Remember the Brigadier, Harry. We've still got a job to do – remember?'

Bastable remembered, and was ashamed and angry with himself.

He had forgotten again. He had been so busy saving his own skin, so preoccupied with his own fears, he had forgotten that the mischief the false Brigadier could do far outweighed this little life in his arms, however defenceless and innocent.

'I'll go first,' said Wimpy.

'No – ' It was all academic, anyway. He couldn't stay here, and he couldn't prise the limpet loose.

'Yes.' Wimpy swivelled awkwardly beside the trap-door opening, and sank to his knees above the top step. 'I'll have to go down backwards . . . my bloody ankle, and all that . . .'

Bastable watched him descend on hands and knees, towards the curtain at the bottom of the steep stair, and was doubly ashamed.

He had always regarded Wimpy as a slightly ridiculous figure as well as an irritating blighter: the archetypal talkative, know-all schoolmaster, full of useless information and Latin tags, over-critical of his seniors and prone to lecturing his equals – equals like Harry Bastable, who had made their way in the real world of business and commerce where there was no captive audience of small boys to tyrannize over and punish . . . a ridiculous figure, too clever by half but often not half clever enough, and never more ridiculous than now, backing down a dusty stair on his hands and knees in ill-fitting black coat and pin-striped trousers and wing-collar.

But the better man, nonetheless: not only cleverer than Harry Bastable, but also braver and more resourceful and more resilient – quite simply *better*, and never more obviously better than now, in the old Frenchman's Sunday best, half-crippled but still leading the way, damn it!

'Okay, then!' Wimpy rose to one foot, steadying himself on the wall with one hand and clasping his white flag in the other, at the bottom of the stair. He looked up at Bastable. 'Now, Harry – give me a minute or two on the other side of the curtain . . . and if nobody starts shooting, then come on down and join the party – okay?'

Bastable watched him disappear through the curtains. The sound of gun-fire in the distance was as continuous as ever, but it was definitely in the distance, he noted with mixed feelings of relief for his own immediate prospects and disappointment for the British Army. In this part of the battlefield the counter-attack had clearly failed: the tanks he had seen, when rescue and safety had seemed for a moment to be only minutes away, must have marked the furthest point of the assault, unsupported by infantry, the final wave of a tide already ebbing. It had been just enough to create a fortunate confusion, without which their madcap escape from the Aid Post would almost certainly have failed – he realized that with a shiver of fear at the so-nearly might-have-been. It had saved them . . .but it had still left them high-and-dry in enemy territory – or in a no-man's-land the enemy had been quick to recapture.

It all depended on how speedily those SS officers returned to hunt for their missing prisoners . . . Unless, of course, the British tanks or the German dive-bombers had accounted for the bastards . . .

The savage hope that they had been shot to pieces, blown limb from limb, or crushed to bloody pulp under steel tank treads flared within him, so that he tightened his grip on the limpet which was attached to his body.

The limpet returned the grip, holding him as though her life depended on it.

And there was no answer to that – except that it did depend on him now.

The moment was up.

Very carefully, blindly but very carefully, forcing himself to concentrate on each narrow tread in turn rather than on the fearful unknown beyond the curtain, Harry Bastable descended the attic stair.

Now the curtain was ahead of him.

It wasn't the unknown: it was the Germans who were beyond that curtain, and this was the last frontier between him and them – and Wimpy was *mad* to make him do what he was doing, quite mad, and he had been just as mad, and weak and foolish too, to let himself be pushed and stampeded into this folly.

Wimpy had to be stopped before it was too late!

He pushed between the curtains.

It was too late: Wimpy was already almost at the bottom of the main staircase; he had changed his method of locomotion from hands-and-knees to hands-and-bottom, sliding from tread to tread with his bandaged foot and ankle stuck out stiffly ahead of him and carrying small avalanches of fallen plaster along with him, the dust of it rising all around.

'Willis!'

It was too late. Even as he cried the name Wimpy

reached the ground floor of the hall, grasped the newel-post, pulled himself upright and started to hop towards the open front door. Four desperate hops brought him within arm's length of the door; steadying himself on one jamb he began to wave the white square of linen frantically with his free hand.

The die was cast, Wimpy had cast it, and there could be no going back to the attic now. This was still madness, but it was madness without choice – he had been conscripted into it and was part of it, and could only go forward with it.

He crunched hurriedly across the landing and on to the main stairs. At least they were less steep than the ones which led to the attic –

The attic! He had forgotten to hide their uniforms in the attic! Their battledress blouses, with their captains' pips plain to see, and their trousers and their gaiters – *they were still lying there in the middle of the floor, for the first German to recognize – oh, God!*

Panic swirled around him half-way down the stairs, starting the sweat all over him. *It was too late* – he couldn't go back now, he had to join Wimpy at the door – *it was too late, but the first German into that attic . . . Oh, God!*

'Good man!' murmured Wimpy out of the corner of his mouth. 'Now – hold the child for them to see and wave the jolly old white flag so they can't mistake us.'

They?

Bastable's awful knowledge of his failure to hide the uniforms thumped simultaneously inside his head and in his chest as he stared out of the doorway.

They were there, unimaginably, in the road outside – in the very garden itself – men and vehicles, only a few yards away. And in the attic above, also just a few yards away –

'Wave it, old boy – wave it,' murmured Wimpy.

Bastable stared hypnotically at the Germans. 'We've got to get away,' he hissed.

Wimpy nodded, and continued to wave his white square.

'I mean *right now*!'

'Soon . . . soon,' murmured Wimpy reassuringly.

'*Now!*'

Wimpy didn't look at him. 'I-can't-walk-Harry . . .' his lips hardly moved as he spoke '. . . we'll-have-to-wait . . . to-get . . . the-cart.'

Bastable focused on the hand-cart in the gateway, with its scatter of bundles and belongings. Not ten yards from it a large grey open car was parked in the track, with a group of German officers in and around it. A long file of soldiers was threading its way along the track, past the car. From behind him, coming from the open fields behind the house, he could hear the roar-and-squeal of tanks.

He was aware of being squeezed by two equal fears, each the more terrible for its inevitability.

They would come . . . and they would search the house, and they would find the battledress . . . which he had left, which *he* had left. And that would be the end of it, then.

That was inevitable. It would happen.

Therefore, because that was his fault – the end of it . . . therefore he had to get the cart first – *now*.

That was also inevitable: he would make it inevitable because he would do it, because he had left himself no choice but to do it. *Now* –

'I'm-going-to-get-the-cart,' he whispered to Wimpy. 'You . . . take-the-child.'

The little limpet held on to him like grim death, as he had known she would, tightening matchstick arms and

292

legs convulsively round him and sobbing wordlessly as he prised them loose.

'Harry – ' Wimpy began doubtfully.

'*Take-her-damn-you!*'

At last he was free of her. For a final instant he met Wimpy's eyes across her shoulder.

'Harry . . . act stupid – dumb . . . and frightened, Harry – '

Bastable turned away, towards the garden and the enemy, lifting both arms above his shoulders, the square of white linen dangling from one hand.

His legs felt weak, yet stiff at the same time, and the sweat lay cold on his face. He could hear all the sounds around him, each one an individual sensation, but they were all meaningless: only what he could see ahead of him mattered.

The hand-cart was nearer.

The German officers were arguing. One of them had a map held open – no, a map-case of some kind –

Suddenly they looked up at him, and in the same instant someone shouted loudly and angrily.

Bastable looked in the direction of the shout and saw a German soldier running towards him. The German shouted again and threw his rifle to his shoulder. Bastable stopped in instinctive terror, cringing from the rifle.

Someone else shouted – it was one of the officers from the group by the car. The German soldier lowered his rifle, but still kept it levelled at Bastable's chest. The officer barked out another order, and the soldier advanced menacingly, until he was within two yards of him.

Now it was finished. It had all been madness from the start, from the very beginning, but now it was finished.

The soldier swore guttural words at him, unintelligible

sounds which could only be questions or orders, but which only served to increase his abject helplessness.

He looked around desperately, taking in the sharp images of his despair, knowing that they couldn't help him: the garden, with its sweet-williams flowering brightly, the trees – chestnut trees – the long grey car and its occupants – its peak-capped officers festooned with field-glasses and pistols and maps – and the pathetic contrast of the hand-cart, with the old couple's belongings – *Oh, God, help me! Help me!*

The soldier shouted at him again, jerking the rifle to point his questions.

Bastable lowered one arm cautiously and pointed at the hand-cart.

The soldier cast a quick glance at the cart, then returned to Bastable wearing an expression of irritation rather than anger on his face.

'Nein, nein – ' The short explosive gibberish which followed was accompanied first by a vigorous shake of the steel-helmeted head and then by a nod towards the house which translated the likely meaning of the words.

'Clear off at once, you stupid bugger!'

Bastable stood his ground. He was still frightened – he was indeed so frightened that even if he had decided not to stand still he wasn't sure that his legs would have obeyed his brain – but he was also prey to other fears which refused to release him.

Simply, he had to have that bloody cart.

He pointed at it again.

The soldier sighed, reversed his rifle, took two quick steps forward and hit Bastable in the chest with the flat of his stock.

The blow wasn't hard, it was more of a push than a thump, but Bastable knew with a sickening certainty that if he still refused to retreat then the next one would be very hard indeed.

'*Halt!*'

The sharp command came from the right, out of his vision, but the soldier's instant obedience to it transformed Bastable's choice of evils into no choice at all: that was an officer-voice, and now it was discovery, not injury or retreat, which he faced.

Not that *faced* was the right word, for he was too scared to lift his eyes from the patch of dirt on which they had focused sullenly after the thump on the chest, a circumference which just included the muddy jackboots of his tormentor.

As he watched the jackboots they came to attention.

The officer spoke sharply again, and the boot-heels clicked.

Every small pebble and fragment of dried mud stood out in high relief in the pathway. A small black beetle scrambled frantically across it, zig-zagging and lurching as though aware of its danger but obstinately determined to disregard it.

'M'sieur – '

Oh God! The German officer was addressing him in French!

'M'sieur . . . kes-ke-voo-voolay, m'sieur?'

Meaningless. The beetle mounted a larger pebble, slithered sideways and rolled over on to its back, its legs waving helplessly in the air. Bastable raised his eyes five degrees, to take in a new pair of jackboots. They were noticeably superior to the soldier's boots, not only recently polished under their coating of dust but also narrower and better-fitting.

'M'sieur?'

The voice went with the boots. There were Germans

and Germans, as he had good cause to know from his own experience now; yet it seemed more strange that any one of them should speak to a French peasant so courteously, thought Bastable suspiciously.

But whatever the question he had no reply to it, only a gesture. Without looking up, he pointed once more at the hand-cart.

'Comment?' There was a moment's pause. 'Ach – so! Mein Gott – ' The German officer rapped out an order so peremptorily that Bastable was startled into looking up.

'Schnell, schnell!' the officer chivvied the soldier.

The soldier grounded his rifle hastily and pushed back the hand-cart, revealing the little old Frenchwoman, who had lain almost hidden among the fallen bundles on the far side of it.

The German soldier bent down and gathered her up into his arms, her head cradled in the crook of one arm, her legs hanging down limply from the other. As he lifted her, one of the carpet slippers dropped to the ground. He looked questioningly at his officer, who nodded towards Bastable. The soldier marched stiffly round the cart and presented the tiny black-clad corpse to Bastable, extending her as though she was weightless.

Indeed, she was a mere featherweight. The child he had held in his arms a few minutes ago had more substance to her, so it seemed, though perhaps that had been an illusion created by the limpet-grip and the beating heart. Either way, he had no experience on which to draw other comparisons, this was his first dead grandmother, just as little nameless Alice had been his first live baby. All he could think of was that, of all the experiences he had tried to imagine, and to steel himself against these last months, no wildest dream had prepared him for such realities.

'Ay be-an, m'sieur,' said the German officer, nodding again at him. 'Noos allons parlay aveck votrer patron.'

Parlay?

Speak.

Bastable didn't want to speak.

He wanted the hand-cart.

He lowered the corpse of the old woman into the cart and swung the handles to point it towards the house, ignoring the Germans –

And stopped abruptly, as he saw that the German officer was already ahead of him, striding purposefully up the pathway towards the doorway, towards Wimpy.

14

Wimpy had acquired a hat from somewhere. When he had got it, Bastable had no idea; but now it was on Wimpy's head – the old Frenchman's Sunday hat, something like an Anthony Eden homburg, but a French version of it from an earlier era, with different proportions of brim and crown.

The trouble was, it suffered from the same defect as the suit itself: it was just one full size too big, so that it came down low on Wimpy's forehead and appeared, indeed, to be resting on his ears; and the net effect of the whole outfit turned Wimpy into a preposterous figure, out of a Charlie Chaplin two-reeler.

But Harry Bastable was a million miles away from the back stalls of the Tivoli Cinema and laughter, as the German officer advanced towards this travesty; half of him wanted to run away, but didn't know where to run, and the other half wanted to help Wimpy, but didn't know how to do it.

Yet he had to do *something*, because he couldn't just stand there holding the cart with the old woman on it.

He had come for the cart, and he had got the cart. Only now he had also got the old woman, because that was what the German officer had assumed he had come for. So *now* he had to behave as the German officer would expect him to behave – he had to behave as the man he was supposed to be would behave!

The decision was like a spark igniting him into action, releasing him from indecision. One moment the cart was stationary, the next it was almost running away with him: it lurched and bucked as its unsprung bicycle wheels rebounded off unseen obstacles. The old woman lost her second carpet slipper, bouncing up and moving horribly as though she was alive again before settling finally among the bundles on which she lay. The German officer heard the sound of the cart behind him just in time to jump out of its way, almost losing his balance in a clump of delphiniums.

'Onri! Onri!' cried Wimpy. 'Non! Non!'

Bastable pulled back at the cart's momentum, swinging it broadside in front of the doorway, almost tipping its contents at Wimpy's feet – he was aware simultaneously as he fought to hold the handles down that the child was struggling in Wimpy's arms on one side of him and the German officer was trampling down the delphiniums in an effort to keep his footing on the other, and that the old woman's black arm had swung out of the cart and was entangling itself in the spokes of the wheel.

For an instant everything was moving. Then everything stopped: the child, imprisoned in Wimpy's arms, the officer, steady in the flower-bed, and the cart stationary, dusty black arm and limp white hand, veined and mottled with old age, hanging down against the wheel.

He caught his breath and stared at Wimpy anxiously, beginning now to doubt the wisdom of his impetuous action. He didn't know what he ought to do next, and – what was worse – he didn't know what Wimpy was going to do either, and it was too late to ask, with the German officer here beside them – which was worst of all.

'Onri, Onri,' murmured Wimpy, shaking his head.

'Onri' was what he had cried out before, but Bastable hadn't the faintest idea what the word meant in English.

'M'sieur.' The German officer stepped out of the flower-bed on to the gravel path lifting his hand in salute.

'Onri – ' Wimpy loosened one arm from the child and pointed towards the cart ' – gabble-gabble-gabble-*madame*-gabble-gabble-gabble.'

Bastable regarded him with appalled incomprehension, sensing the German officer's scrutiny at the same time, and knowing only that the German understood what had been said to him, but that he did not. He lowered the cart handles to the ground gently, to avoid bringing the old woman to life again, and wiped his sweaty hands nervously on the seat of his trousers.

Wimpy frowned back at him, pointed at the old woman, and then swept his hand towards the interior of the house.

Suddenly the meaning of his words became crystal clear to Bastable. In fact, it was obvious – it was so obvious what he ought to do that he understood also why Wimpy had risked addressing him in French, on the assumption that he couldn't fail to take that meaning. It was so absolutely and utterly obvious that it shrivelled him with embarrassment that he had been so slow on the uptake and so quick once again almost to give everything away, to ruin everything, with his slowness.

He bent forward between the handles of the cart and lifted the body of the old woman from its resting place among the bundles and packages.

The interior of the house seemed much gloomier than it had been on the first occasion he had entered it, as though the light which penetrated it from outside had lost some quality of brightness which it had possessed only a short time before.

Bastable stood irresolutely by the newel-post, wondering which way to go, where to lay down his burden, yet held back at the same time by the sound of the voices behind him – Wimpy's voice, so instantly recognizable, yet at the same time so strangely different as that ever-ready tongue curled round those alien French sounds; and the German's voice, slower and deeper, tackling the same sounds less confidently, yet adding a harsh Teutonic abruptness which somehow made each of them even more forcign.

He strained for a minute to try for at least some inkling of what they were saying to each other. But once again he could make no sense of any of it, from the German's carefully-constructed phrases, in which each word was preceded by a momentary hesitation, to Wimpy's fluent replies, in which all the words ran together in one continuous torrent of language.

Les anglais and *les anglais* were all he could distinguish from either of them – they must be talking about *les anglais*, but that was as far as he could get.

And yet . . . and yet – there was no hostility in the German's voice, only a note of polite enquiry. Indeed, if there was an anger, it was in Wimpy's replies . . . and Wimpy *did* also sound impressively and eloquently French – even arrogantly French, with no more concession to his interrogator's understanding of that language than the Tynesider had made to the SS officer back in the operating theatre.

He closed his ears to the voices, and concentrated on his own problem to the exclusion of everything else, and the answer to it came to him immediately. There was only one place to take her, because there was only one place where she would wish to be – even though she wished for nothing now, and knew nothing, and felt nothing.

He blundered forward past the hat-stand, down the passage.

This time the parlour door required no brute force to open, he had swept the floor clean behind it when he had put his shoulder to it the first time.

The old man in the chair hadn't moved, he had only lost his watch-and-chain; and the bowl of artificial fruit hadn't moved, it still sat in the middle of the table amid a litter of fallen plaster from the ceiling.

Still cradling the old woman, he bent forward and caught the edge of the table-cloth and twisted sideways, dragging the bowl and debris with him; and then dropped that edge and caught another part of the cloth, and dragged it further, and then repeated the action, until the cloth slid from the table, carrying the bowl and the plaster with it. The bowl fell and splintered, out of sight beneath him, and a cloud of plaster-dust arose from its ruin. He stepped forward quickly and unloaded the little black-clad corpse on to the bare polished surface, which had been swept clean by the slide of the table-cloth across it; and turned and fled from the room before the dust could settle on her, and on her table, and on her husband, slamming the door fiercely behind him, leaving them alone together.

The slam of the door echoed inside his head for an instant, then was lost in other sounds outside him: the insistent far-distant *pop-pop-pop* and *thud* which was still a continuous background to every other sound, but which he instinctively sought to filter out the better to reassure himself with the closer sound of Wimpy's voice.

He turned his head to look and listen in the same direction, towards the open doorway at the end of the passage. There was no one blocking it now, but the lack of brightness beyond, the pale light outside, suddenly registered the passing of time, of which he had altogether

302

lost track. This endless day was crawling at last out of its long afternoon into its long summer's evening.

But the doorway was not empty – or, it was empty, the rectangle of its opening, but just within it, pasted against the door itself, stood the child.

So Wimpy didn't need the child any more. So now she was plainly alone and terrified again; he could see that by the way the poor little mite had flattened herself against the door, her small fists clenched across her chest. And he knew, from his own experience of being held motionless by the equal forces of different terrors, why she couldn't move. Outside, in the garden and on the road, was all the dust and noise of the whole German Army on the march, a thing beyond her understanding . . . but inside . . . *inside*, in her own ruined home, was another nightmare no less daunting to her – less physically terrifying, but surely more unnerving, beyond his ability to imagine.

How had it happened? Had she been in the house, in the parlour, when the old man's breath had rattled that last time, like Major Audley's under the blood-stained blanket, and she hadn't understood, any more than Harry Bastable – the great Harry Bastable – had understood – ?

'Grandpa? Grandpa?'

Or in the road? Or in the dust beside the cart, when that other old heart had missed a beat, crushed by the concussion of the bombs, or by fear or by desolation at the loss of home and husband, or by all that addition of calamities, which it was incapable of withstanding – ?

'Grandma? Grandma? Grandma!'

It didn't matter now.

She would get in the way – and that mattered.

She would be a burden. Escaping the Germans was bad enough, but to be saddled with a child as well – he could recall vividly how little Alice had weighed him down, and how glad he had been to be rid of her at last – but to be saddled with a child was an unfair burden. She might be the very difference, the last straw of the burden, which held them back and betrayed them.

But it didn't matter, because there wasn't any choice any more than there had been a choice leaving little Alice crying by the roadside. He hated it, and he hated the damned child, and it was stupid, and he despised himself for the irrational sentimentality of it – there must be hundreds of children like this one – bloody hundreds of them – children lost, or left behind, or orphaned – bloody hundreds of them – and this one was only one more among them . . . and maybe one of the lucky ones at that, because she was still alive, and because someone would look after her, sooner or later.

So what he was about to do certainly didn't make any sense.

But it didn't matter: there still wasn't any choice.

He couldn't reach her quickly enough. Even before he was within arm's reach of her he opened his arms to her. Then she was in them again, and holding him tightly again, and sharing her fear and her need with him.

For a moment her hair was in his face, obscuring the view until he shifted one hand to press her head gently against his shoulder.

Nothing had changed outside. There was Wimpy, standing awkwardly on one-and-a-half feet, and there was the German officer; and beyond them there was the group of officers beside the staff car, still engrossed in their argument; and behind them, on the roadway, the dust and the din rose together from moving vehicles and marching men in an endless single file.

Nothing had changed. For an instant Bastable forgot

everything else in the sickened realization that this was the enemy – this was the German Army – and that he was still a helpless spectator, a fugitive from a defeated army.

No! He tightened his grip on the child. *No! It was impossible that it could happen like this. This was only one corner of the battlefield, and he wouldn't believe it – he must force himself not to believe it, never to believe it!*

He could hear the guns in the distance, and his head ached, and he was bone-weary.

The German officer looked at him briefly, just one quick dismissive glance, and then turned back to Wimpy, raising his hand to the brim of his cap.

'M'sieur – je vous rr-mercy.'

He was turning away.

'M'sieur!' cried Wimpy suddenly. 'Siv-oo-play, m'sieur – Capitaine!'

Please?

The German caught himself in mid-turn, and turned back. 'M'sieur?'

Was Wimpy mad? For Christ's sake – the German had been leaving them, and Wimpy had stopped him – for Christ's sake!

Wimpy hopped forward towards him painfully. 'M'sieur – Capitaine – ' – and plunged into another stream of French, of which Bastable could only catch the pleading tone.

'Kommon?' The German frowned, following the words and the gestures doubtfully – Wimpy gesticulated to himself, and to his bandaged foot as he spoke, and to Bastable himself, and to the child, finally towards the road.

'Colembert,' concluded Wimpy.

Colembert?

'Kolombert?' repeated the German.

'Oui, m'sieur,' Wimpy nodded obsequiously, pointing again. 'Sate-oh-sood . . . oon-peteet-vee . . . va-kilomatre – Co-lem-bear . . .' He pronounced the name with appalling clarity. 'Pray de Belléme.'

The German consulted his map, still frowning. 'Kolem-bear . . . Ach-so! Kolembert! Oui!'

This time Wimpy really was mad – stark, staring, raving mad! There was no other possible explanation. On the outside he still presented the nervous and voluble servility to be expected of a French civilian in his predicament. But on the inside . . .

The German officer looked up again from his map, pursing his lip as though he shared Bastable's doubts. 'Hmmm . . .'

The moment of doubt and uncertainty elongated, stretching Bastable's nerves with it until their tautness became a physical sensation quivering down his back. With the child in his arms, he knew that it would be useless to try and run. But with his knees trembling like this he couldn't have run if he'd wanted to. And there was still nowhere to run, anyway.

The German stiffened suddenly. 'Zair-voll – ' he gave Wimpy an abrupt nod, and reversed the map-case ' – votre nom, m'sieur?'

Wimpy swallowed. 'Ah-ahem! – Laval, m'sieur – Gaston Laval.'

The German had produced a stub of indelible pencil: he was writing on a piece of greyish paper – on a message pad clipped to the back of the map-case.

He nodded towards Bastable. 'Ay votre fee?'

'Alys – Alys Dominique Marie Laval – '

'Alys . . . Laval . . .' The German looked at Bastable again.

'Bloch – Onri Bloch,' supplied Wimpy.

306

Onri?

Henri, damn it. Fool! Half-wit!

'Bloch . . .' The German continued to write, moistening the tip of the pencil from time to time on his tongue – an action which reduced him from a figure of terrifying menace to one of everyday ordinariness, who had the same problems with army-issue indelible pencils as Harry Bastable himself had experienced.

'Say sar!' The German signed the paper with a flourish.

But . . . Gaston Laval, and Alys Laval – Alys! and *Henri* Bloch –

Onri Block-headed Bastable . . . what the blue-blazes had the German written?

And now he was handing the paper to Wimpy – and Wimpy was gabbling effusive gratitude, and bobbing and bowing over the scrap of paper in his hand, until the German finally cut him off with a curt 'M'sieur', half-embarrassed and half-contemptuous (or maybe simply scared, like any British officer in the same position, thought Bastable, that he was about to be embraced and kissed on both cheeks by an unshaven, garlic-breathed Froggie).

But whatever it was, it turned him away hastily, and marched him back down the pathway towards the group by the staff car at the roadside. Bastable watched him incredulously, aware that he had understood only a tenth of what he had seen with his own eyes, and that even that tenth was unbelievable.

'Quite a decent fellow, that,' murmured Wimpy. 'For a damn Jerry . . .'

'W – –'

'Sssh, old boy!'

The German had reached his colleagues. He presented

the map to the most formidable of them and pointed to something on it.

'Better not show too much interest in the proceedings,' said Wimpy softly, swivelling awkwardly towards Bastable, trying to keep his weight off his bad ankle. 'Don't stare, old boy – come on and get some of the things out of this damn cart, and help me into it – the sooner we remove ourselves from the scene, the better, I shouldn't wonder. *Don't stare, Harry!*'

Bastable started guiltily, aware that he had been watching the Germans pore over their map with a fascination unbecoming a French peasant.

'Put the child down – here, give her to me – ' Wimpy held out his arms.

The limpet was again unwilling to leave Bastable's arms at first, and Bastable himself was almost as unhappy to surrender her; but with reassuring squeezes and comforting noises the thing was done again at last.

He started to unload the cart.

'Leave me something soft to sit on,' murmured Wimpy at his elbow. 'And . . . that parcel there looks like the one in the kitchen – if it's food, we need it . . . Is it?'

Bastable tore at the corner of the long package.

'It's bread – leave it in,' hissed Wimpy. 'And those bottles of wine – leave them in too.'

Batable grunted irritably at the unnecessary instructions. The schoolmaster in Wimpy, which was never far below the surface, seemed to have assumed control of both of them.

'Hurry it up, old boy – hurry it up!'

Damn the man! thought Bastable hotly. There was a welter of unanswered questions in his head, jostling each other furiously for precedence.

What had Wimpy said to the German?

What was written on that piece of paper?

And . . . Colembert – for Christ's sake – Colembert!

'That'll do. Now . . . help me in . . . Not that way, you idiot – ' Wimpy resisted Bastable's efforts to manoeuvre him towards the rear of the hand-cart, between the handles on the ground ' – the front end, man, the front end!'

Bastable frowned at him, and then at the cart. Because of its makeshift construction and its lack of supporting legs at the back, it was canted on to its handles with its body at an angle of sixty degrees.

'Don't just stand there!' Wimpy mouthed desperately at him. 'I want to get in at the front so I can see where we're going – I'll navigate . . . you just push the bloody contraption – right?' He glared at Bastable. 'So-just-lift-your-bloody-end . . . and let-me-get-in . . . eh?'

So that was the idea: Harry Bastable was to be the donkey betwen the shafts, pushing rather than pulling, and Wimpy would hold the reins, and do the thinking. Which, to Wimpy, was the natural order of things.

Bastable sighed, and stepped between the handles, and lifted them. It *was* the natural order of things.

Wimpy clasped the child to him firmly with one arm and hopped painfully round the cart, supporting and steadying himself on it with his free hand.

He looked at Bastable for a moment. 'Sorry I was rude just then, Harry, old boy – ' the corner of his mouth twitched ' – bit of nerves . . . the old wind-up, eh?' The twitch was trying to turn itself into a smile. 'Can't all be like you, old boy – eh?'

Like me? thought Bastable, with a bitter pang of self-knowledge. It was hard to accept that Wimpy was a member of the same secret club of cowards, to which he belonged. But then . . . perhaps the membership was bigger than appearances suggested if they were each so deceived by the other. Maybe everyone belonged to it?

Wimpy looked away suddenly, towards the road, and Bastable followed the glance. Everything was still happening there: the whole German Army seemed to be flowing past, only a couple of dozen yards away, regardless of them. He had been aware of it all the time he had been listening to Wimpy and obeying Wimpy's orders, he had never been free of the knowledge of it for a second. It was as though that part of his senses which handled such information was full of it, and could handle no more. It was terrifying, but neither more nor less so than it had been at first sight.

Their eyes met again, and Bastable knew and shared Wimpy's thoughts: *at the moment they were French refugees, but every second's delay increased the danger of discovery.*

The German officer might come back to them.

The SS officers who had spotted them might still be alive.

'I'll have to talk French out there, Harry. If I say, "arraytayvoo" that means "stop". "Ah-gowsh" is "left" and "Ah-droowa" is "right" – got that? And "on-avon" is "go" – right? "Arraytay-voo", "ah-gowsh", "ah-droowa" and "on-avon",' said Wimpy, projecting the words at Bastable with painstaking clarity. 'Have you got that, Harry?'

Have you got that, Batty?

Bastable flinched at the memory.

'I'll signal as well – okay?'

Just do as I say, Batty!

Bastable ground his teeth. 'Get in the cart, Willis. Just get in the cart.'

The handles jerked violently and the frail contraption

310

shuddered and creaked as it took the strain of twelve stone of British officer, and three stone of French girl.

Batty Bastable, thought Bastable as he swivelled the cart.

The German Army was still on the march up the road on which they were about to travel.

Batty Bastable, right enough. Only a mad idiot would do this – and maybe that was the only thing they had going for them, at that: the last place any sane German would expect to find escaping British officers was right in the middle of their army-on-the-march.

But which way?

'Ah-gowsh, Onri!' commanded Gaston Laval to Onri Bloch, and pointed against the tide of grey.

The cart shot through a gap, under the nose of a soldier bowed down under the weight of a light machine-gun.

The grey lines flowed by on each side, but Bastable didn't dare look up, to run the gauntlet of their eyes. Yet, though he didn't dare look at them, they filled his mind so that he could see nothing but Germans, all looking at him: they were there inside his head, in his mind's eye, like a newsreel film synchronized with the actual sounds he could hear of them on either side of him – boots crunching and cracking and dragging, equipment clinking and clanking and clunking, voices muttering and calling out and laughing and jeering – but mostly no voices at all, mostly no human sounds . . . because they were tired – they must be tired, because it was evening now, and also because they were trudging not towards their billets and a meal but towards –

Towards the British Army.

That was a thought arousing pain, not fear.

It was painful because, wherever he was going (and at the moment that wasn't a matter of choice and decision),

311

he was going away from the British Army – away from the certainty and comfort and safety of khaki uniforms and English voices . . . and that was a desolate pain beyond anything he had experienced, like the homesickness of the first, lost night at boarding school multiplied by an infinitely greater loneliness which he felt now –

He was aware of·laughter again, and suddenly the pain *was* fear, because of the realization that there was no more any certainty and comfort and safety in France, even where there was khaki, even where there were English voices –

They were laughing at him, and at Wimpy in his ridiculous hat, with his legs dangling ridiculously over the front of the ridiculous orange-box cart.

But they were really not laughing at him at all: *they were laughing because they were winning*.

No. Damn it – no, no, no, no, no, *no, no, no* –

Yes. All those tanks, in the field.

All those bombers – those bloody bombers – and he hadn't even seen an RAF plane . . . he hadn't even heard an RAF plane, let alone seen one – all those bloody planes –

All those tanks in the field –

The field –
  The farm –
  The Brigadier!

Bastable raised his eyes from the old Frenchman's black hat on Wimpy's head, which he had been staring fixedly

312

at, and not seeing at all, and forced himself to look into the faces of his enemies.

And saw only the Brigadier.

The damned, treacherous, false, murdering, Fifth Columnist, fucking-bastard-swine-shithouse Brigadier.

He had forgotten –

It seemed impossible that he should have forgotten, even for a second. He had forgotten, and then remembered, and then forgotten again, and then been reminded – reminded by Wimpy, too – and then forgotten again.

It seemed impossible, but it had happened.

But now it would never happen again. Even when he was thinking of other things it would be there, like a great hoarding erected inside his head advertising what he would never forget again – never, never, *never*.

Everything that had happened to him was because of that damned traitor –

Traitor?

'*I shall make allowances for the fact that you are a Territorial officer, Major –* '

(The crushed, bloody thing under the blanket: that was another thing to remember.)

No German, German-born, could achieve that accent, that ultimate Englishness!

Traitor.

Everything that had happened to him, and to that crushed thing under the blanket, and to the PROs – every humiliation, every agony, every death – was because of that damned traitor.

Traitor, traitor, traitor, traitor –

He looked down again. The sound of the word inside his brain was superimposed on all the other sounds, just as the face had been superimposed on all those faces which were passing him. He could still hear all those sounds, and he had seen the faces –

Big, thrusting nose . . . bushy eyebrows . . . fierce pale-blue staring eyes: the face of authority, staring him down even when it wasn't turned towards him – it had only been turned towards him once, for one surprised instant, in the farmyard –

Traitor!

All those other faces . . . young faces and older faces; tired, incurious faces looking through him; eyes looking at him, dismaying him with their curiosity; pale faces and swarthy faces . . . all different faces, with different expressions, but all the same face, all the faces of his enemies, all German faces.

But *that* face – *that* face was different from all of them: *that* face was the face of *his enemy!*

He was sweating.

Traitor!

He could feel the sweat swimming on his forehead, gathering and soaking up on the damp-greasy line of the Frenchman's cap across his brow, except at one place on the left where it escaped and ran down the side of his face, like the brush of a cobweb, until the breath of an evening breeze cooled it at his jawline; and he could feel it under his armpits, squeezing wetly as the cart bumped him from side to side over the uneven road surface, and he could feel it running down his back, and down his throat and neck, and down his chest – the sweat of fear and anger and desperate exertion saturating him.

Noises –

But also another noise, a new one hornet-snarling at him from the distance ahead –

He looked up again, simultaneously aware that Wimpy had been trying to twist round to attract his attention. It was like a grey rippling funnel down which they had been forcing themselves against the flow of movement on either side of them, but now the distant end of the funnel was no longer empty.

Bastable blinked and narrowed his eyes to adjust their focus. The road was arrow-straight, but the blue haze of evening obscured its furthest point – it was that sound which made up the picture of what was beyond his vision.

And now the hammering of the powerful motor-cycle engine was fuzzed by that of bigger engines labouring in low gear –

Bastable pulled back at the cart, trying to slow it down.

'Non! non!' exclaimed Wimpy, pointing ahead. 'Par la, par la – ah-droowa – veet! veet!'

Ah-droowa? Bastable looked left, and then quickly to the right – ah-droowa! – and saw nothing but German infantrymen, and was the more confused because Wimpy was still pointing straight ahead – or even pointing more to the left than to the right –

Then he saw it, to the left, above the line of steel helmets bobbing up and down, what Wimpy was pointing at: the arm of a signpost directed *ah-droowa* across the road, twenty yards away – fifteen yards – ten yards –

Bastable swung the cart sideways and halted, waiting for a gap in the grey line which would let him into the opening of the side-road.

No gap appeared.

315

The sound of the approaching vehicles increased.

No gap. They saw him – they stared at him, the same mixture of faces and expressions – and ignored him, and dismissed him, and passed on without sparing him a thought.

No gap.

He pleaded silently with each face: *please – oh, Christ! – please –*

The sound was a roar now, motor-cycle and lorries together drowning all other sounds.

No gap –

Please –

A boy – a mere boy, with cropped blond hair, his helmet hanging from his slung rifle – threw out both arms to hold back those behind.

Gap!

There was no time for recognition or gratitude – the boy wasn't even looking at him, he was merely letting a piece of flotsam dislodge itself – there was the momentary glimpse of another pale anonymous young face, and of grey uniforms and dusty jackboots only inches away as Bastable drove the cart through the gap to the safety of the side-road, from under the very wheels of the motor-ized column.

The roar of the engines enveloped him for a moment. Then, almost abruptly, it fell away into the background behind him, further and further away, losing its identity in the sound of the blood thumping inside his brain.

He continued to push the cart at top speed, like an automaton, without any conscious thought of where he was going, or why he was pushing, and even without any awareness of his surroundings. In so far as he was aware of anything, it was a mixture of physical discomfort in his arms and shoulders and emotional exhilaration which made light of the discomfort. His arms were slowly being pulled out of their sockets by the cart, but that seemed quite natural, and only to be expected, and didn't matter at all really . . . Or didn't matter at all when compared with his miraculous escape from the middle of the German Army.

All he had to do was to keep on pushing –
It was more than an escape . . .
All he had to do was to keep on pushing –
It was a deliverance –

> Nor lead nor steel shall reach him, so
> That it be not the Destined Will.

A deliverance!
The sound behind him was no more than an intermittent hum now – *Nor lead nor steel shall reach him* – punctuated by the faraway murmur of gun-fire – *so that it be not the Destined Will!*

'Julian Grenfell,' said Wimpy.
Bastable came to himself with a jolt as Wimpy spoke. He had been staring at the black hat on Wimpy's head – he knew he had been staring at it because when he leaned forward to keep the cart moving it was only a foot from his nose, and it was all he could see, that black hat . . . the old Frenchman's Sunday hat – but he was not aware of doing so until now, when Wimpy tried to turn towards him, and couldn't quite manage it.

'What?' The word was hard to say: he hadn't spoken a word for so long, the sound of his voice was unnatural to him.

'Julian Grenfell, Harry –

> he shall know,
> Not caring much to know, that still

317

> Nor lead nor steel shall reach him, so
> That it be not the Destined Will.

Very apposite, old boy – I . . . didn't know you were poetically inclined . . . other than a bit of the old *Play up, play up, and play the game!* You're . . . a bit of a dark . . . horse, old boy – a dark . . . horse.'

Bastable felt the blood rise in his cheeks beneath their coating of clammy sweat. He must have spoken those words – those lines from that secret poem of heart-breaking beauty which was utterly private to him – he must have spoken them aloud, without knowing that he had done so. He must take a grip of himself, a much firmer grip – it was fatigue on the surface that had made him light-headed for a moment, but there were accumulated layers of gibbering cowardice under that, and if he let go of himself they would surely take over.

Wimpy was still trying to turn towards him, while continuing to hold on to the child on his lap. The child's face was turning towards Bastable, and she was staring at him with huge dark eyes devoid of expression. Where it wasn't smudged with grime, her skin showed very pale, contrasting with Wimpy's, which was greyish and etched with lines he hadn't noticed before.

'A dark – ' Wimpy started to repeat himself, but then clenched his teeth and grimaced as the cart bumped over a pot-hole ' – horse.'

The fellow was in pain. Although he had appeared to be lolling back in comfort, with his legs dangling over the front of the cart, every time the cart bumped – which was all the time – his bad ankle must have been jarred against the frame. And, although he hadn't made a sound, the addition of those clenched teeth and that grey complexion to the memory of the angrily-swollen joint produced a

318

degree of painfulness which made Bastable ashamed of his own minor aches.

He pulled back at the cart, trying to slow it. For some time now he hadn't really been pushing it at all, it had been travelling downhill of its own accord, carrying him along with it.

He looked around him, seeing the landscape for the first time. How far he'd come from the road, it was impossible to tell, for they were down in another of those long, shallow folds of damned, featureless, foreign countryside in the middle of nowhere, devoid of comforting houses and hedges and telegraph poles. The trackway along which they'd come – it was hardly wide enough to be called a road – stretched straight from one blue-misted crest behind them to another equally indistinct one ahead; there were woods, already dark and uninviting, a few hundred yards to the right, and to the left the fold curved away out of sight.

The moment of exhilaration was entirely gone. As the cart finally creaked to a standstill the leaden weight of responsibility took its place, bowing down Bastable's spirit. Even the thought of their recent deliverance rang empty in his mind. It was still a miracle, in a succession of miracles, but it was a miracle in the midst of a far greater catastrophe – a catastrophe so huge that he was unable to imagine its full extent, but could only guess at it.

'Ahhh . . . that's better!' said Wimpy, easing himself gingerly into a more comfortable position, and then finally succeeding in turning his head sufficiently to look at Bastable. 'Still bright-eyed and bushy-tailed, old boy?'

'I'm all right.' Bastable returned the look without betraying himself. 'How's your ankle?'

'Ah . . . inconvenient, let's say.' Wimpy considered the bandaged extremity in silence for a moment. 'I think . . .

if you could help me to alight . . . we might make a structural adjustment in my chariot which might make life easier for me, if not for you . . . Also . . . I think it's time for a spot of refreshment, too.' He swivelled to Bastable again, smiling lopsidedly. 'And then we can discuss the Destined Will perhaps, eh?'

The old, well-worn feeling stirred within Bastable's breast, half irritation, half admiration. Even in pain and weariness, the blighter couldn't resist mocking him. But also, even in pain and weariness, the blighter was still unbeaten, and thinking for himself when Harry Bastable was full of despair and self-pity.

He was the better man still, damn it!

Wimpy shifted his hold of the child. 'However . . . if I help our little Alice Mark Two over the side first – and if she helps to steady my descent – do you think you could avoid unloading me like a ton of coal this time, Harry, old boy?'

Without the child's weight, it was easy. Or maybe it was easy simply without the onlooking presence of the German Army?

He rubbed his aching arms and looked at Wimpy.

'But first things first while it's still light enough to read . . .' Wimpy balanced himself on one leg, steadying himself with one hand on the cart, and felt in the top pocket of the Frenchman's jacket. 'It's here somewhere – '

'What?'

'What everyone needs – what Mr Chamberlain brought back from Munich . . .' Wimpy dug down deeper. 'Ah! And what we need most of all, Onri Bloch, mon ami – '

A scrap of paper?

The German officer's note – of course!

'What did you – ' Bastable broke off helplessly as too

many temporarily forgotten questions came flooding back.

Colembert?

'What did I ask him for?' Wimpy shook the paper one-handed in an attempt to flutter it open. 'I asked him for our ticket, Harry – damn thing! – for a *laissay-passay* – ' He looked up at Bastable ' – for a pass – a chit – a bit of paper . . . What all armies run on – and all schools, too – "Have you got your chit?" – oh, damn!'

He had dropped the paper. Bastable stooped to retrieve it. It was some sort of German Army message form, not unlike its British equivalent – except for the stylized Wehrmacht eagle which clutched a wreathed swastika in its talons, and for the totally indecipherable foreign scrawl slanting across it.

Wimpy reached out and snatched it back. 'Thanks, old boy. Now . . . let's see . . .' He squinted at the scrawl. ' "*To all whom it may concern*" would be a nice start, but I don't see that – '

'You asked him for a pass?'

'Yes . . .' Wimpy frowned at the paper. 'Chap writes as illegibly as Tetley-Robinson, almost – but . . . "*To all German troops*" – well, that's actually better than "To all whom it may concern", I shouldn't wonder – yes, I asked him for a pass . . . *der Vorzeiger* – because one good turn deserves another – *der Vorzeiger?*'

'One good turn?'

'*Der Vorzeiger dieses* . . . "the bearer of this", that must be, with our old friend Gaston Laval following, and his daughter Alys, and his servant Onri Bloch – *Vorzeiger* must be "bearer", it can't be anything else – '

'What good turn?'

'What good turn . . . *Vorzeiger* . . . I told him where the British Army was – '

'You did *what*?'

Wimpy continued to frown at the paper.

'You *told* him where the British Army was?'

'Ye-es . . . Dug in on Vimy Ridge, I said – told him I'd seen 'em with my own eyes: lots of tanks and little guns – didn't think I ought to be able to identify them as anti-tank guns, being a civilian, but I described them so he couldn't be in much doubt . . . but surely "bear" is *tragen*, isn't it?'

Bastable was appalled. 'Why did you do that?'

'It must be "bearer" – because he asked me, old boy,' Wimpy looked up at him, 'and I thought it prudent in the circumstances to be as helpful as possible. And also because it put the fear of God up him – all those imaginary tanks and anti-tank guns – so maybe they'll think twice before trying to outflank Arras. What the hell would you have done?'

There was no answer to that.

Wimpy regarded him obstinately. 'He came up and said he regretted what had happened to the old lady – "une tragédie de guerre", he called it – and that was when I guessed he was after information, if he could get it. So I blamed the British – I gave him a bit of the old perfidious Albion fighting to the last Frenchman, and then betraying France – and he liked that. He said Germany wasn't the enemy of France, and I agreed with him. I said France had been betrayed by Daladier and the British, and the sooner we got rid of both, the better – and the Communists too.

'And I also let slip that I was an assistant deputy subprefect, and I implied that if God and the Germans spared me I would work for a better Franco-German understanding, preferably against the British.

'And he liked that too. Because the next thing he asked

322

me was if I had been in Arras, and what things were like there. So that was when I gave him a cock-and-bull story about tanks and guns – and lots of Scotsmen with kilts playing bagpipes, because that ought to put the fear of God into him too – and he was *grateful* . . . and *that's* when it occurred to me to ask for *this* – ' Wimpy lifted the paper ' – so, for Christ's sake, Harry, let me read the bloody thing and find out what he's written before it gets dark!'

Bastable opened his mouth, and then shut it again. What Wimpy had done was . . . it was beyond his imagination, and there was no word for it – cheek? treason? daring? – and no words, either!

'*To all German troops . . . The bearer of this . . . Gaston Laval . . .* et cetera, et cetera . . . *Onri Bloch . . . is to be permitted and assisted* – by God! that is "assisted" – *assisted . . . to proceed to Colembert* – signed – squiggle-squiggle, *staff-captain* et cetera . . . *permitted and assisted* – splendid fellow! If I really was the assistant deputy sub-prefect I'd be half-way to heiling Hitler for this piece of paper – ' Wimpy waved the paper under Bastable's nose ' – wouldn't you, Harry? wouldn't you, by God?'

Colembert?

Bastable goggled at him: the lines of fatigue were twisted into an extraordinary mask of elation, and the fellow was bobbing on his one good leg as though the paper in his hand was the winning ticket in the Irish Sweepstake –

Colembert!

In all the world, from Berlin to Abbeville, Colembert was the very last place Bastable wanted to go to – to go back to. It was unthinkable, and Wimpy was stark, staring mad to think of it.

'Harry – '

'I'm damned if I'm going back to – to Colembert – I'm damned if I will!'

'Not *back*, Harry – don't you see?'

Not back?

Harry Bastable didn't see.

'I saw his map – he showed me his map – so I could show him where our chaps were, on the Ridge . . . I told him I'd come from Calais to collect my daughter from her grandparents – I told him I wanted to take her to my sister at Colembert – to the south, inside the German lines, don't you see? It didn't worry him – he didn't know what's happened there, why should he? And even if he did . . . why should he worry?'

Why indeed? thought Bastable bitterly. 'I'm . . . not going back to Colembert – and that's final.'

'So . . . where do you want to go, old boy?'

So where did he want to go?

Harry Bastable stared at Wimpy for a moment; and beyond him, to the closing-in distance behind him.

This alien place – this filthy nowhere-in-France – this empty no-man's-land which might as well be that country-of-the-dying with which Wimpy had frightened him yesterday –

'So where do you want to go?' Wimpy looked at him slyly, as though he already knew, lifting his damned scrap of paper again.

'Not to Colembert!'

'No?'

Bastable looked at the child, and then back to Wimpy. He knew now that he hated Wimpy, but that he still needed him more than he hated him – he was so tired that he couldn't think straight, but he needed Wimpy all the more for that reason, to think for him, to make his decisions.

And yet now he had to think for himself, to dissuade Wimpy from returning to Colembert.

So – why should Wimpy want to go back? *Why?*

Of all places, Colembert was the last one in which the Germans would look for them now! But even if that was a reason for going back there he still wasn't going back.

The damned paper waved under his nose. *Damned paper!*

'If anyone catches us with that – anyone other than the Germans – they'll shoot us,' he snapped.

'They will?' Wimpy echoed the thought carelessly. 'You think so?'

'They'll take us for Fifth Columnists.' Bastable pressed his point without quite knowing how it might help him.

'They will?' Wimpy looked at the paper. 'I hadn't thought of that . . .'

'You bet your life they will!' Bastable stared at the paper. 'If I caught a damn Frenchman with that – or an Englishman – I'd put him up against the nearest wall.'

'You would?' Wimpy continued to study the paper. 'Hmm . . .'

There were no British troops between where they were standing in a darkening nowhere and the ruins of Colembert, so the execution was purely hypothetical, thought Bastable hysterically. And even if there were, and he was the officer-in-charge, he wouldn't shoot a dog on such evidence, never mind a lame Frenchman with a child in tow.

Or would he?

'Without a second thought, man!' he said, trying to inject brutality into his voice. 'The nearest wall. And no damned court martial, either.'

Perhaps he would.

Wimpy looked at him. 'You would too – wouldn't you!'

325

For his own sake he had to believe it. And . . . damned Fifth Columnists – damned traitors! . . . he was already more than half-way to believing it. 'Yes, I would, Willis.'

Wimpy smiled at him – and that was the last bloody straw on the donkey's back: weak, stupid Harry Bastable not capable of shooting a damn traitor, the last bloody straw –

'F – '

'I believe you!' Wimpy cut off the obscenity. 'You're a genius, Harry! I'd never have thought of it – and that makes it perfect . . . the reward – and the risk . . . the risk – and the reward . . . absolutely *perfect*! You-really-are-a-genius!'

'What?'

'To catch a traitor – and that's what it's all about – and it doesn't matter what happens to us . . . to catch a traitor – ' Wimpy started to crumple the paper in his fist, and then caught himself doing it, and opened his hand guiltily. 'God! We mustn't spoil the ticket to Colembert, must we!'

'W-what?'

Wimpy pointed into the cart. 'Get the wine – get the bread . . . bread and wine for the last communion . . . We have to reach the St Pol crossroads as soon as possible, old boy, and we need to stoke your boiler for pushing me there.'

The *what* clogged in Bastable's throat that time.

'There's bound to be Jerry transport moving that way,' said Wimpy. 'And there's a road – I saw it on the map – pretended to be short-sighted, and civilian . . . St Pol to Fruges, Fruges to Desevres . . . Desevres to Colembert. And then – what's the word? – hitching? No – hitch-catching? To catch a traitor, anyway – eh, Harry?'

326

The names meant nothing to Bastable – except Colembert; but Wimpy's eyes were feverish; or, it was Wimpy's voice, and he was imagining the look that went with the voice.

'I didn't think we could do it. And maybe we can't . . . but we can try, Harry – we can try!'

And there was only one traitor.

Damned, bloody *traitor*!

But not at Colembert –

'But he – he won't be at Colembert, Willis,' he heard himself. It was what he should have said all along, fuck it!

'Of course not, old boy. If he's anywhere, he'll be on the bridge between Les Moulins and Carpy at noon tomorrow. So let's hope there's only one bridge, and we can be there too – if that's the Destined Will, Harry.'

He was mad. He was insane. They were both insane – in the middle of nowhere.

'The bridge between Les Moulins and Carpy – Carpy's on the map, I saw it. It's just off the Route Nationale from Arras to Boulogne – the Germans must think they'll be there by tomorrow.'

'Boulogne?' The insanity was catching – even the Germans had caught it. Boulogne was as unthinkable as . . . as Colembert?

Wimpy drew a deep breath. 'I know. It doesn't seem possible . . . But if they've reached Abbeville today – or Amiens today – they can reach Boulogne tomorrow, can't they? *Can't they?*'

It wasn't insanity any more: it was the terrible logic of defeat struggling against hope. If there had been nothing to stop the Germans from driving all the way across Northern France to the Channel, then perhaps there was also nothing to stop them pushing northwards to Boulogne?

But Boulogne!

That wasn't a lost battle – that was the war itself – that was the British Army itself – lost!

And that was impossible: after Boulogne, only Calais was left on the map.

He shrugged the impossibility off. And besides, there was another impossibility to set against it: Colembert was to the south – Wimpy was an idiot –

And that was another impossibility –

Christ! He was the idiot!

There were two Colemberts: the right one and the wrong one – the one he knew and the other one – and the other one was the right one – near Boulogne – the real Colembert!

'Harry. Get the wine – I need a drink if you don't, old boy. Because I'm going to need some dutch courage, I think. I certainly don't think I can do it stone-cold sober, anyway.'

Do what?

Idiot, idiot!

But not idiot alone: because Wimpy had reversed the trick on the German officer – pointing to Colembert-les-Deux-Ponts, but intending Colembert-near-Boulogne all along, and getting it on his piece of paper, *and no one would know the difference.*

Do what?

'But – how are we going to get there?'

'By trusting our luck again – and my French, *Onri*.' Wimpy wasn't smiling: the twitch couldn't be called a smile by any stretch of the imagination, even in the gathering twilight.

It occurred to Bastable that the German officer had been a decent sort of fellow, doing his duty with a foolish touch of humanity, as he himself might have done.

Or, as he might have done if he had been winning.

But losers couldn't afford to make mistakes, and be decent.

He must remember that.

'And also by saying "Heil Hitler" at the right moment,' said Wimpy. 'As of now, Harry, we're joining the Fifth Column.'

15

'Harry. Wake up, Harry. It's time.'

Time?

Bastable awoke to greenness swimming before his eyes; which, when he blinked the sleep from them, resolved itself into a primeval forest of grass, impenetrably thick and tangled.

'It's time, Harry.'

The voice in his ear and the hand on his shoulder were both so gentle as they reclaimed him from sleep that they confused him for a moment. He moved his own hand, which had been resting on his cheek to shield his eyes from the light, and pushed at the grass, only half-conscious of what he was doing.

'Harry – wake up, old chap. It's past eleven hundred – it's nearly eleven-thirty.' Not so gentle now, the voice.

The back of his hand was tingling very strangely – no, not so much tingling as itching . . . and more than itching –

Christ! The back of his hand was on fire! The bloody grass was full of stinging nettles, damn it!

And it was time – dear God! – *it was past eleven hundred – Wimpy must have let him sleep on quite deliberately – and now it was nearly eleven-thirty already!*

He sat up abruptly, looking round about him quickly with the beginnings of panic, at once fully and horribly awake.

'What – ' He lifted his other hand from the ground

quickly, but too late, feeling the crushed nettles bite into his palm. 'Oh – damn!'

'It's all right, old boy,' Wimpy reassured him. 'There's nothing moving. A bloke on a cycle about half an hour ago, that's all. You were sleeping like a baby.'

'Did he see you?' Caution was second nature now.

'No.' Wimpy turned back to the corner of the bridge's brick parapet. 'I thought it safer to lie very low, just in case.'

'In case of what?'

'We-ell . . .' He craned his neck cautiously round the corner to look up and down the road '. . . just in case he wasn't as innocent as he appeared to be. We are rather in the middle of no-man's-land again, it looks like. So Jerry may be indulging in a spot of reconnaissance out of uniform, I don't know . . . Anyway, he didn't see me, so it's quite all right. Nothing to worry about.'

It wasn't quite all right, and there was everything to worry about, thought Bastable desolately.

'Where's the child?'

'Under the trees, where we left her – with the chariot. Don't worry. When I last looked at her she was asleep too. Quite worn out, poor little soul, I'd guess. So just don't worry.' Wimpy's voice was relaxed and strangely distant. 'There's nothing to worry about.'

'How's your ankle?'

'About the same.'

'You can't walk on it?'

'Uh-huh.' Distant, and quite unconcerned.

'You can't walk on it?'

'That's right.' Wimpy peered round the parapet again. Not just unconcerned.

The nettle stings on Bastable's hands had risen as

painful white blotches in the middle of raspberry-coloured stains. It struck him as ridiculous that they should bother him, such little childish pains – *Don't scratch it, Henry, it'll only make it worse. Wrap a dock-leaf round it* – at a time like this.

Not just unconcerned. Serene.

His mouth was full of a foul taste, made up of sleep and the stale fumes of alcohol: at some stage last night he hadn't been quite sober, if he hadn't actually been drunk.

Last night –

The night hadn't been dark, as night should be. It had been full of greyness, and black shapes and the flicker of war to the north, like distant thunder and lightning.

And finally the loom of the blacker shape on the road ahead, and the different, slower light of torches –

'Achtung! Achtung!' The guttural warning and the torch-beam swung towards him simultaneously, terrifying him and blinding him at the same time. '*Halt!*'

Stop –

'*Heil Hitler!*' shouted Wimpy confidently.

'Hände hoch! Halt! Halt!' Boots scraped on the road.

'Heil Hitler!' Wimpy shouted again, his voice cracking. 'Kameraden! Kameraden!'

The night was now blinding light and blind darkness, and absolute fear though Wimpy had prepared him for it ('*The moment when they'll be as scared as we are, old boy*').

'Heil Hitler!' Wimpy positively shrieked out the password this time ('*Would you shoot someone who shouted "God save the King!", old boy? Would you?*').

They were about to find out, anyway – once and for all!

332

'Schprekken zee Franz-oh-sisch? Kameraden – Kameraden?' shouted Wimpy. 'Ich bin Froind – ich bin Froind – ja!'

The boots scraped uneasily, left and right – and closer – in the glare-and-blackness filling Bastable's brain.

More German words – but this time they were beyond his script and meant nothing.

'Ja! Ja!' exclaimed Wimpy eagerly.

The torch-beam left Bastable's face in preference for Wimpy's, dancing the familiar black hat in silhouette in front of him.

For an interminable moment there was no reply. There was only fear crawling around in the silence, and what made it worse for Bastable was that he knew he was sharing it with the Germans: in their place, in the middle of a hostile country, at night and alone – even if he'd been winning – he would have been petrified and trigger-happy. And what made it worst of all was that he wasn't in their place: he was at the end of their rifles, and they plainly didn't know what to do next.

No – not worst of all! Worst of all was that there was nothing he could do about it, he was harnessed to the cart like a dumb animal.

'Kameraden!' Wimpy's voice cut through the silence, and Bastable was astonished at the change in it: it wasn't pleading, it wasn't trembling with fear – it was sharp with authority!

'Kameraden!'

'No half-measures, old boy – we've got to go for broke – I shall tell the buggers I'm on a Fifth Column mission of the highest importance, delayed by the damned Englanders of Arras – game leg, and all that! – sent by General Rommel in person – signed and sealed by one of his own staff

333

officers – with an order to prove it – piece of bloody bumf,
but it's bloody bumf that makes the world go round! Bumf,
and the bloody cheek to go with it, Harry!'

And Wimpy had both. But would they be enough?

The torch came towards them.

'Franzozisch – Frong-say?'

'Oui. May-ma-gron-mare-est-dalsass – El-sar-ssich, ja?'

And Wimpy was even enlisting his Alsatian grandmother to serve with his bit of paper and his bloody
cheek . . .

The beam of light played over them nervously. 'Voz
papiez, m'sieur?'

'Non. Nicht owsschwhyce – ' Wimpy produced – produced with a decisive flourish – the magic piece of bloody
bumf on which their lives depended, from which all his
great lies were stretched.

The torch illuminated the crumpled piece of paper, and
Bastable strained his eyes to make out the rank of the
torch-bearer.

Please God – not an officer . . . but not a complete
fool, please God! Someone in between . . . say, an NCO
with a little imagination, but not too much. Say, just
enough to see how useful a Fifth Columnist could be to
an advancing army – that had been Wimpy's reasoning.

The torch-bearer was making heavy weather of the
paper – he was summoning assistance out of the darkness.

Assistance also studied the note. And Assistance also
had a map.

'Colembert,' said Wimpy. 'Entre St Omer et
Boulogne.'

'Ja – ja . . .' said Assistance, midway between irritation
and doubt. 'Colembert – ja!'

There was something wrong, and it could be any one of
a hundred reactions –

334

1. A vital mission? Pushing a cart, with a child and the village idiot – in the middle of nowhere? You must be joking!

2. All the way to Colembert? Do me a favour – the bloody British are still there!

3. Piss off, you bloody Frog!

Or even –

4. You don't sound like a Frog to me – you sound more like Captain Willis, of the Prince Regent's Own. And there's a 'Dead or Alive' SS warrant out on him, I seem to remember –

Wimpy spoke, and he was answering Number 2, by the sound of it: *Take us as far as the St Pol crossroads, and we'll get another lift there* (just so we get as far as possible from Arras and Number 4, Kameraden!).

'Ja . . . ja . . .' More doubt than irritation now: Assistance manoeuvred the map and the torch-bearer's light alongside Wimpy and embarked on what sounded – God! What actually sounded! – like a hesitant question . . . in a mixture of German and French.

'Oui – oui!' Wimpy nodded, and bent over the map. 'Ici – ' he pointed to the map ' – nous sommes ici – *là!*'

'Ah – ach ssso!' exclaimed Assistance gratefully. 'Gut! Bon! Bon!'

The Germans had been lost – hopelessly lost in a darkened France! Lost – just as the Prince Regent's Own had been hopelessly and fatally lost three days before!

'St Pol?' said Wimpy. 'Le carrefour de St Pol?'

'Ja, ja – der Karrefour de St Pol – komm – '

It had been easier, after that.

It hadn't been less frightening – it had never been less than altogether terrifying for Bastable, even after they had shared one of their bottles of wine with the crew of the lorry, whose relief at discovering their whereabouts was so great that they had shared one of *their* bottles in return (and they at least had a corkscrew!), which had added to the wine he had already consumed beside the road, in that other middle of nowhere (after having smashed off the top, very unskilfully, with a stone at the roadside); which had added an insufficient measure of dutch courage to his overmastering English cowardice.

Even, although they had almost ignored him – Wimpy had explained that he was short on wits, and even shorter on words, and one of them had patted his shoulder ('*Doitsches soldarten – Doitsches soldarten ammee!*') – even when they had made much of the child, like family men far from home; very ordinary men – men like his own dead fusiliers – ordinary men who would have killed him a few hours before, and might still kill him, if things went wrong.

No, it had never been less frightening.

It had even been more frightening, in the first place where they had stopped, where there had been a great fire burning, illuminating faces and uniforms and vehicles.

But it had been easier –

It had been easier because Assistance had assisted them to another vehicle – speaking to another Assister, explaining how they had helped him find his way in the darkness, giving substance to their lies –

. . . *permitted and assisted* . . .

– even putting Wimpy's case to a harassed German MTO in the firelight –

'General Rommel – '

'Le *Gaynayral* Rommel – '

336

They were French firemen fighting the fire – in polished brass helmets which flickered red-gold on their heads!

'Kolembert – ja!'

A German soldier actually helped him to transfer the cart from one lorry to another, snapping instructions at him, while Wimpy stood beside the tailboard, holding the child close to him, supporting himself on her shoulder.

'Kolembert – *nine!* Frooges – Frooges?'

'Frooges?' said Wimpy eagerly. 'Frooges – oui!'

Easier. But not less frightening.

For the second leg of their journey had been in silence, and in bumping darkness, with the child wedged in his arms and the sharp edges of things gouging into him – the child shivering at first, cold as death, and then so still and silent that he had shifted himself deliberately once to make her stir to reassure himself that it wasn't a small, cold death he was cradling in his arms, but only the sleep of exhaustion which he himself had to fight against because there were Germans also in that darkness with him, and he dare not release himself from their presence.

And then – somewhere else in the limbo of night.

There was no fire here, only shielded lights. The fire in his memory was a recollection of a happier time – everything which happened was better than what was happening.

He stood in the darkness with the child in his arms, watching the lights move – flicker – go out – move – flicker . . . and the German voices, and the sounds . . . until one of the lights and the sounds came towards him.

The light flashed into his face. The child turned away

from it and he buried his eyes into her hair, lifting her up to block it off.

'Laval – Gaston Laval?'

'Eessee! Laval – say mwa!' said Wimpy. 'Heil Hitler!'

Not less frightening. But there was simply a limit to fear, that was all.

They stood beside the cart, at the side of a road, against a brick wall, in the darkness, to let the German Army pass by.

Bastable finally dared to lean against the wall, which seemed a daring action, but which was almost a necessity in the end, as his knees weakened and the petrol fumes filled his head and his lungs. And it was a little easier then.

Slowly, the shape on the other side of the road ceased to be a shape, and became a building; and then a house, with a shop underneath it; and then a shop with a sign above its front – POMPES FUNEBRES EL - - - - the last letters of the owner's or company's name were obscured by a queer metal-latticed pole at the edge of the pavement, and the vaguer shapes inside its windows provided him with no clue to its merchandise – it could be selling Paris fashions or sanitary-ware for all he could tell, and it would certainly benefit from a lick of brighter paint and a more enticing window-display of the sort that he had introduced to BASTABLE'S OF EASTBOURNE –

'Laval! Gaston Laval!' snapped a voice.

The last part was the easiest of all – the most friendly – and the most frightening.

It was easy because they didn't even expect him to hoist the cart into the back of the lorry – and because they helped him in after it – took the child out of his arms, and helped him in, and handed her up to him, too.

But then they tried to talk to him.

It wasn't night any more, it was grey half-light, and he looked desperately to Wimpy for support.

Wimpy tapped his temple meaningfully. 'Eel ay dumkopff, miner hairen – dumkopff!'

They looked at Bastable with added interest.

One of them leaned forward until his face was six inches from Bastable's, and pointed to himself. 'Oo-see, oo-see – je . . . swee . . . dum-kopff!'

Everyone burst out laughing, including Wimpy. The joke was lost only on Bastable and the French child.

And apparently also on the speaker himself, who held Bastable's attention with poker-faced gravity for a moment, and then pointed at his comrades in turn. 'Too – too lay soldaten – dumkopff!'

More laughter. The soldier pointed at Wimpy.

Bastable looked at Wimpy, and Wimpy stopped laughing.

'Der Foonfter Kolonner – ' The soldier waved his finger negatively in front of Bastable's face ' – nicht Dumkopff!' The finger pointed at Bastable. 'Ay-byan – voos-*nicht*-Dumkopff!'

Even more laughter. They positively fell about – all except the poker-faced soldier, who made great play of disagreeing with them and even of trying to restrain them, shaking his head and waving his hands extravagantly before squaring up to Bastable again.

Bastable didn't know what to do. The best thing might well be to laugh, like everyone else. But his face wouldn't laugh for him, it was frozen stiff with fright.

'Voos – ' The soldier reached out and tapped him on the chest.

'Voos – ' The laughter died away and the rest of the audience suddenly became hideously attentive. 'Voos – '

The child in Bastable's arms gave an explosive sob and then burst into tears, burying her head in his shoulder.

The effect on the poker-faced soldier was instantaneous: the poker-face fragmented into anguished concern.

'Leebshun! Leebshun!' But the touch of his hand on her head only increased the weeping to wailing and the same convulsive clutching and burrowing that Bastable remembered from their first coming-together in the attic. The sound filled the back of the lorry for a moment, against the background of the engine and the tyre-hum, and it was the most beautiful music he had ever heard: he opened his ears to it, and closed his eyes to concentrate on it, and hoped that it would go on for ever.

Much too quickly, the engine-noise came back. But then, to his relief, no one dared to break the silence which the child had created around both of them, protecting them both, until at last the engine-noise itself changed, as the lorry slowed to a snail's pace.

Someone in the cab up front hammered on a door-panel.

'Kar-pee! Kar-pee!'

Carpy!

The poker-faced soldier, no longer in the least poker-faced, was foremost in helping to unload them, winking encouragingly at Bastable and totally ignoring the officious NCO who tried to hurry them up.

They were at another crossroads, amidst a scatter of mean houses and a decrepit garage boasting one antique petrol pump. It was almost full daylight at last, but the sky still had its grey early-morning look, and apart from the Germans, there wasn't a soul in sight, and the only sound was of lorry engines idling.

Bastable and the soldier between them assisted Wimpy to the cart, and while Bastable held the handles (the familiar aches protested, and then surrendered) the soldier fussed Wimpy into his throne of bundles. It was almost too easy to bear.

'Merci – danker,' said Wimpy.

The officious NCO looked down at him belligerently, obviously about to speak.

'D'low, seevooplay,' said Wimpy. 'Vasser?'

The NCO snapped his fingers at the soldier. 'Vasser!'

The soldier handed Wimpy his water-bottle, watched him drink, and brought it to Bastable in turn. Bastable looked at him helplessly, unable to let go of the handles of the cart.

'Ach-sso!' The soldier held the water-bottle to his lips and he glugged thirstily, the water running down his chin. He hadn't realized how thirsty he had been, and that seemed very strange to him. And, at the same time, he felt guilty at drinking all the soldier's water; drinking another man's water wasn't right.

But the soldier grinned at him. 'Goot? Goot?'

It tasted rather odd, with a chemical tang to it, and it was stale and luke-warm. But it was good.

'G – ' Bastable started to say as much, but cut off the word just in time, turning it into a guttural sound. 'G-g-g!' he nodded at the soldier, who nodded back at him as though delighted.

'Schown!' snapped the NCO, pointing to the queer French signpost at the crossroads. 'Rraymee-der-soo – Dayzayvrez-huh?'

Bastable squinted at the signpost.

REMY-DEUX-SOUS 5.5 – to the left.

341

'Desevres – oui!' said Wimpy, nodding.

'Les Moolinz – ' The NCO pointed to the right ' – verboaten – verboaten! Nicht Les Moolinz – ja?'

LES MOULINS 6.5 – to the right!

'Desevres – Colembert!' Wimpy pointed to the left.

'Ja!' The NCO nodded vigorously, and started to turn away.

'Mo-mong!' exclaimed Wimpy, stopping him. 'Mine hair – jay bezwa'n dern pistolay – rayvolvur . . . *kanone* – comprenay?'

The German NCO frowned at him, and then shook his head.

What the devil – ? thought Bastable, swivelling the cart handles in already-sweating palms. *Pistolay?*

'Nine! Nicht pistole!' The NCO shook his head again.

The meaning came to Bastable with a rush of blood to his brain: Wimpy was mad again – he was spoiling everything, just as they had achieved the impossible! *He was asking for a gun!*

Things happened simultaneously. Wimpy was mad, and the NCO was shaking his head, and the no-longer-poker-faced soldier, who had been watching events with interest while reattaching his water-bottle to his equipment, was banging on the tailboard of the lorry and shouting into it.

Wimpy had produced his piece of paper again, and was gabbling a mixture of French and German at the NCO with the same pedantic, schoolmasterish obstinacy as he so often used on Bastable himself.

The soldier returned to them, and promptly presented a revolver to his NCO – an odd-shaped thing – with a nod of his own towards Wimpy.

The NCO stared at the revolver in his hand as though it was a snake about to bite him; and then fumbled with it

– and swore at it, and finally changed hands before succeeding in breaking it open and swore again.

Somebody shouted from up ahead, and banged his hand on the side of the lorry insistently – it was the driver leaning out of his cab, eager as all drivers were to get moving again.

The NCO snapped the revolver again, and shook his head, but with resignation this time, and slapped the weapon into Wimpy's hands – while the soldiers in the lorry cheered and stamped their feet – and swung away angrily, pretending to ignore the noise – and the soldier winked again at Bastable and said something meaningless; and turned away himself, and was hauled into the lorry by his comrades – legs, boots, disappearing into the darkness – even as it started to roll forwards again . . . and someone was waving from the back of the lorry; and then the next lorry cut off the view, and the next, and the next, and the next – noise and dust swirling around them – until the last one, with curious white faces peering at them out of it, disappeared in its own cloud of dust and fumes, and they were alone.

Bastable looked around him.

'French?' Wimpy addressed himself as he examined the revolver. 'Probably French – but made for a contortionist . . . no – made for a left-handed contortionist – ' He fumbled with it just as the German NCO had done, and finally found the release button of the cylinder ' – but – fuck it! – only two bullets . . . so that's why he let us have it, the sod! Just a souvenir – ' he raised the weapon close to his eye ' – something *d'armes* – *St Etienne* – a souvenir from a left-handed French contortionist!'

There still wasn't a soul in sight. The whole of France might be empty: the long columns of refugees of yesterday

343

– the day before yesterday? – had disappeared like flies in the wintertime of the German Army's advance.

The sound of the lorries was fading into the distance, but there were other sounds now to take their place – the rumble and drone of aircraft ahead of them and away to their right . . . and their left . . .

'But two will have to do.' Wimpy twisted towards him. 'Come on, old boy – right for Les Moulins – at least they've given us that on a plate, thank God!'

Bastable stared at him.

'Les Moulins, Harry – ' Wimpy pointed to the right. 'At the bridge between Les Moulins and Carpy' – remember? And, by Christ, if it's forbidden for us to go there, then by golly that's where it is, Harry – at the bridge between Les Moulins and Carpy, that's where the bastard's going to be, and they're keeping it clear to make sure of it, the crafty swine!'

Bastable thought he saw a curtain move in the house on the right-hand corner of the crossroad. So there was perhaps somebody still alive in France, besides themselves.

Wimpy pointed to the right with the revolver. 'Come on, Harry – no more time to admire the countryside. Just look for the next river, old boy – '

But there had been no river.

Bastable looked at Wimpy's back, the stale taste of the alcohol furring his tongue, as Wimpy peered round the edge of the bridge again.

'Still all clear,' said Wimpy over his shoulder, and then consulted the old Frenchman's watch. 'Eleven-forty-two, and all clear!'

Bastable raised himself on his stinging hands and peered down to his left, into the railway cutting. The fall of the bank beside the bridge was much steeper than where the cutting began, so that this side was invisible to him beyond the edge of the thirty-foot drop to the line, and he could only see the cliff on the opposite side, with the rails of the single-track line itself hidden from view where they disappeared under the bridge.

He looked down to the south – so far as he could make out it was north–south that the line ran, with the road crossing it east–west. The further away, the less steep the sides of the cutting, until it ceased to be a cutting and became an embankment: that was the logic of railway building, he remembered, to iron out the rise and fall of the land into a billiard-table; and the smaller the gradients, the more economical the line – that was the logic.

And Wimpy too was very logical . . .

It had been Wimpy who had first realized that it wouldn't be a river, but a railway line. Bastable had only known that he was sweating to push the cart upwards on to a plateau, not holding it back from running away into a river valley; and he had drawn no conclusions from that, except that he was sweating.

But then Wimpy had worked it all out, after he had made sure that the roofs and the spire a couple of miles ahead down the road must be Les Moulins, with no other bridge to cross before they could reach it.

Wimpy was very logical.

'If the Germans are in Carpy, then Les Moulins must be still ours – they've left it, to let the Brigadier get to the bridge!'

Was that logic? Bastable's head ached too much to deny it, anyway.

'Which means . . . they're coming up, round the coast

345

– Le Touquet, Boulogne – Christ!' Wimpy had trailed off, leaving the implications of that unsaid. 'No wonder they want to know what's up ahead of them!'

It was all beyond him. Or, not quite –

'Then we can go on to Les Moulins – if our chaps are still there. We can stop him there.'

'No, Harry.' Wimpy considered Bastable-logic, and rejected it. 'If our chaps *are* there . . . But if they *aren't* – if the Germans are simply passing him through to talk here – then we'll have had it, by God! All we know is that he's coming *here*.'

Bastable had lost the thread of it there. Wimpy was too clever for him, too logical, and he was too tired to argue.

'We know he's coming *here*,' repeated Wimpy.

'We know?'

'I *heard* it. When we were under the table – *the bridge between Carpy and Les Moulins – midday* – that's what they said. And *this is the bridge, Harry – and all we have to do is wait!*'

Bastable was too beaten to argue, but not too beaten to want not to go on living when there was still a chance of life.

'But – '

'No, Harry. I know what you want to do – you want to go at everything like a bull-in-a-china-shop – '

That wasn't what Harry Bastable wanted at all. But there wasn't any way of admitting what he wanted, now that what he had dreamed of had actually happened – and had become a nightmare.

' – but it won't do – with only two bullets . . . it won't do. Being brave isn't enough – we have to think – '

It wasn't being brave at all – that was what Harry Bastable was thinking.

Wimpy shook his head. 'We can't risk it, that's all. He's coming here, so we're staying here.'

Think –

Wimpy looked at him. 'The Destined Will, Harry – you thought of it first. You always think of everything first! And when there wasn't a chance in hell of getting here, you still thought of it.'

But that wasn't it at all! Or, if he had, then he had thought of it when he thought it couldn't happen.

Think –

He saw the child staring at him with her solemn eyes out of her dirty face. What would happen to the child?

'What about her?' She had always helped him: she would help him now! 'You can't look after her – you can't bloody well walk, Willis!'

Wimpy looked at him, and at the child, and then back at him, and smiled – that was the first glimpse of that terrible obstinate serenity.

'Harry, Harry . . . trust you to get it wrong, old boy!'

'What?'

The serene smile. 'That's the point, Harry – trust you to want to do it!'

Do it?

'*I* can't get away – that's the whole point – the jolly old Destined Will, old boy, eh?'

'What d'you mean, Willis?'

Wimpy pointed towards Les Moulins. 'The Brigadier – our own special Fifth Columnist, the bastard – has to come up *that* road, to *this* bridge – *there* – ' he pointed to the middle of the road, at the mouth of the bridge ' – while Jerry trots along from his side – from Carpy – eh?'

Bastable stared down the empty road towards Carpy, and then back to Wimpy.

Serene smile. 'And since when could you ever hit a

347

barn door – at point-blank range, Harry, old boy? Since when?'

Since never. The only shot he'd ever fired in anger – two shots – had been at point-blank range, at the German soldier two yards from the Brigadier's shoulder, and God only knew where they had gone, but they certainly hadn't hit anything.

'Since when?' challenged Wimpy.

A smaller part of Bastable wanted to deny the truth. But only a smaller part.

'We wait here until the Brigadier turns up – you take the child and the cart and snug 'em down in the wood there first – ' Wimpy pointed into the undergrowth ' – and then we wait until he comes in view – ' Wimpy pointed down the road to Les Moulins ' – and you scarper and keep the child quiet . . . and *bang-bang*! – you lie low until the coast is clear again – right?'

Logical.

Wimpy couldn't run away.

Wimpy couldn't run anywhere.

'And if I can't hit a barn door – you take the child and head for home, and tell 'em what happened. Which makes you the small print on the bottom of the Destined Will, old boy. Like . . . an insurance policy, eh?'

It did seem a very good idea –

'Logical?' suggested Wimpy serenely.

Very logical. A very good idea, and also logical.

'So . . . you take the child – and the chariot – and tuck 'em away out of sight . . . and come back and have a bit of a kip until eleven hundred hours, or thereabouts – ' Wimpy consulted the Frenchman's watch – 'because you'll need all the rest you can get – off you go then, there's a good fellow.'

He watched Wimpy survey his surroundings critically.

'An absolutely ideal spot . . . plenty of cover right up to the roadside . . . if I crawl around from the back, without disturbing the front – I can see up and down the road for half a mile too! Ideal!'

Unarguably logical. So why argue with it?

Wimpy turned back to him. 'Look, Harry – I know what you're thinking. But you don't have to prove anything to me, my dear fellow . . . It's simply that this makes sense, that's all.'

So it did, of course.

'It isn't as though you'll be running away – it's just as vital that someone gets through with the information as it is that someone else puts the kibosh on the bastard. Swopping jobs . . . that would be a nonsense.'

And so it would be, of course.

Wimpy half-smiled. 'I always used to tell my boys that nonsense must be wrong – all they had to do was to think logically, because Latin is a logical language. *Patriam amamus: eam servabimus* – illustrating the use of the pronoun – so I'll do the job. End of lesson – class dismissed, Harry.'

Class dismissed.

The nettle stings throbbed as Bastable turned away from the railway line, back to the contemplation of Wimpy's black-suited back half-shrouded by the tall grass and nettles in which he lay.

He had slept without dreaming at all, but before he had slept he had recalled something which until that moment he hadn't remembered for half his lifetime.

Mr Voight had promised Form Vc, the bottom French division of no-hopers, that the last class before the exam would be painless – he would read them Maupassant's *La*

Dernière Classe ('classe' feminine – 'dernière' e-*accent grave*-e).

Not that Vc cared a toss for accents – but wasn't Maupassant that writer of sexy stories who had died of the clap practising what he preached . . .? Good for Old Voighty!

Except that he hadn't understood a word of the story; and even those who had puzzled out some of it had dismissed it as a shameless 'have on'; because it wasn't about *filles de joie* (Vc knew about them) at all, but about boys like themselves having a last French class before the Prussians conquered Alsace-Lorraine and abolished the French language there – and Good for the Prussians was Vc's considered verdict on that!

Only now, by the bridge from Carpy half a life later, Harry Bastable remembered what Harry Bastable had instantly forgotten – the difference Old Voighty had painfully taught them between *la classe dernière* and *la dernière classe!*

Only now it was Wimpy who was teaching him the difference: Wimpy's very last lesson – the last lesson he would teach anyone – wasn't about logic, or about Latin. It was about what sort of man Harry Bastable really was – that was what it was about.

'Give me the gun, Willis,' said Harry Bastable.

'They're a bit late,' said Wimpy. 'What?'

'Give-me-the-gun.'

Wimpy looked at him quickly. 'Don't let's go through all that again, Harry.' And turned away.

Bastable crawled alongside him.

'There isn't time to fuck about now,' said Wimpy.

'Give me the gun.'

'Don't be an idiot.'

350

'I'm the senior officer.'

'Balls!'

'Give me the gun, Willis. That's an order.'

'Balls.'

'I'm taking the gun, Willis.' Bastable reached out through the nettles. 'Give it to me.'

'No, you're not – there isn't time.'

'I'm taking it!'

'Watch out! Christ, man! It'll go off – mind what you're doing!' hissed Wimpy.

Bastable had the barrel, but Wimpy still had the butt. They wrestled with each other silently, each pushing against the other, fighting for control of the revolver.

'It'll go off!' gritted Wimpy.

'Then let go of it.'

'No!' Their cheeks rasped against one another, sandpaper against sandpaper. 'Don't be a fool, man!'

Bastable dug his heel into the ground to anchor himself. It occurred to him that Wimpy couldn't do that, not with his bad ankle. In fact . . . all he had to do was to kick at that ankle with his other foot –

Suddenly, Wimpy relaxed against him. He didn't let go of the revolver – he still held it as firmly as ever – but he relaxed, as though the fight had gone out of all of him except that one hand which held the weapon.

'G – '

'Sssh!' whispered Wimpy. 'Sssh!'

Bastable held himself rigid. For an instant he could hear only his own heart thump inside his chest. And then –

A faint crunching? Was it?

The crunching faded, and then became more distinct.

I am an idiot, thought Bastable. *He's quite right –*

Wimpy was staring at him: their faces were so close

351

that he could see every detail of Wimpy's features with microscopic sharpness, sweat beaded among the bristles, dirt ingrained into the lines crinkling the skin, the crater of a pock-mark on the cheek-bone – eyes huge with surprise questioning him.

'Sssh!' Wimpy's free hand pressed down on his back.

There was something wrong – something more wrong than just that Wimpy was looking at him like this, and not fighting any more. Even his hold on the revolver was weakening.

'They're . . .' Wimpy's mouth opened on the word so softly that it was more like a breath than a whisper '. . . not . . . on the road . . . they're . . . in . . . the cutting – *Harry!*'

In the cutting.

At the bridge – but not *on* the bridge.

Under the bridge.

Logic, thought Harry Bastable emptily.

The line ran north–south. The Germans were advancing to the north. It was a good place to meet, under a bridge, out of sight.

Oh, shit! thought Bastable. The matter had been settled for them by the Germans.

'Take good care of the child, Willis,' he whispered.

The revolver came out of Wimpy's hand – Wimpy wasn't even holding it.

Crunch-crunch-crunch . . . from below them.

He rolled sideways silently, and then crawled the last yard or two to the fringe of grass-and-nettles at the edge of the cutting.

There were three of them: one in German uniform, and two in brown leather coats, belted at the waist, and dark snap-brim hats – civilians of some sort – German civilians. This was the German end of the tunnel under the bridge.

352

The soldier halted, saluted someone under the bridge, and disappeared from view.

The civilians also disappeared from view.

Logic.

Oh, shit! thought Harry Bastable, and then stopped thinking.

He got up and stepped over the edge of the cutting, steadying himself for the first second with his free hand on the brickwork as he dropped into space.

He was conscious in the same second of several physical sensations: the surprising warmth of the bricks under his palm, and their roughness against the nettle stings; the brightness of the sunshine in the cutting beneath him; the sound of an aeroplane engine droning somewhere up above him.

The cutting was very steep, but not altogether vertical: it was a green cliff layered in a succession of narrow terraces; and beside the bridge itself, between the terraces, a series of crude footholds had been trodden into slopes.

His body, not his mind, was in charge of movement and balance. Nevertheless, the fall of the cutting was too great, the terraces too narrow and the footholds too smooth and sloping for him to be in full command of his descent; he could only try to beat gravity by denying it the chance of betraying him – since he was unable to descend slowly he had to do so in a succession of extraordinary leaps, far beyond his normal capabilities.

The last leap almost jarred the breath out of him as his boots crashed into the granite chippings beside the railway lines. Yet his body had been already turning in the air as it fell, and his legs straightened again, driving him into the shadow of the arch above him before the shock wave could register.

Someone shouted –

He had expected the tunnel to be dark – it had seemed pitch-black from the angle above – but it wasn't dark at all; it wasn't a tunnel at all – it was only a high-arched bridge, with the sunshine streaming into it –

There were men left and right of him, staring at him in astonishment. He swung the revolver left and right, searching for khaki-and-red tabs – but encountering only a brown leather coat: it fell away from him as though it had been jerked from behind – but there was no khaki-and-red tabs that side – Christ! There was no khaki at all – only civilians – *Christ!* –

'What the devil – ?' began the Brigadier angrily.

The brigadier was wearing a pork-pie hat, and a sports jacket, and a striped tie.

'Traitor!' shouted Bastable, and pointed the revolver at the Brigadier, stiff-armed across the railway lines, and shot him twice in the face.

The force of the bullets hurled the Brigadier backwards into the civilian behind him. Bastable's head was filled with a loud ringing noise, but he was aware of the other brown coat coming at him. He dodged sideways and threw the empty revolver at the German soldier, who was standing in his way – *and ran* –

Sunlight burst around him.

And ran –

He was twenty yards – thirty yards – out into the cutting before any shred of thought came back to him.

He was running, his boots crashing and crunching into the granite chippings beneath him. The silver railway lines stretched away ahead of him, shimmering into infinity – there was a small concrete hut recessed into the side of

354

the cutting just ahead, which he didn't recognize – it was alongside – he had passed it –

He had run right through the bridge, and now he was heading north, towards the British lines! Towards safety!

The cutting was coming to an end; he could see the edge of it dropping, and the land opening up on each side –

There was someone running behind him!

The air pounded in his chest painfully – *he must go on running – if he could only go on running – he had run away before – he had escaped before!*

But he was weaker now. All the weary miles and hours, and the lack of sleep and proper food, and all the fears which had sapped his strength, were accumulating in his legs now, slowing him down.

He looked from one side of the shallower cutting to the other, to the lines of the embankment ahead: on this side was open country, but there were trees and there was undergrowth on the other. His pursuer would run him down in the open, but in those bushes – perhaps – *perhaps* –

'Stop!'

The bushes were nearer. Just a few more yards, and he could cross the line and throw himself into them – down the embankment –

'Stop . . . or I fire!'

– only ten yards away. Nothing in the world was going to stop him now – *nor lead nor steel* –

He altered direction slightly, to leap across the lines.

First one line – the sleepers were black and greasy-looking, and he judged their distance to match his running strides, to avoid them . . . Now the other one – he heard the shot behind him as he leaped, and knew that it had missed him a fraction of a second before the toe of his boot caught the edge of the line. For the following fraction he was airborne, legs lost behind him; then he crashed headlong into the granite chippings, their sharp edges tearing into his chin and his palms and his knees.

He tried to get up, scrabbling at the chippings, but his leg gave way under him.

'Halt! Don't move!'

The voice was at his back. He stared at the bushes in front of him with utter despair.

'Are you hit? Did I hit you?'

Bastable sank sideways on to one buttock and one hand, and looked his pursuer in the face.

Sandy hair – no hat – double-breasted grey suit, badly cut, with a foreign look, but the voice was unmistakably British.

The sharp-faced staff captain, remembered Bastable belatedly. *He wasn't there in the farmyard with the Germans so I forgot all about him! I should have saved the second bullet for him!* But now it was a million years too late.

'English?' Sandy-hair was sweating, red-faced and breathless.

He didn't have to answer. It was all the same now. It was finished. It didn't matter what he said.

'Get stuffed!' he said.

Sandy-hair nodded. 'English. Who are you?'

Damn! He should have held his tongue.

'Ten seconds.' Sandy-hair pointed to the pistol.

Bastable was disappointed to discover that he was still very frightened, even though it didn't matter any more. On the other hand, maybe it did matter: if the swine was still on the look-out for Wimpy – for Captain W. M. Willis – there was one thing he could do that might help. One last thing.

'Willis,' he said.

Sandy hair's jaw dropped. 'Willis?'

Bastable nodded. 'W. M. Willis. Captain, Prince Regent's Own South Down Fusiliers,' he said defiantly. He was rather pleased with his own cleverness; it was satisfying to know that he had done one clever thing, worthy of Wimpy himself, even if it was the very last thing he did.

Now all he had to do was to keep his mouth shut, so as not to give himself away. But as he usually didn't know what to say that shouldn't prove difficult.

Sandy-hair was frowning at him. 'Willis?' he repeated to himself as though he couldn't believe his ears. And then he looked quickly down the track and held up his hand. 'Go back! It's all right – go back!'

He looked at Bastable again. 'Willis?'

It was as good a name as any other to die under.

'My God!' murmured Sandy-hair. And looked down the line again quickly – and back to Bastable again. '*Fall* – like you're dead – *now!*' He raised the pistol. 'Now! Willis – *now!*'

The order was so categorical that Bastable obeyed it without thinking, letting himself fall flat on his back. And before he could question his own irrational obedience the pistol jerked above him with a loud cracking sound – the blast from its muzzle hit his face and granite chips struck his ear like stinging nettles. He flinched at the shock and tensed himself against the impact of the bullet he would never hear.

'*Lie still!*' Sandy-hair hissed, bending over him, fumbling at the buttons of his denim jacket. 'Where's your identification?'

Identification?

He had no identification –

357

'For God's sake – where's your identification?'

'Trouser pocket!' Bastable heard himself say to the blurred red face and blue sky above him, without knowing what he was saying.

The hands left his chest: they patted the pockets of his denim trousers, and felt a lump in one of them – a knotted lump which, until this confusion of light and thought in his brain, hadn't been in any conscious reckoning there.

Sandy-hair retrieved the lump – the lump unravelled itself above Bastable as Sandy-hair stood up, into the primrose-yellow-and-dove-grey lanyard of the Prince Regent's Own South Downs Fusiliers – *the symbol of pride and privilege!*

'Lie still . . .' Sandy-hair looked down at him again – and then away again, and waved down the track. '. . . stay dead until I come back . . . if I come back . . . or we'll both be dead, Willis – *savvy?*'

Bastable heard the chippings crunch once more, away into a distance of sound made up of aeroplane-drone and the blood in his own eardrums.

He had been dead so many times that being dead was no longer a burden, it was a memory drilled into him by long practice and experience. So many pieces of him had died along the way, during these last hours, that another piece made no difference. One piece lay under the carrier, and another was among the Tynesiders and Germans on the grass behind the field hospital, where he had dropped the lanyard – and picked it up; and another piece remained in the attic, with his uniform, where he had consciously-unconsciously transferred the lanyard from one pocket to another – the last surviving piece of his identity as himself.

And now even that was gone. He was stripped bare to the bone in the sunlight, full of separate pains – hands and knees and face stinging, the unyielding stones beneath him digging into his aching back.

Yet the pains were as nothing compared with the utter bewilderment he was experiencing, rather, they were the spur to an awareness that he was still alive, when he should be finally dead at last. For although he could otherwise have argued with himself that some fragment of consciousness might still continue after death – that the brain might continue kicking and twitching with thoughts as darkness closed in – he could not reconcile such an imagining with the ordinary discomfort he continued to feel.

He was alive, when he ought to be dead.

Sandy-hair had quite deliberately spared him, when that should have been the coup-de-grâce –

And more, and more confusing than that: Sandy-hair had quite deliberately *pretended* to kill him –

'*Lie still! Stay dead until I come back!*'

It didn't make sense.

For it had been Sandy-hair who had fired at him from behind, as he had jumped the rails; and it had been that which had made him miss his footing and fall.

But then Sandy-hair had fired that second time – but to miss –

It didn't make sense, and the nonsense of it made his head ache with the effort of thinking about it.

And now Sandy-hair had returned to his German friends, to complete whatever treason he was transacting with them . . .

It didn't make any sense at all.

Time was passing.

He toyed with the idea of seizing this opportunity to start running again – to spring to life and start running –

but finally rejected it as unsound. He dare not move to test the strength of his leg, which he had damaged in his fall, but he could add its likely weakness to the greater tiredness and lassitude which enveloped him, and to the doubts within him; and the addition told him that if he ran he would not run far before they caught him.

And, also, if he ran he would be disobeying Sandy-hair's explicit instruction: *Lie there! Stay dead until I come back – or we'll both be dead. Savvy?*

So he lay there, and stayed dead, even though he didn't *savvy* at all. Because it didn't make sense at all.

Eventually he heard the familiar crunching footfalls again, far away but coming closer.

He thought: *Now it will make sense*, and the thought so filled his mind that there almost wasn't room in it to be frightened.

He closed his eyes and held his breath.

'Don't move,' murmured Sandy-hair above him. 'They've gone, but I said I'd dispose of you, and it's not safe in the open, so that's what I'm going to do – for appearances' sake . . . I'm going to drag you off the line into the bushes – right?'

If it was right it was also decidedly uncomfortable as Bastable felt his wrists being seized and his arms stretched, and his boots bumped and scraped over the granite chippings of the railway track. But at least he knew what was happening to him.

Then the going became softer, and the light penetrating his eyelids was shadowed.

He opened his eyes, and beheld a nightmare, and closed them again instantly because the nightmare was impossible.

Bushes swished around him, and twigs cracked underfoot ahead of him.

He opened his eyes again fearfully, and saw that he was in a small clearing enclosed by bushes.

The bushes parted and the nightmare came back, scowling frightfully at him.

The Brigadier was alive.

16

'Sit up, Willis!' said the sandy-haired staff officer.

Bastable stared up through a tracery of leaves at the blue sky far above. He didn't want to sit up. He wanted to die.

He had failed.

'Sit up!' repeated Sandy-hair sharply.

He had not merely failed: he had failed miserably and shamefully and impossibly. He had failed at point-blank range.

'Don't play silly buggers with me, man!' rasped the Brigadier. 'Sit up this instant!'

Harry Bastable raised himself on to his elbows and faced his failure.

Its extent was printed on the Brigadier's face, across his cheek and the side of his neck in a fiery red powder-burn – and also in the ferocious expression of anger on the rest of the Brigadier's face.

And finally in the pistol in the Brigadier's hand which pointed unwaveringly at his heart across the little clearing in which they lay.

'Now then – ' The Brigadier spoke through clenched teeth, as though his face hurt him. 'Now then – '

'Sir!' The sandy-haired staff officer raised his hand. 'If it's all the same to you, sir – he's mine.'

'Yours?' The Brigadier started to turn towards Sandy-hair, and then winced as the movement creased his powder-burn. 'Well . . . he's certainly your responsibility,

Freddie – I grant you that. Because when you deceived Obergruppenführer Keller you risked both of us getting the kibosh. God only knows what you would have said if he'd decided to examine the corpse!'

'I should have said that I wanted to interrogate him myself, sir – without delay and without interference,' said Sandy-hair suavely.

'And you think Keller would have let you?'

'Our need is greater than his, sir – he isn't going straight back to the British lines, and we are. So it's our risk . . . Besides which, Keller's got a far more urgent job than interrogating British agents; the sooner he gets the details of Operation Dynamo back to Berlin, the better.'

'Hmmm . . . well, I'm glad you didn't have to put that theory to the test. Keller's awkward enough as it is.' The Brigadier lifted his arm to bring his wrist-watch level with his eyes. 'And we've not got a lot of time, anyway.'

'The railway line will be safe until thirteen-thirty hours, sir. Keller was positive about that. We've a clear thirty minutes.'

'If you say so . . . But I wouldn't like to come a cropper at the last fence.' The Brigadier lowered his arm. 'Very well – he's yours. Only just remember that my vote is for shooting him here and now. Better to be safe than sorry is my motto.'

His wish was going to be granted, thought Bastable bleakly: they were going to kill him.

'But he did try to shoot you, sir,' said Sandy-hair. 'That's pretty strong evidence on his behalf.'

'True.' The Brigadier fixed his fierce pale eyes on Bastable. 'But he missed.'

'Only by a hair's-breadth.'

'Also true.' The Brigadier lifted his free hand to touch his neck gingerly. 'It undoubtedly wasn't for lack of trying

363

. . .' The eyes bored into Bastable. 'You're a monstrously bad shot, whoever you are.'

'Willis, sir,' said Sandy-hair quickly. 'Captain, Prince Regent's Own – those Terriers at Colembert, remember?'

'Yes. The ones the Huns scuppered.' The Brigadier's eyes flickered. 'I remember.'

'Do you recognize him?'

The eyes ran up and down Bastable, chilling him. 'Never saw him before in my life, so far as I can recall, Freddie. Looks a damned ugly customer – doesn't look like a British officer to me, even a Territorial. They used to be fairly presentable.'

'He's not the one who took a shot at you in the yard at Beaumont Farm, then?'

Again the eyes flickered. 'Can't honestly say for sure, you know – it all happened rather quickly, as I recall. It was a British officer – captain's pips . . . and a fancy lanyard like the one you showed to Keller back there under the bridge, right enough. But he had his tin hat tipped over his eyes and the strap across his chin . . . Could be him, I suppose – and he was a damn bad shot too, that's a similarity if you like! But I can't say for sure, Freddie . . . my eyes aren't what they were . . .' He squinted at Bastable. 'But you say he's Willis?'

'He says he's Willis.'

'And you're inclined to believe him? Hmmm . . . Keller would have found out quickly enough, with his experience from Poland. And Spain . . .' He started to nod again, and caught himself just too late. 'Damn! Just get on with it, Freddie – that's all!'

Sandy-hair stared at Bastable. 'You are Captain Willis?'

Bastable stared back at him sullenly. The Brigadier seemed older and tireder, and far less formidable, but the sandy-haired staff officer had become larger and foxier, and infinitely more dangerous. And yet together they were outwardly a typical enough pair of British officers, and somehow that made their treason infinitely more despicable.

'Go to hell!' he croaked, before he could stop himself.

Sandy-hair continued to stare at him. 'How did you get here, Willis?'

It was a silly question, and its silliness surprised Bastable. Of all the things which might matter, the fact of his arrival at the bridge between Carpy and Les Moulins mattered least. And then it struck him that if Sandy-hair – Freddie – wanted to know the answer, then it couldn't be a silly question; it was simply that Harry Bastable was too stupid to see its significance.

'How did you get here, Willis?' repeated Freddie patiently.

Therefore . . . if Freddie wanted an answer, then he wasn't going to get one. Because, in a world of defeat and failure, one thing was certain: Freddie was the enemy.

And because they were going to kill him anyway – that was another certainty.

Why they hadn't killed him already was beyond him. But they hadn't turned him over to the Germans, and they couldn't take him with them when they returned to the British lines, and they couldn't leave him here free. So they had no choice in the matter.

'How did you get here?' Freddie paused. 'Last time, Willis.'

Bastable was about to say, 'Go to hell' again, if he could find enough moisture in his mouth to do so, when it came to him suddenly that he hadn't any choice in the matter either.

Wimpy and the child were up there somewhere, by the bridge; and they couldn't help him, but he could still do something for them; and, what was more, it was something that he could do.

All his life he had never – or very rarely – been able to find the right words, the clever words, in an emergency. He could think of them afterwards, but never at the time. But now, in this last emergency, it didn't matter. Because now words could only betray him – or, what was worse, they could only betray Wimpy and the child. So all he had to do was to say nothing. And then, however frightened he was, he would be doing the right thing.

The Brigadier stiffened. 'Hold on there, Freddie – I know the answer to that one. He must have overheard us at the farm – that was what Keller was afraid of, when he told his chaps to kibosh those poor devils at Colembert. He insisted on fixing the next rendezvous – I didn't think they'd get so far, but he was confident they would, Keller was . . . And when he speaks in English he always shouts at the top of his voice as though I'm deaf – and this fellow, if he's Willis . . . he was only a few yards away, behind the wall. He could easily have heard. So there's your answer, eh?'

Freddie gave him a weary look. 'I didn't ask him how he knew where to come, sir. I asked him how he got here.'

'Same thing. Does it matter?'

'If he's Willis it does, sir.'

'Why?' The Brigadier's bushy eyebrows quivered.

'He's covered fifty miles – through the whole of the German Second Army Group. And with a price on his head, dead or alive . . . And . . . if he went back to Colembert first – and somehow got away from there again – that makes more than fifty miles in less than forty-eight hours . . . sir.'

The Brigadier gazed at Bastable from under the eyebrows. 'You mean . . . he's covered a lot of ground, with the Huns crawling all over the place?'

'Too much ground. He couldn't have done it without help. It isn't possible.'

'Good point, Freddie!' The Brigadier turned stiffly towards Bastable. 'Well?'

Stupid old bugger! thought Bastable, anger momentarily driving out fear. Perhaps if he was rude enough, that might finish the thing quicker, before he could disgrace himself – as he surely would. Or perhaps there was an even quicker way – if he could summon up enough courage for it.

'Go to hell!' he said, with all the contempt he could muster.

Freddie leaned forward. 'We probably will. But I'll make sure you get there first, Willis. Only you'll travel more slowly, that I promise you.'

Bastable watched him draw his pistol out of his coat, from his gangster's holster. Now there were two pistols, and any movement now would be suicidal.

'There are a lot of ways of shooting a man, Willis,' said Freddie unpleasantly. 'Painful ways – painful places.'

The fear came flooding back, but the anger remained: Bastable was too frightened to move, and angry with himself for having put off moving until the fear had come back to unnerve him.

'G-go to hell!' he whispered. 'F-fucking traitors!'

The Brigadier made another of his awkward half-turns towards Freddie. 'That's a damn good answer – in his place I'd have said much the same thing, I hope. Short and to the point. So . . . I agree with you, and I take back my vote. He's one of ours.'

He swivelled back to Bastable. 'Here, Captain – if it makes you feel any better – take it!'

He had reversed the pistol.

'Take it, man!' The Brigadier leaned forward painfully. 'Go on – never refuse a free gift.'

Bastable took the pistol.

'Just don't point it at me.' The Brigadier gently deflected the barrel. 'Though I don't know . . . I suppose you could still manage to miss me at even this range.'

Bastable looked down at the pistol in his hand, then back at the Brigadier, unbelievingly.

'Tell him, Freddie,' said the Brigadier.

Freddie nodded. 'You want to know what Brigadier Carter's been doing?'

In default of being able to speak Bastable nodded.

'He's been handing over the details of the Allied counter-offensive to the Germans,' said Freddie. 'Plus the British order of battle behind the Aa Canal and the French one south of the Somme River.'

It was dead quiet in the wood. Far away, to the north, there were familiar sounds, and there was the high drone of aircraft engines in the distance. But in the wood around them nothing stirred.

'There are three full-strength anti-tank regiments dug in behind the canal, at a distance of between five and seven miles. Behind them we have an armoured division equipped with Mathilda Mark Twos, and a French DMI. Plus three fresh infantry divisions, one British, one Canadian straight from the UK, and a French one.

'He also told them that the Guards landed at Boulogne yesterday – although as the Germans are on the outskirts of the town they probably know that already . . . and also that two battalions of the Rifles and a tank brigade are landing in Calais today. Which they will presumably discover tomorrow . . . Are you with me, Willis?'

Bastable tried to swallow the lump in his throat.

'He told them also that once they are fully committed beyond the canal, against us, so that they can't easily disengage, then the whole of the French Seventh Army will attack northwards across the Somme in the south, spearheaded by the Fourth Armoured Division, across their lines of communication. And at the same time the British will launch another attack southwards from the Arras area – a bigger one than they launched yesterday, which was merely designed to draw the German armour away from the Somme. Right?'

Right? Bastable no longer knew which was right and which was wrong.

'The code name for this operation is "Dynamo". The British originally wanted to call it "Waterloo", but the French objected to that on historical grounds.'

'And I don't blame them,' murmured the Brigadier. 'Do you know your history, Willis?'

Bastable closed his mouth, which had fallen open.

'No? Well, the Waterloo campaign began the same way for the Allies. Napoleon humbugged them at Ligny and Quatre Bras, just as Hitler humbugged us on the Dyle and the Meuse. But then Wellington held Napoleon at Waterloo, and the Prussians came from the flank and finished the job. And that was the end of the war.

'Until now the Hun has found it easy to advance. But that's because we've made it easy for them – because we want them to commit their armour over the Aa Canal, in the waterways there – with the rest of their army strung all the way back to the frontier. It's a trap, Willis.' The Brigadier paused. 'Do you understand?'

Harry Bastable didn't understand. He felt the weight of

the Brigadier's pistol in his hand – and in his chest the greater weight of the black treachery he had been listening to.

But why were they telling him all this?

The pistol lifted to point midway between the Brigadier and Freddie.

'That's what the Brigadier has told the Germans,' said Freddie.

Bastable steadied the pistol.

'And there isn't a word of truth in it,' said the Brigadier.

Freddie looked sideways at the Brigadier. 'Actually there is a word or two. The Guards *are* in Boulogne – and the Rifles *are* landing in Calais today. And they'll fight there too.'

'And they'll die there, too,' said the Brigadier.

'And we did counter-attack at Arras yesterday,' said Freddie. 'But there aren't any anti-tank guns behind the Aa Canal. Or any tanks – or any fresh divisions. At this moment there isn't a corporal's guard to stop the Germans between Calais and Dunkirk.'

'And there isn't going to be any great French counter-attack across the Somme. Because there isn't any great French army to attack with – the French are finished. The Germans could be in Paris within a week,' said the Brigadier.

'And in Ostend by this weekend – which is what matters to us,' said Freddie. 'Because then the BEF will be finished – they'll be surrounded.'

'And then we shall have lost the war,' said the Brigadier.

'No!' Bastable found his tongue. 'I don't believe it!'

'Neither do the Germans – *that's the whole point, man*,' said Freddie. 'That's what the Brigadier and I have been doing – trying to feed them lies to keep them from realizing it. If we can just *delay* them for a few days – if Gort can pull the BEF back to form some sort of line protecting Dunkirk and Ostend . . . Then maybe the Navy can save some of them. At least if we've got our backs to the sea, we've got a chance. Because that's what "Dynamo" is about – the real Dynamo, Willis.'

'Dynamo?'

'The evacuation of the British Army from France. We need four days to start it – and at the moment we've only got two before the Germans reach Dunkirk – three at the outside. But as we can't stop them we've got to make them stop of their own accord.'

The Brigadier grunted. 'For sound military reasons.'

Bastable grappled with the sound military reasons, but they were too big for him. *The French are finished . . . if Gort can pull back the BEF . . . we need four days . . .*

'And we've given them some sound military reasons, by God!' said the Brigadier. 'They've got plenty of their own, but we've given them a better one – we've warned them of a trap which doesn't exist.'

'But – ' Bastable felt the sweat on his forehead.

'But why should they believe us?' Freddie's lip twisted as he looked at the Brigadier. 'Because we've been supplying them with sound military information since Czechoslovakia was occupied last year – the Brigadier and I, Willis. We've been working for them for over a year – so they think.'

'What?'

'Since they broke the Munich agreement,' said the Brigadier. 'Before that . . .'

'Before that Brigadier Carter was just a genuine practising Fascist,' said Freddie.

'No. Not practising – that's not permitted for a serving

371

officer.' The Brigadier eyed Freddie balefully. 'Just convinced.'

'He didn't like Jews and Communists,' amended Freddie. 'And he made no secret of it.'

'Still don't. Too many Jew-boys and Reds in high places.' The Brigadier held himself stiffly. 'But that doesn't mean that I'll betray my country to the first Hun who approaches me.'

Freddie half-smiled. 'A reasonable mistake on their part. But a mistake, nevertheless . . . Because then he came to us. And now he's fighting for the Jews and the Communists instead.'

'That I'm certainly not!' snapped the Brigadier.

'Well, maybe not, sir. But you joined us – and I joined you, anyway.'

'To keep an eye on me, eh?' The bushy eyebrow on the left lifted sardonically. 'In case I was one of your "doubles"?'

'If you say so, sir. Perhaps at first.'

The Brigadier scowled at Bastable. 'They never trust anyone absolutely, his people, it's their occupational disease. And neither do the Huns, for much the same reasons, only more so. Which is where you came in, my lad!'

'Where? I beg your pardon – ?'

'You may even have saved the day at that, in fact.'

Bastable stared at the Brigadier in astonishment. 'What?'

'I told you – they never trusted anyone. And Obergruppenführer Keller is no exception to the rule; he simply couldn't quite bring himself to believe that we were offering him authentic information. Which is hardly to be wondered at, with their front-line commanders wanting to go hell-for-leather up the coast, and telling them there's nothing in their way . . . whereas we simply couldn't give him enough corroborating facts to back our version. Because we're not running the show, Willis. We're just mixing what little truth we've got with a lot of damned lies.'

'The Arras attack has shaken 'em up, I think,' cut in Freddie. 'And Boulogne will help.'

'And Calais too – the Rifles'll die hard – ' The Brigadier nodded and flinched. 'But there isn't enough – or there wasn't enough until you descended out of nowhere, Willis, like the wrath of God – shouting, "Traitor" at the top of your voice – *and shot me!*'

'And were shot in your turn, too!' supplemented Freddie.

The Brigadier just managed to stop himself nodding. 'That's right. Positively heroic . . . I suppose it would have been even better if you'd actually killed me . . . But you did the next best thing, Captain: you did your incompetent best, by God!'

Bastable licked his lips and looked from one to the other.

'Don't look so unhappy, my dear fellow,' said the Brigadier. 'Don't you see – *you shot me as a traitor*. And that does rather suggest that I *am* a traitor – someone worth killing. And someone worth dying for, too, by God! And that's about the strongest corroboration you can give to a man's story, to my way of thinking.'

Freddie nodded agreement. 'Keller was certainly a lot more friendly after that.'

'And so he damn well should be!' snapped the Brigadier. 'He was supposed to have suppressed Captain Willis – and I told him so in no uncertain terms, the incompetent swine . . . But you, Willis – you just may have tipped the balance our way, that's the long and short of it. So what do you say to that, eh?'

Bastable looked down at the pistol in his hand, which he was embarrassed to discover was still pointing more or less at the Brigadier. He lowered it hastily.

'I – I don't know what to say, sir,' he said lamely.

'You don't feel like trying a third shot, then?' The left eyebrow lifted. 'While you've got the chance, eh?'

Bastable swallowed.

The Brigadier reached forward and lifted the pistol out of his hand. 'Wouldn't have done you any good if you had. No bullets in it. Freddie prudently removed them.'

Bastable looked at Freddie.

And at Freddie's pistol, which was covering him.

The Brigadier also looked at Freddie. 'Well, Major Clinton, I've played my last charade for you. But whoever he is, if he won't press the trigger after what we've given him then he can't be one of your damned Abwehr men – or any other sort of Hun, for that matter, if you ask me.'

Bastable opened his mouth.

'I warned you, Willis,' murmured the Brigadier. 'Major Freddie Clinton is no different from Obergruppenführer Keller. He never trusts anyone.'

Any other sort of Hun?

'You don't think he made me tell you all this because he liked the cut of your jib, do you?' continued the Brigadier. 'I told you – '

'Do shut up, sir,' said Freddie, lifting the pistol until its muzzle looked Bastable in the eye. 'Who are you?'

'Thinks you're maybe a German – doesn't trust anyone else to make sure,' continued the Brigadier, quite unabashed. 'Maybe not SS – but possibly Abwehr . . . sent to shoot me and double-test him. Or just to kibosh the SS. Never did quite follow his reasoning, but then I frequently don't. I just do what I'm told. And it's you who've been tested, whoever-you-are, eh?'

'Shut up, Brigadier!' snarled Freddie. 'Who-the-hell-are-you?'

Words deserted Bastable.

'Just don't tell me that you're Captain Willis,' said Freddie. 'If you'd been Willis then I might well have shot you back there on the line, just to be on the safe side. But Captain Willis had brown hair – brown hair, five-foot-seven, slightly-built – and you don't fit that description by a mile.'

'A schoolmaster from Sussex.' The Brigadier nodded at Bastable. 'First thing the Major did after the Hun picked up those field-glasses – checked up on W. M. Willis, of course . . . schoolmaster and former classics scholar of University College, Oxford: Willis, William Mowbray. *Dominus illuminatio mea – est summum nefas fallere.* Funny, really . . . if you'd been Willis, you'd probably be dead – and if he'd identified you, you'd probably be dead too. But he couldn't – so now he's going to shoot you unless you can decline *nefas* for him, I suppose. There's an irony there somewhere, don't you think? Or are you a classsicist too?'

Bloody Latin, thought Bastable wildly.

And – *bloody Latin master!*

'Time's up,' said the Brigadier. '*Tempus fugit!*'

The Brigadier talked too much, thought Bastable bitterly, like –

Like –

'I never was any good at Latin, sir,' he said to the Brigadier. 'But I know someone who is.'

They both frowned at him.

'If I could introduce you to the original Captain Willis – would that do?' he enquired politely.

375

'Who the hell are you, then?' snapped Freddie, lowering his pistol.

'Bastable,' said Bastable. 'Harry Bastable. Acting-captain, Prince Regent's Own South Downs Fusiliers, sir.'

Epilogue
Saturday, 24 May 1940, and
ever after

'On the morning of Saturday, 24 May 1940, the German panzer divisions advancing up the Channel coast were ordered to halt on the line of the Aa Canal, just short of Dunkirk.

'Although opposed by only weak British and French units, the Germans remained on the canal line for three days, and when they were at last permitted to resume the offensive it was too late: the defences of the Dunkirk perimeter had hardened sufficiently to delay their advance, allowing the British Expeditionary Force to retreat to the beaches off which an armada of little ships had assembled.

'On 24 May Winston Churchill himself believed that the Allies would be lucky to save as many as 45,000 men from those beaches; between 26 May, when the "Operation Dynamo" evacuation began, and 4 June, when the last of the gallant French rearguard was overwhelmed, a total of 338,226 Allied soldiers were rescued. These included the bulk of the BEF, which provided the trained nucleus of Britain's future armies.

'An unparalleled military disaster thus ended with what the British ever after regarded as a miracle – "The miracle of Dunkirk".

'What might have happened if there had been no such miracle must remain a matter of conjecture. Supposing that Britain had fought on – supposing that Churchill's shaky new government had survived the greatest British surrender of all time and that the RAF had still won the

Battle of Britain – it is very difficult to imagine how she could have reinforced and held the Middle East while defending her own islands with the depleted wreck of her army; and the loss of the Middle East must surely have signalled the end of the war.

'But since the miracle did take place the more important conjecture shifts inevitably to that "Halt Order" of 24 May, which Adolf Hitler in person confirmed when he visited Colonel-General von Rundstedt's Army Group Headquarters that morning.

'No one now believes (as was rumoured at the time) that Hitler deliberately allowed the British to escape, on the grounds that they would be more likely to make peace if he left them their pride intact, for his subsequent actions do not support such a theory.

'Goering's offer to finish the job from the air may well have influenced the decision. Certainly, this would have combined a political merit – unlike the Wehrmacht, the Luftwaffe was very much a Nazi creation – with the military virtue of preserving the travel-worn panzer divisions from further loss at the hands of a defeated but still dangerous foe when there were important battles to come.

'Yet if that was the case, the military consideration was even more certainly the stronger of the two. For the fog of war, which had utterly confounded the retreating Allies, equally concealed many things from the advancing Germans – above all, the completeness of the brilliant victory which they had already won.

'Indeed, what appeared to the rest of the world to be a new type of warfare, devilishly conceived and ruthlessly executed, was in fact a campaign plagued by doubts and hesitations, and by arguments between conventional commanders and innovators. It was Hitler's supreme insight that the French Army of 1940, and France herself, lacked the will to re-fight the battle of the Marne. But his insight went no further, and on that fatal 24th both he and von Rundstedt believed that the Battle of France was as yet only half-won. As a result, both were deeply and not unreasonably concerned for the vulnerability of their flanks to counter-attack, and for the concentration of their scattered forces for that final supreme effort.

'Also, one other factor needs to be remembered (and not least by the beneficiaries of the miracle that was to come), imponderable though its contribution must always remain in the historian's calculations.

'Although by comparison with the "contemptible little army" of 1914 the British Expeditionary Force of 1940 was lamentably ill-equipped to handle the army of Rommel and Guderian, the quality of the British rank and file was as high as ever.

'The gallant, haphazard, hopeless British tank attack at Arras on 21 May undoubtedly played a part out of all proportion to its actual size in raising doubts in Hitler's mind; it is unlikely that the self-sacrificial heroism of the garrison of Calais was altogether in vain; and who knows what unrecorded acts of defiant bravery by individual units, or even single soldiers, contributed to the sum of events which in the end tipped the scales of decision?

'But so much for conjecture. What is certain is that the "Halt Order" of 24 May was given – and confirmed. And in that hour the final victory which was within Hitler's grasp, which his soldiers had won for him, began to slip through his fingers, and the last days of his Thousand-Year Reich had begun.'

– from Sir Frederick Clinton's *The Dunkirk Miracle*
(Gollancz, 1959)